AMPARO GARCÍA-CROW:

THE SOUTH TEXAS PLAYS

(Between Misery and the Sun)

Cocks have Wings and Claws to Fly

Under a Western Sky

The Faraway Nearby

Esmeralda Blue

<u>NoPassport Press</u>

Dreaming the Americas Series

Amparo García-Crow: The South Texas Plays

Copyright 2009 by Amparo Garcia-Crow.

"Introduction: Between Misery and the Sun" copyright 2009 by Octavio Solis.

"Spirited Geographies: Amparo García-Crow's Trans-regional Views of South Texas" copyright 2009 by José Limón

NoPassport Press, Dreaming the Americas Series

First edition 2009 by NoPassport Press

PO Box 1786, South Gate, CA 90280 USA;

e-mail::NoPassportPress@aol.com,

ISBN: 978-0-578-01913-0, US List Price: $30.00

Contents

Acknowledgements, 5

Introductions

Between Misery and the Sun, 7
Octavio Solis

Spirited Geographies: Amparo García-Crow's Trans-regional Views of South Texas, 19
José Limón

Standing By and Letting it all be, 31
Amparo García Crow

The Plays

Cocks Have Claws and Wings to Fly, 37

Under a Western Sky, 169

The Faraway Nearby, 281

Esmeralda Blue, 413

Biographies, 559

Acknowledgements

I wish to thank the 'nothing' sky of South Texas; my parents, grandparents, siblings (especially Anna for being such a muse!). My great-grandmother Elvira whose mantra was "cada cabeza is otro mundo" and whose dharma was feeding people. Thank you Bhagirit, David Rose, Vinnie and Todd; especially my diamond children Ali and Surya and best friends Melba, Charlie, CK, Mishon, Darla and star students Jackie, Andre, Soham, Chris Alonzo and Brandon D.---all teachers who have inspired and supported me with their beings! Thank you David Cohen, UT's Texas Center for Writers, South Coast Repretory's Hispanic Playwriting Festival and the TCG Director's fellowship that got me on the writing path! And to my heart---'head doctor' KD and our beloved Baba, Bhagwan(s)and the ever she-Gods that guide our lives, I will never find the words or enough gratitude for the Grace. Thank you Caridad (and No Passport Press) for your extraordinary vision, talent and generous invitations to all of us to keep in "forming" ourselves. I feel doubly the artist, always, in your presence. Thank you Octavio for being ever the mentor, gifted writer and friend that we all want to grow up to be and Dr. José Limón who comes from the holy stix of Laredo where all of Texas was formed---you more than most, know what it means to be this elegant animal we can only call---Mexican, American---Tejano.

To my children---Alejandro and Surya:

I may have brought you here but you
are the ones that deliver me
to my deepest heart.

Introduction

Between Misery and the Sun: The South Texas Plays

Texas often yields its creative fruit reluctantly. It's a harsh state, filled with hard-knuckled people living hard-scrabble lives. An arid place still caught up in its own myth of the Old West, but a myth no less confirmed in the outlaw attitudes and two-fisted ways of its citizens. I come from there, and I know its terrain as well as any Texan, a dry sun-roasted landscape for which the cowboy boot seems to have been invented. But out of this land have come some amazing writers whose works are as hard-bitten and prickly and stunningly beautiful as the desert blooms of the Southwest, writers such as Dagoberto Gilb, Sandra Cisneros, Robert Wilson, Benjamin Saenz, Naomi Shihab Nye and John Rechy. Add to this distinguished company the name of playwright Amparo García-Crow.

This volume of four of her works tracks the kind of tough living that marks the Texas Chicano/a experience, and she comes by it the hard way. The real way. She's lived it. She knows it and respects it. But in her plays, she conducts her own imaginative transmutation to see it new and give it meaning beyond what seems obvious. She finds grace and beauty in the severely overwrought lives of doomed, washed-out people. And she accomplishes this with a dash of humor by simply taking *la vida extremis** of Texas to its own illogical *extremis*. Where other writers dream up their own Tejas, Ms. García-Crow allows Tejas to dream her.

Her extensive credentials have prepared her for this journey. She's an experienced actor, a director, and she's taught many workshops in playwriting. It's the writing, though, that has really called on her powers. I first became aware of her work when I attended a reading of her play, *Cocks have Claws and Wings to Fly* and I was struck by how instantly familiar the world was to me and yet how brilliantly re-imagined. Firmly rooted in the realism of the Texas small town, the characters readily dispatch that grounding with some disturbing and often comical hallucinations of both the narcotic and spiritual sort. I thought, this is the kind of play I would have loved to write, but soon the professional envy gave way to solid admiration. Here was a writer who knew my home state well.

Then, upon reading her other works, my suspicions about her were confirmed. Amparo García-Crow, like myself, suffered from Texas on the brain. She writes with a sense of its oppressive mythologies, both past and present, and with the added prescience of the changes to come for that way of life. In the plays contained herein, there's the isolation of the small town set against the isolation of the individual. Concepcion, Texas or San Diego, Texas — it's all really "Nowhere, Texas." The stories that take place here will be heard by no-one; they happen in the vacuum of the open sky and the closed heart; they happen in the silent murderous thud of the lonely. And yet, they have a immediate resonance far beyond the state-line; mythological resonances, from the myth of the wild, wild West to the myth of the Viet Nam; resonances that make even the whisper of a rape hiss across the country on the pages of a newspaper. Hers is a world of people who must depend on their own belief structures, value systems, and network of lies to come to terms with each other. Large civic institutions are meaningless in the small Texas town where things have been ever so for who knows how long. In her works, the law and the outlaw become curiously merged, and redemption is as elusive as rainfall.

There were about ten guys at the ranch, I
think more. It all happened when
Monkay's car drove up. I remember
because the muffler was loud, man. It
sounded like a tractor or something like
that. It got all the roosters squawking like
crazy. Kicking up dust all over the place.
She was already in the car. I think she came
with them. She was the only girl there. She
looks like my sister, but more built, so I
take a second look. Monkay gets out first.
They were gonna try out this new killer
bird or something like that. So Monkay
checks it out in back of the trailer house but
Jessie stays in the car the whole time. She
tries to get out but he doesn't let her, he
grabs her by the hair and slams her on the
car. . .

In these straightforward unadorned terms, Javier
begins to tell his account of a monstrous gang rape
on a teenage girl in small Texas town in her play
Under a Western Sky. Merging two separate real-
life events, this attack on the girl and the discovery

of a lost cache of early watercolors by Georgia O'Keeffe in another small Texas town, Ms. García-Crow portrays a community thrown into upheaval by events that thrust them into a national spotlight. But instead of getting overly poetic and dangerously polemical, she keeps the language spare and true to the region and the backgrounds of her characters, and she employs a simple but truly effective theatrical performance style akin to the "talking newspaper" of the mid-century U.S. The ensemble is plainly presented as a group of players who narrate the sequence of events as they slip in and out of various guises and voices amid a slate of shifting slide projections as demonstrated below in the scene introducing Veronica and Elisa.

Projection: STANDING NUDE

`ACTRESS ONE

VERONICA CONCEPCION GARCIA-MORALES, 40, reads the latest issue of Cosmopolitan. It is her day off. Usually she works a forty -eight hour week, plus, at the Post Office.

ACTRESS TWO

ELISA MERCEDE GARCIA, ninety plus years old, sits in her rocking chair at La Hacienda Nursing Home. She lost most of her sight many years ago. Her back is still unusually straight, rigid even. She moves very little, except for her hands which work at molding a piece of clay.

(Actor One sits in front of an imaginary easel and pretends to paint.)

ACTOR ONE

A great artist Elisa knew as a young woman sits at the foot of Elisa's bed painting. The artist appears exactly the way Elisa remembers her, when they were both in their early twenties. Only Elisa can see and hear the Great Artist.

ELISA

Pos when you give your children the milk of animals, you raise a pack of little animals. I'm not saying animal milk is not good for the bones. But you do not take the

place of the milk of the mother with the
milk of a cow or goat!

Even though this depiction eschews any lyric and
didactic impulses, there is still something
strikingly beautiful about the directness of the
spoken text. It has the effect of producing its own
simple home-grown poetry and an instructive
mode which, far from being off-putting and
preachy, lends a humanity to the proceedings in
the play. This performance style has its
antecedents; the early works of El Teatro
Campesino and El Teatro de la Esperanza both
used this dynamic method to accommodate their
bare-bones aesthetic. But Ms. García-Crow takes it
a step further, allowing a deeply spiritual
dimension to form layers into the frontal
presentation of the work. The character known as
the Great Artist moves through the plateaus of the
piece as a ghost and a reminder that there are
resonances for everything we do far beyond the
present and the realistic, a lesson that is not lost on
Yolanda, the victim of the rape, nor on her
attackers. It is even a lesson that is meted out by
the cosmos, in the way weather reacts to the
passing of verdicts and the passing of life:

As the sun readies to rise on this morning,
the wind is blowing something terrible…
The ground rising up in a kind of fury as
the wind whips away like something in a
mad rage.   The weather man is
predicting more heavy rains today and a
tornado watch remains in affect till noon
for all of Duval County and several of the
surrounding areas.

This same sense of spiritual reverberation takes on
a more historical aspect in her play, *The Faraway,
Nearby: A Day with Juan, Parts 1 &2*. The subject of
this work, which is really two plays bundled in
one, is Vietnam, the memories of that war, and its
concomitant scars on the individual and national
psyche. But Amparo is more concerned with how
old war wounds heal with the application of the
balm of love. In the first work of Act 1, Juan is a
vet living in a rat-nest in some beaten-down
isolated Texas town, and is about to commit
seppuku with a real Samurai sword, when he is
interrupted by Evelyn who returns him his lost
dog tags. When she realizes what he is about to
do, and for which she must be witness, she asks
why. Juan's convoluted reply is "I'm just trying to
say to you. . . not everything that's wrong. . .has to

stay wrong." His act is an act of correction. As she tries to save him, and he resists, they fall in love. After an unplanned, spontaneous kiss between them leaves them both stunned...

JUAN: Evelyn. . .please. Say something. Anything. What just happened here?

EVELYN: I'm sorry. It's been---

JUAN: No apology necessary.

(They stare at each other for a prolonged moment. Without either leading, they both move towards the other. Again they kiss. This time clothes quickly get pulled at and flung off. They don't take them all off, just enough to penetrate the other, much to their own shock and disbelief. After a moment of frantic exchange, there is total silence. As they pull away from the other and quickly compose themselves, as best they can, they move away from the other, as far as possible, in the space. Evelyn will not look at him. He attempts to walk towards her.)

EVELYN: Don't. Nothing happened.

She wants to save him, but won't admit to loving him, even though that's precisely what he needs, because she holds fast to the belief that her own MIA husband is still alive. So Juan falls back on the nihilistic writings of Yukio Mishima, from whom he gets his cue. In the end, love isn't enough for either of them, and he disembowels himself before her. In the second act, the second play, takes place thirty-two years later, with Frank, Evelyn's estranged husband and former POW, returning to Southeast Asia to find his illegitimate son. He enlists the help of Phun, a young Viet-American woman to locate his whereabouts. What occurs to Frank as he become more infatuated with Phun, is a spiral downward into the most hellish memories of his imprisonment in North Vietnam. He becomes cruel and belligerent and mistreats Phun, rebuffing her most loving pleas with the foulest imprecations. Ironically, he finds solace in the memory of the friendship of a mouse he kept in his cell:

> FRANK: I only got what's under the fingernails today, little buddy. A flake a rice maybe and you're gonna need all the strength you can round up. We're starting

with the wings. That's as good a place as any. The first thing you do, we start with the ribs first. So we need, first. . .I need to build a jig to build the ribs. Let's cut the spruce strips and shape them. They're quarter inch square, see the ribs are like sticks put together with plywood gussets, they're the curve of the wing. And there are like. . .twenty. . .I'd have to go back. . .they're not all the same, there's about twenty eight ribs altogether. You have to make a jig, or modify a jig for each one that's different. . .for the different sizes.....

Under the observation of this mouse, Frank painstakingly constructs a small plane from banana leaves and other found materials, a plane on which he plans to escape his prison. It is a meager fantasy but enough to keep him hoping, to keep him alive. But in the present day, he is hardly even that, and every attempt Phun makes at offering her love draws him further into his own painful world. His plea to the mouse is as close as he can come to articulating his condition.

What happened, sweet buddy, I'll ask. What happened to us? How did we make living ghosts of the other? And when the

loving arms that would comfort us appear. .
.why do we send them empty-handed on
their way---without us? What happened to
us? And what would it take to make it
right?

These are the resonances Amparo García-Crow
explores in her plays. The places we never leave.
The places that never leave us. The acts that ring
inside for retribution and redemption, and the acts
that echo far beyond the single moment. Her plays
are about lonely people in very desolate places,
but they know that history has a way of folding
back on itself, on making the invisible seen and
secret known; they know that the ghosts they are
being haunted by are actually themselves; they
know they are trapped by a destiny malignant to
their redemption. Maybe it's a Texas thing, but I
understand it completely. There's sky and there's
earth. And that thin line in-between is where we
live.

--Octavio Solis

Spirited Geographies:

Amparo García-Crow's trans-regional views of South Texas

In *Under a Western Sky*, one of Amparo García-Crow's marvelous plays contained herein, a defense attorney is addressing a judge and jury hearing a gang rape case in the small town of San Diego in southern Texas, an area that is the core setting for these plays as well as the playwright's home region. Speaking of the confluence of local moral factors that led to the rape, the attorney says to them in Spanish: *"Pueblo chico, infierno grande,"* but quickly translates: "small community, big hell!" As becomes evident in all of the plays, most of the characters are Mexican-Americans, as is the attorney and likely the jury and judge, reflecting their demographic and social predominance in south Texas and for whom, in this area, a vernacular Spanish is often a second language, indeed sometimes a first. The attorney's translation into English is more than likely for the benefit of the legal court record and for a few local Anglos who might have wandered into the courtroom (although they often also speak some

Spanish) but also for the outside media in attendance such as perhaps the Anglo writer for Texas Monthly who appears as a character even as the translation also serves for the Anglo-phone reader of these plays.

That such a Mexican-American attorney is addressing a judge and jury of his cultural peers sometime in the late twentieth century is all by itself revelatory of the historical changes that have come to this area. San Diego is within a few miles of the Nueces River that traditionally has been the boundary line between south Texas and the central and northern part of the state, a river where the famous Texas Anglo writer J. Frank Dobie tells us, "Mexicans were shot on sight and pitched into *Agua Dulce* Creek", one of the Nueces' tributaries, reflecting in bloody fashion the racial domination of Anglo over Mexicans beginning at the end of the U.S.-Mexico War of 1846-47 whose initial phase was fought in southern Texas. (1) Indeed, it is altogether instructive that one major Mexican-American armed rebellion against such Anglo domination was launched in San Diego, Texas in 1915. (2) In earlier times even through the 1950s, the attorney's comment might well have referred to this domination, the metaphor of hell entirely appropriate in a moment when Anglos were referred to as *diablos Tejanos* (Texas devils) among other choice epithets. But such an attorney in such a culturally defined courtroom would have been a rarity in such past times.

However, for these plays the time is now, at least since the 1960s and in this "today," such attorneys are much more in evidence reflecting that at least some of these citizens are getting a higher education as also becomes evident in the characters attending and graduating from the University of Texas at Austin in other of the plays as well as in the playwright's own education. In these times - our times – the moment some have called post-modernity – change has come to southern Texas and Mexican Americans are now dominant and enjoying some large measure of social and cultural mobility. But, in this playwright's thematic estimation, it would appear that such mobility is morally and socially fraught, and the "hell" that envelops this south Texas *"pueblo chico"* now has other references and meanings but which cannot be grasped without a consistent sub-textual referencing to a past culture now slowly slipping away even as new possibilities also emerge.

In *Esmeralda Blue,* such a past culture appears to be symbolized by a great stone house personally built by an early Mexican settler although the playwright also carefully shows us that even "tradition" can be a site of contradiction and sexual oppression. But perhaps the central example of decisive change occurs in the realm of the maternal. Consistent with the traditional symbolism of the now abandoned stone house, grandmothers- the repositories of tradition – appear but on their deathbeds in their final days to be replaced by younger women, some mothers. However, three of these works do not indulge the culturally iconic figure of the warm, loving enveloping mother allegedly at the heart of Greater Mexican culture. (3) Rather, these mothers and key characters are themselves already products of change, born certainly during or shortly after the Second World War and now displaying themselves in cultural contradiction; as still drawn, for example, to traditions such as a folk Catholicism even as they offer for dinner, not some sumptuous, traditional Mexican home-cooked meal, but rather Kentucky Fried Chicken as does the character, *Mama,* in *Cocks Have Claws and Wings to Fly.* The infliction of such fare on the physical health of the young has its symbolic parallel in a greater infliction: her distorted use of this folk Catholic base to overlook pedophilic priests, engaging in illicit sex even as she passes invidious homophobic judgment on the young who are examining new forms of sexuality and loving even as they are also now crossing the racial barrier in intimate relationships with the Anglo. If there is any hope in these plays, it is indeed with the young who, though still rooted in southern Texas, are nevertheless exploring new cultural paths though not always fruitful ones.

It is not at all a coincidence that such explorations occur away from south Texas with the University of Texas at Austin and Austin itself as one such site but also San Antonio, New York and even Vietnam. Yet as a troubling counter-point, the plays seems to suggest that those who remain do so at some considerable risk to their humanity as do those who return from afar to stay. In addition to the dysfunctional *mama* of *Cocks Have Claws and Wings to Fly*, the former, those who stay, include *Guero*, her drug-addicted son from an illicit affair; Francisco, the scheming homophobe of *Esmeralda Blue* but also many of the other homophobic citizens of San Diego in that play; and, the gang rapists of and their victims of

Under a Western Sky. (Only *mama*'s husband, Santiago, emerges as a quiet exception as if the playwright is still searching for some native meaningfulness in this otherwise morally questionable world). Among those who return to stay, we have Beto Aleman, the sleazy lawyer of *Under a Western Sky* and Juan Sandoval, the haunted Vietnam vet in *The Faraway Nearby* who commits suicide not far from San Diego in a decrepit shack in a village with the ironical name of *Concepcion* (Conception). In *Esmeralda Blue,* suicide is also the final destination for Clara, the cultural preservationist from the University of Texas Institute of Texan Cultures in San Antonio with her intense but stigmatized love for Carmen paralleling her also stigmatized intense interest in a traditional culture of no interest to the locals except for its monetary value. These suicides also seem to underscore a sense of the corruption and morbidity of the region best exemplified by the career and also shotgun suicide noted in *Under a Western Sky,* that of the famous south Texas political boss, George Parr, he, who in dubious fashion, launched the career of Lyndon Johnson. In *Esmeralda Blue,* the aptly named Dolores, the central character, knows that love and sexuality in New York can be fraught, but that hardly persuades her to extend her visit to a deeply problematic southern Texas into anything resembling a permanent return to her mother's ancestral home. In the same way that, in *Cocks Have Claws and Wings to Fly*, we hardly expect Sofia and her gay brother Pedro to return permanently to south Texas from Austin.

Such then are my thematic discernments for these thoughtful if troubling plays. But something should also be said about the stylistic manner through which García-Crow achieves her vision and her relationship to other fine literary representations of southern Texas in an expanding universe of such writing. Though her fictive world has much of the aura of post-modernity, stylistically she writes under the still very productive sign of a high modernism, in drama, one characteristic of O'Neill, Tennessee Williams, Arthur Miller, Albee, but a high modernism utterly innovative when brought to bear on her regional-cultural and US Latina dramatic concerns. Experimental and innovative techniques for dialogue and monologue, poetic stage directions, unusual props and scenery, shifting actors and roles, are all effectively brought to bear in the vivid and compelling creation of the world

we have described above. But above all is her use
of unanticipated, sometimes jarring historical and
cultural juxtapositions to philosophically and
culturally de-center her mostly Texas world so as
to persuade us of the deep and enlarged
seriousness of her people. I mean more here than
the already mentioned transcontinental and
transnational use of New York and Vietnam. In
The Faraway Nearby we can much better appreciate
the depth of Juan Sandoval's learning, his trauma
and his loss of love when he commits suicide
using the ritual of *hara-kiri* perhaps acquired in his
experience in Asia even as his subjectivity through
the mediation of Evelyn from Idaho intersects
with that of the complex Anglo, Frank, and his
lover-guide, Phun, in Thailand. As a culturally
different anchor to a better past, the figure and
work of Georgia O'Keefe enter into the dying
vision of the grandmother, Elisa, in *Under a
Western Sky*. In *Cocks Have Claws and Wings to Fly*,
the death of the dysfunctional *mama*'s first
husband and his sons' tribulations is given more
thematic salience through the playwright's
inventive use of Shakespeare's *Hamlet* and its
haunting ghosts. In the New York- San Diego axis
of *Esmeralda Blue*, our interest and absorption are
enhanced by the monologic commentary of the

American soldier of fortune, Emil Holmdahl, from the Mexican Revolution of 1910.

Such a modernism but also her particular regional focus also give Amparo García-Crow a distinctive and welcome place in the growing field of fine literary artists who have undertaken the representation of south Texas. Even though these are plays and they write fiction, I think the comparison is valid. Among these we count Jovita Gonzalez, Americo Paredes, Rolando Hinojosa, Tomas Rivera, Sandra Cisneros and Oscar Casares. (4)

Four of these – Gonzalez, Paredes, Hinojosa and Casares set most of their fictional work in the Lower Rio Grande Valley on the south Texas border with Mexico where the Rio Grande meets the Gulf of Mexico (hereafter, "the Valley"). Rivera works the southwestern part of the state whereas Cisneros writes of the San Antonio, Texas area. For her part, as we have noted but must now specify, García-Crow has focused on that upper part of the south Texas world that lies immediately along Texas Highway 44 between Laredo and Corpus Christi and extends south for some fifty miles but not quite to the Valley. Many would argue that it has its own distinctive historical and cultural characteristics and it is refreshing to now see it in such capable literary hands.

With the exception of Gonzalez who wrote a historical romance, the others may be said to practice varying forms of realistic writing so that García – Crow's experimental modernism also grants her a welcome distinction although in no way do I wish to valorize modernism as a "better" way especially given the marvelous accomplishment of the others especially when one, Rivera, may be said to be practicing a form of his own restricted modernism. However, their general realistic practice may be related to two broad thematic tendencies in these other writers that generally emerge with occasional and limited exceptions. The first of these is the theme of Anglo-Mexican conflict in Texas at the heart of the work of Gonzalez, Paredes, Rivera, and a bit less so with Hinojosa. The second, to be found in Cisneros and Casares but also to some degree in Hinojosa, is one much less concerned with such conflict but rather focused on the internal workings of the Mexican-origin community with some tendency toward a sympathetic and valorizing representation. Within these internal workings, however, none of these authors fully explore the domain of women and sexuality although Cisneros may be a partial exception.

By considerable contrast, García-Crow's eschews either alternative in the clear belief that they are not as, or no longer as, true of her world. Her skillful modernist practice seemingly allows her to focus on her own yet small strip of geographical territory and yet to explore far beyond, not only trans-regionally and trans-nationally, but perhaps more importantly inter and intra-psychically and across cultural, historical, and sexual experience while still telling us so much about the changes that have come to her native ground. The human yield is not always pleasant, but it is fiercely honest, finely discerning, a pleasure to have read and whose live performance I am most eager to see for the first time.

-- José Limón

ENDNOTES

1) J. Frank Dobie, <u>A Vaquero of the Brush Country</u>.
   Austin: University of Texas Press, 1981 (1929). P. 62;
   David Montejano, <u>Anglos and Mexicans in the
   Making of Texas, 1836 – 1986</u>. Austin: University of
   Texas Press, 1987.

2) Benjamin Johnson, <u>Revolution in Texas: How a
   Forgotten Rebellion and Its Bloody Suppression
   Turned Mexicans into Americans</u>. New Haven: Yale
   University Press, 2005.

3) The concept of Greater Mexico was first voiced by
   the late, distinguished Mexican-American, south
   Texas folklorist, Americo Paredes to refer to all
   people of Mexican-origin whether in national
   Mexico or the United States.

4) Of course, one other obvious axis of comparison is
   toward other Mexican American playwrights such
   as Carlos Morton and Cherrie Moraga, the latter
   with clear interests in sexuality although no such
   published playwright focuses on Texas. For the
   moment, I think my cross-genre but regionally
   focused comparison may be more interesting and
   fruitful. However, one might also consider a Texas,
   cross-cultural comparison by way of Horton Foote's
   plays keyed on the small town of Wharton and
   southeast Texas.

Standing Back and Letting It All Be

In 1990 I received a TCG/NEA Director's fellowship which changed my life completely. When they gathered the five directors and designers for our first meet and greet/retreat somewhere in the Catskills, playwright-teacher Maria Irene Fornés happened to be on the premises working on her opera. To our good fortune, the TCG folks invited her to do a writing workshop for the directors and designers while we all shared the same retreat center. She began the workshop with yoga stretches and then asked us to draw a picture of whatever came to us, as I recall. My drawing looked like a David Lynch landscape from his movie "Mullholland Drive," maybe perhaps because I was living in Los Angeles. It had an eerie desert like feel with a Hopi eternity circle within a circle serpent coiling into itself. When we were done rendering, she then asked us to start writing. I don't remember what I latched onto as an idea---but whatever it was---I wouldn't let it go. The purpose of the writing exercise, as it turned out, was to interrupt and disrupt our process constantly and randomly. And when she would do that, she was would ask us to include into the writing whatever random phrases or ideas she would threw at us. And more importantly, we were not to stop writing.

I liked my initial idea so much, I wouldn't

let it go---even when she would interrupt us to do exactly that. When it came time to share what we'd written, everyone who did exactly as Maria Irene asked, generated some pretty great stuff. It was dynamic, imaginative and unpredictable--- as she had hoped. Mine however, which thankfully she didn't make me read aloud----was horrible! The idea was redundant, one-track minded and very quickly, predictable. Needless to say, I fell completely in love with writing because I had failed at it so completely.

I returned to Los Angeles, after the fellowship, pumped to start a writing group for actors. At that point, I was always waiting for the phone to ring for my next Prostitute #3, Drug Dealer Girlfriend or Mexican maid role auditions that would pour in. "You're too exotic, you'll never work!" one casting director predicted early on. And yet when I got a call back for the role of the Mexican prostitute in Oliver Stone's "Born on the 4th of July" (which beds the invalid Tom Cruise), I was later told I didn't get the part because I had "an Anglo nose!" That's when I knew it was time to write about the Latin people I knew I loved, as opposed to the Latin people, non-Latin (Hollywood) writers didn't know how to give a life to. I don't mind prostitute, drug dealer girlfriends or Mexican maids as characters to portray, direct or write---I just want them to have a name and an arc. I want to know what their hopes and dreams and struggles are so that I find myself in them. What a character 'does' for a living (or what their ethnicity is) doesn't define their soul.

The group I started in Los Angeles the month after having Maria Irene open my 'third eye' (as a writer) as they would say in other realms, I invited a group of actors to meet weekly to write at my home. The idea was to write what we hoped would be the parts we could sink our life and souls into. In my case, a scene would materialize and while I thought, these scenes were not related whatsoever, the mother character that showed up from the first scene on---which ended up becoming the mother character in "Cocks Have Claws and Wings to Fly"---was a hit. Right from the first read. The actors loved putting that role in their mouth. "She's funny!" they kept saying. "Not really," I kept arguing, quietly---knowing that as the play unfolded, that it was far too close to home. It's actually the most autobiographical play I've ever written.

I was still on my TCG/NEA Director's fellowship at that point. Because I had expressed a desire to work with established directors and/or theaters that were working on New Play Development , the TCG people introduced me to Jose Cruz Gonzalez at South Coast Repertory Theatre. And that's when I heard about their Hispanic Playwrights Project Festival. Jose asked if I had any plays of my own, which seemed like an odd question because even though I had just 'accidentally' written my first play---I didn't yet think I was a playwright. I still have to pinch myself to make certain its even my own hand---writing them. "Yes, I do---!" something or someone spoke through my mouth. So I sent the play to their Literary Manager the following day and much to my surprise, they chose it for development. When it came time for the public reading, Latino Chicago Theatre was in the audience and they invited me on the spot to premiere the play at their theater the following year. At that point, I wasn't completely sure that there would ever be, necessarily, another play in me. But I did remember that just like Jean Paul Sartre brought into awareness his existential ideas, waiting for the bus as an eight year old child. For me, it was riding in the backseat of my parents Galaxy, as they argued like the two passionate, young and shattered lovers that they were---probably something about my father staying out too late at the "Alibi Club" and letting gay men buy him drinks if he did who knows what on their behalf. Why my mother allowed him to drive, drunk as he did, only to slide into the oncoming traffic momentarily, sparing us at the last second---I will never know. I remember, as clearly, as I'm writing this today---hearing a voice saying: "I'm going to have to write about this, cause NOBODY is going to believe it otherwise." I think the reason I remember this voice speaking is that it was a voice---speaking. The voice I heard, it turns out, is the one speaking right now, the mature woman who just turned 50, who started writing at 33. Nobody 'writes' or makes 'a writer' of themselves where I come from, they 'just stand back and let it all be' as Bruce Springsteen "Jungleland" (1975) lyric goes. And while it appeared like I would do everything else but write for many years, I did begin one day---to finally 'write' about what other people were never going to believe otherwise.

Amparo García-Crow;

Austin, Texas;
January, 2009

Cocks Have Claws and Wings to Fly

This play was developed at South Coast Repertory 's "Hispanic Play Festival" in 1993 as "Cocks Have Claws and Wings to Fly" and then produced by Latino Chicago (Chicago, Ill.) the following fall under the same title. Live Oak Theatre in Austin, Texas awarded the play the Larry King "Best Texas Play" award that same year. The Planet Theatre, in San Diego, California in co-production with San Diego State produced the now completed (final) draft in the Spring of 2003.

CHARACTERS

SOFIA   22 years old, Hispanic. Stocky and feisty. A senior at the University of Texas in Austin, majoring in psychology.

SCOTT   Early twenties, White. Boyfriend of Sofia. A musician. Wiry. A very artsy fellow.

PEDRO   33 years old, Hispanic. Gay. Brother of Sofia. The "successful" son, who makes a lot of money being an accountant. He is an avid athlete. Lives with his lover Alfredo, except when his family comes to town, then he makes Alfredo move out.

ALFREDO   45 years old. Pedro's live-in lover. Elementary school teacher. A kind-hearted man who loves children. This character can also be portrayed by a non-Hispanic actor who can speak Spanish and present the part as someone who grew up in the barrio knowing all the cultural slang

and informalities his character uses.
(Can double as Father Boots/Father's
Ghost or R.D. Laing)

GUERO 18 years old. Brother of Pedro and
Sofia. He looks different from the
rest of the family. He has light
brown hair and is lightly
complicated. He's an acid head. New
father of a baby girl.

MAMA Mirta. 48 years old. Would have
liked to have been a nun except she
ran off to get married at 14. A
licensed vocational nurse by trade
and an avid "soldier" in the Army of
the Virgin. Mother of Sofia, Pedro
and Guero.

SANTIAGO Tio. Vet who lost his soul in the war.
Over medicated, withdrawn, lost in
his own thoughts. A slow-tempoed
man. Much humility and
unconscious dignity.

FATHER Parish priest. Recently deceased.
Now wears colorful Nigerian robes

BOOTS. Originally from Spain, speaks with a Castilian accent.

FATHER'S GHOST We only see his body in a black tux with a red cummerbund.

R.D.LAING Famous psychotherapist/author. Must be able to impersonate Groucho Max. (Can double as Santiago)

DUENDE: The figure in black, much like the one you meet in "noh" theatre which moves things--- props, scenery etc. when necessary. She can also personify disembodied characters like the 'little girl' that Santiago is haunted by. She steps in when necessary to represent "that" which cannot be explained but nonetheless moves things--- forward or back.

FATHER'S GHOST/HAMLET'S VOICE A famous recording of Sir Lawrence Olivier as Hamlet or some such BBC rendition of. These voices may also be performed live offstage through a microphone, affected with English accent and high melodrama.

PLACE -Pedro's House, Sofia's Apartment in Austin, Texas

-Mama's House, St. Francis de Assisi church in a small town in South Texas

-Scott and Sofia are depicted in two separate bedrooms. Only the headboards need to be changed.

Preshow

Act I, Scene 1

(Lights come up on a white spiral staircase. The
FATHER'S GHOST, dressed in a black tuxedo
with a red cummerbund is at the very top of the
stairs. His face is not easily distinguished. **GUERO**
a young man with light brown shoulder length
hair enters. He wears jeans and a rock and roll t-
shirt, he seems dazed and very scared. Offstage a
scratchy BBC rendition of Hamlet's ghost can be
heard crackling. Now and then it skips at certain
key places. Guero stares out into the audience as if
the sight of his father is projected here.)

VOICE: I am thy father's spirit, doomed for a
certain term to walk the night, and for the day
confined to fast in fires, till the foul crimes done in
my days of nature are burned and purg'd away.
But that I am forbid to tell the secrets of my prison
house I would a tale
unfold(skips)…unfold…unfold…

(Guero bumps into a piece of furniture which
releases the voice.)

VOICE: whose lightest word would harrow up thy soul(skips)thy soul…thy soul…thy soul…

(He hits his head with his hand, again releasing the voice.)

VOICE: freeze thy young blood, make thy two eyes like stars form the start from the spheres, thy knotted and combined locks to part and each particular hair to stand on end like quills upon the fearful porpentine. But this eternal blazon must not be to ears of flesh and blood (skips)…and blood…and blood.

THIS TIME HE STOMPS HIS FOOT ON THE FLOOR, RELEASING THE VOICE ONCE MORE.

List, list, O, list! If thou didst ever thy dear father love---

GUERO: (shouts with the Hamlet recording) Oh, God!

VOICE: Revenge his foul and most unnatural murder.

GUERO (continues to shout with the recording): Murder! Murder!

VOICE: Murder most foul, as in the best it is, but this most foul, strange, and unnatural.

HAMLET'S VOICE: Haste me to know't, that I with wings as swift as meditation, or the thoughts of love, may sweep to my revenge!

(After his shout of "revenge" Guero hurries up the staircase to follow the figure. Lights fade as Guero reaches the top.)

Act I, Scene 2 –

Pedro's Kitchen - Austin, Texas

(**SOFIA LOPEZ** and her boyfriend, **SCOTT ANDERSON** are unpacking groceries in the kitchen/dining room of Sofia's brother's house. The rooms are decorated with taste and style. Above the modern dining table hangs a print of Salvador Dali's "Last Supper.")

SOFIA: She turned the garden hose on me so I bit her.

SCOTT: (laughing) Unbelievable! God knows there's plenty of times you should have bit her but I can't believe you actually bit her.

SOFIA: Oh, shit, he's out of milk. Did you get some? She's been bugging me about it all day.

SCOTT: It was on the list, right? Then I got it.

SOFIA: It's time somebody humiliated her for a change, you know?

DIGGING IN THE BAGS.

I just see sour cream and coffee beans.

SCOTT: Oh shit, I left a bag there?

SOFIA: She can use half-and-half in the meantime.

SEES A BAG ON THE FLOOR.

Here it is, never mind, we're safe.

SCOTT: Doesn't your mom have a weak heart, Sofia?

SOFIA: So she says. What she has is a mongrel mouth. Just cause she's old doesn't mean I have to put up with it.

PEDRO, SOFIA'S BROTHER ENTERS. HE IS A STRIKINGLY HANDSOME GAY MAN AND VERY AWARE OF HIS BODY.

PEDRO: It's chewed up again.

SOFIA: Mother, probably.

PEDRO: The neighbor's dog. I'm about this close to poisoning it. Wish I had my BB gun. Thanks for shopping for me, I haven't even had time to work out this week. Oyes, is mother acting pretty strange or what? She has to be going through the change of life or something.

SOFIA: Worse. The same old life.

SCOTT: Sofia bit your mother. (to Sofia) You'll go to hell for that.

SOFIA: As long as I don't have to run into her there.

PEDRO: What?

SCOTT: The Mother's Day massacre.

SOFIA: I didn't mind the hose really, but when she went for my hair, I lost it.

PEDRO: What happened?

SOFIA: She's pregnant, Pedro. She drops the bomb on me outside while she's watering your rose bushes. I told her she was nuts and she turned the hose on me.

PEDRO: You actually bit her?

SOFIA: Shut up! After she pulled my hair. Did you hear me? She's pregnant.

PEDRO: No wonder she's been acting so crazy. That woman eats saints and shits devils, I swear to God. You know what she did to me, when she got here, unannounced, mind you? Now it makes sense, sort of. She gets here at dawn and wakes me up, right, it's Saturday, for God's sake, so Alfredo and I are sleeping late, we're laying there, bien dormidos...and she just walks into our bedroom.

SOFIA: No knock or nothing?

PEDRO: (shakes his head) She tries to be sweet at first, talking like it's totally normal to barge in that way. I don't have my contacts on, but I notice that she's come into the room with a box about yea size. Like a damn fool I think, "Oh how sweet, Mama finally got me a birthday present." Like an innocent child I actually allow myself that fantasy. (to Scott) She's never bought me a gift in my life, okay? Never. Christmas, birthday, nothing, not even my college graduation, right? All my life she hands me a $10.00 bill and tells me to buy myself something, which takes all the fun out of it.

SOFIA: It's never enough to buy anything anyway, she should just forget it.

PEDRO: It got to where Sofia and I would go buy each other something with our ten dollars just so that we'd have a surprise under the tree.

SOFIA: So what happened?

PEDRO: So I'm laying there, touched, thinking she finally went and got me a real present. But then, very dramatically she puts the box down...and she says, "This is the virgin that will stomp the snake."

SCOTT: What the hell was she talking about?

SOFIA: Wait, wait, wait...what was in the box?

PEDRO: The Virgin, in this Barbie sized wooden box about yea size. The army of the virgin loaned her out.

SCOTT: Army of the virgin?

PEDRO: There's an army of the virgin. That is what they call themselves. In all of my years in this city I have never run into a single soldier for the virgin, right? But mom's here one week and just like that, at the supermarket, she runs right into them, like radar and they trust her with the portable traveling virgin. They loan her out I think like a library book or something.

SCOTT: So that was the gift?

PEDRO: No, I would have even appreciated that gesture, but she brought it to my house to exorcise the snake.

SCOTT: What snake is she talking about?

PEDRO: I don't know, all I can figure is that Alfredo gave me this ring. It's a snake, you know the eternity symbol of the snake biting its own tail, pos anyway, ever since she saw it on my finger, it's made her nervous. To make things worse, Alfredo's elementary school is having their annual fundraiser right, so we had all this Halloween looking stuff all over the house when she got here, real hocus pocus stuff.

SCOTT: No way you guys, you're not giving her enough credit.

SOFIA: Scott! She's very superstitious. (to Pedro) I saw her giving the hairy eyeball to your Omni magazine. The one with the snake on the cover.

SCOTT: Oh my God, yes…the giant snake eyes…magnified…

SOFIA: And…underneath, in bold letters it says "the occult."

PEDRO: No way. That explains it right there. Se le puso que es del Diablo, the occult can only mean one thing…

SCOTT: What?

PEDRO: Sodomy. She wants the virgin to kick the snake's butt…what do you think? She wants to believe that Alfredo and I do not exist. We were even under the sheets, Alfredo and I, when she came into my room and the whole time she's pretending he's not there.

SCOTT: No way.

PEDRO: Even when I confronted her she says to me, "Pos no lo vi."

SOFIA: (to Scott) : She didn't see him.

PEDRO: "O nomas vi las almohadas."

SCOTT: She just saw the pillows?

PEDRO: That's right and she standing right over handing me her hand, you know, like the stewardess from hell, deadly sweet and then she leans that cheek over to me.

SOFIA: I hate when she does that. It's so gross. She just plants that fat cheek on your mouth so you have to kiss her. It makes me want to throw up. Why doesn't she use the virgin on herself to stomp out the snake that got her pregnant.

PEDRO: So who got her pregnant?

SOFIA: The saint himself. Santiago.

PEDRO: Tio? I'm impressed. I didn't think he could still get it up at his age. So why do I have to sleep on the couch to let her have my bed? The deed has been done. They should both just shack up in the guestroom.

SOFIA: Not with Guero in the house. They play this charade for his benefit, I think.

PEDRO: I almost did a terrible thing, had I not been naked...I have this rubber snake in my closet about yea long and this thick, it looks real and weighs about as much as a real snake, okay? When she made her pronouncement I wanted so much to grab it likes Moses or something and hold it over my head like I had wrestled it down with my bare, brute strength. I wanted to throw it on top of the virgin in the box, just to see who would stomp who...

SOFIA: Aye no, Pedro, it would have given her a heart attack, as much as I want to kill her sometimes (knocks on wood)...I don't want her dead, yet.

SCOTT: Did she bring the virgin to our house?

SOFIA: Never, I bit her, remember?

SCOTT: More reason.

MAMA: (offstage) Did you get the milk?

SOFIA: I didn't know she was back. (to Mama) Yes!! (to Scott and Pedro) You think she heard us? Is Santiago here too?

PEDRO: (Pedro nods.) They never leave the den, they watch TV all day long.

MAMA ENTERS. SHE LOOKS OLDER IN THE WAY SHE CHOOSES TO DRESS. SHE IS A BULKY WOMAN, DYES HER HAIR TO COVER THE GRAY. HER HAIR IS SHORT AND KEPT SO

TO BE THE LEAST AMOUNT OF WORK. SHE WEARS NO MAKE-UP EXCEPT RED LIPSTICK NOW AND THEN.

MAMA: The doctor says I can't be drinking that fat milk. You got the low fat milk I hope. (spots Scott) Mira nomas.

MAMA TURNS INSTANTLY INTO HER SWEET SELF.

Scott, how are you?

MAMA OFFERS SCOTT HER CHEEK AND HER WEAK HANDSHAKE. SOFIA AND PEDRO GIVE EACH OTHER AND SCOTT A KNOWING LOOK, TRYING NOT TO LAUGH.

SCOTT: Mrs. Lopez, so good to see you.

MAMA: And your mother? How is she?

SCOTT: The arthritis slows her down a lot.

MAMA: Ay, probrecita. It killed my father. It stops you in your tracks and freezes you like a statue till you dry up and die. Que lastima. At least that's what happened to Papa, pero Nancy is a strong woman isn't she?

SCOTT: I hope so.

MAMA: (to Pedro) I know so.

RUMMAGES THROUGH THE GROCERIES

Tell your maid not to cook tonight, I want to take you all to Kentucky's. She works too hard Pedro, don't make her cook so much.

PEDRO: Mama, I do most of the cooking. She just cleans. Either way, I cook everyday around here, that's why me and Alfredo eat so well.

MAMA: Pos you need your protein too. If you don't eat meat you get weak blood.

SOFIA: Kentucky's is too much fat for your heart Mama, now that you're pregnant...

MAMA: (ignores Sofia) Pos esa mojadita is a good girl, Pedro. She does good work and she's cute too. I thank God for that. And she's very cute.

SOFIA: Ma, I'm talking to you. Listen, I'm sorry I bit you.

MAMA: You're trying too hard to be as skinny as that boyfriend of yours. No matter how much you try you're not ever going to be as small as him. Eat!!!!

SOFIA: I can't believe you.

MAMA: (to Pedro) That's what makes her crazy. (to Scott) Those diets, they make her bien hyper. (to Sofia) You snap at me like a mad dog.

SOFIA: What are you doing right now?

MAMA: I'm peaceful, I just want peace. It's better not to argue. I'm getting too old to argue.

SOFIA: But not too old to get pregnant.

MAMA: (to Sofia) I feel sorry for you. Probrecito Scott, (to Scott) what you must have to put with. It's a waste of all that education.

SOFIA: Attacking me with the hose and pulling my hair is peaceful? And then you tell me you're pregnant? I'm out of here.

SCOTT STAYS SITTING.

You can stay if you like Scott.

HE SITS RIGHT UP. SOFIA EXITS.

MAMA: (to Scott) She's anorexic.

MAMA HAS SCOTT'S ARM.

PEDRO: Sofia is not overweight for God's sake.

MAMA: That doesn't mean she can't be anorexic. (to Scott) Don't chase after her Scott, it just encourages her.

PEDRO: Let's drop it, please. Out of respect for Scott.

MAMA: (laughing sweetly) Scott knows we argue just in fun, he knows. It's better than holding it in. (to Scott) It's good to see you mijito. Let me take you to Kentucky's too.

SHE GRABS HIS CHEEKS, DOES A SPIRALING ACTION WITH HER HAND OVER HIS HEAD AND GIVES HIM ANOTHER DRAMATIC SQUEEZE OF THE CHEEKS.

No te quiero hacer ojo. The evil eye. You know not to take me personal, verda? Your skinniness is healthy, you should be glad you don't have to worry about fat, but for Sofia, it's different.

SOFIA: (Sofia enters.) Scott!

MAMA: (to Scott) You're as cute as ever, those beautiful eyes. (to Pedro) Aye, que lindo. Se parece a San Martin.

SUDDENLY MAMA IS TWENTY-FIVE YEARS YOUNGER, LOST IN A ROMANTIC REVERIE, PERHAPS.

SOFIA: Yeah. The black saint of lost causes. Let's go!

MAMA: (to Scott) Anda hombre. (to Sofia) You're talking about Saint Jude. He's the one for lost causes.

SOFIA: Yeah, and San Martin is the saint of animals.

MAMA AND SOFIA GLARE AT EACH OTHER. MAMA REALIZES SOFIA IS RIGHT AND IS SPEECHLESS.

Don't you get it Scott? Let's go!

(Sofia and Scott exit.)

Act I, Scene 3 -

Still Pedro's House

(Guero, the young man in Scene 1 is staring at Dali's "Last Supper.")

GUERO: I was there.

SOFIA: Where?

GUERO: (indicates the painting) The Last Supper, man. I know what it is to be asked: take his body, drink his blood…wanting me to dig into him, like I was Pedro or something. But I'm not that naïve, I'm too street smart, you know?

SOFIA: No, I don't know.

GUERO: I've heard every line before. It's a dog eat dog shit world, so what if he's a man of God, you know? He's still just a man. I know a fucking snake when I see it. I'm the son of Judas, man. It's stamped on my forehead.

SOFIA: You sure it's not a number, like 666?

GUERO: Yeah, it's a number to call, 1-800-666-6969. (laughs) It takes a Judas to make anything happen, don't forget that.

NOTICES SOFIA'S BRIGHT RED SCARF AROUND HER NECK.

You've got blood around your neck and shoulders, too… you know about sacrifice. Frailty thy name is, Sofia.

SOFIA: Can you speak English? Why are you so fucked up?

GUERO: (Reaches for scarf.) He's asking me for something very simple. Does he show up for you too?

SOFIA: Judas?

GUERO: Dad. Does he ask you to avenge his blood? "O that this salivated flesh would melt..."

SOFIA: Are you so starved for attention or what? You're worrying everyone.

GUERO: I see him all the time, Sofia. He stands there showing me the way...like an imprint...I'm to follow the moving object. He's the only one that knows about the fucking snake. The snake finds any way he can to get into your pants. But next time...and believe me, there won't be another next time ever never...should it happen again...I won't be afraid...

MAMA ENTERS

...even when they come with pins and needles.

MAMA: Guerito, there you are mijito. I've got your B-12. It'll make your blood strong.

GUERO TAKES HIS PANTS DOWN, EXPOSING
HIS BEHIND ON WHICH HIS MOTHER PLANTS
A B-12 SHOT. HE GIVES SOFIA AN "I TOLD
YOU SO" LOOK.

GUERO: I need all the strength I can get Mama.
For what I have to do, it's going to take the
strength of 10,000 bulls. God bless my mother, for
she knows what she does.

MAMA: You could use a shot to make your blood
healthy too, Sofia.

SOFIA: One of these days they're going to arrest
you.

MAMA: It's not against the law to give shots. I'm
a licensed nurse. This is a prescription.

SOFIA: From that crazed pharmacist that gives
you anything you ask for. It's not right. You're not
a doctor.

MAMA: He's a good man. If it wasn't for him, we
wouldn't be so healthy, all the tetracycline he's
given us over the years, mala gradecida.

GUERO: Can you see the stuff crawling up my
vein...it feels like ice, melting, turning my blood
into turbo, man..."Take this my blood, eat this my

body." I used to love that part. They still say that in public too, right?

MAMA: Who mijito?

GUERO: The priests. The pimps. Selling the meat of Christ.

MAMA: Ay, mijito, vente, don't talk like that. You need to sleep.

THE STAIRCASE COMES ON WITH THE FATHER'S GHOST, GUERO AGAIN STARES OUT, AS IF IN A TRANCE.

GUERO: I'm to follow the moving object…trust the king of shreds and patches…save me, father…hang over me with your wings.

MAMA: Vente, mijito…

MAMA GRABS HIS ARM AS SHE CONTINUES TO TALK BUT HER WORDS ARE MOUTHED AS WE HEAR INSTEAD THE VOICE OF HAMLET'S MOTHER SUPERIMPOSED OVER HER LIKE A BAD LIP-SYNCH JOB.

"O, Hamlet, speak no more! Thou turns'st my eyes into my very soul and there I see such black and grained spots as will not leave their tinct!"

GUERO STOMPS, HOPING HE CAN MAKE HAMLET'S MOTHER'S VOICE STOP. INSTEAD THE FATHER'S GHOST DISAPPEARS AS MAMA'S REAL VOICE PICKS RIGHT UP AS IF SHE HAD NOT MISSED A BEAT.

...pos, si, mijito, I heard you walking all night long. Wrestling is on, I know you don't like to miss that. Santiago is in Pedro's den watching it, go on, I'm running to Kentucky's to get supper. Andale, or you'll miss it.

GUERO: (Guero grabs her hand to kiss it.) My poor angel mother of mercy.

WHEN HE LOOKS UP FROM THE KISS HE SPEAKS OUT WITH UNEXPECTED SPITE AS IF MOMENTARILY POSSESSED.

"Confess yourself to heaven, repent what's past, avoid what is to come..." (back to his sweet self)...don't make the weeds nastier, ama.

MAMA: Bueno mijito.

GUERO: (Guero gets overly affectionate with her, she laughs self-consciously.) What would I do without you?

MAMA: Andale, mijito, Santiago needs company. He likes your company.

GUERO EXITS.

SOFIA: I can't believe you can laugh. Guero is sick. Really sick.

MAMA: We'll never get him back if we take him to the state hospital.

SOFIA: But mother, he needs help.

MAMA: Santiago is begging me not to. He knows. He's been there. Ruben too…

WHO'S RUBEN? NOW SOFIA IS EVEN MORE CONFUSED.

…with the Army of the Virgin, one of the regulars…he used to be a drug addict, so he knows what Guero is going through. Guero will be alright, we're praying every night.

SOFIA: I've never seen him this far gone.

MAMA: Those psychiatrists are crazier! Look how they messed up Santiago by using him like a guinea pig at the Veteran's Hospital. Just because you lack faith, and you have no need for the help of the saints for your sanity, you shouldn't be criticizing, instead you should be happy and on your knees giving thanks. Guero will get better, you'll see.

SOFIA: Did you tell him about the wedding?

MAMA: Yes.

SOFIA: And the baby?

MAMA: No, he's not ready for that.

SOFIA: What do you mean he's not ready for that? He just had one of his own.

MAMA: And he wasn't ready for that either.

SOFIA: And we are?

MAMA: He says he sees your father and you father wants him to avenge his death.

SOFIA: That's what I'm talking about.

MAMA: He's always been very sensitive, Sofia and you have always been jealous.

SOFIA: Of what? That he's a drug addict?

MAMA: He has no skin. He is not tough like you. He is sensitive and you know he has never been the same since your father's death. He saw it happen por dios. You cannot begin to understand what that does to a person.

SOFIA: You think I have to have seen my father sliced up in order to be affected? What about the rest of us? I've lived in a fucking asylum of a house all my life and now, as if we didn't have a full house of locos, you're marrying a crazy man too.

MAMA: You could only hope to be as crazy as Santiago. He's a saint. He never hurt anybody. He's a good man.

SOFIA: He's schizophrenic!

MAMA: Those military doctors label everybody that!

SOFIA: So why are you gonna have his baby? Mama, women over 40 have retarded children, all on their own. Now add Santiago's mental illness to the pot and there's no telling what kind of a monster you're going to bring in to the world.

MAMA: Santiago's a good man, Sofia. Just because the war broke his nerves…

SOFIA: I didn't say he wasn't nice.

MAMA: You'll never find a better man with a bigger heart anywhere.

SOFIA: I like him, okay? I just don't want him to be my father. I think you're only marrying him because you think you have to. This isn't the 50s anymore, you don't have to have all your mistakes. Why would you want to bring another opinion into the world, Ama?

MAMA: Que dices? I never understand what you say to me.

SOFIA: Haven't you brought in enough mistakes into the world, already?

MAMA:I understand Guero so much more easy than you. He might be crazy but he has a heart.

SOFIA: Think! For the first time in your life, Ama.

MAMA: I know I'm stupid, Sofia. You don't have to smear the dirt in my face. I am not as smart as you but let me tell you something, genius is borderline insanity, that's what Dr. Garcia used to say when I worked in the emergency room. You think too much and you are just as crazy for it!

Act I, Scene 4 –

Sofia and Scott's Apartment

(The apartment is collegiate but artsy. Scott sits on the bed picking on an unplugged electric guitar.)

SOFIA: I came this close to slashing my wrists.

SCOTT: Oh, come on baby, it can't be that bad.

SOFIA: It's so humiliating. She's going to have to get married.

SCOTT: Maybe it's a good thing, don't you think? Someone to take care of her?

SOFIA: Someone she can terrorize you mean? You know what she told Guero? She told him they were already married, that she snuck off to Mexico to get married secretly because she didn't want to hurt him and that they have actually been married for several months.

SCOTT: Why would she do that?

SOFIA: To explain the pregnancy.

SCOTT: It's not like Guero doesn't know the facts of life, I mean he just went through all that nightmare with his girlfriend.

SOFIA: Believe me, if I could understand what goes through my mother's head. All I can figure is that she thinks she has to marry him.

SCOTT: Is it safe for someone her age to have a child?

SOFIA: Her own mother didn't have her till she was 48. How could she be so stupid? All of my life, she's done these adolescent things, I'm the one that's supposed to be doing those stupid things, like Guero. We've got every right, too.

SCOTT: So Guero bought the made up secret elopement story?

SOFIA: Who knows? Even if he hears you there's no guarantee that he's heard you. He's getting worse, every time I see him. And my mother won't get him the help he needs.

SCOTT: Is it acid, or what the hell is he taking?

SOFIA: Who knows, but whatever it is, he takes it like aspirin. I wish they would commit him but Santiago has convinced my mother not to because of what he went through after the war. They tortured the poor guy, electric shocks and every kind of mind drug they could think of. So since, my poor uncle is a basket case…

SCOTT: You said uncle.

SOFIA: Yeah, he was my father's uncle. Grand uncle.

SCOTT: It's hard to keep track of all your family babe, you got cousins that are aunts, sisters that are grandmothers, it's not exactly the neat little Brady Bunch thing I'm used to. So your mother is marrying your uncle, is that legal? Sounds like incest.

SOFIA: (screams!!!) They're not related!!! He's my father's uncle.

SCOTT: Okay, alright already, its confusing, that's all. You don't have to bite my head off.

SOFIA GIVES HIM AN "OH THAT'S SO FUNNY I FORGOT TO LAUGH" LOOK.

Sorry. So when's the wedding?

SOFIA: Who knows? I can't get her to talk about it.

SCOTT: What about Guero?

SOFIA: What about him?

SCOTT: Don't you think he'll figure it out? Especially if they have this wedding?

SOFIA: Who cares if he does, now you sound like my mother.

SCOTT: How old is your mom anyway?

SOFIA: I don't know, forty?

SCOTT: Amazing, and your uncle?

SOFIA: I think he's sixty.

SCOTT: Fucking amazing sperms! They just keep going, don't they? That's a frightening thought.

SOFIA: Yeah, especially when you think how long Santiago's sperms have been on the shelf. I worry for them. They can bring a Mongoloid into the world and actually that's the best case scenario.

SCOTT: Come over here and catch your breath at least.

SIGNALS FOR HER SIT ON THE BED.

You get so stressed out when your family is in town. You need to relax.

STARTS TO STROKE HER.

All that talk about sperms…

SOFIA: Gross!

SCOTT: It'll relax you.

SOFIA: (Starts to hug and kiss her.) I feel weird.

SCOTT: Why?

SOFIA: You're weird to say what you said.

SCOTT: (Still stroking her seductively.) Forget what I said, Sofia. Take a deep breath.

SOFIA: There's no way I can get turned on talking about my mom.

SCOTT: I just miss you, sweetie. Take a deep breath…come back, come back wherever you are.

SOFIA: (Kisses her gently. She suddenly pulls away.)You are too skinny, Scott.

SCOTT: Ooooh honey, I love it when you talk dirty to me.

SOFIA: (Kisses her again.)No, you really are.

SCOTT: And you're chubby, so?

SOFIA: Fuck you Scott! That really hurts my feelings.

SCOTT: And just when I'm all hot and bothered and feeling pretty damn good, you tear into me, "You're too skinny, Scott," that hurts my feelings. You know I'm sensitive about that. How come I'm only skinny when your mother is in town?

SOFIA: You have no idea what I've been through. You start feeling me up like that's supposed to feel good right now...

SCOTT: Excuse me?

SOFIA: The last thing I want to do is "do it" right now.

SCOTT: How long is she going to be here?

SOFIA: I don't know.

SCOTT: Don't think I can take it, babe.

SOFIA: You're gonna leave me aren't you?

SCOTT: Well, I'm thinking about it.

SOFIA: Then don't think about it, do it! Get the fuck out!

SCOTT: Why don't you?

SOFIA: Because I asked you to.

SCOTT: It's my apartment, remember?

SOFIA: (Sofia grabs the nearest item and throws it against the wall.) Not if I can help it.

SOFIA PROCEEDS TO GO FOR OTHER ITEMS, SCOTT GRABS HER ARMS, THEY STRUGGLE TILL SHE BITES HIM.

SCOTT: God damn it, you bitch! What did you do that for?

SOFIA: Oh my God…

SCOTT: Your family is possessed, all of you. Now you're turning into a rabid dog.

SOFIA: I'm sorry…

SCOTT: Get out of here, before I call the police.

SOFIA: (to herself) What's happening to me?

Act I, Scene 5a –

Pedro's House

ALFREDO: (Alfredo, Pedro's lover has stopped by. He is conservatively dressed.) Well, I see things are all in one piece at least. Give or take a thing or two. (spotting Kentucky bucket) Oh God, carcass. You're not eating this shit are you? Just paying for it, I hope.

PEDRO: I told you to call before just appearing, unannounced.

ALFREDO:I live here for God's sake. I'm not the one that came unannounced if you recall. Besides, I've run out of clothes, that's why I'm here, excuse me.

PEDRO: I know I'm asking a lot...

GESTURES FOR ALFREDO TO LOWER HIS VOICE.

ALFREDO: (raises his voice) Well don't then! Ask more of <u>them</u> for a change. Check <u>them</u> into the Holiday Inn, they'd probably love it. I hate it. Stop shhing me.

PEDRO: I'm a wreck. A real wreck, God I wish they'd leave.

ALFREDO: And...

PEDRO: We'd be back to normal.

ALFREDO: Oh God forbid. It's my fault for going along with it. You know, putting me out makes you look real bad. Worst of all, it makes me look like a fucking door mat that says, "You're welcome! Come again!"

PEDRO: Mama's pregnant.

ALFREDO: (bursts out laughing) Well, well, well, well, well...

PEDRO GESTURES FOR ALFREDO TO QUIET DOWN BUT STOPS HIMSELF HALFWAY SINCE IT ONLY ENCOURAGES ALFREDO TO GET LOUDER.

Babies everywhere. Well, its practical, in some ways, we can share the baby clothes. What did she say when you told her about our baby? (no response) I see. I guess it can keep till the next unannounced visit and she trips over the baby when she walks in with who-knows-what-saint-in-a-box.

PEDRO: It's your baby, not mine.

ALFREDO: Why of course, just like its your house and not mine. Oh my God, this woman is unbelievable.

PEDRO: Don't blame her for this.

ALFREDO: I do! You regress the minute she's around.

PEDRO: I don't want this baby, you do. I don't think its right for two men to raise a little girl, its not...natural.

ALFREDO: You wait two weeks before the baby gets here to tell me this crap? Okay. Where is she, I think its time we had a little talk.

PEDRO: I will blow my brains out, I swear I will. I don't want this baby, Alfredo.

FINALLY IT'S OUT IN THE OPEN.

I don't. I don't want this baby, I don't like you fucking Blanca, even if she's your best friend and it's just to do "the deed" I can't deal with it.

ALFREDO: I can't believe you waited this long to tell me all this.

PEDRO: I'll help you with money if you need that but...

ALFREDO: Give me a fucking break, your money can't fix everything every time, Pedro. You can't buy your way out of this one, my friend.

PEDRO: It's about time you knew who you're living with then.

ALFREDO: (explodes) Oh give me a break.

PEDRO: You give me way too much credit.

ALFREDO: First "Insult me, I'm an asshole" then "Put up with me, I'm an asshole." Make up your mind, hombre! (beat) Look, we're under a lot of stress, let's don't talk about this right now, I just came for some clothes. So if you'll excuse me I'm going to go to <u>our</u> room now, into <u>our</u> closet…

PEDRO: Don't go up there.

ALFREDO: I thought you said she's at her fanatic meetings at this time? Did I get it wrong?

PEDRO: Her fiancé is up there.

ALFREDO: I won't come on to him, I promise.

PEDRO: You are so disgusting.

ALFREDO: Just pack me some clothes and bring them to me then.

PEDRO: Fine.

ALFREDO: Tonight.

PEDRO: Tonight.

ALFREDO: It will do you good to leave the house for a while. They haven't been messing with my things, have they?

PEDRO: What things?

ALFREDO: My knick-knack stuff.

PEDRO: They wouldn't know that...

ALFREDO: Exactly, they're expensive. You're the one who said they're pigs.

PEDRO: Please, Alfredo, I can't deal with this right now.

MAMA: (Mama enters through the front door.) Ay dios mio, I got lost.

PEDRO: You remember Alfredo?

MAMA: (nods to him)Don't let me disturb you.

GOES TO REFRIGERATOR TO POUR SOME MILK.

I must have turned right instead of left. I thought I would never find your street.

PEDRO: Why didn't you call?

MAMA: Pos I prayed real hard and it worked. Do you want some chicken, Alfredo?

ALFREDO: No, thanks.

MAMA: Oh that's right, Pedro says you don't eat meat.

ALFREDO: Well...it depends...

MAMA: There's some potatoes and corn, you can take some with you. It's good to have things to snack on late at night.

ALFREDO: Yes, that's true but no, thank you. I just had a big dinner.

MAMA: (to Pedro) He reminds me so much of Father Boots.

PEDRO: The priest back home.

ALFREDO: I'm flattered, I'm sure?

MAMA: (Pedro shakes his head.) He's been coming over a lot to talk to Guero.

PEDRO: (panics) Guero needs a doctor, Ama, not...that priest.

MAMA: But he's good...

PEDRO: He's...not the one to help Guero, Ama.

MAMA: But he's not like those other priests that just show up on Sunday, you know?

ALFREDO: You're talking about the pervert...

MAMA: Que dice?

PEDRO: Tio is still up, Mama, I think he's been waiting for you.

MAMA: Pos it's his nerves, Santiago worries so much. I better tell him I'm alright.

ALFREDO: I hear you're having a baby. Mira nomas, congratulations.

MAMA: We've been married for many months.

ALFREDO: Deveras? Why didn't you tell anyone?

PEDRO: Ama, you don't have to make anything up for us. Alfredo doesn't care.

ALFREDO: But I do care. So you got married, already, then?

PEDRO: They are going to get married.

ALFREDO: But she said they're already married.

PEDRO: Ama, its okay that you aren't married.

MAMA: Pedro, callate! You don't let me finish.

PEDRO: What is there to finish? I'm trying to save you the trouble.

ALFREDO: So if I'm hearing you right, you are already married, nobody knew, so you eloped or something like that and now you are going to get married...again?

MAMA: Through the church, that's right.

ALFREDO: I see.

PEDRO: No, you don't Ama, I'm just trying to tell you that its okay to just tell the truth, if you want to. Alfredo and I could care less about whether or not you got pregnant when you weren't married. It takes so much energy to remember lies, might as well just tell it like it is.

ALFREDO: It must run in the family.

MAMA: (to Pedro) Que dice?

ALFREDO: Pedro is asking you to do something he doesn't even know how to do himself.

MAMA: (ominously) I would not judge if you do not wish to be judged yourself, Alfredo.

ALFREDO: Oh, please, do senora (he laughs), somebody please, do me the favor.

PEDRO: Alfredo, please...

ALFREDO: I'm agreeing with what you just told your mother, mi amor. Tell it like it is.

MAMA: There is something in the way you say that Alfredo, that gives me a very bad feeling, se me paran los pelos...

PEDRO: Ama, he doesn't mean anything.

MAMA: I can feel it Pedro, I feel something evil in the way he stands there picando.

ALFREDO: Yo no le estoy picando nada, maybe the truth is what you are calling evil, senora.

MAMA: Only God speaks the truth Alfredo.

ALFREDO: Well thank God for that. Then I don't have to listen to your...

MAMA: Let me tell you something Alfredo. The way you behave is more on the side of the animal.

ALFREDO: Excuse me?

MAMA: What you do is unnatural, God did not wish for that to happen because if he did...

SHE REACHES INTO HER PURSE.

…Adam and Eve would not have been a man and a woman. You take advantage…

ALFREDO: I take advantage?

MAMA: You're old enough to be Pedro's father…

PEDRO: Ama, please…

MAMA PULLS OUT A CRUCIFIX FROM HER PURSE AND HOLDS IT UP AS IF ABOUT TO DO AN EXORCISM.

Oh why of course, oh my God…I'm suppose to cringe right, like a vampire or some bad devil… (to Pedro) Can you please call her off?

MAMA: Mira Pedro, he can't even look me in the eye.

ALFREDO: Not with that thing in front of your face.

MAMA: That's because you're ashamed.

ALFREDO: (still laughing) No, because it's so fucking big, bigger than your mouth even, of course, I can't see you when you hide behind it.

PEDRO: Alfredo, you need to leave.

ALFREDO: (explodes) This is my house damn it! Get this bitch from hell to go!

MAMA CROSSES TO ALFREDO ABRUPTLY AND KNOCKS HIM IN THE MOUTH WITH THE CRUCIFIX. THE BRASS CRUCIFIX CHIPS ALREDO'S TOOTH AND CAUSES HIM TO START BLEEDING.

MAMA: Malo desgraciado!

ALFREDO: My tooth! God damn it, she broke my fucking tooth.

PEDRO: (Pedro grabs the crucifix from her.) Ama! For God's sake.

ALFREDO: (to Mama) I want you out of my house or I'll throw you out.

PEDRO: Alfredo, please.

ALFREDO: Stay away from me!

PEDRO: She didn't mean it.

ALFREDO: Senora, you better hope your prayers get heard. People like you are already in hell and they want to drag everyone else there with them.

PEDRO WALKS TOWARD ALFREDO.

Stay away form me, I'll kill you, I swear to God! You and that crazy woman. If they are not gone by tomorrow, I will call the police and press charges.

ALFREDO EXITS ABRUPTLY.

MAMA: Esta endiablado. He's brainwashing you, mijito. You are doing things with him that are against your will. It's not right, mijito.

PEDRO: No Ama, hitting someone is not right. All my life I've had to put up with it, we'll I won't. Not anymore.

MAMA: I never hit you. Not any more than any mother does. God forgives, even if you can't.

PEDRO: Well then ask him to, I don't know if I can.

MAMA: See how you sound like Alfredo?

PEDRO: You used to hit yourself with the frying pan and knock yourself out! I would sit there hysterical, thinking you were dead for God's sake. I was just a kid.

MAMA: That was then mijito, now is now, you have to forgive and forget.

PEDRO: But you're still acting like a maniac and I'm not a kid anymore.

MAMA: Ruben, probecito, he was worried, tonight at the meeting. He thinks because the drugs didn't kill him and he was spared that he has to pay a debt of some kind because he can't believe God has forgiven him.

PEDRO: Who the hell is Ruben?

MAMA: The drug addict I've been telling you about. He was the one that the virgin saved.

PEDRO: There you go again.

MAMA: (painfully) I told him that if God can forgive me he can forgive anyone!

Act I, Scene 5b –

Still Pedro's House, Scene continues

GUERO: (Guero enters.) Pack of wolves, chewing on the fat ese.

MAMA: Are you hungry, mijito?

GUERO: I don't need food, Ama. I breathe what I need, one long breath goes a long way.

SEES PEDRO.

Pedro, my main man…

MAMA: There's still some Kentucky left, mijito.

GUERO: (very jolly) All work and no play makes my brother a strange, a stranger man in a strange land. You want to know what the problem is carnal? You're invisible. If it wasn't for the bells on your toes, I wouldn't know where to look.

MAMA: Mira, there's some mashed potatoes and corn, mijo.

GUERO: (Looks at his mother intently.) How is it with you old lady?

MAMA: (Hamlet's mother/the recording) "Alas, how is't with you that you do bend your eye on vacancy and with th' incorporeal air do hold discourse?"

MAMA'S BEEN TALKING ALL ALONG LIKE BEFORE.

Que te paso mijito? Your soul has flown away, que lastima?

GUERO: Mommy dearest, I'm looking for an eraser. You got one? I can't write all the checks and balances without a pencil. A red pencil. For check marks!

MAMA CLOSES HER EYES AND PLACES HER HANDS IN THE PRAYER POSE. SHE PRAYS QUIETLY.

See what I mean? (to Pedro) She's always on the phone… whispering all that long distance 911-can-I-help-you-please God help him bullshit…

WALKS UP TO THIS MOTHER AND GESTURES A KNOCK AS IF HIS MOTHER'S HEAD IS A DOOR.

Rap-a-tap-tap-mom. They're coming for me and this time I'm signing up. (to Pedro) Even if he did have you on your knees, bro…you were just being yourself, you know that?

AT FIRST PEDRO THINKS GUERO IS UP TO HIS USUAL NONSENSE, BUT SOMETHING ABOUT THIS "TRANSMISSION" IS NOT ONLY MESMERIZING, BUT TRUE.

(points to Mama) Can you believe she sent me there? But I could see it coming, man. From a mile away. So I left him there with his pants down and his hand on his own dick. You know what I'm saying?

MAMA: (Hamlet's mother) "O, Hamlet, thou hast cleft my heart in twain…"

GUERO: (to Mama who is still praying) Throw away the bad part of it and live purer with the other half…assume a virtue if you have it not, Ama…

GUERO LOOKS AGAIN, OUT INTO THE AUDIENCE. FATHER'S GHOST APPEARS MOMENTARILY IN THE STAIRCASE, AGAIN GUERO LOOKS OUT TOWARDS THE AUDIENCE.

…look bro…here it comes! "Angels and ministers of grace defend us! Be thou a spirit of health, or goblin damn'd, bring with thee airs from heaven or blasts from hell, be thy intents wicked or charitable, thou com'st in such a questionable shape."

THE VISION DISAPPEARS. GUERO TURNS TO PEDRO.

Whoa, Pedro…you look like you just saw a ghost, man. It gets easier when you stop fighting it…really.

MAMA HANDS GUERO A PENCIL.

Yes!!! I have found what I have come looking for…it's that simple…if you set out to seek, you will definitely find. (points to Pedro) By heaven, I will make a ghost of him that let's me!

GUERO EXITS.

PEDRO: He needs help, Ama.

MAMA: I blame myself.

PEDRO: Whatever you do, don't send him to Father Boots, anymore.

MAMA: I don't send him. He comes to see Guero. At the house.

PEDRO: Worse.

MAMA: I have felt sorry for Guero…over-protected him…all of his life, mijo.

PEDRO: He's getting worse, mother.

MAMA: He doesn't look like the rest of you.

PEDRO: So? What Mexican family looks alike?

MAMA: He's not like the rest of you. I've done such bad things.

PEDRO: Somehow it always ends up being about you. I don't know how you do it mother.

MAMA: (continues to try to explain) It wasn't other men, just one man.

PEDRO: What?

MAMA: He was from Mexico City…muy chulo…as white as Scott…I was a stupid girl…20 years old…with already two babies…and your daddy running around with women all over town.

PEDRO: We were talking about Guero, Ama.

MAMA: Pos we were talking about forgiveness, mijo…

PEDRO: So you had an affair with the guy?

GUERO: Pos that's why I protect Guero so much, because he's not one of you.

PEDRO: I have to make my bed down here…I've got a horrible headache.

MAMA: Si, como no…rest mijito. You need a good rest.(beat) Maybe you're hungry. There's more Kentucky…

PEDRO GOES TO THE SOFA AS MAMA WAITS, HOPING HE WILL CONTINUE TO BE AUDIENCE TO HER. PEDRO, WHO LOOKS LIKE HE'S BEEN THROUGH A BOXING MATCH, FORGETS SHE'S THERE. FINALLY AFTER A MOMENT, SHE CALLS OUT.

Asta manana. Mijo...

PEDRO HASN'T HEARD A WORD SHE HAS SAID. HE LOOKS AT HER, DISTRACTED.

Asta manana?

PEDRO: Si dios quiere.

MAMA: Si…si dios quiere.

Act I, Scene 6a –

Pedro's House - The day after - Evening

SOFIA: (Pedro is pouring himself another drink. He's pleasantly drunk.)

I thought you weren't drinking anymore.

SHE OBSERVES PEDRO A MOMENT

PEDRO: I don't. Except on special occasions.

SOFIA: (He offers to fill up Sofia's glass.) No thanks. I can ask them to leave for you…

PEDRO: It's my house, Sofia.

SOFIA: And Alfredo's.

PEDRO: Fuck him, he can't call the police if they're still here when he comes back.

SOFIA: Oh yes he can. He can file charges, Pedro. She broke his tooth and she could have put his eye out. I don't understand why you enable her this way.

PEDRO: I don't enable her.

SOFIA: Yes you do, you enable her.

PEDRO: Please don't psychobabble me right now.

SOFIA: Well it pisses me off and frankly, I think you're in shock or denial about the whole thing.

PEDRO: Well at least I don't go around biting people.

SOFIA: No, but you make it okay for your mother to batter your significant other.

PEDRO: Just because you can label it Sofia, doesn't mean you know anything about it. Why do you think Guero's so fucked up right now?

SOFIA: He's having a delayed grief response. It's pretty obvious.

PEDRO: No, Sofia. I think it's something worse than that.

SANTIAGO ENTERS. HE IS A VERY SHY, OLDER, NICE LOOKING MAN. HE IS TALL BUT CARRIES HIMSELF APOLOGETICALLY AND QUIETLY

SANTIAGO: Pedro, como estas?

HANDS HIM HIS HAND TO SHAKE.

SANTIAGO: Sofia…

HUGS HER.

Mucho gusto en verte. It's been a long time.

THEY SIT. THERE'S AN AWKWARD PAUSE TILL SOFIA STARTLES EVERYONE BY CALLING OUT.

SOFIA: (screams) Ama! Santiago is already downstairs, come on down.

PEDRO: Estas bien?

SANTIAGO: Oh si. I can't complain.

PEDRO: Well that's good.

PEDRO NODS A LOT NERVOUSLY.

Can I get you something to drink? A beer?

SANTIAGO: Si, thank you.

PEDRO DISAPPEARS TO GET A BEER.

It's not as hot here in Austin, verda?

SOFIA: No, it rains more here.

SANTIAGO: Si.

*PAUSE. SOFIA LOOKS NERVOUSLY FOR
PEDRO WHO FINALLY RETURNS.*

SOFIA: Mama says it's been very dry down there.

SANTIAGO TAKES THE BEER

SANTIAGO: (to Pedro) Gracias.

SOFIA: Lots of fires, I hear.

SANTIAGO: Si.

PAUSE

PEDRO: That's terrible.

SOFIA ROLLS HER EYES OUT OF VIEW OF TIO

SANTIAGO: Si.

PEDRO: It's such a shame.

SANTIAGO: Oh, si.

(PAUSE.

You're busy, no?

PEDRO: Oh, si.

SANTIAGO: I keep missing you.

PEDRO: Yes, I had to work late all this week.

SANTIAGO: And I go to sleep with the chickens.

PEDRO: I hope you've been able to find your way around.

SANTIAGO: Oh yes, it's a very nice place. Very beautiful. very beautiful.

PEDRO: Thank you, Tio.

MAMA ENTERS ACTING LIKE A SHY TEENAGE GIRL. SHE HESITATES TO SIT BY SANTIAGO, WHO HAS STOOD UP. SHE SITS IN ANOTHER CHAIR. HE SITS AGAIN.

PEDRO: Okay, we're all here.

SOFIA: (to Santiago) You're gonna marry her, right?

PEDRO: Sofia, can you hold off one minute.

SOFIA: I think you're both making a mistake to think you have to have this baby.

PEDRO: Sofia, can I please ask you to be quiet? Please?

SOFIA NODS, RELUCTANTLY.

I need to hear from the two of you what you <u>want</u> to do.

SANTIAGO: Pos, yo quiero ser lo que sea major...

PEDRO: Yes, but what do you <u>want</u> to do Tio? He wants to marry in the church. (to Mama) s that what <u>you</u> want to do?

MAMA: He wants to do what's right.

SOFIA: Obviously what is right has nothing to do with anything. Why is it so important to lie about it and tell everyone you're secretly married. Why?

PEDRO: Okay, okay, before we get distracted again...

SOFIA: Pedro, you've had too much too drink. I'm trying to move this along. I'm not going to lie about it. If anyone asks me, I will not lie about it.

MAMA: I have to protect your brother.

SOFIA: By keeping him away from the medical help he needs?

PEDRO: Sofia, I'm not drunk, yes I've had something to drink but if you don't mind...

MAMA: (to Sofia) ou're not going to be happy till you send Guero over the edge.

SOFIA: Excuse me, I think he's already there.

MAMA: He wants to kill the guy that killed your father, but you ...oh no, you won't be happy till he does something more stupid. Father Boots is helping him.

PEDRO: He's not helping...him.

MAMA: Anda hombre. He knows how to help young people, especially, the difficult ones.

PEDRO: That's how he covers his tracks, Ama. By taking the difficult ones that no one else knows what to do with. That makes it easier for him to do whatever he wants to do with them.

MAMA: Que dices?

SOFIA: Please, we don't need to get into this issue right now. We're here to talk about the wedding, first.

A KNOCK IS HEARD OFFSTAGE.

MAMA: Quien sera? Are you expecting someone, mijo?

PEDRO: I don't think so.

PEDRO GOES TO THE DOOR.

SOFIA: I think you and Tio are making a terrible mistake.

ALFREDO IS AT THE DOOR.

PEDRO: Oh my God, I forgot…

SOFIA: (Sofia sees it Alfredo.) Oh great.

ALFREDO: You couldn't even call?

PEDRO: Let's meet later.

ALFREDO: Have you been drinking?

ALFREDO SEES THE FAMILY.

Buenas noches.

SANTIAGO RISES AND WALKS UP TO
ALFREDO TO SHAKE HIS HAND.

PEDRO: Alfredo, this is Santiago.

SANTIAGO: Mucho gusto. You have a beautiful, beautiful place.

ALFREDO: (surprised) Oh thank you, I hope you're enjoying it.

SANTIAGO: Oh, si, gracias.

ALFREDO: I don't want to disturb you, I'm here to pick up some things. I can help myself. (to Tio) It was nice to meet you.

SANTIAGO: Thank you.

MAMA: Ya, no more talk Sofia. We will marry back home on a weekday when the church is free, I just want family, no reception or anything like that. You are invited, if you can make it, we would love to have you there. Vamos, Santiago.

SANTIAGO PROCEEDS TO FOLLOW HER.

This gives us time to confess and start all over again, verda Santiago?

SANTIAGO: Si, como no.

MAMA: He's not used to these late, big city hours.

SANTIAGO: (laughs self-consciously) Pos I go to sleep with the chickens. Con permiso.

MAMA: Hasta manana.

SOFIA: Si dios quiere. I'd like to take everyone out to breakfast in the morning.

PEDRO LOOKS AT HER DUMBFOUNDED.

(to Pedro) To celebrate. If you can't beat them...

MAMA: Bueno mijita. Did you hear that Santiago?

SANTIAGO: Oh, si.

MAMA: We are going out in the morning with Sofia. She's such a good girl. No te preocupes, mijita.

SOFIA: No, I want to Ama. (to Pedro) I do.

ALFREDO ENTERS HOLDING A CHEWED UP CORN COB JUST AS MAMA AND TIO ARE EXITING UP THE STAIRS.

ALFREDO: (very upset) What is this?

SANTIAGO: (innocently takes the cob) It's my corn. Thank you.

HE EXITS. MAMA STAYS BEHIND FOR A MOMENT TILL PEDRO URGES HER UP.

PEDRO: (herding them out) There's some clean towels on the bed, Ama.

HE LEADS HER UP AND AWAY FROM THE SCENE.

ALFREDO: (to Sofia) I was just bitten by at least a thousand hormigas swarming in my bedroom! Luckily I'm not allergic or I'd be dead.

PEDRO RETURNS

SOFIA: (to Pedro) I can't believe you. You know how she feels about Father Boots.

PEDRO: I can't believe you. "I want to take you out to celebrate."

ALFREDO: This cob was on our silk comforter, Pedro. And now they're ants all over the fucking place.

ALFREDO IS FRANTICALLY PUTTING THE PLACE IN ORDER.

SOFIA: Father Boots is the only help Guero's getting.

PEDRO: Father Boots is a fucking pedophile, Sofia.

SOFIA: Oh please.

ALFREDO: (to Sofia) Sofia, why don't you let them stay with you for a change? At least you already have ants running around in your place.

PEDRO: Sofia, I need you to leave.

SOFIA: We have a lot of mama business to take care.

PEDRO: (totally out of character) Get the fuck out! Now!!!

SOFIA IS STUNNED. SHE EXITS

Act I, Scene 6b –

Still Pedro's House, Scene continues

PEDRO: (calls after Sofia) I'm sorry…

NO RESPONSE

I've never talked to her that way.

ALFREDO: Oh please. My fricking tooth is gone, I don't see you worried about that. I have yet to hear an apology from anyone for anything. And now look, my fricking hand is ballooning up.

PEDRO: I'll get you some ice.

ALFREDO: Something!

PEDRO: Can you sit…for a moment?

PEDRO GOES TO GET AN ICE PACK TOGETHER.

ALFREDO: Only if you promise me I don't have to deal with that woman.

PEDRO: They've gone to bed.

ALFREDO: Your mother is a psychopath, I need to hear you say it.

PEDRO RETURNS WITH THE ICE PACK. ALFREDO NOTICES THE LIQUOR.

ALFREDO: You <u>have</u> been drinking.

PEDRO: I brought it out to toast the happy couple…

ALFREDO: You're drunk, Pedro.

PEDRO: You really do look like him. It never even registered.

ALFREDO: What?

PEDRO: Till Mama said it. How much you look like Father Boots.

ALFREDO: She thinks everybody looks like somebody she knows.(beat) I have to go.

PEDRO: But then Guero, out of the blue…talking his crazy talk…(suddenly very emotional)…standing there telling the total truth of it all.

ALFREDO: The truth of it all what?

THE MEN SIT QUIETLY FOR A MOMENT.

Pedro…I really have to go. The baby's early. Blanca's in labor, I just needed some clean clothes.

PEDRO: Did you hear what I said?

ALFREDO: Did you hear what I said? I told her I would be there. (pause) And you should be there too.

PEDRO IS FROZEN, UNABLE TO SPEAK. ALFREDO GETS UP TO LEAVE.

Besides, I don't like talking to you drunk.

PEDRO: But that's when I speak my truth.

ALFREDO: No, because after you speak your truth, you won't even remember doing it. I have to go.

PEDRO: Please...

ALFREDO STOPS TO LISTEN.

I can't trust myself. Not with a baby. Not with anyone.

ALFREDO: (suddenly fearful) Okay.

PEDRO: Maybe I can be the uncle.

ALFREDO: As opposed to?

PEDRO: The psychopathic mother, what the fuck do you think I'm talking about? You're the father, that can be clinically proven in a court of law even but what the hell am I?

ALFREDO: What do you want to be?

PEDRO: I know what I don't want to be. But, regardless, the baby will be taken care of. I promised you that.

ALFREDO: It takes more than money, Pedro. Babies have no skin, they feel everything. I don't want you around if you don't wanna be there. She'll know it and all her life she will feel it and she'll go around feeling pissed off or worse and not knowing why. Why do you think you feel like slashing your wrists every time your mother comes to town?

PEDRO: That's what I'm trying to tell you.

ALFREDO: Do you think she was happy to have you at fourteen? To this day, you're going around feeling all of her shit and you don't even know it.

PEDRO: (violently) It was the fucking priest that fucked me up!!! That's what I'm trying to tell you.

ALFREDO: The curse stops here then.

GETS UP TO LEAVE.

I'll pick up the rest of my stuff when they're gone.

PEDRO: The rest of your stuff…

ALFREDO: All of my things. I have to get moved out and moved in somewhere in time to set up a place for this baby. Call me when they leave.

PEDRO: You're moving out?

ALFREDO: You're off the hook.

PEDRO: No, goddammit! Just wait....

ALFREDO: I have to go.

PEDRO: (sobering up) Let me move, then...it's easier.

ALFREDO: That's not easier...

PEDRO: For the baby. I have to be gone for the...wedding anyway.

OUT OF THE BLUE.

You know how I hate the drive down there. There's nowhere to eat, mother's house is...

ALFREDO: Will you see him?

PEDRO: Who?

ALFREDO: Won't he be the one doing the service?

PEDRO: Oh my God. No. I don't think so. God, I hope not. Please...

(beat) Alfredo...just wait a moment...please? Don't move out, bring the baby here...while I'm gone. We can figure it all out when I come back.

ALFREDO: Call me when they're gone.

Optional: Duende

Scene 6 (b)

This is a moment in which "duende" can complete the dots---be it movement or just the simple act of bringing Act I to a close---animating whatever "stage" design or business might be necessary to touch upon the "other world." This is where duende has its say, even if it's never with words.

Act II, Scene 1 –

Mama's House - South Texas

(A sharp contrast to Pedro's home. Hanging over the bargain house dining room table is a print of Da Vinci's "Last Supper." On each side of the print, which has a cheesy metallic gold frame, are two black wrought-iron guitars Mama bought from traveling Mexican importers. There are several ceramic saints in various shelves as well as a gallery of Sears-made portraits of the family. Plastic flowers and other tchotckes, such as plaques proclaiming "Today is the first day of the rest of your life" hang prominently on the walls. Santiago sits quietly staring at the audience, as if not present, lost in his own (Duende)world. One of the Duendes, having taken on the persona of a young "flower girl" enters. She scatters tiny blooms around Santiago. She takes the plastic wedding bouquet that sits on the table and stands slightly away from Santiago, with his back to him. After a moment, she throws him the bouquet, startling him back to reality as the whole family assembles after the wedding service. That is, everyone, except Mama. Everyone is wearing Sunday attire. Pedro is holding a bouquet of fresh cut flowers.

The South Texas heat is oppressive, they all sweat through their clothes. Santiago, regardless of whether he caught the bouquet or not, sits as still as before. But this time, he holds the flowers in his hands.)

SOFIA: Why does mass have to be so long? Even when nobody's there? At least Father Boots makes it interesting when he does mass, he's so dramatic

- 110 -

but this guy taking his place is the pits. I could barely hear him.

SCOTT: That's really his name? Father Boots?

SOFIA: (shakes her head) Father Saludenio. He wears these huge cowboy boots.

SCOTT: But does he actually answer to Father Boots---to his face?

SOFIA NODS.

SOFIA: It's a small town. Every year he visits his family in Spain so they bring in a substitute who doesn't speak English. I'm sorry you couldn't understand the service.

SCOTT: English wouldn't have helped that, babe.

PEDRO ENTERS. SOFIA ALTERS HER MANNER.

PEDRO: Is there a vase for these? Let's use that one, take the plastic flowers out, they're so tacky! Scott, can you put water in that thing?

SCOTT DOES AS HE'S ASKED.

SOFIA: Do you realize how bossy you're being? Maybe you're the boss of your company...

SCOTT: I really don't mind.

SOFIA: But I do.

NOBODY SPEAKS FOR A FEW MOMENTS.

PEDRO: (to Scott) Have you seen the bride by any chance?

SCOTT: Not since the service, we thought she was with you.

PEDRO SHAKES HIS HEAD.

PEDRO: Did you take a look at her face?

SCOTT: Not really.

PEDRO: (to Sofia) Have you?

SOFIA SHAKES HER HEAD.

It's been the twilight zone around here. Her eyes are glassy, like she's stoned and when you try to talk to her, she doesn't blink. And she's doesn't say very much. This morning Santiago and I had to drag her out of the bathroom, she was mumbling and frantically dumping everything out of the medicine cabinet, including his medication, when he tried to stop her she slapped him.

SOFIA: That's the way to start a marriage, isn't it? I told you we shouldn't have allowed this to go this far, it's pretty obvious she doesn't want to be married. I'm sorry, Tio, but it's true.

SANTIAGO DOESN'T REACT.

SCOTT: Your mom said something weird to me at the church. I saw the look you're talking about, I think. I sort of blanked it out because I didn't know what she meant or whether I heard her right. I was standing at the church waiting for you to park and she came up to me and says: "cocks have claws, you know?"

SOFIA: What has claws?

PEDRO: You heard right.

SOFIA: Does she mean roosters?

SCOTT SHRUGS.

PEDRO: That's what I'm talking about. Guero-talk, I swear to God, she's acting like Guero.

SOFIA: He didn't slip her something did he? Where is he?

SHE WALKS UP TO TIO, IT'S NOT TILL SHE TOUCHES HIS ARM THAT HE EVEN BECOMES

AWARE OF WHERE HE IS OR WHAT HE'S DOING.

SANTIAGO: Que paso?

PEDRO: Do you know where Mama is?

SANTIAGO: Pos at the church, I think. That's where she goes, with the dogs. Everyday.

PEDRO: Shouldn't today be the exception, it's your honeymoon.

SANTIAGO: She wants Guero to get well.

PEDRO: So, what is she doing there?

SANTIAGO: Pos I think she prays, tu saves.

PEDRO: Have you noticed anything strange, Tio? About Mama?

SANTIAGO: Pos she's been very nice.

SOFIA: Well that's strange enough but what he means is has she been talking like Guero to you?

SANTIAGO: Pos, no…not really. She threw the pills out for my nerves. She said it was like eating broken glass and if I kept taking them they would cut me up inside.

SOFIA: That's what I mean, Tio.

SANTIAGO: Pos, she's probably right. Last night she kept kicking my feet, telling me I had hooves.

PEDRO: Hooves??

SOFIA: Like a goat or what?

SANTIAGO: Pos no, like the devil, that's what it sounded like.

SOFIA: That is strange, Tio. That is what we are talking about.

SANTIAGO: Pos most days, she treats me real good. It's other people. She's not always so good with them, como Crucito. He was here yesterday, cutting the grass, you know and she goes outside from behind and pulls his hat off and throws it to the ground. "You have horns," she tells him. Pos, it scared the little old man very much. I had to go outside and bring her back in, she gave me some good scratches...(shows his arm to everyone)...pero I had to pull her inside por que it looked like she wanted to push him down, y pos he's very skinny, very old. He turned white as a sheet and you know how black he is. So...she must be seeing devils everywhere. I don't take it personal, you know.

PEDRO: Tio. It's late, isn't it a little too late for her to be at church alone?

SANTIAGO: Pos the dogs are with her.

PEDRO: Si, Tio, but it's your honeymoon. You two need to go somewhere, I'll pay for it. Maybe Corpus, to the beach...something.

SANTIAGO: Bueno, pos, let me take the truck, that way we will all fit, the dogs can get on the back.

TIO BEGINS TO EXIT.

PEDRO: You two have to go somewhere, it would do you good to get away.

TIO EXITS.

SOFIA: It's a loony bin, I'm telling you.

GUERO: (Guero abruptly enters.) A party? Nobody invites around here. What's going on...hey Scott!! My man...

SCOTT AND GUERO EXCHANGE AN EXOTIC HANDSHAKE.

SOFIA: We're worried about mom. Did you…

INTERRUPTS…BIG REACTION

GUERO: She's acting WEIRD, man. Giving me the willies. She needs help. Bad.

Act II, Scene 2a –

St. Francis de Assisi Church, sort of…

(Duende world: Mama sits alone on a pew, looking hypnotized. There is no one else in the church. She is lit mostly by candlelight as she sits in the shadows of saints looking on from above.

In the center hangs, we presume, Jesus himself. But after a moment, the statue is very much alive. At first, Mama cannot believe what she's seeing. As the statue starts to move, Mama, in terror, rises and proceeds to get away.)

MAMA: Ay dios mio….

FATHER: Don't be afraid, Mirta. It's me. Father Saludenio.

MAMA: Father? I didn't hear you come in. I didn't know you were back.

FATHER: You're going to have to come closer.

MAMA: I didn't know you were back. Where are you?

FATHER: Right here. You know I'm hard of hearing. I need you to come closer.

MAMA IS AFRAID TO ASK THE OBVIOUS. SHE DOES AS HE ASKS, SHE APPROACHES HIM AND OUT OF HABIT, KNEELS AT HIS FEET, AT THE ALTAR

No, no, no…sit down where I can see you.

SHE'S NOT COMFORTABLE WITH THAT IDEA, BUT DOES AS HE ASKS. SHE GIVES HIM HER BACK…SHE LIKES LISTENING TO HIM, MORE THAN HAVING TO LOOK AT HIM, IN THIS STATE.

I see you're still praying and waiting for the soul of your son to be returned.

MAMA: But he's not dead.

SHE TRIES TO IGNORE THE FACT THAT FATHER BOOTS IS HANGING ON A CROSS.

FATHER: That's what that drug does, it pushes the soul out of the body.

MAMA: It started the day he saw his father cut up like an animal.

FATHER: Pos si, es el susto. When someone gets scared to death, they die, although their body can still look very much alive. That's why you're here, too.

MAMA: (surprised) In the church?

FATHER: With me.

MAMA: At the church.

FATHER: No, your body is still sitting at the church but your soul is roaming my dear. Lucky we found one another.

MAMA: Where is your body then?

FATHER: Where do you see it?

MAMA: (Mama does not want to look.) I can't really…say.

FATHER: I really want to know, Mirta. Can you look at me?

SHE LOOKS BACK FOR A MOMENT. IT FREAKS HER OUT.

MAMA: I can't, Father...

FATHER: Why? What do you see?

MAMA: What do you think I see?

FATHER: I can't know. Really. That's why I need you to tell me.

MAMA: You're hanging, Father.

FATHER: From a rope?

MAMA: On the cross.

FATHER: I'm hanging on a cross?

MAMA: Like Jesus, I thought you were Jesus, till I heard your voice.

FATHER: A car hit me as I crossed the street.

MAMA: In Spain?

FATHER: Si, in front of my mother's house.

A MOURNFUL, SOBBING WOMAN IS HEARD OFFSTAGE.

MAMA: Ay dios mio, who is that?

FATHER: That's you.

MAMA: I'm crying.

FATHER: You're mourning my death, I think.

MAMA: But I don't feel anything. It all feels so far away.

FATHER: When you're roaming you don't feel in the usual way. The body is the only place you feel. And since you're right here with me right now...

MAMA: Where's your...real body...right now, Father?

FATHER: Laid out, waiting to be buried.

MAMA: Why am I seeing you...hanging that way...if you're not really...hanging?

FATHER: Do you know the story of the thieves that were crucified next to Jesus that day?

MAMA: I'm sorry...no...que?

FATHER: They were in the right place, at the right time. It didn't matter that they lived their lives like barbarous criminals. In that moment...one of them knew to say: "Lord, remember me when You come into Your kingdom."

MAMA: He was forgiven, you mean.

FATHER: No, there was just suddenly nothing to forgive.

MAMA: But Father, you're not a criminal.

FATHER: Pick up the rod that was turned into a serpent, Mirta. Take it in your hand. Because until this moment, you haven't been willing to hear that.

MAMA: Hear what, Father?

GUERO IS SUDDENLY SEEN DESCENDING THE WHITE STAIRCASE. MAMA WANTS TO SAY SOMETHING BUT THE PRIEST SIGNALS TO HER TO STAY QUIET AND TO REMAIN SITTING. GUERO CONTINUES HIS DESCENT AS MAMA AND FATHER BOOTS CONTINUE THEIR VISIT. HE MOVES SLOWLY AND DELIBERATELY, AS IF IN SLOW MOTION AND WHEN THE VISIT COMES TO AN END, GUERO HAS FINALLY MADE IT DOWN ALL OF THE STAIRS. WITHOUT ACKNOWLEDGING THEM,

HE WALKS INTO THE DARKNESS RIGHT AS SANTIAGO ENTERS THE END OF THE SCENE.

FATHER: Every step is important. He'll find his way back. When you worry like you do, it forces you to live far away, somewhere far outside yourself, roaming like the living dead…and if you're here with me…who is living your life?

SANTIAGO: (offstage) Mirta!

MAMA: But Father…

LIGHTS GO OUT ON THE ALTAR AND FATHER BOOTS.

Act II, Scene 2b –

Still the Church, Scene continues

SANTIAGO: Are you there? Mirta?

SANTIAGO APPEARS.

Did they lock you inside, que paso?

MAMA: Where am I?

SANTIAGO: The church. It's closed, I got the janitor to open the door

MAMA: (suddenly overcome) Father Boots is dead.

SANTIAGO: (She looks back to where the altar was.) No, Mirta, he's in Spain, on vacation, remember?

MAMA: I just saw him…he was hanging on a cross. He didn't know he was hanging on a cross, but he didn't mind, once I told him.

SANTIAGO: Mirta, please. Let's go home. It's late.

MAMA: (Mama suddenly becomes very still.) He asked me to pick up the rod, Viejo…to strike the waters that were in the river, in front of God and his servants and everyone.

SANTIAGO: You're tired, mujer, its time to rest.

MAMA: All of the waters that were in the river have turned to blood. Did you hear me?

SANTIAGO: Everyone's waiting for us.

MAMA: We're not going to have this baby, Santiago.

SANTIAGO: Pero como no?

MAMA: The baby has died. I feel only emptiness. Like there was never any body there.

SANTIAGO: Ay dios mio, Mirta, that is enough death talk for one day. Pedro wants us to go somewhere, for our honeymoon. Vamos.

MAMA: We all go there, when we worry or when we're scared.

SANTIAGO: Where, mujer?

MAMA: (totally manic) Where Guero was. Where you go, when you just sit there for hours. I know where you go when you don't talk. I saw it through your eyes, Santiago, you <u>have</u> lived a living death, so it's easier to roam, Viejo. But Guero is going to come down and stay down, I saw it with my own eyes. That's why the Father has to hang like that. He was hanging on a cross.

SANTIAGO: Like the Christ?

MAMA: No, like the criminals that were hanging, next to the Christ…that's what he said…take me home, Viejo. I feel like I could sleep till Christmas.

Act II, Scene 3 –

Mama's House – the next day

(Guero is sitting at the kitchen table. He sits very still, something about him has shifted. After a moment, Sofia enters. Guero doesn't acknowledge her but she watches him like a hawk.)

SOFIA: There's a tropical storm headed for Corpus, maybe we should tape down the windows, can you help us?

GUERO DOESN'T ANSWER.

The TV said we could get up to ten inches of rain and lots of strong winds. Thank God the creek and everything is so dry right now, I don't want to have to sleep in the courthouse if it floods. So much for a honeymoon. We wanted Mama and Tio to go to Corpus, but now, all the roads are closed down. Are they home yet?

(Guero shrugs.)

Did your airplane land or what?

GUERO: The plane crashed, man. What do you think?

SOFIA: That's why I don't do drugs, it feels like I'm dying afterwards.

GUERO: How long was I gone this time?

SOFIA: A couple of weeks, maybe. You were high as a kite the whole time you were in Austin.

GUERO: Two weeks? No way, it felt like a couple of days, tops.

SOFIA: We came this close to taking you away in a straightjacket.

GUERO: Something happened to me.

SOFIA: No shit.

GUERO: I'm not talking about the drugs. I saw daddy. He was talking to me, it didn't sound like him, exactly, but I knew it was him. Did Miss Pena ever play those Shakespeare records for you, when you took her English class?

SOFIA: All the time…they make the shit easy to follow.

GUERO: Well that's what she's doing in class right now, playing those records, everyday…so like they're in my ear…those voices…but every time I see the old man, he's as real as you are okay…he's wearing this black tux with a red band…

GESTURES HIS WAIST.

right around here…right where he was stabbed! Whoa…I hadn't even made that connection, till right now, man! Wow.

SOFIA: You were hallucinating.

GUERO: But he was more real than that…he looks real concerned but he doesn't say nothing, but then like in a movie I start to hear that Shakespeare shit, some guy with an English accent, in my ear telling what I already know to be true.

SOFIA: You're not still hearing all that are you?

GUERO: When I'm in class, yeah and it stays with me…but it's the coincidences, man, there's no way to ignore it.

SOFIA: What is, you're losing me again.

GUERO: Mom, she doesn't even wait for the corpse to rot, man. Too many coincidences.

SOFIA: (confused) What?

GUERO: It doesn't look right. No respect. I got nothing against Tio, he's a damn good man, but she's running off with the uncle and shit.

SOFIA: You're joking, right? You know you're not Hamlet…

GUERO: No shit…but…something is definitely stinking in Denmark, Sofia.

SOFIA: (to herself) Oh my God. (to Guero) You know Tio didn't do it, right…you are clear about that at least?

GUERO: (violently) I hate it when you condescend to me, I ought to slap you. I know the man who did it, I was there. I know exactly who killed him and how and the fucker is going to be out in six months. I'm supposed to avenge his death. Father's ghost is asking me to, okay?

SOFIA: It's out of our hands, Guero.

GUERO: The way my hairs stand up when I hear those voices, you just can't know what I'm trying to say. It's like seeing very clearly. Knowing. I don't know how to explain it better than that.

SOFIA: So all of this time you've been thinking you have to avenge Dad's death?

GUERO: Who else could?

SOFIA: Oh my God, Guero, you're crazier than I thought.

GUERO: See, I knew I shouldn't have said anything. You only listen to me when I'm fucked up.

Act II, Scene 4 –

Still Mama's House, Scene continues

(Pedro, Scott and Santiago enter with Kentucky Fried Chicken buckets and bags.)

SCOTT: Hey babe, you need to check out the clouds out there, they're green.

SOFIA STARTS TO PULL OUT THE STUFF TO SET IT UP.

PEDRO: There's a tornado warning.

SOFIA: I'm glad you got home before the downpour. Did you get more masking tape for the windows?

PEDRO PULLS IT OUT.

Great. We'll cover the windows after we eat.

SOFIA IS ABOUT TO PUT DOWN PAPER PLATES.

PEDRO: Can we use real plates?

SOFIA: If you're willing to wash them?

PEDRO: I'm kind of plastic and papered out.

SOFIA: (Sofia brings down the plates.) Scott, can you grab some silverware?

SANTIAGO: Here are the forks and spoons.

PULLING THEM OUT OF THE BAG.

SOFIA: Pedro has requested the real thing, Tio.

PEDRO: I don't like to eat off plastic, that's all.

SANTIAGO: Okay. No problem.

SOFIA: Mom, come eat, it's gonna be gone if you don't hurry. Actually, eat up everybody. She shouldn't be eating this greasy stuff. That's all they eat.

SCOTT: Pass me the tub of gravy, please.

SANTIAGO PASSES IT

MAMA: (offstage) Save me a seat on the wheel!!

EVERYBODY LOOKS AT ONE ANOTHER WITH A RESPONSE.

SOFIA: (to Mama) O.K. (to everyone) Oh God, pass me the potatoes.

PEDRO: (Pedro obliges.) Mmmm, paper potatoes. My favorite.

DUENDE WORLD: MAMA ENTERS, FOR ALL PRACTICAL PURPOSES LIKE "OPHELIA"...WITH ONE FOOT IN THIS WORLD AND THE OTHER IN VERY MUCH IN THE NIGHTMARE OF POSSIBILITY.

MAMA: (enters) I hear your bones crying, Pedro.

PEDRO: For potatoes?

MAMA: For truth.

SOFIA: Guero, did you or did you not slip her something? Tell us now.

GUERO: She's the walking pharmacy, man, maybe she took too much of her own medicine.

MAMA: Ay mijito. You have been released, thanks to God. You're a free man. Go where you will. With wings on your feet, don't look back. You made it out alive, don't look back. It's not easy to come down all those steps.

SANTIAGO: Pass me a drumstick, por favor Sofia.

MAMA: (points at Tio) That man looks for a leg to stand on. Help him. Viejo, you are a chicken without feathers, without the wings to fly for safety. They forced you to shoot at all those innocent people. Mothers, fathers, old, old people…I see it, oh my God, and that little tiny girl, that they left for dead, you saw her moving. Scared to death that they would see her alive and shoot her again. Her mother dead beside her…she was starving to death and you went back, to give her your own food. From your very own mouth. I can see it…like I'm looking through your eyes, Viejo. You are a saint, you have suffered, maybe without feathers but the one mouth you fed lives and breathes to this day because of you. She gives thanks for you.

SANTIAGO FREEZES AS IF HE JUST SAW A GHOST.

Tell them so that they too will see.

SANTIAGO: Por favor, Mirta. Be quiet.

MAMA: They need to know, Viejo that they are among the highest in your presence. That little girl gives thanks every night for you.

SANTIAGO BEGINS TO BREAKDOWN, QUIETLY.

SOFIA: Mother, please stop. It's bad enough that you don't know what you're saying.

MAMA: But he knows. Ask him. ASK HIM!!! She brings him flowers like he's dead. But she's alive, Viejo, because of you. Thanks to you, don't you see?

GUERO: Why don't you just SHUT UP mother. For once.

MAMA: And you…you have died and been born again mijito and you don't even know it. You died, alongside your father and have just now returned to us like Lazarus. Santiago died with that little girl holding his hand so that she would live, tell them, Viejo.

GUERO: I can't stand to see him cry, you've made him cry, isn't that enough?

MAMA: You're the one that needs to drown in your tears. That's why you want me to shut up.

SANTIAGO: Ya. Por favor, callate mujer.

SANTIAGO GETS UP AND LEAVES THE ROOM.

What gives you the right, Ama?

MAMA: Your sickness opened the gates of hell and I have gone there and made it back in one piece. Your father will kill you if you avenge his death. Like a cancer it will eat you up.

GUERO: You're a crazy woman.

MAMA: And you are an idiota who likes to be crazy so that he doesn't have to feel nothing. Let the dead be dead! Once and for all live!!!

GUERO: You're one to talk, marrying and fucking around before the body of your husband has even decomposed.

MAMA: You want me to dry up like a skeleton or a rotting corpse or what? Well you have another thing coming before I would try to live the way that you would like me to. That's why Father Boots is hanging. Because of you.

GUERO: I didn't touch that faggot. You're mistaking me for Pedro.

PEDRO: Oh great, let's just get all the shit out at once.

MAMA: When are you going to cry?

GUERO: Why are you changing the subject, Ama?

MAMA: It has been a year. Your father is dead. You saw him slaughtered like an animal. That is what you have to live with.

GUERO: Fuck you bitch! FUCK YOU!!!

GUERO PULLS OUT A KNIFE.

Why don't I just do you the honor!

MAMA: Of what? You would do me a favor. Go ahead. Send me to my peace once and for all.

GUERO: Its gives you peace to pimp your children, huh?

SOFIA: Guero…

GUERO: SHUT UP!!!

PEDRO: Give me the knife…

GUERO: Shut up faggot. (to Pedro) She sent us both to the slaughter, man. (to Mama) But you don't even have a clue, Ama. (parodies Mama)

"When are you gonna cry?" You're fucking blind. When am I ever gonna stop? So when I'm drowning, holding this knife to my wrists, day in and day out, daddy laid out and the kid who killed him, riding up and down the street like nothing happened...you bring me that fucking snake of a priest. "He can help you, mijo, he can help you..." Help me what? You already got a one faggot in the house, Ama. He had me all wrong, sitting there jacking off, man...(to Pedro) He thought I was you.

PEDRO GETS UP AND LEAVES. MAMA HAS FROZEN. UNABLE TO MOVE, SHE SLOWLY SITS DOWN, IN SHOCK.

I'm the one that should have died. I'm the one that wanted to.

GUERO STARTS TO CRY. SCOTT APPROACHES GUERO FROM BEHIND AND GRABS THE KNIFE AWAY FROM GUERO.

SCOTT: (gently) It's okay, buddy...I got it...just let it go.

KNIFE FALLS FROM GUERO'S HAND. SCOTT TAKES THE KNIFE, AS GUERO FALLS INTO A GRIEVING, UNCONTROLLABLE SOB.

Act II, Scene 5a –

The Void

DUENDE WORLD: LIGHTS UP ON THE WHITE SPIRAL STAIRCASE. THE FATHER'S GHOST APPEARS. HE'S DRESSED SLIGHTLY DIFFERENT THAN BEFORE. HIS FACE IS NOT EASILY DISTINGUISHED LIKE BEFORE, BUT INSTEAD OF STANDING THERE, RATHER FORMALLY LIKE BEFORE, THERE IS AN UNEXPECTED SHIFT IN HIS POSE. AT FIRST HE CAN'T QUITE FIND HIS FOOTING AND AS HE ATTEMPTS TO, HIS POSES BECOME OVERLY RELAXED AND COMICAL UNTIL SOFIA, RATHER TENTATIVELY, ENTERS. THE "FATHER'S GHOST" HEARS HER ENTER AND INSTANTANEOUSLY FREEZES INTO A POSE. THERE'S SOMETHING VERY UNUSUAL ABOUT SOFIA AS WELL. SHE IS PLAYFUL AND INNOCENT, AND FOR THE MOST PART, A "LITTLE GIRL." AFTER A MOMENT, THE "FATHER'S GHOST" SNEEZES, STARTLING SOFIA, OF COURSE.

SOFIA: Who's there?

*THE "FATHER'S GHOST" MAKES HIMSELF KNOWN BY STEPPING DOWN THE STAIRCASE INTO THE LIGHT. HE IS ACTUALLY **R.D. LAING** WITH A GROUCHO MARX MOUSTACHE AND CIGAR. HE ALSO WEARS GROUCHO'S CLASSIC COSTUME.*

R.D.: Knock, knock!

SOFIA: (irritated and scared) Who's there?

R.D.: Interrupting cow.

SOFIA: Interrupting cow wh..

R.D. OFFERS HER HIS HAND WITH HIS LEG HANGING OVER THEIR HANDSHAKE, DELIVERING HIS LINES AND GESTURES IN GROUCHO FASHION.

R.D.: Moooooooooooooo!!!!!

SOFIA: (to audience) Last thing I remember is falling asleep reading…

R.D.: Yes, you were wondering if prayer, too much of it, can cause madness? Page 69. Second paragraph.

SOFIA: That's right.

R.D. TAKES A PIECE OF CHALK FROM HIS POCKET AND BEGINS TO DRAW A PATTERN OF HOPSCOTCH ON THE FLOOR AND THEN HANDS HER A TOKEN.

R.D.: First of all, all experience is either invalidly mad or invalidly mystical.

SOFIA: How can you tell them apart?

R.D.: Who wants to know?

DOES A GROUCHO BACK AND FORTH SHIFTING OF THE EYES AND HEAD.

SOFIA: I'm worried about my mom.

SOFIA FROM THIS POINT ON MIRRORS R.D.'S MOVEMENTS AS HE LEADS HER THROUGH THIS MULTI-LAYERED DREAMSCAPE. THEY PLAY FOLLOW THE LEADER SPONTANEOUSLY, CLIMBING IN AN UNRESTRICTED WAY OVER THE FURNITURE, ETC. CONVERTING IT FROM THIS MOMENT INTO A JUNGLE GYM LIKE ENVIRONMENT.

R.D.: I take it there are fragments…a few memories…

SOFIA: Well actually my younger brother…

R.D.: Sounds, the void is not empty my dear.

SOFIA: My stepfather…he lives in his own world.

R.D.: Peopled with visions, voices…(points to staircase) perhaps a ghost, strange shapes and apparitions…you certainly know your way around.

SOFIA: Wait a minute, I'm not the crazy one.

R.D. BECOMES MOMENTARILY MENACING, MOVING TOWARDS HER…AND SINCE IT IS SOFIA'S NIGHTMARE, SHE WORRIES HE MIGHT BE A RAPIST. HE OBLIGES HER FEAR BY CONTINUING TO MOVE TOWARD HER.

R.D.: When you leave the world as you know it, you're an alien, a stranger signaling from the void…go ahead, scream…who's gonna hear you?

SOFIA: (suddenly resourceful) I will! (the tables turn) I'll wake myself up!

THIS GENUINELY STARTLES HIM, CAUSING HIM TO RETURN TO THEIR ORIGINAL PLAYFULNESS. THEIR ACTIONS SHOULD BE VERY PHYSICAL, ALMOST LIKE A DANCE OR A GYMNASTIC OR ACROBATIC ROUTINE.

R.D.: Maybe. Maybe not. The thing to remember Sofia is madness doesn't have to be a breakdown. It can also be a breakthrough.

SOFIA: Yeah…but she's seeing things we don't even dream of.

R.D.: They used to call them demons…and spirits you see, they used to be known and named. It all had dignity…but now, if you're lucky…we all experience in different ways, you dream or imagine and such, (indicating their conversation, for example) your mother has visions, your brother has hallucinations and your uncle is disturbed.

SOFIA: He's schizophrenic.

R.D.: Disturbed, meaning his family is disturbing. So what if he's invented a strategy, a way to live in an unlivable situation.

SOFIA: I'll say.

R.D.: It's all hypothetical. The perfectly adjusted bomber pilot is a greater threat to our species and survival as a whole than a gentle schizophrenic like your Tio who thinks the bomb is inside him. Page 91.

SOFIA: I've lost my page. But I see what you mean. It's a very crazy world.

R.D.: And those who act like its not are the insane ones. You even underlined that twice. Page 44. Your mother's experience…let's call it…transcendental, to get back to your real concern.

SOFIA: Trance what? Like being in a trance.

R.D.: That'll work…what do you think is at the heart of all religions my dear.

SOFIA: I'm not on that chapter yet.

R.D.: Chances are, your mother has never had this kind of experience before and she probably never will again, so you don't have to worry that she'll join a cult or anything.

PERHAPS THEY'VE BEEN SUSPENDED ON THE STAIRCASE OR A PIECE OF FURNITURE. WHATEVER HE'S DOING, HE SHOULD JUMP DOWN TO STRESS THE GROUNDED POINT. EVERY IDEA IS PHYSICALIZED, TO BE EFFECTIVE.

She wanted your brother grounded…so she took on all his symptoms…that's very impressive.

SOFIA: But now this Father Boots thing…I don't know if she'll ever recover.

R.D. HAS LEAD SOFIA BACK TO HER BED. THE PHONE RINGS.

R.D.: Right on cue.

PHONE RINGS AGAIN.

Why don't you answer it?

Act II, Scene 5b –

Sofia and Scott's Bedroom

SOFIA SUDDENLY WAKES UP, STARTLED. SHE IS OUT OF BREATH. SHE SITS ON THE BED, HER PHONE IS REALLY RINGING. SCOTT SLEEPS BESIDE HER. ON THE OPPOSITE SIDE OF THE STAGE, PEDRO ENTERS AND FACES THE AUDIENCE AS HE TALKS TO SOFIA. ELSEWHERE ALFREDO ENTERS, HE'S CARRYING A TINY INFANT. HE TOO ANSWERS A PHONE.

SOFIA/ALFREDO: (in unison) Hello? Oh God…Pedro…

REACHES FOR THE CLOCK.

…what's wrong…are you okay? I can barely hear you. Where are you?

SCOTT'S NOW AWAKE, HE LOOKS AT THE CLOCK BESIDE THE NIGHT TABLE.

SCOTT: It's four o'clock, where's he calling from?

SOFIA: He's in jail!

ALFREDO REMAINS ON STAGE LISTENING ON HIS OWN PHONE.

PEDRO: I let myself into the rectory. They thought I was breaking in. But I have a key.

SOFIA: (to Scott) Father Boots is dead. It's all over the news. Somebody ran him down in Spain.

PEDRO: He liked to take pictures. I wanted to spare the families …it's a small town. He's got quite the collection of all his escapades, over the years. But they caught me before I could get to them. Someone's going to be in for quite the surprise.

SOFIA: (to Scott) Hand me that piece of paper, I just remembered my dream. Pedro…I was in a church, right now, in my dream…it must have been an altar that then turned into this staircase, sort of? Anyway…the virgin was there, a statue of her…but she had those…bullets on her chest, like Poncho Villa…when then suddenly, there's an earthquake or something like that.

PEDRO: Do you remember the flood after Hurricane Celia…the night Mama's house was swallowed up by the creek. Twelve feet of water…all you could see was the roof of the house the next day?

SOFIA: Everything toppled over, after the earth shook…including the virgin…and when she falls to the ground, her head breaks off right as Groucho Marx shows up, but it's not really Groucho…(reaches for the book on the night table) I fell asleep reading R.D. Laing's book…so I knew I was talking to R.D. Laing, but it was Groucho at the same time…I know, I know…I'm sorry…but it's just that while you're talking to me…

PEDRO: It took us a week to get back home…and the day we finally set foot in the house again, it was me who opened the front door. There was an inch of mud everywhere…on everything… and when I opened the front door…a snake came slithering out. And right where it left its "s" shape on the mud…there was a ring, embedded in the dirt. It was a woman's engagement ring that had washed away with the flood and of all places, it had ended up buried right there…on the threshold…and I notice it right when the snake slithers past it. Does that mean I'm engaged…to the snake? I actually remember thinking that.

LIGHTS ON SOFIA AND SCOTT ARE BEGINNING TO GO OUT…SLOWLY…

SOFIA: …it's like some freaky déjà vu or something. Everything you're telling me…it's familiar somehow.

Act II, Scene 5c

LIGHTS OUT. ONLY PEDRO REMAINS ON STAGE.

PEDRO: That was the first night I spent at the rectory. Do you remember? I called Mama, right as all of you were getting ready to evacuate, there was already a foot of water in the front yard…you were running for your lives. I told her it wasn't safe to walk or drive through all that rain, so Father Boots was asking me to stay…and for her, that was an honor, or at least that's how she acted at the time. To have her beloved priest take such good care of me, to take such an interest in me, it was some kind of special acknowledgment that I was on the right track. Maybe I'd be a priest after all. She had no earthly idea that up until then, Father was sneaking me into the rectory, sometimes several times a day... we would even do it in the confessional, late into night...but on that night, the whole town was deserted, all closed up. Everyone was at the court house for safety, there were tornado warnings left and right as the town sunk deep into the murky creek water...it was like we were the last two people alive on the earth...we were finally free to stay, all by ourselves...at the rectory. Like husband and wife, on a bed, my very first time to sleep with a man through the whole night. There's something about being inside a rectory, after hours...when there's nobody there...the smell of candles burning, the shadows of ceramic saints magnified against the wall...but mostly, knowing that what you are getting away with...is all so very bad. But good, in that...you're in God's house. With God's special servant...by then, I was 15 and madly in love...you never consider...if you're gay, anyway...and realizing that for the first time, as a kid...that when someone, old enough to be your father...who is also a kind, good priest to everyone else...offers himself to you...he used to tell me that he wanted me to use <u>his</u> body as I saw fit...he didn't want me sneaking off into dark alleys and dirt roads with strangers ...I loved how concerned he was, like the father I never had...daddy wasn't even talking to me in those days. He knew what I was...I wasn't going to be the ladies man so...he was pretty harsh. So when Father Boots was so willing to sacrifice himself on my behalf...or so I was convinced...I told myself it was consensual...I had seduced him somehow...and after confessing my sins to him, it was between him and God and nobody else unless I made the mistake of telling someone. That's why he kept all those pictures. It was his way of having leverage. Besides, he knew how confused I was, I tried to slice my wrist that year, remember? I thought I was his only...tryst, but God in heaven, that man had tentacles. It was a rare young man he didn't try to mess with. He definitely took "advantage" of me. I was ten years old when he stuck his hand down my pants and masturbated me. (beat) I would be the last person on earth to give Mama any credit...but in her own crazy way...when she brought the virgin over to my house that day...she knew what she was talking about...she <u>knew</u> the virgin would stomp the hell out of that snake and by golly...she's done that. Like your dream, about the virgin losing her head, she's even gone that far...it's really freaky how right she can be when she goes about it...so wrong.

Act II, Scene 5d –

Sofia and Scott's Bedroom

SCOTT: What happened?

SOFIA: (without a break) Father Boots is_ dead.

SCOTT: What?

SOFIA: Mama was right. Just like she saw in her vision. Oh God, when she's psychic and right, it just encourages her. You watch, she'll be in a great mood!

SCOTT: You family, babe, does not fail to amaze me. They make soap operas look pretty tame.

SOFIA: Oh shut up! It's so humiliating.

SCOTT: It's colorful.

SOFIA: Well that's easy for you to say. Whose side are you on anyway?

SCOTT: I meant it as a compliment.

SOFIA: You try living with a freak show every day of your life. They are so sick!

SCOTT: No they're not! I like your folks. They sure don't act like my family!

SOFIA: Thank God for that. Your folks are decent. You've had it good all your life Scott.

SCOTT: Maybe.

SOFIA: You're so ungrateful.

SCOTT: Maybe. But you're arrogant and that way you don't have to feel anything. (out of the blue) I wanna do you babe.

SOFIA: (surprised) What do you mean arrogant?

SCOTT: I want to do you.

SOFIA: Is doing it all you can think of? I'm not arrogant.

SCOTT: Yes. I can hardly ever look at you and not think about that. Sorry and you are arrogant. You turn me on so much. What do you want me to say?

SOFIA: That you're sorry you are unable to sympathize with anything but your dick!

SCOTT: What don't YOU for a change.

SOFIA: I want you to listen.

SCOTT: That's all I've been doing...with everyone in your family...for some reason I'm the only one they all want to talk to.

SOFIA: How you can say I'm arrogant!

SCOTT: You think you're the only one hurting! Can you try to enjoy it? You're a little wild cat...(very sweetly) you just weren't held enough as a kitten so now when anyone tries to hold you, you just want to scratch their eyes out...I can take it...I like it...I just want to hold you, make you know it's alright...I'm crazy about you.

SOFIA: Why can't you hear me? I can't communicate with you.

HE KISSES HER NECK.

I can't think about that right now.

SCOTT: (affectionately) It's late. Everyone's asleep. We've got some time to kill, we can't go out in this weather right at this moment, so why don't you just...relax...let it go babe...just let it all go...its okay...I love you so much.

SOFIA: (giggles unexpectedly then lets out a frustrated "fit" sound) GODDAMMIT SCOTT! That feels good.

SCOTT: (imitates her with a gruff) Good.

SOFIA: (makes unexpected sensual sound) I HATE this.

RUMBLES OF LIGHTNING ARE HEARD.

SCOTT: I do too.

SOFIA: Don't go making this a habit.

SCOTT: What?

SOFIA: Trying to take my misery away. (she teases him physically) It keeps me going.

SCOTT: (Finding it hard to complete a sentence) You…drive…me…absolutely nuts.

SOFIA: Yeah?

SCOTT: Yeah…I'm crazy about you.

THE LOVERS END UP IN HYSTERICAL LAUGHTER TOGETHER AS THE RUMBLES CONTINUE TO BE HEARD IN THE BACKGROUND. LIGHTS FADE.

Act II, Scene 6a –

Mama's House

THE TWO WORLDS: DUENDES AND HUMAN INTEGRATED SOMEHOW. THE FATHER'S GHOST FINALLY MAKES IT DOWN THE STAIRS AND AS A THE SCENE UNFOLDS, HE MAKES HIMSELF COMFORTABLE. PERHAPS HE SITS AT THE KITCHEN TABLE. MAMA DEFINITELY TALKS TO DIRECTLY TO HIM EVERY NOW AND THEN.

THE WINDOWS ARE NOW ALL TAPED UP. MAMA IS WALKING AROUND HER LIVING ROOM WITH A CAN OF GOLD PAINT. THE DUENDES HOLD UP THE EMPTY PICTURE FRAMES THAT MAMA SPRAYS, AS IF THEY WERE HANGING ON THE WALL. SHE OBVIOUSLY DOESN'T BOTHER TO TAKE THE FRAMES OFF THE WALL. SHE SPRAYS THEM RIGHT WHERE THEY HANG. RIGHT AS SHE REACHES THE EDGE OF THE ROOM, SHE LOOKS UP AT THE CEILING. MAMA IS LOOKING AT THE CEILING. A LEAK HAS SPRUNG ON THE CORNER OF THE HOUSE.

MAMA: (looking at the ceiling) There's definitely a leak right here. Get the bucket, Viejo. From the porch.

SHE LOOKS OUT THE WINDOW.

Ay dios mio, the tree fell down. Right on top of the house. Viejo, a tree fell down on the house.

SOFIA AND SCOTT ENTER WITH THEIR LUGGAGE.

SOFIA: Where Ama?

MAMA: On top of the house, that's why it's leaking right there.

SCOTT: Should we go out there and move it?

MAMA: No, no, no…then the hole will just be left showing and the rain will pour in real bad. Just leave it. The City will come and take care of it.

SOFIA: Are you sure Ama?

MAMA: Ay que lindo el Scott…those Jesus eyes of yours…

SHE DOES THE GYRATING MOVEMENT WITH HER HANDS ABOVE HIS HEAD.

Para no hacerte ojo.

SOFIA: She doesn't want to give you the evil eye.

MAMA: I have to touch what I admire, Scott.

SOFIA: It can cause a person harm if she doesn't touch you.

SOFIA SHRUGS. MAMA TOUCHES SCOTT'S FACE.

MAMA: You're a good boy, Scott. You bring color to Sofia's face. (to Sofia) You be good to him, Sofia. You can be difficult.

SOFIA PICKS UP THE SPRAY OF GOLD PAINT.

SOFIA: Ama...Guero's not sniffing this stuff, too, is he?

MAMA: No, Sofia...don't even say that.

MAMA TAKES THE CAN OF SPRAY BACK

SOFIA: (to Scott) She's into graffiti...

POINTS TO THE WALLS.

She sprays halos around the pictures.

MAMA: (laughs) Ay, Scott, no...they fade...the picture frames...I spray everything to make it look new, pos you know…it's the gold color I love so much…metallic gold, it's a royal color.

SOFIA: You could take them down first, Ama.

SHE SHOWS THE CAN TO SCOTT.

SCOTT: (what else can he say) It's nice…

MAMA: The rain's a good sign, Scott, a blessing. Especially if it rains when somebody dies.

SOFIA: Are you feeling okay, Ama?

MAMA: Pos I'm a nurse, mijita…this baby wasn't going to be alright. That's all. I'm just glad I didn't have to go to the hospital. They stick those things up a woman's insides, Scott…they're like vacuum cleaners, I'm surprised all the organs don't come flying out.

SOFIA: (doesn't mean it) I could stay a few extra days, Ama…

MAMA: You have things to do. No. We're fine, verda Viejo?

SANTIAGO SITS LIKE BEFORE, STARING OUT INTO SPACE. HE DOESN'T RESPOND.

Act II, Scene 6b –

Still Mama's House, Scene continues

PEDRO ENTERS. HE'S GOT HIS BAG AS WELL.

SOFIA: A tree fell on top of the house, Pedro. That wind was spooky.

HE DOESN'T RESPOND.

But at least the creek didn't flood again.

MAMA: (to Pedro) I got up early but you were already gone, mijito. Did you go to church?

SOFIA (wanting to change the subject): Scott, do you mind helping Pedro pack up the car?

SCOTT QUICKLY OBLIGES.

It takes three hours to get back to Austin. Ama, I have a class tonight.

MAMA: O si, the rain is going to be bad all the way back.

PEDRO: I was in jail, Ama.

MAMA: Que dices?

PEDRO: This morning. I spent the night in jail.

PAUSE.

You're enabling her now, Sofia.

SOFIA: What is going on with you?

PEDRO: You didn't tell her. (to Mama) I broke into the rectory, Ama.

SOFIA (To Pedro): Can you please...just let it go.

PEDRO: Neither of you can take your own goddamn medicine. You're both full of shit. (to Mama) I have my own key. To the rectory. So I really didn't break in, the cops just thought I did.

PEDRO TAKES THE KEY OUT OF HIS POCKET. HE PLACES IT ON THE TABLE.

Maybe you can return it.

MAMA DOESN'T SAY A THING. PEDRO GOES TO TIO, GIVES HIM HIS HAND.

Tio, I just wanted to say goodbye.

SANTIAGO, STARTLED, OFFERS HIS HAND BACK TO PEDRO. HE RISES. REMOVES HIS COWBOY HAT.

SANTIAGO: Oh si, que le via muy bien.

PEDRO: Thank you for everything.

SOFIA GOES UP TO GIVE TIO A HUG.

SANTIAGO: Thank you.

MAMA: I blame myself, Pedro.

PEDRO: For what, Ama. We don't have all day.

MAMA: Dr. Garcia used to say that it's the mothers who are to blame. If they overprotect their sons and never let them out from beneath their skirts.

PEDRO: In that case, Guero should have been the funny one.

SCOTT ENTERS.

Where is he, I want to say goodbye.

MAMA: He's at the cemetery. He likes to go there on Sundays, takes the paper and talks to your father. He reads him the comics.

PEDRO: Right.

MAMA: When something innocent suffers a sacrifice, it is blessed forever.

PEDRO: Is that right?

SOFIA: Pedro, we really have to get going. (to Scott) Is the car ready?

MAMA: I have faith in the man Guero's going to be.

PEDRO: You'll get a real man in this house yet, won't you mother? Or you'll at least die trying.

MAMA: (has totally run out of patience) Now you sound like Alfredo. That man has a hold on you, mijo...he brainwashes you.

PEDRO: There's no hope for you, Ama. Alfredo has been...(stops) was... Alfredo was my only saving grace. But you couldn't stand him, because he was good to me.

SOFIA: Pedro...

PEDRO: (to Sofia) She needs the face of evil...the devil himself...to feel good about herself. (to Mama) You like to forgive, Ama. More than you like anything or anyone else. (to Sofia) She's still trying to deny it.

MAMA: Anda, hombre...

PEDRO: The priest you loved so much, Ama. He raped one of your sons and bought the other one drugs.

SOFIA: Pedro, stop…

PEDRO: So that Guero would keep going back for more. I can only imagine what he had to do in return. (to Mama) And you were the one that kept making us go back to see him…when are you gonna get it? (to Sofia) I'll be in the car.

SOFIA: Scott, can you check the room one more time, to make sure we got everything?

HE IS RELIEVED TO OBLIGE.

MAMA: (to Sofia) I've done so many bad things.

SOFIA: Ama…Pedro's just…

MAMA: You can't play God in this life, mijita. I had no business having another one…ever. Nothing was wrong with her but the life she would have had.

SOFIA: It's all for the best, Ama.

A CAR HORN IS HEARD.

MAMA: She had been moving the whole time…

SCOTT RE-APPEARS.

SOFIA: Scott, can you go tell Pedro, I'll be right there.

SANTIAGO IS STILL, AS ALWAYS FACING OUT. DEEP IN A REVERIE THROUGHOUT.

MAMA: She was perfectly formed, a little girl...

SOFIA: It's hard to lose a baby Ama...you're going to have to give yourself some time.

MAMA: (extremely agitated) I have the little tube, Sofia. They show you in nursing school.

SOFIA IS STUNNED. ANOTHER CAR HORN IS HEARD.

God doesn't forgive a killing, mijita. No matter what you say. I know I have to pay for that.

SOFIA CAN'T MOVE. MAMA RETURNS TO THE WINDOW.

It's going to rain all day, till tonight. Make Scott drive, so you can rest, mijita.

SOFIA HESITATES, BUT SHE FINALLY WALKS OUT. MAMA TAKES THE SPRAY OF GOLD

PAINT AND SPRAYS ONE MORE FRAME. SHE LOOKS AT TIO.

I don't know why you feel sorry for yourself. Here I am bleeding like the Red Sea, but you don't see me sitting there, feeling sorry for myself. I get tired, hombre. But do you see me sitting there asking why? Looking like I don't even deserve an answer?

LOOKS OUT AT THE TREE THAT HAS FALLEN.

That tree was our only good shade out there, we'll never get that air conditioner to do anything. Not without that shade. It looks like somebody picked it up like a stick and threw it on top of the house. Look at that. All those roots sticking out.

MAMA IS GETTING DROPS OF RAIN ON HER HEAD.

It's getting worse, hombre. Maybe if we put some plastic down, stick some newspapers in the hole, I don't want that possum thinking he can move in up there. It might be winter before we can fix it.

SANTIAGO IS STILLER THAN EVER, ALMOST LIKE HE HASN'T EVEN BLINKED.

The TV says it's gonna rain all night…

*THE LIGHTS SHOULD BEGIN TO COME DOWN
VERY SLOWLY...AS MAMA TRAILS ON,
WITHOUT HARDLY A BREATH IN BETWEEN.*

I can feel it in my bones. I get that pain in my
knees.

STILL LOOKING OUT THE WINDOW.

The creek could still swell up. Putting the house
underwater...for a week. Mario drowned down
the street, did you now him? Mario Sandoval? He
was trying to help people evacuate, pobrecito. I
remember Roberto's pigs, from next door. They
were squealing louder than the sirens, running as
fast as they could as the water was chasing them
down the street. The water was up to here...

SHE INDICATES HER KNEES.

...when we got in the car. What if it doesn't start?
What if the water makes it die on us? But I prayed
and prayed...all the way to the courthouse...and
we all made there, fijate... all in one piece. Thanks
be to God.

*MAMA HAS FOUND HER WAY TO TIO.A
MOMENT OF PEACE AND
UNEXPECTED"ROMANCE" BETWEEN THEM,*

*AS SIMPLE   AS MAMA REACHING FOR HIS
HAND. FATHER'GHOST TAKES THIS MOMENT
AS HIS CUE TO LEAVE. THE DUENDES HELP
THE FATHER SIT ON THE GROUND, ALMOST
AS IF HE'S FINALLY GOING TO ALLOW
HIMSELF "TO REST". THE BODIES OF THE
DUENDE(S) WRAP AROUND THE FATHER,
BECOMING IN ESSENCE HIS GRAVE.*

Act II, Scene 7 –

Epilogue - Cemetery

*THE DUENDES WRAPPED AROUND THE
FATHER ARE NOWTHE ABSTRACTED
"GRAVESTONE" THAT GUERO ADDRESSES.*

GUERO: (reads) "Sir, in my heart there was a kind
of fighting that would not let me sleep."

*HE REPEATS THIS PHRASE WITH DIFFERENT
INTENTION AND INFLECTION INCLUDING
THE ONE HEARD EARLIER OF THE BBC
RENDITION.*

"Sir…in my heart there was a kind of fighting that
would not let ME sleep…sir…in my heart…there
was a kind of fighting…that would not let me
sleep…"

HE LAUGHS CURIOUSLY, LOOKS UP AND STARES OUT DEEP IN THOUGHT AS HE REACHES FOR A CIGARETTE.

"I lay worse that the mutines in the bilboes." You and your damn cigarettes man...I had a bad feeling ...a real bad feeling that day in the pit of my stomach...I knew something had gone wrong...but the worst part of it was that I ran into Debbie Finch on the way to the store...pure accident...and that was it. Nothing else mattered. I wanted her bad...back then...I could barely look at her, you know? ...But shit, man. . .nothing lasts,...nothing...but we started talking and talking and that's when I saw Jose running down the street..."He's cut really bad, man...he's sliced up, he's hurt real bad"...I acted dumb, 'who man?' But by then the sirens were coming from all over the place...And I froze. Right in my tracks, my mouth moving, babbling about who knows what...till finally she left...but it was too late...(pause) I didn't want her to know it was you. Nobody's father gets sliced up. Not if he's decent...(pause)

(With no emotion whatsoever) I'm the one who should have died.

*GUERO MOVES AWAY FROM THE
HEADSTONE FOR A MOMENT TO CONTINUE
TO READ SHAKESPEARE AS IF THIS IS WHAT
HE HAS BEEN LEADING UP TO.*

"Rashly and prais'd be rashness for it...let us
know our indiscretions sometimes serves us well
when our deep plots do pall, and that should learn
us there's a divinity that shapes our ends, rough-
hew them how we will...that...is most certain."

*DUENDE STIRS. SHE UNWRAPS FOR A
MOMENT FROM THE GRAVESTONE AND
TURNS TO OFFER GUERO A FLOWER. HE
RAISES HIS HEAD SLOWLY IN SILENT FRIGHT
AS THE LIGHTS FADE.*

END OF PLAY

UNDER A WESTERN SKY

This play was originally developed at South Coast Repertory's Hispanic Play Festival under the direction of Jose Cruz Gonzales in the summer of 1995. It received its world premiere Off-Broadway in a co-production with INTAR and the Women's Project under the direction of Loretta Greco in the Spring of 1997.

Characters

The play is performed by four actors that portray eighteen characters.

Javier Zuniga…lanky thirteen year old boy with tattoos on his fingers. He witnessed the gang rape and is the only one who reports it to the authorities.

The Sheriff…middle-aged but boyishly finds it hard to listen without wanting to interrupt constantly.

Frankie…nineteen year old, tattoo artist, husband of rape victim, Yolanda.

Arturo Ramirez…middle-aged, owns a burger stand, boyfriend of Veronica

Veronica C. Garcia-Morales…forty, works at the Post Office, granddaughter of Elisa

Elisa Mercede Garcia..ninety plus years old, she is on her deathbed, she can see and hear the Great Artist.

The Great Artist…eventually we discover she is Georgia O'Keefe in her twenties. Must be played by the actor who portrays Jesus.

Jessie Gomez…twenty-one, accused ringleader of the rape, has a "Carmen" tattoo on his arm.

Carmen Valdes…eighteen…wears too much make-up and clothes that she knows will accentuate her "Valentine" butt.

Estella Gomez…mid-thirties, Jesus' mother. The wear and tear of having too many children makes her look fifteen years older.

Father Reyes…Catholic priest, reads murder mysteries between confessions in the privacy of the confessional.

Mandy Feinstein…forty…a reporter for the Texas Monthly. She's writing an article about the rape.

Beto Aleman, III…elderly lawyer whose hair is blacker now than it was twenty years ago.

Evelina Gonzalez-Parr…the "child" bride of the town's white political boss; tends to over-dress for the occasion.

Beatrice Zuniga...young grandmother of Javier Zuniga, fierce but protective of her grandson.

Chuy...town "idiot", witnessed the rape. For his "love of God" wants the victim's husband to know that he did not participate.

PLAYWRIGHT'S NOTES:

The play was inspired by two separate true stories that occurred in Texas. One was the gang rape at an illegal cock fight that took place in my hometown in 1988. The other incident took place elsewhere in West Texas, also in 1988 when twenty-eight watercolors painted by Georgia O'Keeffe were supposedly found wrapped in a brown paper bag in a garage. These paintings were previously unknown and unpublished. There is now some question about whether this work is a hoax but if authentic, the work was produced in the period during which O'Keeffe taught at West Texas State Normal College in Canyon, Texas. When she left Canyon in 1918 to move to New York, it is believed that she gave the watercolors to a close, possibly intimate friend.

The changes in locations and characters are meant to be fast. Instead of trying to make rapid costume changes, for example, the actors make very few, subtle changes like using the varied possibilities of a scarf, a vest, apron, or at hat, etc. The convention of the actors announcing their stage directions is meant to be a story-telling device. The purpose is to set tone, irony and in many cases, the scene itself in lieu of props. This piece is meant to celebrate the magnitude of an actor's capacity to create a reality simply, but magnificently, by portraying various characters with the most efficient means: his body and voice.

The projections are meant as inspiration more than they literally have to be projected. The paintings can be found in a collection entitled "Canyon Suite."

I would also like to acknowledge <u>Texas Monthly</u> writer Mimi Swartz for her outstanding coverage of the cock fight incident and my hometown in her article, "Macho Gone Mad" which provided fuel and inspiration for creating many of the imaginary characters of this piece.

ACT I

Scene 1.

Projection: Somewhere in this space, there is a screen projecting Georgia O'Keefe's <u>LIGHT COMING ON THE PLAINS.</u>

Enter four actors. They greet the audience simply, allowing themselves to be seen. They bring all of their attention to the space.

ACTRESS ONE: Space.

ACTRESS TWO : Wide-open space. Mostly sky.

ACTOR ONE: On this night the sky is all gray-blue. . .

ACTOR TWO: The whole thing lights up, first in one place. . .

ACTOR ONE: Then another. . .with flashes of lightning.

ACTRESS ONE: Sometimes flashes of lightning. . .

ACTRESS TWO: Sometimes just sheer lightning. . .

ACTOR TWO: And sometimes sheet lightning with a sharp bright zig zag flashing across it.

ACTOR ONE: You can see nothing here but sky and flat prairie land. . .

ACTRESS TWO: Land that seems more like the ocean than anything else.

ACTRESS TWO: POSITIONS HERSELF TO WATCH THE FOLLOWING SCENE. THE POSITION SHE TAKES SHOULD BE THE EXACT LOCATION THAT THIS ACTRESS WILL TAKE FOR THE LAST SCENE OF THE PLAY WHEN SHE PLAYS ELISA ON HER DEATHBED.

ACTRESS ONE: Somewhere in this space a young Mexican-American woman, YOLANDA VASQUEZ, 18, sleeps and dreams alone.

ACTRESS ONE TAKES A SLEEPING POSITION SOMEWHERE ON THE STAGE, INDICATING THAT SHE IS YOLANDA

Her slip is torn and filthy. There are scrapes and scratches on her elbows and knees. Her body is caked with dirt and other debris.

ACTOR ONE: Elsewhere, JAVIER ZUNIGA appears. He is a lanky thirteen year old boy with tattoos all over his fingers. His face is broken out and a straggly mustache is starting to darken over his full lips. He chews gum and is very nervous to tell his story to the authorities.

ACTOR ONE TAKES A SEAT INDICATING HE IS JAVIER. ALTHOUGH JAVIER IS NERVOUS, EVEN TERRIFIED, HE IS FLAT AND EMOTIONLESS ON THE SURFACE.

ACTOR TWO: The SHERIFF is middle-aged but boyishly finds it hard to listen without wanting to interrupt constantly.

ACTOR TWO SITS BESIDE ACTOR ONE AS JAVIER, INDICATING HE IS THE SHERIFF.

The reason is he drinks too much coffee and there is usually not enough going on in the town to merit that kind of consumption. (to Javier) Sit down. Don't be afraid.

JAVIER: (terrified) I'm not afraid.

SHERIFF: Okay, good. Whatever you have to tell me is between you and me and nobody else.

LONG PAUSE.

JAVIER: I seen something. . .bad.

THE SHERIFF EXPECTS JAVIER TO EXPLAIN
HIMSELF. THE SHERIFF WAITS. JAVIER
SAYS AND DOES NOTHING. THE WAIT
SHOULD FEEL AWKWARD AND
UNCOMFORTABLE.

SHERIFF: So. . .what can I do for you?

JAVIER: You cain't do nothing. For me.

SHERIFF: Okay. So what's the problem then? Do you need . . something?

JAVIER: I don't need nothing. The whole town maybe.

SHERIFF: What's your name?

JAVIER: Javier Zuniga, Jr.

SHERIFF: Javier, Payaso's boy?

JAVIER NODS.

I went to school with your dad up until the seventh grade. He dropped out. But he was a smart kid. How's he been doing?

JAVIER SHRUGS.

Good. Now Javier, you're not telling me anything. . .specific. I don't know what you're talking about exactly. You need to start from the very beginning, you know what I mean?

JAVIER: They went crazy.

SHERIFF: Who? Who went crazy?

JAVIER: The whole town. The guys. They went crazy. I never been to one of those rapes before. . .

SHERIFF: Rapes?

YOLANDA WAKES UP IN TERROR, BREATHING FAST AND HARD. SHE SITS UP DISORIENTED. HER POSITION ON STAGE SHOULD BE CENTRAL AND DIRECTLY IN THE SPACE OF THE TWO MEN, AS IF IN THE SCENE WITH THEM. JAVIER SHOULD RELATE TO HER BY LOOKING AT HER, AS IF REFERRING TO HER IN HIS MIND

What rapes?

JAVIER: Frankie's old lady. Somebody called her Yolanda.

SLOWLY, YOLANDA STANDS UP AND TENTATIVELY RAISES HER SLIP UP AS IF TO LOOK BETWEEN HER LEGS. SHE
    SCREAMS WHEN SHE REMEMBERS

*THAT SHE HAS BEEN RAPED. WHEN THE
SCREAM HAUSTS ITSELF, HER FACE RELAXES
FOR A MOMENT. THERE IS A PAUSE. A
STILLNESS. AFTER A MOMENT, ACTRESS ONE
LIES DOWN LIKE BEFORE AND THE WHOLE
SERIES OF GESTURES BEGINS TO REPEAT
ITSELF AGAIN LIKE A GHOSTLY DANCE OF
SORTS. WHEN SHE REACHES THE SCREAM
SEQUENCE NEXT TIME, IT IS IN SILENCE BUT
NONETHELESS AS REALISTICALLY PAINFUL
AS THE FIRST TIME THE AUDIENCE
ACTUALLY HEARD IT*

SHERIFF: What Frankie?

JAVIER: The tattoo guy.

SHERIFF: The one that lives over there by the
Laundromat?

JAVIER NODS.

You're saying his old lady got raped?

JAVIER: Last night at the cock fight. With
everybody watching. I never been to one of those
rapes before so. . .

SHERIFF: Nor do you hope to ever be, you
understand me?

JAVIER: They acted like they'd done it before or something.

SHERIFF: They better not have, or at least I better not find out about it. Who are "they?"

YOLANDA WAKES IN TERROR LIKE BEFORE.SHE REPEATS THE WHOLE SEQUENCE AGAIN.

JAVIER: The regulars, you know, the guys that hang out there. Monkay, Jessie. . .

SHERIFF: Try to start from the very beginning, if you can. (to the audience) The Sheriff pulls out a tape recorder.

ACTOR TWO THEN RESUMES THE ROLE OF THE SHERIFF, HARDLY SKIPPING A BEAT.

Don't let this bother you. I'm not too good with notes. I get it all wrong. I think I'm . . .what do you call it?

When you turn around letters and things, your eyes, they scramble the letters on the page?

JAVIER SHRUGS.

Dyslexetive. Okay, there's tape in there. Go.

JAVIER: There were about ten guys at the ranch, I think more. It all happened when Monkay's car drove up. I remember because the muffler was loud, man. It sounded like a tractor or something like that. It got all the roosters squawking like crazy. Kicking up dust all over the place. She was already in the car. I think she came with them. She was the only girl there. She looks like my sister, but more built, so I take a second look. Monkay gets out first. They were gonna try out this new killer bird or something like that. So Monkay checks it out in back of the trailer house but Jessie stays in the car the whole time. She tries to get out but he doesn't let her, he grabs her by the hair and slams her on the car. . .

YOLANDA WAKES IN TERROR LIKE BEFORE,BREATHING FAST AND HARD. THE WHOLE SEQUENCE BEGINS AGAIN.

hard, I heard her head hit the top of the car. The hood. He pushes her back in the car. Slaps her hard. He's on top of her when Monkay comes back out and goes "save me some of that" or something like that. He pulls his pants down too.

JAVIER DOESN'T KNOW HOW TO SAY THE REST.

I ain't never heard anybody scream like that. I don't like to see nobody cry, loud like at a funeral. Her legs hanging out. No pants when Jessie grabs me. I guess I was standing there looking stupid. Frozen. "This is what you can look forward to," he goes, throwing me on top of her. Everybody laughing at me. I kick him hard but he holds me on top of her when she bites me, right here.

INDICATES HIS ARM NEAR HIS ELBOW. THIS MOMENT IS TOTALLY SYNCHRONOUS TO ONE OF YOLANDA'S GESTURES. FOR A MOMENT IN TIME, JAVIER AND YOLANDA MIRROR THE EXACT SAME GESTURE, IN PERFECT MOTION, TOGETHER.

Takes a big chunk out and I didn't even do nothing to her, man. Not like those other guys. So I get on my bike and ride home. There's big holes all over the place since the flood so I almost crash when I blow a tire. I guess it's about four in the morning cause the train gets stuck. I wait a long time for it to pass. There's no way around it out there in the middle of nowhere.

Scene 2.

<u>Projection: Abstraction, Dark</u>

ACTOR ONE TIES A RED BANDANA AROUND HIS HEAD.

ACTOR ONE: On the other side of the railroad tracks, Yolanda's husband FRANKIE (19), puts a tattoo on an unidentified customer's butt who lies on his stomach, bare-chested.

ACTOR TWO: The middle-aged man, ARTURO, raises his head and lets out a yelp of pain.

ACTOR TWO/ARTURO: EEEEEEEEhole, man! Take it easy.

ACTOR ONE/FRANKIE: Don't be moving on me, man. One move and you got a whole different picture on your butt.

ARTURO: I cain't take it much longer, vato. How much more you got?

FRANKIE: Well if you want a half-assed job, it's done. But if you want a work of art, ese, you're gonna have to shut up and put up with it.

ARTURO: Can I see at least?

FRANKIE: There's a mirror in the bathroom, it's not gonna reach. I don't think you'll see nothing. You either trust me or you don't.

ARTURO: I trust you. I just cain't take it too much longer, that's all I'm saying, man.

FRANKIE: Quit being a pussy and let me do my thing. Otherwise, don't waste my time, it insults me, man.

ARTURO: Okay, okay, I'll shut up. But it's worse than having a baby, man.

FRANKIE: Oh, yeah? Like you know all about that?

ARTURO: Movies don't lie about that shit. My sister said it's like trying to shit a watermelon.

FRANKIE: You're grossing me out, vato! I got to concentrate, man! Do you think you could shut up for maybe five minutes at the most? That's all I got left, then I got to stop. I'm going cross-eyed. I got to pick up Yolanda. She'll kill me if I'm late. She locks me out. She throws all my stuff out the front door when she gets mad at me, man. It's a bad habit she's gonna have to break.

ARTURO: I don't know man, you got to tell a woman everything three times or they pretend they didn't hear you.

FRANKIE: You sure Veronica's gonna like you having a pair of tits on your ass?

ARTURO: Hell yes!

FRANKIE: You're lucky, man. Mine would scratch'em off.

ARTURO: Yolanda? You make her sound like somebody totally different, man. She's pretty shy.

FRANKIE: If she doesn't know you. But I'm her husband, man. She's got her music on the inside, vato. She'll bust my balls if I get out of line just with the silent treatment, you know?

ARTURO: Tell me about it! AYYYYYYYY!!!! Chingao! Watchale, man. You're peeling off my skin!

FRANKIE: You moved your ass. I'm telling you, you make it hard on yourself. Just shut up and lay there so I can do my thing and I promise you, it won't hurt. . .as much. (to audience) Tears are rolling down Arturo's eyes, faster than he can stop them, almost like they do when he cuts up onions for the burger stand he owns on the edge of town. He things about his girlfriend Veronica. . .

ACTRESS ONE READIES TO PLAY VERONICA IN THE NEXT SCENE DIRECTLY IN FRONT OFARTURO. THEY MAKE EYE CONTACT AS ACTOR TWO COMPLETES HIS ASIDE.

. . .who just broke up with him for the hundredth time. He's thinking she better appreciate the gesture he's making on her behalf. . .meaning the tattoo with her tits on his butt.

ACTRESS ONE WALKS AWAY, UNIMPRESSED.IT BOTHERS ACTOR TWO WHO RESORTS TO EMPTY THREATS.

. . .or else!

Scene 3.

<u>Projection: STANDING NUDE</u>

ACTRESS ONE: VERONICA CONCEPCION GARCIA-MORALES, 40, reads the latest issue of Cosmopolitan. It is her day off. Usually she works a forty -eight hour week, plus, at the Post Office.

ACTRESS TWO: ELISA MERCEDE GARCIA, ninety plus years old, sits in her rocking chair at La Hacienda Nursing Home. She lost most of her sight many years ago. Her back is still unusually straight, rigid even. She moves very little, except for her hands which work at molding a piece of clay.

ACTOR ONE SITS IN FRONT OF AN IMAGINARY EASEL AND PRETENDS TO PAINT.

ACTOR ONE: A GREAT ARTIST Elisa knew as a young woman sits at the foot of Elisa's bed painting. The artist appears exactly the way Elisa remembers her, when they were both in their early twenties. Only Elisa can see and hear the Great Artist.

ELISA: Pos when you give your children the milk of animals, you raise a pack of little animals. I'm not saying animal milk is not good for the bones. But you do not take the place of the milk of the mother with the milk of a cow or goat!

VERONICA LOOKS AT HER GRANDMOTHER, CONCERNED. SHE'S AFRAID HER GRANDMOTHER IS GETTING SENILE

VERONICA: I'm talking about those awful boys, ama!

ELISA: Pos that's what I'm saying, nina! A cow is not so smart. A goat. . .well, it pretends it has horns three times bigger than its size.

VERONICA: That poor girl. She just had a baby, too.

ELISA: (shakes her head) The day they started to put women to sleep, mijita. When they bring their babies into this world, that's when the bad was done.

VERONICA: They're saying they raped her three times, ama. Three different places. After the cock fight.

ELISA: If the mother does not feel the pain, the child comes in feeling nothing too.

VERONICA: Ama, I'm talking about those boys. They beat up the ones that wouldn't touch her. What kind of devil is that, ama?

ELISA: (frustrated) Pos that's what I'm saying.

VERONICA: This has nothing to do with their mothers.

ELISA: If they cannot feel their mother's pain, they will never feel anybody's pain. That's why they can cause it. When your mother had your brother in the hospital, I cried so much your grandfather thought I had gone crazy.

VERONICA: Why ama?

ELISA: He wouldn't wake up. The doctor beat him black and blue. Two of his little fingers got broken. Whatever drug they gave your mother to put her to sleep, nearly killed him. So now to feel anything, he thinks he has to have drugs. That's why he sells them and takes half of them himself. And don't think I don't know he beats his wife.

VERONICA: Ama, it's not as bad as all that. He's getting better. He found Jesus Christ.

ELISA: Pos Jesus Christ was never lost, it's the children that are growing up lost. (to the Great Artist) She tried to kill herself, too!

VERONICA: I haven't tried to kill myself. (lying) Ever.

ELISA: (to the Great Artist) When that boyfriend of hers left with another woman y quien save que! (to Veronica) We never forget the first thing that happens to us when we are born, Veronica. It stays with us until the day that we die.

VERONICA: (lying) I would never kill myself, ama!

ELISA: You came into this world with the umbilical cord around your neck. . .thinking you were dying and you're not happy until you are dying one way or another. Those animals that killed that girl. . .

VERONICA: They didn't kill her, Wela. . .

ELISA: She may still be walking around but her soul will never return to that body of hers! That is a killing, they were animals to take advantage. If you look into their eyes, there is nobody there. Like that boyfriend of yours.

VERONICA: Wela, Arturo is good to me. Has been. Good. To me.

ELISA: Until you disagree with him or some woman lets him take advantage. Es mejor estar sola que malacompanada.

VERONICA: Well I am alone, are you happy now?

ELISA: Until you stop bleeding. So long as your body can make a baby, mijita, the men will look better than they are.

ELISA ADDRESSES THE GREAT ARTIST AS VERONICA LOOKS ON, CONCERNED.

ELISA: Does this look like anything? (to the audience) Elisa has turned the lifeless lump of clay into a beautiful winged shape.

THE GREAT ARTIST: I see a world as if you were the first woman looking at it...

ELISA SMILES, PLEASED. VERONICA LOOKS ON, CONCERNED.

VERONICA: Everybody in this town is married, too young or God forbid, a rapist, ama.

ELISA: Pos when babies are taken from their mothers the moment they are born and put into those tiny prisons alone, those cribs. They grow up wanting to be behind bars. Over and over again.

VERONICA: Cribs are not prisons, ama!!

ELISA: For all of the bad to stop, mothers are going to have to remember their jobs in this world.

VERONICA: Not everybody is here to take care of babies.

ELISA: Pos no, but my babies never slept alone, mijita. They stayed in the bed with me. Where they were born. Till they were not afraid. (To the great artist) Those boys died, alone. The moment they were born. (to Veronica) That's why motherless animals have ears but have no souls to feel. That is what the end of the world is about. I never thought I would live this long to see it.

THE GREAT ARTIST: I have come to the end of something...

ELISA SITS UP TO LOOK AT WHAT THE GREAT ARTIST IS PAINTING. SHE IS ECSTATIC TO SEE THE FINISHED PAINTING.

ELISA: I wish you could see what I see, Veronica. (to the Great Artist) You have painted all of my life in one solitary, beautiful flower. Mira nomas. And those bones. Those beautiful bones.

ELISA SMILES PEACEFULLY AT THEGREAT ARTIST.

I can sleep peacefully now. Thank you.

ELISA LIES BACK TO SLEEP.

VERONICA: (to audience) Veronica worries that her grandmother's hallucinations have gotten out of hand. She doesn't want to tell the doctor because her grandmother does not like to take the medication that they give her. She says her angels stop talking with her when she does. Veronica tucks in her grandmother appears under the covers, like she has shrunk in stature practically over night.

VERONICA KISSES HER GRANDMOTHER ON THE CHEEK.

SCENE 4.

Projection: RED HOUSE/FENCE & DOOR

ACTRESS ONE SITS AND PANTOMIMES A PHONE TO HER EAR AS ACTOR ONE TAKES THE BANDANA OFF HIS HEAD AND TUCKS IN HIS FRONT POCKET, ALLOWING IT TO HANG THERE ORNAMENTALLY.

ACTRESS ONE: (to the audience) A pretty CARMEN VALDES, 18, is on the phone with her best friend Ninfa. Her hair is up in electric curlers. She's wearing a little bit too much make-up and applies nail polish onto both hands and feet.

ACTOR ONE: (to audience) JESUS "JESSIE" GOMEZ, 21, sits in the confessional at the church talking to the priest. He is short and stocky. His front tooth is gold and he stutters slightly. Even with a T-shirt on, his tattoo with the name "Carmen" (points to Actress One) can be seen.

ACTOR TWO: (to audience) FATHER REYES is surprised anyone is confessing. Usually he has time to read murder mysteries between confessions in the privacy of the confessional. But this afternoon he's has to close the book and put it away. That pains him of course, since he's only a few pages away from finding out who done it.

CARMEN: I mean if this is true, then they should cut all their balls off, did you see that? (laughs) Spray painted in big letters, I mean big, all over the church walls, yes! "Cut the rapists' balls off!"

ACTOR ONE SHOULD ACKNOWLEDGE CARMEN'S PRESENCE ON THE STAGE IN ORDER TO MAKE THE AUDIENCE AWARE OF THE RELATIONSHIP BETWEEN CARMEN AND JESSIE.IN THE SAME WAY ACTRESS ONE SHOULD OPENLY REFER TO JESSIE WITH LOOKS, FROWNS AND WHATEVER, AS IF CONJURING HIM IN HER MIND. IN REALITY,

HE SITS RIGHT IN FRONT OF HER SOMEWHERE ON THE STAGE WITH HIS BACK TO HER. THE PRIEST SITS TO THE SIDE OF JESSIE, WITH AN EAR TOWARDS HIM. EVEN THOUGH THE ACTORS ARE IN A CONVERSATION WITH SEPARATE PEOPLE, IT SHOULD APPEAR LIKE THEY ARE IN A CONVERSATION WITH EACH OTHER, PARTICULARLY IN THE WAY THAT THEY LISTEN TO EACH OTHER.

JESSIE: I didn't touch Yolanda...after...ever...never. I didn't even look at her. I offered her a ride, yes, but it was Monkay who drove us all to the cock fight.

CARMEN: Ninfa, it can't be true. Yolanda just had a baby. It doesn't make no sense. She's pretty . . . but she's not as pretty as some of those guy's wives. I mean Monkay's wife is beautiful, why would he want to do it with Yolanda when he's got her at home? It doesn't make no sense.

JESSIE: How should I know, man. I left early. She was just laying there when I left. Fainted, I think. "You sure you're taking her home," I tell Monkay. (imitating Monkay) "Yeah, yeah, man, don't worry, man. I got to be at work at 6:00" or I don't know what, like he's all of a sudden real responsible, right? He can't keep a job for more than a day to save his life.

CARMEN: Everybody knows she had a thing with Jessie, they went to the prom together? She wore that tacky lacy bridesmaid dress we wore for Rosa's wedding, remember? I still have those awful purple shoes, it's such a waste of money, I mean when will I wear those dumb things again? At least Yolanda wore them somewhere.

JESSIE: He didn't take her home, he took her to his cousin's property, over by the water work and he rapes her again. I heard him bragging the next day at the pool hall. "Mind your own business if you don't want this pull cue up your ass," excuse my language father, but he can be a real asshole sometimes, when all I did was ask him if he got her home alright.

CARMEN: He always had a thing for me, all during their thing. Yes ma'am, he did. Leaving me notes and stuff in my locker, he couldn't spell for nothing but it was the thought that counted. You know how he flirts like crazy, looks you up and down like he's taking your clothes off, he's so fugly!

JESSIE: I invited her nice, you know. That's the only reason she got in the car. Those guys don't even know her, man. But then Monkay's cousin, this retard guy that acts like his bodyguard these days, does that guy stink or what? Armpits, man. "Take a shower, man." He gets right in my face, Father, hers too...real crazy like...that's why I left, right when we got there, so I don't know what to tell you. I didn't really see nothing. I'm only here cause my mother made me. Nothing personal, father, I think you're doing a good job and all that but it's just not my...thing.

CARMEN: I think she was out with Jesus that night, two timing Frankie and somebody caught them so this rape thing's a cover-up. Because!

JESSIE: I'm just sorry that I didn't beat the you know what out of that retard guy. Monkay too. Cheek for a cheek and all that, father, otherwise you see what happens when you don't stand up for what you know? People get away with murder, man.

CARMEN: I'm just glad Jessie finally left me alone.

SCENE 5.

<u>Projection: Abstraction, Pink & Green appears</u>.

ACTRESS TWO: (to the audience) Outside the confessional, Jessie's mother, ESTELLA GOMEZ, kneels at a pew praying, waiting for her son to be done with his confession. Although Estella is only in her early thirties, the wear and tear of having too many children, one after another makes her look ten or fifteen years older. In spite of that, Estella's face remains beautiful and innocent in a distraught sort of way. Her nose is red and her face wet from hours of crying.

ACTOR ONE: Jessie leaves the confessional, relieved it's over with. The priest has asked him to do way too many Our Fathers and Hail Mary's. He figures he'll fake it.

JESSIE KNEELS TO BEGIN HIS PRAYERS AS ESTELLA APPROACHES HIM, PLACING HER HAND ON HIS SHOULDER BUT HE RECOILS FROM HER AND LEAVES ABRUPTLY. SHE ENTERS THE CONFESSIONAL, DEJECTED.

ESTELLA: Forgive me father for I have sinned. My last confession was two years ago.

SHE SUDDENLY BURSTS OUT CRYING.

I'm sorry, father. I'm sorry.

FATHER REYES: Please, my daughter...don't cry.

ESTELLA: That girl asks for it, father. My son's no angel, but she never left him alone when they were boyfriend and girlfriend. Ask anybody, father. My son hated that skinny husband of hers so even when she got pregnant, father, Jesus would go see her. He says no. But at all hours of the night? When her skinny husband wasn't home? He plays deaf. Like his father if you tell him no.

ACTOR ONE RETAINS JESSIE'S ATTITUDE THROUGHOUT THE FOLLOWING NARRATIVES

ACTRESS TWO: (to audience) Estella cries more. Her tears are endless. (to Father as Estella) I didn't even know who he was. My husband. He would come looking for my brother when nobody was home. I would push his hand away...but there is only so many times you can do that to a man before he goes, you know... crazy. I didn't know about babies. Where they come from. My mother has eight but...but nobody says anything. (pause) I had to cover my ears with my pillow but I would still hear them.(to audience) Father Reyes seems preoccupied.

ESTELLA CRIES MORE HYSTERICALLY THAN BEFORE.

ACTOR TWO: (to audience) Father Reyes regrets not having gone to the nursing home this afternoon to visit the sick and dying instead. He suspects the worst. (to Estella as Father Reyes)Hear who, my daughter?

ESTELLA: My father . . . my mother... (hesitates, more gestures. But she can't say it.) He's a big man, my father, a giant...I was just a little girl...

FATHER REYES: (to audience) Although Estella is not necessarily making herself clear, Father Reyes doesn't necessarily want her to either. (to Estella)God forgives . . . everything and everyone, my daughter. Please, do not suffer for nothing.

ESTELLA: It's like seeing a ghost, father, every time I look at Jesus...his nose, the way he acts just like my father. But's it's the sins of the father, Father, the children are the ones that suffer, no?

FATHER REYES: Your son . . . (hesitates, gestures awkwardly) he can also be forgiven. God forgives all sinners.

ESTELLA: Is it true that if someone kills you, you go right to heaven? That would be his only chance.

FATHER REYES: (to audience) Father Reyes rubs his forehead. They sit in silence until an old woman who was lighting a candle a few moments ago, pulls open the door to the confessional, thinking nobody is in there.

FATHER REYES AND ESTELLA MIME A RESPONSE TO THE INTRUSION.

Estella, feeling perpetually guilty, exits quickly. She avoids making eye contact with the old woman and runs out of the church like a frightened rabbit. Father Reyes, so overwhelmed by Estella's concerns, forgets to tell Estella that she needs to pray three Our Fathers and Four Hail Marys.

SCENE 6.

Projection: Landscape with Crows

ACTRESS TWO: (to audience) Elsewhere MANDY FEINSTEIN, 40, walks into Sammy's

Restaurant, the fancy restaurant in town. Actually, it's the only restaurant in town. She is a reporter for the TEXAS MONTHLY. She is writing an article about the rape.

ACTOR TWO: BETO ALEMAN, III, an elderly lawyer whose "hair is blacker now than it was twenty years ago," sits in a nearby table reading the newspaper. Everybody knows everybody in this town, so when Beto spots Mandy, he assumes without question, that she is the one he has been waiting for.

BETO STANDS UP TO GREET HER ODDLY, THEY FIND EACH OTHER, UNEXPECTEDLY, ATTRACTIVE. IN THE BACKGROUND LITTLE JOE AND WILLIE NELSON SING THEIR DUET: SOLAMENTE UNA VEZ.

BETO: Sit down, sit down, Miss . . .

MANDY: Feinstein.

BETO: Of course, Miss Feinstein, I enjoy your articles very much. Very, very much. Please.

BETO STANDS UNTIL SHE TAKES HER SEAT.

ACTOR ONE: Sammy, the owner approaches the table with two hot plates. He always wears a western shirt buttoned all the way up to his neck. A large gold crucifix of Jesus resting on an anchor hangs prominently on his chest.

SAMMY: Hot, hot plates. Very hot. Enjoy.

BETO: I have ordered for us. I hope you don't mind. I'm diabetic.

MANDY: I'm really not hungry....

SAMMY: It's on the house, please. Enjoy.

BETO: Take it with you. You'll want it later. I know you will. Ms. Feinstein is going to need her order to go, Sammy.

Make sure you give her a lot of your corn tortillas. (To Mandy) He makes them from scratch . The coffee's nice and hot. Please.

SAMMY EXITS. THEY EACH TAKE A MOMENT TO TAKE IN THE OTHER.

BETO: I think you've been in the business long enough, Miss . . .

MANDY: Feinstein.

BETO: Miss Feinstein, to know that the press has built this whole rape way out of proportion. They bought her a car for God's sake. (He laughs)

MANDY: I'm sorry, who bought who a car?

BETO: Out of towners. Righteous do-gooders with money to spend. They've bought the young woman a car.

HE LAUGHS.

They have turned this into a crisis because the whole town here knows that she knew all the men better than she should have.

MANDY: You were George Parr's lawyer, is that right?

BETO: (to audience) Beto did not expect this line of questioning. He's out of Camels and hates that Sammy only carries Menthol lights.

(to Mandy) Yes maam. Twenty five years of service.

MANDY: According to this article you were implicated in a murder of one of Parr's enemies.

BETO LAUGHS.

Can that be right?

BETO LAUGHS UPROARIOUSLY.

BETO: Enemies? That's very dramatic, my dear. You've been talking to some envious people around town.

MANDY: Why were you implicated?

BETO: What are you referring to exactly, Ms . . .

MANDY/BETO: Feinstein.

MANDY: The murder.

BETO: That is exactly what I am talking about, (mispronounces it again.) Ms. Feinstein! The press going way out of line and then nobody and I mean, nobody, questioning their assumptions. I don't see what this has to do with the rape. I believe we were meeting to talk about that.

MANDY: I don't believe any story can be told about this town or the rape without talking about the last of the white, benevolent patrones.

BETO: I'm sorry but I fail to see the connection.

MANDY: What the Parr's did to this town, politically. It's not that different than what those boys did to Yolanda, emotionally.

BETO LAUGHS UPROARIOUSLY.

BETO: Call it whatever you like but I can tell you this rape business would have never happened if George Parr was still alive.

MANDY: Because nobody would have been able to talk about it without his permission, you mean?

BETO: That's tabloid mentality and you know it, Ms. Feinstein. I don't want to try the case in the newspapers but that young woman had been keeping company with one of the accused on the QQT. That's the story you got to get right.

MANDY: And that gives twenty men permission to violate her?

BETO: The press, my dear, is making the young woman appear innocent, a young, virginal mother. That's a contradiction in terms, unless you're the Holy Mother of God herself. (he laughs.)

MANDY: One of the accused is related to you?

BETO: He's the best example for what I'm saying, yes. His uncle is the president of the school board, his whole family is devoted to the good of this community.

MANDY: But the fact is that he's a relative of yours . . .

BETO: That doesn't excuse his behavior. But he has no prior offenses. Never been in trouble then suddenly he has one night of bad judgment . . .

MANDY: Bad judgment???

BETO: (overlapping) God knows, a teenager has many nights like that if he's normal. Assuming he even did it in the first place. . .

MANDY: Most are repeat drug offenders, one has an armed robbery charge! The youngest was ostracized to the point of being thrown on top of her, practically forced to penetrate her and you're calling that bad judgment?

SAMMY ENTERS WITH MS. FEINSTEIN'S FOOD.

BETO: Miss...

MANDY: Feinstein! Jesus. Feinstein.

BETO: Of course. (getting it right) Miss Feinstein. Mrs.?

MANDY: Ms.

BETO: (to Sammy) Uh-huh. Ms. Feinstein is a great writer, Sammy besides being a charming, attractive young woman.

SAMMY: Very good. Welcome, enjoy, please. I have put extra tortillas in there for you.

HANDS MS. FEINSTEIN A TO-GO BAG.

BETO: You think the town got raped, Sammy?

SAMMY: (to audience) Sammy freezes, not understanding the question.

BETO: Ms. Feinstein says the Parrs raped this town.

SAMMY: (misunderstanding) The Parrs, yes. Good people. Good, good people. (to audience) Sammy rushes to the wall and grabs a picture of himself with George Parr. (to Mandy) He call Sammy, three in the morning. "I want enchiladas, Sammy." I meet him here. Make enchiladas. He was the happy go lucky type, you know.

BETO: (to audience) Beto has taken a large bill and rolled it up neatly. Very ceremoniously he hands it to Sammy as if to commemorate the story.

SAMMY: You two have a nice day, okay?

BETO: The green sauce, Sammy. Give her a lot of that. (to Mandy) You've never tasted anything like it. You'll come begging for more. I guarantee it!

SCENE 7

<u>Projection: Abstraction, Black and Blue</u>

ACTRESS TWO: An hour later, Mandy drives up to biggest house in the town. It is a two-story white-washed Spanish colonial which might as well be the White House on Congress Avenue sitting oddly out of place between the main highway and the brush country to the southwest. There are several imported bald palm trees around the house; a tall, cement wall encloses an empty, littered swimming pool. Clearly at one time, this property was grand. It was the home of George Parr, and it is now for sale.

ACTRESS ONE: Parr's widow EVELINA, gives Ms. Feinstein a tour of the mansion. She is a bit over-dressed for the occasion. Tall heels, expensive gold jewelry, looking like she might be going out on the town instead. She wears a little too much make-up for her age and dyes her hair blonde to make herself appear whiter. She points to a window that's been shattered by a rock.

EVELINA: We have a man in town who doesn't like glass. He goes around breaking everything. Did you see the city-hall windows boarded up, too? It's gotten worse since the rape. I vacuumed it. Real good. But I keep finding little pieces. So be careful. Just in case.

MANDY SPOTS A HUGE PORTRAITOF THE COUPLE ON THE WALL. EVELINA ALWAYS PRONOUNCESGEORGE AS "CHO-CHE".

An artist from New York, New York painted that. It was so hard to sit (she imitates herself trying to hold still) you know, without moving or nothing. I think it looks just like (pronounced cho-che) George. (pronounces it once in English just in case) George. But I'm too fat there.

MANDY: It's a lovely portrait of both of you.

EVELINA: I'm too fat there.

MANDY: Not at all.

EVELINA: Baby fat.

MANDY: How did you and George meet, if it's all right to ask?

EVELINA: On my fifteenth birthday. My father was his gardener. George gave me this. It's a real ruby on a real diamond. Emerald cut. He had asked my father for my hand but nobody had told me nothing. (Still looking at the ring) Everybody tells me I should sell it. The back taxes. You know.

MANDY: You were fifteen? When he asked you to marry him?

EVELINA: Yes ma'am.

MANDY: How old was he?

EVELINA: Fifty-four. No, fifty-five.

MANDY: And your father?

EVELINA: He was forty, I think.

MANDY: No, what I mean is, what did you father think about George at his age, asking you to marry him?

EVELINA: He didn't have to work another day in his life after that. My father was thrilled. It was like being asked to marry the king or something like that. The wedding reception lasted all day. The governor came, all kinds of big wigs.

A KNOCK IS HEARD.

EVELINA: I'm expecting someone to fix the window. Excuse me please.

EVELINA LEAVES MOMENTARILY.

ACTRESS TWO: Mandy is left alone for a few minutes. It gives her an opportunity to look at several photographs on the wall. She is drawn to the picture of George Parr smoking a cigar with his legs kicked up on a desk sitting across from Lyndon Baines Johnson. It was Parr that helped collect dead people's names from the town's ancient cemetery and then listed them as alive and well and voting in the infamous Box 13 that got LBJ his fated senate election. The rest is history.

EVELINA AND ACTOR TWO ENTER.

ACTRESS ONE: Evelina leads CHUY LONGORIA into the room. He chews tobacco and carries a toolbox.

ACTOR TWO: Chuy is a handy-man, the local simpleton who can fix anything at the extra economical price. He's very uncomfortable in the company of the opposite sex, so he goes right to work, pretending he didn't see Mandy standing there.

MANDY: I just interviewed Beto Aleman...

EVELINA: Oh, yes, Beto. He's a very good lawyer. The best.

MANDY: Oh I'm sure he is, he just . . . I don't know. You know how some people can remind you of somebody else sometimes?

EVELINA: Oh yes.

MANDY: Well he reminds me of my grandfather.

EVELINA: Oh that's nice.

MANDY: Well not really. Did you know Yolanda? The young lady...

EVELINA: (shakes her head) They happen in Corpus and Houston all the time, Ms. Feinstein. These rapes. My daughter says in college, too. They happen. But do they get this kind of attention? Like when George (cho-che) killed himself. Now that I can understand but my goodness, the tv trucks. Up and down the streets looking for something to put on the news. I look horrible. Everytime.

CHUY: I know Frankie. Yolanda's husband. I don't know her but I pray for her. And her babies.

THE WOMEN BOTH STOP TO LOOK AT CHUY. SELF-CONSCIOUSLY HE LOOKS AWAY AND SPITS INTO HISCHEWING TOBACCO CUP.

EVELINA: This rape is a bad thing, Ms. Feinstein but it's not as bad the pool hall, remember? Up north. That was in a public place for God's sake.

CHUY: I pray for Frankie too. I say a rosary for them. Every morning.

CHUY DOES THE SIGN OF THE CROSS. MANDY WAITS TO SEE IF CHUY IS GOING TO SAY ANYTHING MORE. HE BECOMESSELF-CONSCIOUS AND SPITS HIS CHEWED UP TOBACCO INTO A PAPER CUP AND TURN HIS ATTENTION BACK TO HIS WORK.

MANDY: Is it true your husband, towards the end of his life. . .several people I've talked to have mentioned this. . .they said he would hide in the bushes and shoot at people? Young men, in particular?

EVELINA: The tv news hate this town, Ms. Feinstein. Because of George. What they say about the ignorant Mexicans here, my god. Like I have anything to do with it. They think George's still alive. That he had somebody else's face blown off so tha the wouldn't go to prison. He would shot into the sky, to scare trespassers sometimes, yes. But that is all.

MANDY: This person I spoke to was standing on the corner getting ready to cross the street when George and you passed him in the car. He says that George then got off the car and slapped him because he said he was looking at you?

EVELINA: In the wrong way, yes. That's why this rape would have never happened if George was still alive, Ms. Feinstein. Never.

MANDY: But the young man says he hadn't even seen you. . .

THE WOMEN STARE AT EACH OTHER, EACH ODDLY UPSET BY THE OTHER.

I just don't see how George could have prevented this particular rape. That's all.

EVELINA: Then you're just like the woman at the bank. The other day. For no reason she tells me, real mean---"when someone commits suicide they can't go to heaven."

MANDY: No, what I'm saying is. . .

EVELINA: So I dream that night, Ms. Feinstein that I'm standing in front of George's casket, afraid I'm gonna see his face, you know, blown up. Without his dentures. They found those by his feet. The force of the gun....But then suddenly I'm the one laying inside the casket...I don't know how I got there but its real comfortable. (She laughs cathartically.) You can't believe how good it felt in there. Man! I hear his voice as clear as Chuy's (indicates Chuy). Right here (she points to her head), "I never felt better in my whole life, mi linda." (She laughs) You can't be in hell and say something like that. (threateningly) You can't. It was a sign.

CHUY STARES AT MANDY. MANDY STARES AT EVELINA, AND EVELINA STAYS FOCUSED ON THE PORTRAIT.

SCENE 8

Projection: Canyon Landscape

ACTRESS ONE: Veronica visits her grandmother Elisa at La Hacienda Nursing Home and attempts to manicure her nails.

ACTOR TWO: But today Elisa is not sitting up in her chair, as usual. She has been in her bed all day, looking longingly out the window. Lying next to her is the Great Artist, who holds Elisa in her arms, very reassuringly.

ACTOR ONE PORTRAYS THE GREAT ARTIST.

ELISA: I have a heavy heart this whole, long day.

VERONICA: What's wrong grandma?

ELISA: Death comes and lays with me, mijita.

VERONICA: But you're not dying.

ELISA: Maybe not today.

VERONICA: I don't like to hear you talk like this.

ELISA: I want you to go to my closet. There is a paper bag full of the great artist's paintings. I want you to have them.

VERONICA: What great artist, ama?

ELISA: In the newspaper. She died in her sleep.

VERONICA LOOKS FOR THE ARTICLE HER GRANDMOTHER IS REFERRING TO.

VERONICA: Are you talking about Georgia O'Keeffe grandma?

ELISA: The ignorant things this town tells the newspaper and the newspaper is stupid enough to print it.

VERONICA: The great artist, ama. Are you talking about Georgia O'Keeffe?

ELISA: Does it have her picture?

VERONICA NODS.

ELISA: Pos then that's her. If she is gone today, I know I am not that far behind. I want you to have her paintings.

VERONICA: I gave you that calendar a few years ago, with her painting on them. Those flowers you liked so much. Is that what you mean?

ELISA: No, no it's her. She was always painting.

VERONICA: What are you talking about, ama?

ELISA: Canyon. She came to Canyon, Texas. Taught at the college. She would say si, no, como estas. Like me, in English. The easy things. So we made signs with our hands.

VERONICA: You would talk with her?

ELISA: I would help your grandfather clean at night. I still have her paintings.

VERONICA: The calendar, you mean?

ELISA: The ones she gave me. Not the hard kind of paint. That you can feel with your fingers. The water kind.

VERONICA: She didn't paint watercolors, Ama. I think you're confusing her...

ELISA: They're in the closet in a paper bag. Under the Christmas decorations. I never forget a face, mijita. Her hair bien dark. I thought she was Mexican, pos Spaniola. Came to Texas by herself. In those days, women did not go nowhere by themselves.

PAUSE.

VERONICA: You have Georgia O'Keeffe paintings in a paper bag.

ELISA: In my closet. They would end up in the garbage. Piles and piles of them. She wasn't happy with them.

VERONICA: But she's famous, Wela, are you sure?

ELISA: Pos I am not sure of anything I have anymore, since I have been put away in this prison.

VERONICA: I thought you liked it here.

ELISA: I was very happy in my own house.

VERONICA: You served me coffee at your house and put the cups face down and poured the coffee on them like they were facing the right way, Ama.

ELISA: If I can see that artist in the newspaper Veronica, there is nothing wrong with my eyes.

VERONICA: When you hold it an inch from your face! It was dangerous. To leave you alone. You could have come to live with me.

ELISA: To hear that man yell at you and take advantage?

VERONICA: I invited you.

ELISA: I'm used to this place, now.

VERONICA: Ama...

ELISA: Remember the first baby, how the last month you tell yourself, "there's no baby in there," even though you are the size of an elephant and the baby is kicking you crazy, you still can not believe that there is a baby growing inside there. That is how it feels to be old and waiting everyday to die, mijita.

VERONICA: But you're not dying.

ELISA: Maybe not today....(she shrugs)

VERONICA: You're gonna outlive everybody!

ELISA: Now you tell me she's famous, fijita. I should have had them framed.

VERONICA STARES AT HER GRANDMOTHER, DUMBFOUNDED.

VERONICA: Ama...

ELISA: Que?

AFTER LONG PAUSE.

VERONICA: Nothing.

SCENE 9.

Projection: Sunset

ACTOR ONE: (to audience) Elsewhere, Frankie is watching television. Yolanda is especially late getting home.

FRANKIE STAYS FOCUSED ON THE TELEVISION.

FRANKIE: Where the hell have you been, I waited at work for an hour.

YOLANDA IS UNABLE TO RESPOND. SHE STARES AT HIM BRIEFLY, DISORIENTED. FRANKIE LOOKS AT HIS WIFE FOR THE FIRST TIME, REALIZING SOMETHING IS TERRIBLY WRONG.

FRANKIE: Where were you?

HE WALKS TOWARDS HER. SHE LOOKS AT THE FLOOR.

FRANKIE: How come you weren't waiting for me?

SHE STARTS TO CRY.

FRANKIE: What's wrong? Hey, hey, shhhhhhhh, it's okay.

HE TRIES TO HUG HER BUT SHE FLINCHES

FRANKIE: What? What the hell is the matter with you? Don't cry, okay, it's okay, whatever it is, it's okay, just don't cry. Oh please, Yolanda, it makes me crazy to hear you cry like that, what did I do? You got to tell me something.

Did something happen to you? (aside to audience) Frankie notices the scrapes on her knees, as well as the scratches, dirt and other debris all over her legs.

FRANKIE: (violently angry) What happened? Somebody do something to you?

HE REACHES FOR HER DRESS TO RAISE IT SLIGHTLY, SHE SCREAMS. THIS SHOULD MIRROR THE BEGINNING OF THE PLAY, CONNECTING AND COMPLETING HER EARLIER MOVEMENTS AS LIGHTS SLOWLY FADE.

ACT II

SCENE 1.

Projection: <u>LIGHT COMING ON THE PLAINS</u>

ACTOR TWO: (to audience) A disoriented Yolanda sits next to her husband at the Sheriff's office. A muted, portable television sits in the corner tuned to "The Price is Right". The Sheriff turns on his tape recorder.

YOLANDA DOES NOT MAKE EYE CONTACT WITH ANYONE.

SHERIFF: So...okay. There was Jesus Canales, Monkay Solis, Chuy Longoria . . .

SHE SHAKES HER HEAD.

Not Chuy Longoria.

YOLANDA: He was there, but no.

SHERIFF: He didn't . . .

CAN'T FIND THE RIGHT WORD TO VERIFY THE INFORMATION.

YOLANDA: No. Sir.

SHERIFF: Okay, what about Javier Zuniga, Jr.?

SHE LOOKS AT HIM CONFUSED.

He's Payaso's boy, thirteen, maybe fourteen years old.

YOLANDA: No. I don't know who he is.

SHERIFF: Did you know everybody else who . . .

YOLANDA: Yes. Sir.

SHE KEEPS FORGETTING TO SAY YES SIR, BUT ADDS IT AWKWARDLY WHEN SHE REMEMBERS TO.

SHERIFF: Was there anybody else?

SHE NODS.

Can you tell me who they were?

YOLANDA: Roel.

FRANKIE: Roel Paiz? He just fixed my van. God, no.

FRANKIE DOES EVERYTHING HE CAN TO RESTRAIN HIMSELF.

SHERIFF: Roel Paiz. Is that all?

YOLANDA SHAKES HER HEAD. BOTH THE
SHERIFF AND HER HUSBAND CANNOT
BELIEVE THE EXTENT OF IT.

YOLANDA: What's Roel's cousin's name?

FRANKIE: Which one?

YOLANDA: The one who works at the Dairy Queen.

FRANKIE: Him too?

SHERIFF: Who works at the Dairy Queen?

FRANKIE: Mando. Armando Rodriquez.

SHERIFF: Sammy's boy? You sure?

SHE NODS.

FRANKIE: That son-of-a-bitch, smiling right to my face. Jesus Christ.

SHERIFF: Okay, is that it?

YOLANDA WANTS TO LIE AND SAY YES BUT
SHAKES HER HEAD AND STARTS TO CRY.

YOLANDA: Luis . . . Salazar.

FRANKIE: No man, I cain't believe it. Not him too.

FRANKIE BREAKS DOWN.

ACTOR TWO: The Sheriff nervously hands him a box of Kleenex. He stands up and gets them both a glass of water. Neither seems interested.

SHERIFF: Here, it calms the nerves.

THE FOLLOWING ACTION, WHEN SPOKEN ABOUT, SHOULDN'T BE PANTOMIMED. IT WORKS BEST IF THE ACTORS JUST STARE AT THEIR CUPS AS THE ACTION IS DESCRIBED.

ACTOR TWO: Frankie and Yolanda take the water. Yolanda just stares at it. Frankie drinks it all like a stiff drink.

FRANKIE: I cain't believe it. These are my friends. Were. What did I ever do to them? I cain't . . . (wants to say fucking) believe it.

SHERIFF: Okay. Do we have everybody?

AGAIN SHE SHAKES HER HEAD. FRANKIE STANDS UP AND KICKS HIS CHAIR.

FRANKIE: This ain't right, no matter what anybody says, this is wrong. Very wrong. They got to pay, man. They got to.

SHERIFF: Frankie, please, sit down. Please don't kick the furniture, okay? No need to get as crazy as the rest of them, you're a good kid. Sit down.

FRANKIE REFUSES TO.

SHERIFF: I have to ask you to sit down. That's an order. Or else.

FRANKIE FINALLY GIVES IN.

SHERIFF: I know this is a very bad thing. But I have to ask you to either leave the room so your wife can tell me everything she has to tell me or you have to sit there no matter what.

FRANKIE: I'm sitting. I'm sitting.

SHERIFF: Okay, good then. Please, continue.

YOLANDA: Sergio.

FRANKIE: WHAT? Sergio Villanueva? No way, Yolanda. No way.

SHERIFF: Frankie, I warned you.

FRANKIE BARELY RESTRAINS HIMSELF.

SHERIFF: Sergio Villanueva. You're positive about that?

YOLANDA: Yes. Sir.

FRANKIE: He better not get away, that one.
They'll never convict him. His uncle is the judge.

SHERIFF: And the lawyer.

FRANKIE: What lawyer?

SHERIFF: Beto Aleman is his uncle too.

FRANKIE: No man, that's like trying to convict
one of the Kennedy's. It'll never happen, man. No
fucking . . . I'm sorry, excuse me. No way in hell.

SHERIFF: They'll be no favoritism here, Frankie.
No mercy whatsoever.

FRANKIE: We'll see about that. I cain't believe it.
He was my best friend. In Junior High but still,
my best friend.

SHERIFF: Okay. I hope that's everyone.

AGAIN YOLANDA SHAKES HER HEAD

No?

FRANKIE BOLTS UP AND KICKS THE CHAIR
AGAIN AND STORMS OUT. THE SHERIFF

LOOKS AT YOLANDA WHO LOOKS AT HER FEET.

SCENE 2.

Projection: GRAY ABSTRACTION (Train/Desert)

Actor One announces: Elsewhere Javier looks out the window as his grandmother BEATRICE ZUNIGA, paces nervously. There is a huge stack of mail on the kitchen table.

BEATRICE: The same car keeps passing by real slow. I don't know why you were so stupid!

JAVIER: They were gonna catch me anyway, grandma.

BEATRICE: Who? Who was going to catch you if you had kept your big mouth shut?

JAVIER: The police.

BEATRICE: Why the police? You didn't touch the girl.

JAVIER: But everybody saw me there.

BEATRICE: More reason to keep your mouth shut. Let the girl tell it, she was there.

SHE SPOTS THE CAR FROM THE WINDOW.

There he goes again.

JAVIER: Get down, ama, get down!

Actor One announces simply: Javier lunges down as if to avoid a bullet.

BEATRICE LOOKS OUT THE WINDOW.

BEATRICE: Your sister cain't even go outside without somebody bothering her too. He's the one who jumped you, right?

JAVIER: He didn't jump me, ama. Get that through your thick head, I fainted.

BEATRICE: Okay you fainted. And since when do you faint? Since your friends turn into psychos? Did you tell the principal?

JAVIER: Don't be stupid, ama. Jessie is my friend.

BEATRICE: Why do they let a rapist ride around the school, making people faint?

JAVIER: How come everybody else cares except you? Every letter here says I did right. Except you.

BEATRICE: I didn't say that.

JAVIER: You said I should have kept my mouth shut.

BEATRICE: No, Javier. I didn't say that.

JAVIER: That's what you said.

BEATRICE: No, I said I wish it had been somebody else. You turn around everything that I say!

AGAIN SHE IMPULSIVELY WHACKS HIM.

I don't want nothing bad to happen to you. Chiwawas, hombre. There's a time to speak and there's a time to stay quiet. A time to plant, a time to sow, it's in the bible. Common sense. There's a time to go. And there's a time to stay. That's all I am saying.

ACTRESS TWO: (to audience) Beatrice reaches for a stack of mail. (as Beatrice to Javier) This one sent a picture.

ACTRESS ONE TAKES THE POSE,
REPRESENTING THE PICTURE.

JAVIER: Eeeehole, she's fine.

BEATRICE: Anda grosero, listen. "Dear Javier . . ."

OPTIONAL: ACTRESS ONE EMBODIES THE
LETTER OR IT CAN BE READ BY BEATRICE.

ACTRESS ONE: "After I read about you in the Corpus Christi Caller I thought to myself, thank God there are still brave people in this world that know how to stand up for what is right. Don't let them get you down. I am praying for you every night. I have lit a special candle at St. Mary's. Sincerely, Tamara Reyes. P.S. Did anybody ever tell you you look like Johnny . . .

BEATRICE: (she pronounces it with a long "e") Depp. Who's Johnny Depp? Is that one of the rapists?

JAVIER: No, ma. Don't be stupid. Can I have it?

BEATRICE: This one didn't send money. When they do, I save the checks. You say you want to move, okay we're going to all move, all of us together but first you finish school.

JAVIER: Fine. A lot of good it's gonna do me dead.

BEATRICE: Anda hombre.

JAVIER: I cain't go back to school. I got to get out of here or I'm dead meat!

BEATRICE: No way, Javier, when you go, we all go. Nobody leaves nobody. And nobody quits school.

JAVIER: They're letting Chuy, down the street, go to school at home.

BEATRICE: Cause he's stupid.

JAVIER: Somebody shows up with books and stuff from the school. Everyday.

BEATRICE: Because he cain't learn nothing at school, that's why.

JAVIER: Someone could come here. I could go to school here.

BEATRICE: So that people think you're retarded like Chuy?

SHE IMPULSIVELY WHACKS HIM ON THE HEAD AGAIN.

As if I hadn't been through enough already with this rape, hombre. Now you want special education!

JAVIER: Chuy's not retarded, Wela! He's just got the love of God in him.

THEY STARE ANGRILY AT EACH OTHER.

BEATRICE: Pos if you got the love of God you don't go to no rape.

BEATRICE STARTS TO READ ANOTHER LETTER.

Somebody wants you to go to their camp, mira. For free. Like the white kids, mijito. Camp Madre or something like that. Come the summertime, all of us will move. Alive. To Corpus, like Frankie and Yolanda. They're happy there. We'll be happy there.

JAVIER: I'm not going to no camp.

BEATRICE: The people in Corpus are . . . different. Es el environment, mijo, como dijo el counselor. They're not ignorant Mexicans there like here. They're educated Mexicans, that finish school, not special education. They go to college. They care what happens to other people. Your grandmother is stupid because she had no choice. You have a choice. There's enough donations here for a down payment for a house, a little house, but we'll have our own house. "No aye no mal que por bien no venga."

JAVIER: (frustrated) What?

BEATRICE: Learn your Spanish hombre! "There is no bad that doesn't bring good with it!"

ACTRESS TWO: Suddenly Jessie's car drives by again.

VOICE: (offstage) Orale pendejo! We got your number!

BEATRICE: (hollers back) Anda cabron! Pick on somebody your own size. (aside to audience)Beatrice runs outside, takes her shoe off and throws it at Jessie's car. She manages to hit the backside of the passenger that rides with him. She watches the car speed off, leaving a puff of caliche dust behind it.

SHE SHAKES HER HEAD IN HESITANT RESIGNATION.

(to herself) Aprovechados!

SCENE 3.

Projection: EVENING

YOLANDA AND FRANKIE SIT ON OPPOSITE SIDES OF THE STAGE. ALTHOUGH MANDY IS "INTERVIEWING"THEM, SHE IS NOT TECHNICALLY ON STAGE. IT IS MORE IMPORTANT TO SHOW THE ACTUAL "PHYSICAL" DISTANCE BETWEEN THE COUPLE AND THEIR ISOLATION NOT ONLY FROM EACH OTHER BUT THE WORLD AT LARGE.

ACTOR ONE: Ten thousand dollars have been raised in Corpus Christi for Yolanda and Frankie. A mere seventy dollars have been collected for them in their hometown. They are being interviewed by Mandy Feinstein in their donated apartment, a small, dark place in front of a trailer park in Corpus Christi.

ACTRESS ONE: Yolanda holds her sleeping toddler in her arms while the oldest watches their donated color television tuned to a re-run of "Gilligan's Island." Donated toys are strewn about the floor and velveteen hangings from Frankie's mother decorate the walls. One is of Christ, the cross inside his heart ablaze. And the other is of kittens frolicking in a basket with a ball of pink yarn.

THE BABY CAN BE SUGGESTED BY ELISA'S SHAWL FROM THE PREVIOUS SCENE

YOLANDA: I don't talk about it.

FRANKIE: But people talk about it. All the time. Like last week, somebody asks me where I'm from. He says, real stupid like . . . You're not one of those rapists are you? I grab him

DEMONSTRATES BY PULLING AT AN INVISIBLE SOMEBODY'S JACKET

and tell him never, never say anything like that to me again, you understand?" Now he tells everybody I have a temper. So nobody talks to me. It's weird.

YOLANDA: I don't go outside. Just to watch the babies in the plastic pool when its hot. There by the door. That's why I want a hand wringer so I can wash clothes here at home. I don't like those laundry places.

FRANKIE: I don't know anybody here. It sucks. They just said, here's the address, this is how you get there. You start on Monday at 8:00 a.m. I don't know nothing about cash registers. Just because people buy something from you in the store, it doesn't mean they're better than you. But they sure act like it. There's always somebody that gets on my nerves, right? Like yesterday, this woman wanted to return something. The store takes everything back, except if you've worn it, right, this woman wouldn't take no for an answer. Let me talk to the manager, young man. Like she's saying . . . .You're in trouble now. Well, she left with her tail between her legs. He stood up for me, man. The customer is not always right. That's the sign I want to put up on the wall. You can't pay me enough to be nice to you, man, so don't even try. But some people, they think they own you cause they buy fucking toothpaste from you.

YOLANDA: They're bringing couch. To morrow. I don't know what else. People are nice, here. I like it a lot. Except this guy.

AS IF ASKING PERMISSION FROM FRANKIE TO TELL THIS

The one that pulled his pants down?

FRANKIE: (to Yolanda) At the laundrymat or what?

YOLANDA NODS.

Some guy downtown. In the daylight, flashing everybody. The perverts, man. It's a big city, so.

YOLANDA: And those birds. You cain't eat nothing outside. They're everywhere.

FRANKIE: Seagulls.

YOLANDA: Yeah, the seagulls. (to Frankie) We found one that time at the ranch? (to Mandy) Before we had to leave to come here. It was bleeding and stuff. No beach anywhere. So Frankie put it in a shoebox. But it died. (to Frankie) Even with bandaids and stuff.

FRANKIE: One of the assholes lives here in Corpus. On my way to work sometimes I wind up at a stop sign across from him. I picture him...(stops, afraid he'll cry) with Yolanda and have to fight the urge to ram his car. He was my friend. In Junior High, but my best friend.

YOLANDA: But the people here. They're nice. The counselor. I like her a lot, but. . .I don't know, it's different I guess.

FRANKIE: But the day he walked in to the store, I lost it. He bought some oil for his car. Looked at the shirts on sale. My neck got real hot. My hands started shaking. I had to run to the bathroom and throw up. My boss got really mad at me, there was a line waiting to check out. I told him I ate something bad. (pause) Seeing one of those guys can ruin your damn day. Your whole damn day.

FRANKIE: Down there I belonged. Here in Corpus I'm just another Mexican. I mean it's a dumb town and everything, there's nothing to do down there, but I've been there all my life. The people here are nice I guess but they act like they're our good friends or something. We don't even know them. It's weird. I mean, it's hard to know how to act back. I don't know these people. Why are they being so nice?

SCENE 4.

PROJECTION: DUSK IN THE CANYON

ACTOR TWO: (to audience) The Sheriff approaches the house of Estella Gomez and her son Jessie. They live in neighborhood known to the locals as "Naked City" because so many children run dirty and wild with only a shirt or shoes on. A mangey pit bull guards the porch.

ACTOR OR ACTRESS ONE EMBODY THE
BARKS OF A VICIOUS DOG.

SHERIFF: Shhhhh! Take it easy, boy. Here boy, come on boy.

THE DOG CONTINUES WITH MORE
INTENSITY.

ESTELLA: (offstage) Waldo, cajate hombre! Come here.

THE DOG HESITATES FOR A MOMENT AND
THEN BEGINS BARKING AGAIN.

Come on, here boy, it's just Gus. Come on. (To Sheriff) Tell him hello.

SHERIFF: Hello.

THE DOG BARKS LOUDER.

ESTELLA: He likes you. You just have to remind him that its you. He doesn't bite but we shouldn't take any chances. Andale Waldo, get in there.

POINTS IN THE DIRECTION OF THE HOUSE AS
IF LEADING THE DOG.

(to audience) Estella is aware that the neighbors are watching them. Now that news about the rape is out, the traffic has doubled on their dead end street. Somebody threw a rock through their front window this morning, missing the Jessie's kid by a hair.

SHE WANTS TO TOUCH HIM BUT THINKS BETTER OF IT.

ESTELLA: Como estas.

SHERIFF: Bien, Bien. Y tu?

ESTELLA SHRUGS. THINGS ARE TERRIBLE.

ESTELLA: I'd ask you to sit down, here on the porch but the fleas are bad right now, very bad.

SHERIFF: No, no, that's fine. Thank you. I'm looking for Jesus. Is he here?

ESTELLA: He's sleeping.

SHERIFF: I need you to wake him, por favor.

ESTELLA: Why?

SHERIFF: I need to talk with him, Estella. Alone.

ESTELLA: You're not believing what they're saying are you?

SHERIFF: Estella, this is a very bad situation. Nobody is happy about it. But I need to discuss it with him.

ESTELLA: Are you going to lock him up?

SHERIFF: I might have to keep him there for a while, yes.

ESTELLA: They're good for nothings. Especially Monkay. They would lie to God himself.

SHERIFF: Estella, please. This is not personal, it's my job.

ESTELLA: If course it's personal. Its my son. I don't want him rotting in jail like his daddy.

SHERIFF: The sooner I speak with him, Estella...

ESTELLA: You have to promise me you'll be fair.

SHERIFF: I always am, Estella.

ESTELLA: Have you picked up Beto's nephew? Or is he to good to lock up?

SHERIFF: Everyone will be treated fairly. Under the law, Estella.

ESTELLA LAUGHS SARCASTICALLY.

ESTELLA: I'll come pull on your toes and scratch your feet, Gus, if I die first. You hear me? I will never let it rest.

ACTOR TWO: (to audience) The sheriff doesn't know how to respond to that.

HE LOOKS AT HIS WATCH IMPATIENTLY.

SHERIFF: I don't have much time.

ESTELLA: (hollars loudly) Jesus! He's a heavy sleeper. He can sleep through anything.

SHERIFF: Can you go wake him up? Please?

ESTELLA: Jessie! He's deaf in one ear. Jesus! Levantate!

JESSIE: (offstage) I told you not to bother me!

SHERIFF: It's me, Jesus. Gus. I need to talk with you.

LONG SILENCE.

ACTOR ONE: Just as Estella starts to approach the house, Jesus surfaces without a shirt on. The Sheriff is shocked to see his daughter's name . . . "Carmen" tattooed on his arm.

JESSIE: What's up?

SHERIFF: I need to take you down to the courthouse.

JESSIE: The jail?

SHERIFF: You're under arrest.

ESTELLA: Gus! You didn't say anything about arresting him.

JESSIE: Ama, stay out of it, please. What for, Gustavo?

SHERIFF: For rape.

JESSIE: Rape? Who do they say I raped?

ESTELLA: Gus, that was no rape. You know the little tramp.

JESSIE BURSTS OUT LAUGHING.

SHERIFF: Yolanda Hinojosa!

JESSIE: Whatever she wants to call it, Gustavo, I can tell you right now, that was no rape.

SHERIFF: Jesus, I have to tell you that anything you say can and will be used against you . . .

JESSIE: Yeah, yeah, I have a right to an attorney, big fucking shit. No man, she gave me whatever she says I took. Ask anybody. Ask her.

ESTELLA: Two times. The phone. I've changed it, Gus. She called so much.

ACTOR TWO: (aside to audience) The sheriff pulls out his handcuffs.

ESTELLA: Why those things like he's animal, a stranger?

SHERIFF: I have to put these on him, Estella, please. We can talk about this later.

JESSIE: Put anything you want on me, Sheriff. There's gonna be some very embarrassed people when all is said and done. I was with my wife for most of the night. Ask her. Bonnie!

ESTELLA: Bonnie! (Beat) She's at work.

JESSIE: Well then, make sure you call her, Gus.

ESTELLA: They watched tv. The whole night long.

SHERIFF: What night would that be?

JESSIE: Whatever night they're saying I raped her. I got to be at work at 6:00 A.M. every morning, Gus. I'm home and in bed by 9:00.

ESTELLA: That girl lies about everything, Gustavo.

JESSIE: How long you gonna hold me for? I cain't miss work without losing my job, Gus. I need you to keep that in mind.

SHERIFF: You'll be done as soon as I can get done with you. I promise.

ACTOR TWO: (aside to audience) The Sheriff places handcuffs on Jesus as a very betrayed Estella looks on.

SHERIFF: (tenderly) I'll call you later.

ESTELLA: Save your quarter.

Scene 6

Projection: ABSTRACTION

ACTOR TWO: (to audience) On the other side of town, Arturo, sits at Veronica's kitchen table, thumbing through a stack of Georgia O'Keefe's watercolors.

ARTURO HOLDS UP GEORGIA O'KEEFFE'S WATERCOLOR, ABSTRACTION.

ARTURO: They look like something your little girl could have painted.

VERONICA: Arturo, for heaven's sake, don't be so ignorant. (aside to audience) Veronica is reading Mandy Feinstein's article about the rape in Texas Monthly.

ARTURO: (suspicious of her reading) Ignorant? So now I'm ignorant. Last night you couldn't get enough of my ignorance. I'm talking about the rainbow Vanessa made for Mother's Day, on your refrigerator. It looks just like this. Either that little girl of yours has got talent or this chick is a little overblown, that's all I'm saying.

VERONICA STARES AT HOME WITH ALOT OF HOSTILITY.

What?

VERONICA: Your fingerprints. They're worth thousands of dollars!

ARTURO: They've been under a pile of your grandmother's nightgowns for seventy years or something and now suddenly, I cain't even touch them with my hand?

VERONICA: Can't.

ARTURO: Can't what?

VERONICA: Your English, Arturo. It's third grade. It's not cain't. It's can't.

ARTURO LAUGHS SARCASTICALLY.

ARTURO: Chingao, Veronica. Now you're my pinche English teacher too. Now I cain't say cain't and now my grease monkey hands aren't good enough all the sudden. You couldn't get enough of them last night and this morning?

VERONICA: Someone from the college is picking the paintings up. I want them to be in good condition when he gets here.

ARTURO: He? Who is "he" Veronica?

VERONICA: A curator, or something like that.

ARTURO: What the hell is that? You got something going with that asshole or something?

VERONICA: Shut up. I've talked to him, this professor, on the phone. One time.

ARTURO: Something's different about you lately.

VERONICA: I cut my hair.

ARTURO: No, something about the way you look at me. They way you talk.

VERONICA: You're the one that knows all about that.

ARTURO: What?

VERONICA: Sneaking around my back.

ARTURO: Who said anything about sneaking around anybody's back, Veronica?

VERONICA: "Mexican men always have something on the side."

ARTURO: If I got all these women on the side, why would I tattoo your tits on my butt? You got a guilty conscience?

VERONICA: They could be anybody's tits.

ARTURO: With your name on them?

VERONICA: Am I suppose to be flattered, Arturo?

ARTURO: I cain't . . . (corrects himself) . . . can't . . . I can't do nothing right, can I? It's a tribute to your beauty, Veronica. To our staying power, but no, you have to turn it into trash in your mind. Well I'm sick of it, really sick of it, you know that?

VERONICA: My beauty on your butt? Am I getting that right?

ARTURO: I'm a tit man. You like that about me, you've told me yourself. You got the most beautiful tits I've ever seen.

VERONICA: Arturo, it takes more than your appreciation of my tits, okay?

ARTURO TEASES VERONICA WITH PLAYFUL, INTIMATE CARESSES.

ARTURO: I picked my butt in the first place because it's private space, Veronica. Only you and me see it and nobody else. It's my way of showing you that you are absolutely the only one for me.

ARTURO KISSES VERONICA, AFTER A MOMENT SHE BITES HIM ON THE LIP.

ARTURO: Ouh!! Goddammit!

FEELS HIS LIP FOR BLOOD.

VERONICA: So you tattoo my tits, with my name on your butt, and that's suppose to make everything all right?

ARTURO: How come you can appreciate this chick's kindergarten paintings and not Frankie's tattoo on my butt? Art can only be on a piece of paper?

ARTURO TAKES THE MAGAZINE FROM HER VIOLENTLY AND THROWS IT.

It's this white chick's article. Brainwashing you.

VERONICA: I can't believe we're having this conversation. I want you to leave.

ARTURO: That ain't gonna happen, Veronica.

VERONICA: I don't want you coming around anymore, Arturo. I don't know how to get that across to you any clearer.

ARTURO: So how come you let me in, every time?

VERONICA: Because I don't want you to push the door down. It's expensive. I'm trying to be your friend.

ARTURO: So this what you do with your friends? Fuck their brains out?

VERONICA: I'm fucking human, too, okay?

ARTURO APPROACHES HER AGAIN, HE TRIES TO KISS HER AGAIN, SHE MOVES AWAY.

ARTURO: This is something you women, I mean, this rape thing is bring it all home, you women got to quit saying yes, when you mean no, goddam it and quit blaming the men when they get pissed off and do something they regret later.

HE GRABS HER. SHE BITES HIM ON THE ARM TO ESCAPE HIS GRIP. HE SCREAMS IN PAIN.

ARTURO: Ouuuu!! What's the matter with you?

VERONICA: Yolanda wanted Jesus to rape her like a hole in the head.

ARTURO: I'm just saying you cain't make love to me that way and not love me.

VERONICA: Jessie head that Yolanda still wanted him. That makes it okay to force himself on her?

ARTURO: Can you look me in the face and tell me I'm forcing myself on you?

VERONICA: It's an addiction.

ARTURO: That hurts my feelings, Veronica. It makes me want to . . .

VERONICA: What?

ARTURO: Hurt somebody! What do you think? You make me that crazy.

VERONICA: I need you to leave.

ARTURO: I'm not going. I know you cain't . . . goddamn it . . . can't understand how I feel but you're gonna have to try.

VERONICA: Don't make me call the police, Arturo.

ARTURO: Not again, Veronica. I haven't broken anything.

VERONICA: Then just go.

ARTURO: No, goddamn it! If I go, you're going with me.

LONG PAUSE. THEY STARE AT EACH OTHER. FROZEN. WHEN VERONICA MOVES SLIGHTLY, HE MOVES TOWARDS HER. SHE STOPS. PAUSE. SHE TRIES AGAIN, THIS TIME HE LUNGES FOR HER.SHE TRIES TO GET AWAY, HE PINS HER DOWN.

ARTURO: Why are you acting like this? I ain't never raped you.

VERONICA: Not physically.

ARTURO: Oh come on, Veronica. You say one thing and do another, goddamn it!!!

VERONICA: Jesus wouldn't leave Yolanda alone either. It didn't matter that she would tell him no.

ARTURO: She was married. The asshole couldn't respect that. That's not what's going on with you and me, unless there's something you ain't telling me.

VERONICA: We've been breaking up for two fucking years. I lie to my grandmother. My mother.

ARTURO: What do you want from me?

VERONICA: I don't want you...I mean I want you to not go crazy like Jessie.

ARTURO: He's a fucking, crazy junkie! How can you compare me to that asshole rapist?

HE LETS GO OF HER. HE STARTS LOOKING AROUND FOR HIS THINGS.

That really hurts my feelings. Where's my coat?

VERONICA: Arturo...

ARTURO: This whole fucking town has lost its mind. I didn't expect you to go crazy too!

THUNDER IS HEARD.

VERONICA: Arturo, wait....it's late.

ARTURO: It's real late. (aside to audience) The blinds are knocking violently against the window frame, as a hard rain starts to force its way through the screen.

VERONICA: My car windows are down. (aside to audience)Arturo runs out in the rain to pull Veronica's car window up and drag several pounds of livestock feed from the back of his truck onto Veronica's porch. She's terrified of the sudden, violent storms that come out of nowhere this time of year. She does the sign of the cross to calm herself, praying that Arturo doesn't get hit by lightning like the kid running to his car after a football game last year. It killed him on the spot.

ACTOR TWO: Arturo is soaked. The heavy feed has winded him. He sits on the porch swing to catch his breath.

ACTOR TWO BREATHES HARD AND AUDIBLY TWO OR THREE TIMES. HE STARES VERY INTENSELY AT VERONICA.

(to audience) He swings back and force, staring at Veronica.

VERONICA: Veronica stares back, standing behind the screen.

LONG PAUSE.

ARTURO: (to audience) Neither can say a word. (Thunder.)

SCENE 7.

<u>Projection: Portrait W</u>

ACTOR ONE: Elsewhere, fifty four miles northeast out of town in Corpus Christi, Frankie is asleep in front of the television. Johnny Carson is on making fun of Quayle's latest blunder...something about how "the future will be better tomorrow"...Frankie, though...is having a nightmare in which he sees himself paralyzed and helpless at the scene of the gang-rape right as

A KNOCK IS HEARD. FRANKIE DOESN'T HEAR IT. A LOUDER KNOCK FOLLOWS. FRANKIE STILL DOESN'T WAKE UP.

YOLANDA: (offstage) Frankie!

FRANKIE ABRUPTLY WAKES UP.

FRANKIE: What!

YOLANDA: Someone's at the door.

FRANKIE PANICS AND IS DISORIENTED AS YOLANDA ENTERS, BUTTONING A ROBE SHE HAS QUICKLY THROWN ON. ANOTHER KNOCK IS HEARD. FRANKIE LOOKS AT HIS WATCH, CONCERNED.

FRANKIE: It's almost eleven.

FRANKIE WALKS TO THE WINDOW AND LOOKS OUT. HE SHRUGS HIS SHOULDERS.

FRANKIE: It's Chuy. (Accusingly) Did you invite him?

YOLANDA: (violently) No!

FRANKIE: I didn't mean nothing bad, he's a good guy, right?

YOLANDA NODS WITH HESITATION.
ANOTHER KNOCK.

FRANKIE: We'll be right out!

YOLANDA STARTS TO LEAVE.

FRANKIE: We have to talk to people, sometime. Put some clothes on then come back out. Don't hide, okay? Chuy's a good guy.

SHE LEAVES THE ROOM. FRANKIE WALKS TO THE DOOR TO LET CHUY IN.

FRANKIE: Hey! What's up?

CHUY ENTERS. HE DOESN'T LOOK COMFORTABLE AT ALL. HE IS RELIEVED TO FIND FRANKIE ALONE.

CHUY: I got lost.

FRANKIE: It's bad, the streets around here don't make any sense, man.

CHUY: I don't know how to get back on the highway.

FRANKIE: Were you just out riding or what?

CHUY: I've been working construction. . .digging ditches. But the rain. . .I haven't worked in two weeks.

FRANKIE: Yeah, it's been pretty bad.

CHUY SHRUGS, EMBARRASSED. THEY NOD AT EACH OTHER AWKWARDLY.

CHUY: It's late. . .

FRANKIE: I don't get to bed till midnight. Sit down, can I get you a beer?

CHUY: What kind?

FRANKIE: (shrugs) Yolanda gets whatever's on sale. Bad as piss, the generic shit but it's cheap. We can drink more and not notice it, you know? So you want one?

CHUY NODS.

CHUY: Just one.

FRANKIE: How'd you find us? By accident or what?

CHUY: Your mother.

FRANKIE: She's not suppose to tell anyone.

CHUY: I know when I told her why....I cain't see as good at night, I mean I see, but it gets a little too . . . dark, you know? Even with the brights.

ACTOR ONE: (to audience) Frankie hands Chuy the beer.

AGAIN ITS NOT NECESSARY TO PANTOMIME THE ACTION OF THE BEER.

MENTIONING IT SHOULD BE PLENTY.

CHUY: But I got the love of God in me, Frankie. You know that. But those other guys, since what happened to Yolanda . . .

FRANKIE: We don't talk about that, Chuy.

CHUY: They don't have nothing good in them. I ain't been to prison, I ain't never asked for food stamps, I ain't never been to jail, you know that.

FRANKIE: So you want me to give you a medal or what, man?!

CHUY: I should have already killed someone. Messed up as I been as a kid, you know. But I got the love of God in me. I'm solvent. It's hard. Not many people are.

FRANKIE: Are what, man?

CHUY: Solvent.

FRANKIE: Solvent?

CHUY: Solvent. You know . . . I ain't had no sex.

FRANKIE: So?

CHUY: Ever. Sol-e-vent, you know.

FRANKIE: What the fuck are you announcing it to me for?

CHUY: It's hard to do. But I got the love of God in me. As hard as it is, you know, I don't do that, with any one. Anytime. I've had my chances. Two lady friends that pray for me, they're married, it's not like that. I got them praying for you and Yolanda, too.

FRANKIE: So is that what you came to tell me or what?

CHUY: Yeah.

FRANKIE: So you're celibate and you're praying for me? Am I getting it right?

CHUY: Yeah!

FRANKIE: It don't change nothing, Chuy. You came a long way for nothing.

CHUY: You know those blue little squares that kill rats? You put them on on the trap and the rat would comes and bites on it little by little and then finally goes off and dies somewhere? My parents put that stuff in my drawer, you know, where I kept my things? I should be dead. Had I accidentally touched it and licked my hand. My aunt finally told me, they're trying to kill you. I had just made my holy communion and my head's all swollen, right? My parents tell everybody I fell but hell no, they used to beat the shit out of me. For no reason. (laughs hard) That was the easy part, you know. You get stuck in shit, you know and then it just gets worse. I do what I can to make it better. Every day I ask God, what did you save me for? For more misery? (He laughs.)

FRANKIE: Chuy, I don't know what the fuck you're talking about.

CHUY: (to audience) Chuy pulls his elbow up, there's a bulge in his skin where his elbow should be. (to Frankie) I put this together myself, Frankie. Six years old. The top bed. Without a rail, man.

Too little to stay put, right? So one night I fall down, blam! And I break the son-of-a-bitch. Right between the elbow so I put it back together myself. That's bad news. But the good news, I didn't have to tell my parents. They would have broken the other one. (laughs) Crazy people, man. Don't have the love of God in them. If they take you away. The county. You're not suppose to see your parents. But I have the love of God in me, so I come see them, here in Corpus.

FRANKIE: So that's why you're here?

CHUY: Yeah. They're old. Hate each other. But ever since . . . what happened to Yolanda . . .

FRANKIE: Chuy, we don't talk about that in the house.

CHUY: I know, I'm not talking about it, I'm just saying, those guys, they went crazy, and if they can do what they did. . . so I stay up here all the time now.

FRANKIE: Look, Chuy, we don't have room here.

CHUY: No, vato, that's not why I'm here.

FRANKIE: And we don't talk about what happened in this house. For the kids, you know.

Yolanda cain't remember, anyway. She shakes I her sleep, man. I feel her in my sleep jump up. It's like I'm living the nightmare she had. I start kicking. Punching. I wake up to make sure I didn't hit her. So, enough is enough. I've had to put my foot down.

CHUY: I know. But I didn't do nothing to her, Frankie. That's what I'm here to tell you.

FRANKIE: But you didn't stop them either.

CHUY LOOKS DOWN, ASHAMED.

CHUY: They beat the shit out of me. The barbed wires.

HE SHOWS FRANKIE HIS TORSO.

FRANKIE: Look Chuy. I'm letting you in my home, you're the first person to set foot here.

CHUY: Swear to God and hope to die, Frankie. I didn't touch her.

FRANKIE: Yeah, but ten thousand other people did, man. And you fucking watched.

CHUY: No, man. It was dark. I don't see too good in the dark.

FRANKIE: Everybody saw you there watching, like some fucking pervert, man.

CHUY: I cain't remember nothing. Swear to God, Frankie. About Yolanda. (to audience) A baby is heard crying in the next room.

FRANKIE: That's because you're a fucking coward, Chuy. Had you remembered anything, you'd have to live with your self. So it's better to forget, like it never happened. Well I will never forget and I will never forgive you, or any of those fucking assholes. I'm suppose to like you just because you didn't touch her? I ought to kill you for not helping her either.

YOLANDA ENTERS, TENTATIVELY. CHUY STANDS UP TO GREET HER, SHE NEVER LOOKS UP. SHE PASSES IN FRONT OF THEM TO GET TO THE KITCHEN WHERE SHE PREPARES A BABY BOTTLE.

YOLANDA: The baby is very hot. There's no Tylenol.

FRANKIE: I'll go get some.

YOLANDA: The drops. Grape flavor.

CHUY: Let me drive you.

FRANKIE: Not in the dark, you won't. We need anything else?

YOLANDA: Creme of Bananas for the morning? I don't think the baby will eat, but if it's hungry, it likes those bananas.

FRANKIE: (to Chuy) Can you remember all that?

CHUY: Tylenol, creme and bananas.

YOLANDA: Creme of Bananas.

FRANKIE: They come in a jar, baby food.

CHUY: Oh, oh, yeah sure. Right. Creme of bananas. Good stuff.

FRANKIE: Is that all?

YOLANDA: Check to see if they have flowers. It's Sunday. They sell the ones nobody bought. Real cheap. I like the yellow flowers.

CHUY STARES AT YOLANDA WHO NEVER LOOKS UP.

CHUY: Tylenol, creme of bananas and flowers.

FRANKIE: Sunflowers.

CHUY: Sunflowers. Too bad it's dark, man, they're all over the highways right now. We could pick them for free.

FRANKIE: Make sure the door is locked. Don't open it for anyone or anything. Not even Chuy. Even if he's with me.

CHUY DOESN'T KNOW WHETHER TO LAUGH OR JOKE ABOUT THAT. YOLANDA DOESN'T LOOK UP. AFTER A MOMENT, THE YOUNG MEN WALK OUT.

SCENE 8.

Projection: EVENING STAR IV

ALL FOUR ACTORS APPEAR ON STAGE AT THE SAME TIME.

ACTRESS ONE: A Duval County jury meets at dawn to return a verdict against Jessie Gomez, the first of the defendants to stand trial.

ACTOR TWO: Sammy delivers the jurors hot coffee and chorizo tacos as they sit and review the dramatic testimony one more time.

ACTRESS ONE: Across the street from the courthouse, at La Hacienda Nursing Home, Elisa sleeps peacefully under the covers. She imagines she is standing on a rocky hill watching a brilliant sunset as Georgia O'Keeffe in her late twenties, paints.

ACTOR ONE PORTRAYS GEORGIA O'KEEFFE LIKE BEFORE.

ELISA: (in Spanish) But I don't speak any English.

GEORGIA: And I don't speak any Spanish.

ELISA: But I understand you.

GEORGIA SMILES AT HER. ELISA LOOKS AT WHAT GEORGIA IS PAINTING WHICH SHOULD BE THE OTHER ACTORS READYING TO PLAY THE FRAGMENTED COURT ROOM TESTIMONIES BEGINNING WITH ACTOR TWO WHO RAISES HIS RIGHT HAND AND SWEARS ON SOME INVISIBLE BIBLE.

SHERIFF: I swear to tell the truth and nothing but the truth so help me God.

GEORGIA: Can you see the holes in the bones of the living, Elisa?

ELISA CLOSES HER EYES AND NODS. A NEWBORN BABY IS FAINTLY HEARD IN THE BACKGROUND.

SHERIFF: Her husband told me about that particular rape but no sir, I didn't file on the incident.

AS IF RESPONDING TO A QUESTION THAT ONLY HE CAN HEAR.

Well. . .I didn't want to cloud the situation but apparently Jessie. . .

DOESN' T KNOW HOW TO SAY IT.

had relations with Yolanda, in her house. Before the rape, yes, sir. Three days before the cock fight situation, but she didn't invite him. I mean, she wasn't happy about it, no sir.

THE SHERIFF LEAVES THE STAND AS YOLANDA APPROACHES IT. SHE TOO TAKES AN OATH. WE SEE HER LIPS MOVING, ONE HAND UP AND OPEN AND THE OTHER RESTING ON THE INVISIBLE BIBLE AS WELL.

ELISA: I feel (takes in a breath) this incredible sadness. An eternity long.

GEORGIA: But it is only a moment in time, Elisa. .
.that passes.

SOUND: FAINT RAINSTORM IN THE
BACKGROUND.

ELISA: I've never seen such a sky.

GEORGIA: We walked into the sunset tonight.

ELISA: Is that what I see?

GEORGIA DOESN' T SAY YES OR NO. SHE
CONTINUES TO PAINT AS ELISA

WATCHES HER PAINT THE CONTINUING
TESTIMONY.

YOLANDA: It was blinding. The spotlight. Like
the ones they use to hunt. Monkay switched it on.
Over me and the guys when they started. . .fifteen,
twenty guys. (Has to defend herself) I was
crying! Yelling for them to get off me. Pushing
them. I got weak and fainted. Then I would wake
up, start crying and pushing again.

ELISA SUDDENLY EXPERIENCES SUDDEN
DISCOMFORT.

ELISA: I feel myself the shadow. . .of a dream. Somebody remembering. . .(in Spanish) But I don't speak any English.

ACTOR I WHOSE BEEN GEORGIA "PAINTING" LEAVES HIS PERCH FOR A MOMENT. HE TAKES THE WITNESS STAND AND SLOWLY TRANSFORMS INTO JESUS. THIS GESTURE CAN BE AS SIMPLE AS THE ACTOR WEARING A WRAP OR ELEGANT SCARF AROUND HIS HEAD WHEN HE PORTRAYS GEORGIA AND THEN TAKING IT OFF WHEN HE'S SUDDENLY JESSIE AGAIN. JESSIE ALSO GETS SWORN IN, MOUTHING HIS OATH IN THE MIDST OF COMPLETING HIS THOUGHT AS GEORGIA

ACTOR ONE: And I don't speak any Spanish.

ELISA: Still I understand you.

ACTOR ONE: (now Jessie) She wanted a ride, we were just driving by. Riding. So when we told her where we were going she's the one that wanted to go. (listens to question) No, she didn't rape me. . .I'm saying. . .she wanted it, you understand me? Yolanda and I had a . . .

CHOOSES WORDS CAREFULLY.

an "encounter" before the cock fight. That afternoon. Other. . .afternoons. I didn't want another round. That night. She did.

ELISA STARES AT "GEORGIA" TOTALLY BAFFLED AS SHE LEAVES THE STAND AS JESSIE AND RESUMES TO PAINT THE SUNSET ONCE AGAIN AS THE GREAT ARTIST.

ELISA: You keep changing on me. One minute you're. . .I don't know. . .who. Then suddenly you're that great artist. (suddenly fearful) How do I know you're not a devil?

GEORGIA PAINTS LIKE BEFORE.

GEORGIA: The same way I know you are not an angel.

ACTOR TWO AS BETO ALEMAN ADDRESSES THE JURY.

BETO: You have hard testimony this week suggesting that the young woman may have been involved in several other multiple sexual encounters. This indicates symptoms of a medically defined disease which causes her to have an abnormally excessive drive which is uncontrollable. To me, it's devastating that a young woman placed herself in a situation where something so extraordinary may have happened. She went out there to that cockfight. . . .ladies and gentleman of the jury. . .because she wanted to be with this man here. "Pueblo chico, infierno grande." For my English speaking counterparts "small community, big hell!" You can't keep skeletons in the closet in small communities.

GEORGIA: Hold those bones up against the sky, against the Blue, Elisa.

ELISA: I've never seen such sky. It knows no kindness with all of its beauty. Am I dying?

GEORGIA: Peacefully, in your sleep.

ELISA: But I feel so alive. I have to tell Veronica. (calls out urgently) Nurse! (to Georgia) It's time for my medicine. (Calls out again) Nurse!

FOCUSES ON JESUS/GEORGIA

Do we take the face of all that we have loved?

GEORGIA: And hated.

ELISA STARES AT ACTOR ONE AS IF REMEMBERING SOMETHING PROFOUND RIGHT AS ACTRESS ONE RESUMES THE

CENTER OF THE STAGE WHERE "YOLANDA" FIRST APPEARED AT THE BEGINNING OF THE PLAY. SHE LIES DOWN LIKE BEFORE, AS IF ASLEEP. ACTOR TWO LIES DOWN BEHIND HER IN A SPOON-LIKE EMBRACE AS ELISA STANDS WATCHING THEM DO THIS, SLIGHTLY DISPLACED.

ELISA: (bursts out laughing) That is so funny. Our dreams. How they hold the bones up. For everyone to see! (suddenly very concerned) I have to tell Veronica. Will she remember the dream that is dreaming her?

GEORGIA: She will never forget.

ACTOR ONE LETS GO OF ELISA'S HAND AND MOVES AWAY FROM HER,

LEAVING HER ALONE MOMENTARILY.

ELISA: Aye que lindo, my mother. . .

GEORGIA: In heaven. . .

ELISA: Pray for our sinners, now and at the hour of our death. . .

GEORGIA: Amen.

ACTRESS ONE CAN NOW PEACEFULLY
RETURN TO HER "DEATH BED."

ACTOR ONE: At that moment, Veronica is having
a nightmare on the other side of town. She
dreams that Arturo is pointing a gun at her as
another man tears off her clothes. Instead of
protecting her, Arturo orders other men to hold
her arms and legs down while several other men
look on.

ACTOR TWO SITS UP AS IF AWAKE. HE
ADDRESSES HIS LINE OUT, AS IF TO THE
AUDIENCE, HIS EYES CLOSED. THERE IS NO
NEED TO PANTOMIME THE GUN. THE WORDS
ARE SUFFICIENT.

ARTURO: I'm the one in the many, Veronica. . .the
many in the one.

ACTOR ONE: Arturo points the gun at Veronica
as Elisa enters unexpectedly. To save her
granddaughter from the assault, the old woman
throws herself between the lovers right as Arturo's
gun fires.

WHERE EVER ACTRESS TWO SITS, PLAYING
ELISA, HER HEAD FALLS UNCONSCIOUS VERY
SIMPLY. ACTOR TWO FALLS INTO THE ARMS

*OF ACTRESS ONE, AS IF THEY ARE STILL
SLEEPING. SHE ROCKS ARTURO IN HER
ARMS, THEIR EYES CLOSED THROUGHOUT.*

ACTOR ONE: (to audience) Veronica sits up on
her bed startled, more asleep than awake, holding
what she believes is her grandmother Elisa in her
arms.

VERONICA ROCKS ARTURO IN HIS ARMS.

ACTOR ONE: At that moment, across town, Elisa
Mercede Garcia, 92 has died peacefully alone in
her sleep at La Hacienda Nursing Home exactly
one day after Georgia O'Keeffe passed away
peacefully at the age of 99 in a nearby state.

ACTRESS TWO STEPS OUT OF THE ELISA.

ACTRESS TWO: Across the street at the
courthouse, the jury has taken less than two hours
to return a guilty verdict against Jessie Gomez. It
has taken another hour for them to sentence him
to twenty years, the maximum punishment for
this offense. Elsewhere, Frankie and Yolanda sleep
soundly in Corpus Christi. Yolanda dreams she's
in a church attending a funeral without her clothes
on. Everyone one in the town has turned up for
the funeral but instead of paying their respects to

the dead, they stare and point at her. She sobs so loudly in her dream, she wakes her husband with a gasp.

ARTURO STEPS OUT OF VERONICA'S ARMS AND JOINS THE OTHER TWO ACTORS.

ACTOR ONE: Frankie sits up terrified, unsure of what it was that woke him. He's relieved to see his wife sleeping, even though he swears he heard her scream. He reaches for the clock which reads four thirty a.m. The alarm will not go off for another two hours. He tries to go back to sleep but can't.

ACTOR TWO: As the sun readies to rise on this morning, the wind is blowing something terrible.

AT THIS POINT, VERONICA IS NOW TRANSFORMED INTO YOLANDA SIMPLY BY HAVING ENDED UP IN THE EXACT SPOT AND IN THE EXACT "GHOST DANCE" SHE DID EARLIER AT THE BEGINNING OF THE PLAY.

The ground rising up in a kind of fury as the wind whips away like something in a mad rage. The weather man is predicting more heavy rains today and a tornado watch remains in affect till noon for all of Duval County and several of the surrounding areas.

YOLANDA SCREAMS SILENTLY LIKE BEFORE, CONTINUING THE SEQUENCE OF MOVEMENTS.

ACTOR ONE: (to audience) End of play.

OPTIONAL: IF THE PRODUCTION MERITS THE "ALIENATION AFFECT" OF ANNOUNCING THIS, GREAT. IF THERE'S A DIFFERENT MOOD NEEDED TO CORRESPOND TO THE VISION OF THE PRODUCTION, THIS CAN BE LEFT OUT ENTIRELY.

THE FARAWAY NEARBY

A Day with Juan, pt. 1 and pt. 2

A Full Length Play in Two Acts

This play received a public reading at Nosotros' New Play Festival, Ricardo Montalban Theatre in Hollywood, California in Sept. 05. It was developed at Texas State University Department of Theatre and Dance's Black and Latino Playwrights Conference, Sept. 18-23, 2006. Reading was directed by Luis Munoz.

Characters: (in order of appearance)

Juan Sandoval.............31 years old, former Lt. in
Vietnam

Evelyn Ross...............genteel, mid-twenties, but
mature beyond her years

Frank Ross................in his early sixties,
although he looks younger under

certain light.

Phun Loan.................a Vietnamese-American
woman in her early thirties,

lovely and almost delicate but with no
nonsense about it.

Act I: Time: Summer, 1974

Place: Concepcion, (La Chona), Texas,
population 120.

Act II: Time: Spring 2006

Place: Udonthani, Thailand, population 330,000.

Playwright's note:

This play has a long title for a couple of reasons. My hope is that Part 1 and Part 2 can also be produced separately, as individual long, one-acts. If produced separately, they should carry the title: "A Day with Juan, Pt. 1" or "A Day with Juan, Pt. 2" depending on which part is produced separately. If Part 2 is produced alone, it isn't necessary to have Evelyn appear---in reality. However, if produced together under the title "A Faraway Nearby: A Day with Juan, Pt. 1 and Pt. 2"---then Evelyn can actually appear in both plays. If produced separately, it should be acknowledged in the program that "A Day with Juan, Pt. 1" (for example) is part of a two act play entitled: "A Faraway Nearby. . . .etc."

ACT I

*THE RADIO IS ON A NEWCAST ABOUT THE
PRESENT RELEASE OF AMERICAN P.O.W.S IN
VIETNAM AS THE LIGHTS COME UP ON JUAN
SANDOVAL, THIRTY ONE. HE IS UNROLLING A
SMALL TAPESTRY ON THE FLOOR. HE WEARS
A VERY FINE KIMINO OVER ARMY PANTS AND
IS BARE CHESTED. HIS HAIR IS LONG AND
SHAGGY AND HIS BEARD IS THE SAME.
BECAUSE HE MISSED OUT ON HIS HIPPIE
DAYS AS A FORMER LT. SERVING IN VIETNAM,
HE IS NOW MAKING UP FOR LOST TIME, HAIR
WISE. A VARIETY OF MUSIC, FROM COUNTRY
TO ROCK IS HEARD THAT WAS POPULAR IN
1974. HE STOPS FOR A MOMENT TO LISTEN TO
THE RADIO BROADCAST AND THEN
CHANGES THE STATION. THERE'S A KNOCK
ON THE DOOR AT FIRST JUAN DOESN'T EVEN
HEAR IT. AFTER A MOMENT, THERE'S
ANOTHER KNOCK. HE'S STILL NOT
CONVINCED IT'S EVEN POSSIBLE. HE LOWERS
THE MUSIC A LITTLE AND LISTENS, OLDING
HIS SAMURAI SWORD CLOSE TO HIM, READY
TO USE IT IF HE HAS TO.*

EVELYN: Hello! (More knocks.) Mr. Sandoval?
Your brother said you're always home.

JUAN: (barely audible) Like it's his fucking
business.

EVELYN: Please answer the door. (pause) Please.

*HE HAS TO TAKE A PEEK. HE CANNOT HE HAS
TO TAKE A PEEK. HE CANNOT FIGURE OUT
WHO IN THE WORLD THIS COULD BE.*

EVELYN: My name is Evelyn Ross. I have
something of yours.

HE TAKES ANOTHER PEEK.

EVELYN: I know you're in there. I just saw you
through the window.

JUAN: I don't even know who you are! Go away.

EVELYN: What's that? Mr. Sandoval. . .(pause) is
that you?

JUAN: I'm trying to sleep.

EVELYN: I'm sorry. I don't want to disturb you. This won't take but a minute.

JUAN: You need to get off of my property right now. It's posted. No trespassing.

EVELYN: I have something of yours that's all. I picked it up in Vietnam.

NOW HE'S REALLY CONFUSED. HE TAKES ANOTHER LOOK OUT THE CURTAIN.

EVELYN: I thought you might like this back.

SHE FLASHES HIS DOG TAGS AT HIM

JUAN: I'm going to give you ten seconds to get your ass off my property, you hear me? (to himself) "I picked this up in Vietnam." Right.

EVELYN: We have the same birthday. I just noticed that. (pause) Look. . .I'm sorry to have disturbed you. I will leave your dog tags on the floor here. I just thought you might like to have them back. That's all.

YOU HEAR HER PLACE SOMETHING ON THE PORCH AND THEN BEGIN TO WALK AWAY. MUCH TO HIS OWN SURPRISE HE OPENS THE DOOR.

JUAN: Hold on!

HE BENDS DOWN TO GET THE DOG TAGS.

JUAN: What in the hell? Is this some kind of sick joke?

EVELYN: No. I took a trip to Vietnam a few months ago.

JUAN: Right, I took a vacation to hell over Christmas.

EVELYN: My husband is missing. He's been missing in action for five years. So I went to Vietnam in search of anything I could find out about him.

HE LOOKS AT HER. SHE'S LOOKING AT HIS SWORD. EVELYN IS IN HER MID-TWENTIES. THERE IS A GENTEEL ELEGANCE ABOUT HER. SHE IS MATURE BEYOND HER YEARS.

JUAN: Take a picture, it'll last longer.

EVELYN: I'm sorry. I've never see anything. . .like that.

JUAN: I make'em. Custom.

EVELYN: It's amazingly beautiful.

JUAN: So are you from around here or what?

EVELYN: Is it alright if I come in for just a moment. It's pretty hot out here.

JUAN: I don't let anyone- - -just stop by. Sorry.

EVELYN: No, I'm from Idaho. I'm not used to this kind of heat. That's all.

JUAN: Well its even hotter in Viet Nam. And you say you went there. . .

EVELYN: It was unbelievable. I have never experienced anything like that.

HE GIVES THE DOGTAGS A REAL LOOKING OVER.

I found twenty of them.

JUAN: What?

EVELYN: Dog tags.

JUAN: Twenty dog tags? Now I know you're pulling my leg.

EVELYN: A street peddler was selling them in Hanoi. I paid a quarter for each one. I've been returning them since I got back last year. You're the first one that's. . .been- - -

JUAN: Been what?

EVELYN: Everyone else has been dead.

JUAN: So what's to return then?

EVELYN: Pardon me?

JUAN: I didn't ask you for these. . . did I?

EVELYN: The families have been really grateful to get them back. For some. ..it's all they'll ever get back. Could I ask you for a glass of water? I'm about to die of thirst.

GESTURES FOR HER TO ENTER. JUAN'S PLACE IS SURPRISINGLY SPARSE. HER ATTENTION GOES TO THE SMALL RUG ON THE FLOOR. THE "RITUAL" HE WAS PREPARING.

JUAN: I don't want you to stay. . .too long. I have. ..an appointment.

EVELYN: Oh. Alright. Of course.

HE GOES AND GRABS HER WATER.

JUAN: And if you think I'm going to thank you for them.

EVELYN: No. That's not why I'm doing it.

JUAN: So you like driving to nowhere places and knocking on people's doors that didn't invite you?

EVELYN: Look. . .I'm sorry. I'm obviously intruding. You've got the tags. That's all I wanted.

JUAN: You said your husband was. . .

EVELYN: In Vietnam. He's been missing since 1971. (beat) So if I take this road back, the one I drove up on, if I take it back to the main road. . . .

JUAN: No wonder.

EVELYN: No wonder. .. what?

JUAN: You think you're doing something for other people but really. . .you're just doing it for yourself.

EVELYN: Doing what...I'm sorry?

JUAN: Running around returning these.

EVELYN: I just know how hard it is. It's a horrible thing not to know anything about someone I love very much. I know what its like to be waiting. And hoping. And because I don't know what happened to him. . . .

JUAN: So the people, when you return the dog tags, do they know where their sons or husbands ended up? When you drop by like this?

EVELYN: Yes. In most cases, they've buried them. I don't just drop by uninvited. I call first. I've been calling you for two weeks, but you're line has been temporarily disconnected.

JUAN: I'm not paying my bills anymore.

SHE STARTS TO LEAVE.

EVELYN: So. . .anyway. I'm sorry to have disturbed you.

JUAN: The mind is like this cup, if you do not empty yourself, how can you expect to be filled?

EVELYN: I'm sorry?

JUAN: Where are you going?

EVELYN: I'm obviously intruding. . . .

JUAN: That's funny. . .

HE WALKS TO THE DOOR AND CLOSES IT.

I was thinking the opposite. One door closes so another door opens. No mistakes, right?

*SHE DOESN'T KNOW HOW TO RESPOND.
JUAN TEMPTS TO DRAW TAP WATER INTO HIS
MUG.*

JUAN: Oh shit. I keep forgetting. (to Evelyn) No utilities.

*HE LOOKS AROUND AND FINDS A MILK
JUG.POURS SOME WATER INTO THE MUG
THEN WALKS OVER TO EVELYN. SHE
HESITATES TO TAKE IT.*

This comes from the well. It's better for you.. There might not be a lot of people in La Chona, but if you go door to door, you'll see how many old folks are still standing. We got a couple of hundred year olds living here. And why do you think?

*HE TOASTS HER WITH THE MUG. THEN
TAKES A DRINK OUT OF IT. HE REFILLS IT
AND OFFERS IT TO HER AGAIN. THIS TIME
SHE TAKES IT. SHE IS VERY THIRSTY, SHE
DRINKS EVERY DROP OF IT.*

There's more.

*HE REFILLS IT FOR HER. THEY STARE AT
EACH OTHER FOR A MOMENT.*

EVELYN: What?

JUAN: What?

*HE HANDS THE MUG TO HER. AGAIN SHE
FINISHES IT OFF. THIS TIME SHE ADMIRES
THE MUG BEFORE HANDING JUAN THE
EMPTY CUP.*

JUAN: My family makes them

EVELYN: Are those handpainted?

JUAN: In laid. By hand. On my mother's side,
since the turn of the century. You want some
more?

EVELYN: No, thank you. I really have to go, Mr.
Sando--

JUAN: Call me Juan.

EVELYN: I really don't drop by on people without
calling first. But since I happened to be nearby.

JUAN: Nobody happens to just be nearby La
Chona, Texas unless they're planning on it.

EVELYN: I'm sorry, La—what?

JUAN: And you came all the way from. . .what did
you say?

EVELYN: Idaho. Stanley, Idaho. What is La Cho--
-I thought this was Concepcion.

JUAN: La Chona, for short---it's the same thing.

EVELYN: It was wrong to just drop by, I'm sorry.

JUAN: What if I told you were summoned here?

*EVELYN DOESN'T KNOW WHAT TO MAKE OF
THAT.*

There's that story about the Zen monk who is
going to die. Do you know that one?

SHE SHAKES HER HEAD.

He's an elder, maybe a hundred years old. He's on
his death bed when he opens his eyes and says,
"Where are my shoes?!" His compadre tells him,
"Where do you think you're going? Are you crazy
in the head? You're dying old man. Even the
doctor has told you so. At the most you got a few
minutes.. The elder says, "That's why I'm asking
you for my shoes. I want to go to the cemetery."
Well, you'll be there soon enough, his compadre
says. "Yeah, but I don't want you or anyone else to
drag me there." We won't have to drag you,
you're a bag of bones, light as a feather, the wind
could blow you there, ese. But the old man, bien

terco doesn't drop it. "I'm gonna walk there by myself. I will meet death there, by myself. I've never leaned on nobody and I'm not going to start now. " But he didn't want to be carried there, right. . . by his good for nothing relatives. So he gets up, finds his own shoes and walks to the damn cemetery. When he gets there. . .he digs his own grave . .with his bare hands. And then he lays down in it and dies. (beat) That's exactly what I'm going to do, durangama! Like Buddha says! Make yourself available to the beyond! But death is never like the movies. If you go there, welcoming the beyond, the beyond welcomes you first. And then what happens after that, is that the beyond keeps echoing you. . . it goes on echoing you. . .for all time. That's why you're here. To echo me. (beat) You want some more water? The facilities are out there if you---

EVELYN: No, thanks. I'm fine. I really have to get going.

JUAN: Let me thank you now. You can't succeed at seppuku without a compatriot.

HE POINTS TOWARDS THE RITUAL DISPLAYON THE FLOOR.

EVELYN: I've already taken up way too much of your time.

SHE WALKS TOWARDS THE DOOR.HE GETS THERE BEFORE SHE CAN.

JUAN: This will just take a moment, please? I could really use your help.

SHE HESITATES.

I just need a witness, that's all. *Seppuku* is a very formal ceremony. There's etiquette and considerable preparation. And its nothing without a witness. And that's where you come in, the *kaishaku*. The assistant. There's generally a close friend of the condemned present, so we're going to assume you're a closer friend than we know right now. Why else would you be here? I mean did come knocking, right?

HE LOCKS THE DOOR. SHE PANICS.

This is only a formality, to secure the environment. We don't want any more interruptions, so we can start.

SHE DOESN'T KNOW WHAT TO DO BUT QUICKLY LOOKS AROUND FOR A POSSIBLE ESCAPE.

I've gone over it many times, everything will work the way its suppose to,

HE GESTURES TOWARDS THE SWORD.
so that it takes the least amount of effort on both our parts.

EVELYN GETS UP QUICKLY.

EVELYN: I need you to open the door.

JUAN: You'll be able to do that yourself. Bushido respects others. I'm not going to hurt you. If that's what you're thinking.

EVELYN: No. I just have to go. I really do.

JUAN: And you will. I promise.

EVELYN STARTS PACING BACK AND FORTH LIKE AN ANXIOUS TRAPPED ANIMAL WHILE JUAN WATCHES HER, IRRITATED.

JUAN: So you got ants in your pants or what? Can you sit down for a moment? I need to…to concentrate.

SHE IGNORES HIM. SHE CONTINUES TO PACE.

EVELYN: I'm diabetic.

JUAN: And that means you can't sit or what?

EVELYN: I had my insulin today. . .but I can't be here long without it.

JUAN: You won't be here long. So if it's alright to ask. . .what did they tell you. . about your husband?

EVELYN: What do you mean?

JUAN: What did the military report to you? (beat) Can you please sit down?

SHE HESITATES, BUT FINALLY SITS.

EVELYN: They said his plane went down.

JUAN: Do you have his dogtags? Your husband's?

EVELYN: No. All that made it back were miniscule fragments of bone and a tooth they couldn't positively identify.

JUAN: So he was buried with full military honors?

EVELYN: The government came up with a coffin, but it was empty. Except for the bone and tooth.

JUAN: Symbolic remains, like it matters.

EVELYN: That's why I know he walked away from the crash.

JUAN: That happened a lot. .

EVELYN: What?

JUAN: Soldiers walking away from the crash. Maybe not walking. . .but- - -

EVELYN: See that's what my heart tells me. And still the government ignores the facts. If they think burying his empty coffin makes it alright to stop the negotiations, they are badly mistaken. The whole thing is starting to be a closed book. And I know in my heart that he's still alive. I feel him very much alive. And now that all the known POWs have been released, they're closing the case on everyone else.

SHE STARTS TO CRY QUIETLY.

EVELYN: I'm sorry. I really have to get going.

HE ONCE AGAIN BEATS HER TO THE DOOR.

JUAN: The warrior protects and defends because he realizes the value of others. I'd prefer the whole thing to go peacefully, if it can. It doesn't have to take long.

GESTURES FOR HER TO SIT. SHE DOES. HE WALKS UP TO HIS RITUAL SPACE.

JUAN: As you can see, the location of an official *seppuku* ceremony is very important. And even more important than that is. . .the state of mind that goes with it. After the condemned empties himself. . .the assistant cuts his head off. I mean that's how it's done traditionally

EVELYN PANICS AND STARTS WALKING AROUND THE ROOM TRYING TO FIND A WAY OUT. HE BLOCKS THE ONLY DOORWAYBESIDES THE FRONT DOOR.

JUAN: I'm sorry. . .is something wrong?

SHE STARTS TO SCREAM.

EVELYN: Help! Somebody help me!

JUAN: The closest house is a mile away. I'm not going to hurt you.

EVELYN: HELP! SOMEBODY HELP ME!!! Please. . . .

HE GRABS HER PRETTY QUICKLY AND COVERS HER MOUTH.

JUAN: I'm not going to hurt you. I am NOT going to hurt you. I don't want to have to tie you up and tape your mouth shut but I will , alright? . Nothing is going to happen to you. And you'll have your insulin. You have my word. You're only here to witness. That's all. That's all I'm asking. Honor for the samurai is dearer than life itself. (Pause.) So. . . can I trust that you're not going to scream if I let you go?

SHE NODS.

JUAN: You promise? (She nods again.) Okay, then.

HE RELEASES HER. AFTER A MOMENT SHE SCREAMS AGAIN. HE HAS TO COVER HER MOUTH IN THE SAME WAY AS BEFORE BUT THIS TIME HE BENDS HER ARM AROUND HER BACK. SHE'S IN PAIN. NOW HE'S PISSED.

JUAN: I told you to shut the fuck up! I ASKED YOU NICELY LADY! I'm asking you to have some integrity, alright? If you say you're not going to scream. . .then you can't scream. If I tell you I'm not going to hurt you. . .you have my fucking word, alright? I'm a samurai, goddammit! I have taken a vow of honor and I'm not going to lose it over a wimpy, waspy bitch like you, you understand me?

SHE NODS

JUAN: So now sit down and shut the fuckup. Not there. Over there.

SHE DOES. SHE STARTS TO CRY.

JUAN: Goddammit! I don't like doing that. I don't talk to ladies like that. No maam. I'm sorry. So please. . .don't push it. You have no idea how lucky you are that your husband DIDN'T come back.

SHE OPENS HER MOUTH TO SAY SOMETHING.

JUAN: Shhheeeeen! Don't argue with me. He wouldn't be the same. Trust me. You'd be the one he'd take it out on

EVELYN: He wasn't like. . .

JUAN: Don't interrupt! Maybe its not my place to say what I said about your husband. What did you say his name was?

EVELYN: Frank.

JUAN: Frank. Maybe Frank was a really good guy. You're out there still looking for him. I mean you went all the way to fucking Vietnam! Shit! I'm just trying to say to you. . . not everything that's wrong. . .has to stay wrong. You have my word on that, okay? There can to be an honorable way out. For everyone. Personally---I can't live in the world this way---I can't live defeated this way. I'm glad you're here to see that. You won't have to read in the paper, you know? Personally. . .my tour in Vietnam isn't something I like to. . rehash, okay? But you bring me the fucking dogtags! I didn't lose them, lady! I threw them away! But that just goes to show you, man---you can't run away from what you've done. Ever. Why else you would be here?

SHE'S ABOUT TO SAY SOMETHING.

JUAN: Sheeeeeen! Please. The Japanese have a sound. . .it's an onomatopeic sound. . Do you know what I mean by onomatopeic?

SHE HESITATES TO RESPOND.

JUAN: What?

EVELYN: I was an English lit major.

JUAN: Me too. Before I took my commission. Wow. Good. So you know that English as a language doesn't have a single fucking nuance to it, alright? It's the language of a machine, right? Shallow. Literal. Everything describes everything else as an object if you think about it. But the Japanese. . .they're fucking brilliant! They have a word for the sound of nothing, okay? The sound that's about to transpire between us, alright? You see it in the Japanese comic books all the time. . . *"manga!"* where there are so many words that resemble the sound they want to express. . .so they draw the sound in. . .but then they have to hire special English translators to come up with words for those sounds. But they take the time to do, right? So there's a Japanese word for silence and that is " s-i-n" . Sin. Yeah. . .like the bad things we do. In Spanish "sin" means ---

EVELYN: Without. Like "sin culpa." I placed out of Spanish. Three semesters.

JUAN: Me too. Wow. Well that's alright then. I'm starting to be impressed I'm sure. But for right now, I need you to shut the fuck up! Sin culpa my ass. Jesus. I'm sorry. I don't talk to ladies like that. You see what I'm talking about? My fucking nerves. Like I'm gonna crawl out of my skin.

THEY STARE AT EACH OTHER FOR A MOMENT. FINALLY SHE LOOKS AWAY.

JUAN: So like I was saying. *"Sin!"* Its pronounced *"sheeeeeen"* in Japanese. . .with the sound kind of trailing off at the end. Like "whoosh" is the sound for a sword cutting through the air and "gurgle" for the sound of blood spurting out the neck hole. You see where I'm going with this? "Sin" is the sound afterwards. . . .after everything is done and you remove my body. . .and then both of us go home.

EVELYN: Juan. . .

JUAN: Sheeeeeen! You can't be talking and listening at the same time. I'm trying to hurry this along. I thought you said you had to go?

EVELYN: You're the one that has an appointment.

HE LIKES HER

JUAN: That's right. I do. With you. I have an appointment with you. That's what I'm trying to say. What did you say your name was?

EVELYN: Evelyn.

JUAN: This is no fucking accident, Evelyn. You get me?

HE RETURNS TO HIS "HARI KARI" ALTAR AND ADJUSTS A FEW THINGS. SHE OBSERVES. A FEW SECONDS GO BY IN SILENCE.

JUAN: To the samurai, *seppuku*- - whether ordered as punishment or chosen, in my case, as a preference to a dishonorable death- - -*seppuku,* unquestionably demonstrates a warrior's honor, his courage, and of course his loyalty and moral character.

SHE'S ABOUT TO SAY SOMETHING.

JUAN: *Sheeeen.* Please? (she stops herself) Yes. Thank you. As you can see, all the little matters relating to the act have to be carefully prescribed and carried out in a very meticulous manner. The only thing stopping me this morning, before you ever got here was that I didn't have a *kaishaku* by my side. An assistant. So now that you're here. . .it can all come together. (beat) So. . .alright. Your husband. His plane went down, right?

EVELYN (confused): Yes.

JUAN: Of course it did. Quang Tri, South Vietnam, right?

EVELYN: Yes. How did you know that?

JUAN: I didn't.

EVELYN: You were guessing?

JUAN CAN'T RESPOND.

JUAN: Why didn't you just tell me that in the first place.

HE SHOWS HER HIS ARM.

JUAN: Se me paran los pelos. Look at the goosebumps. I get these when it means something.

EVELYN: Were you there- - -?

JUAN: Cut the bullshit about dogtags, alright? Holy Jesus and Mary.

HE GETS VERY PENSIVE. SUDDENLY DISTRACTED.

EVELYN: I spent a week of salary to get here!

JUAN: You can drop the fucking charade, alright?

EVELYN: And for bullshit? Is that what you said?

JUAN: You want me to believe this is all an accident? That you had no idea who I am?

EVELYN: I just know what your dog tags tell me. Name, rank and serial number.

JUAN: Oh come on, you don't expect me to believe that.

EVELYN: Call up the others. Their families. They'll tell you.

JUAN: Was he shot down? Your husband?.

EVELYN: I'm not here to talk about my husband. It's none of your business, really.

JUAN: I mean I can tell you what I saw that day. When his F-4 went down.

EVELYN: What F-4?

JUAN CAN'T BELIEVE WHAT HE'S HEARING.

JUAN: What do you take me for lady? A total idiot? Like I don't know why you're here?

EVELYN: I told you why I'm here.

JUAN: Do you know what I see when I look at you, Evelyn? I see your original face. That's what the Japanese would call it. The total innocent face.

I mean how many people get to make amends with the person they hurt the most in this lifetime, huh? How many?

EVELYN AND JUAN SIT STARING AT THE OTHER FOR SEVERAL LONG, STRAINED MOMENTS.

EVELYN: I said nothing about an F-4.

JUAN: You're here to echo me, I told you that.

EVELYN: *HE WALKS UP TO HER AND OFFERS HER THE HANDLE OF THE SWORD.*

EVELYN: No thank you.

JUAN: Just hold it.

EVELYN: I'd rather not. Juan, I didn't say anything about my husband's F-4.

JUAN: If you take hold of the handle like this. .

EVELYN: I'm terrified of knives.

JUAN: It's like looking into an abyss, I know. Its hard not to tremble. I start feeling sick myself thinking about it. So don't think about it.

AGAIN HE EXTENDS THE SWORD TO HER.

EVELYN: Get that away from me.

JUAN: But you're strong, Evelyn. I can see that. You're stronger than you know. Here. If you hold it right here. . .like this, there's no danger whatsoever. Please.

EVELYN (She snaps at him.): I told you I fucking can't! (beat) Thank you.

JUAN: I don't' know how Mishima did it.

EVELYN: Yukio Mishima?

JUAN: The Japanese Ernest Hemingway. How he took the beyond by the horns, man! Durangama!

HE GOES AND GRABS ONE OF MISHIMA'S BOOKS AND HANDS IT TO EVELYN.

He committed hari kiri.

EVELYN: Hari-kari.

JUAN: No, it's Hari-kiri. People mispronounce it all the time. It's Hari-kiri. And yes. He committed Hari-kiri.

HANDS HER THE BOOK.

EVELYN: I read this one.

JUAN: You read this?

EVELYN: He was psychotic.

JUAN: Because death comes anyway and he chose to seize it on his own? Why psychotic?

EVELYN: He liked dressing up like St. Sebastian for God's sake. The saint with all the arrows piercing through him. He masturbated to the painting of St. Sebastian.

JUAN: Oh come on. How would anybody know that?

EVELYN: It's in that very novel thinly disguised as fiction.

JUAN (very impressed): Oh come on. . .that's ludicrous.

EVELYN: I was in college the year he disemboweled himself. I read everything of his I could get my hands on. It was the same year Frank left for Vietnam.

JUAN (smitten): And why would you do that ?

EVELYN: Do what?

JUAN: Read everything you could get your hands on about a psychotic?

EVELYN: It's not every day somebody commits hari-kari.

JUAN: Kiri.

EVELYN: Whatever! And then he makes that poor kid, my God! Cut his head off! That's a horrible. He was psychotic.

JUAN: You sure know a lot about him.

EVELYN: It was all over the news. He was a freak.

HE GOES AND KNEELS IN FRONT OF HIS MAKESHIFT ALTAR.

What are you doing?

JUAN: I'm disappointed with you Evelyn. I wanted you to understand the nobility involved. That's all.

EVELYN: Meaning. . .

JUAN: A martian lands in Manhattan, alright? And a bystander goes up to him and asks: "Mister, have you got a dime?" The Martian asks:

"What's a dime? To which the bystander says: "You're right! Have you got a quarter?"

EVELYN: What is that suppose to mean?

JUAN: It means. . .you haven't understood a word I've been saying.

EVELYN: Well you don't exactly talk. . .

JUAN: What?

EVELYN: In simple terms.

JUAN: Look. . .are you here to help me or not?

EVELYN: Help you what?

JUAN: I need you to pick the sword up. . . .

EVELYN: It looks really heavy. No!

JUAN: Well that's what it takes to do the trick.

EVELYN: What trick?

JUAN: To cut my head off afterwards.

EVELYN: Very funny.

JUAN: Just try.

EVELYN: To cut your head off?

JUAN: To pick it up.

SHE HESITATES. FINALLY SHE PICKS IT UP BUT DROPS THE SWORD ON THE FLOOR, STUNNED.

JUAN: Oh my God! No! Did that crack the handle? For God's sake woman!

HE PICKS IT UP. FOR A MOMENT HE LOOKS LIKE HE MIGHT STRIKE HER WITH IT.

JUAN: Do you know how long it took to make this? And how?

EVELYN: I'm sorry.

JUAN: Jesus!

EVELYN: I told you I didn't want to.

JUAN: You did that on purpose.

EVELYN: What?!!!

JUAN: You're just wanting out, never mind that you destroy everything in the process.

EVELYN: I'm terrified of sharp objects. I told you. I said I was sorry.

HE INSPECTS THE SWORD CAREFULLY.
THERE'S NOT A SCRATCH ON IT AFTER ALL.
HE TAKES A MOMENT TO COLLECT HIMSELF.
AS IF SAYING A MANTRA TO HIMSELF. . .

JUAN (as if praying quietly): "My work is done. I am fulfilled. I am leaving this world contended. My work is done…" (looks straight at her) I should be thanking you.

HE WALKS OVER TO HIS ALTAR AND KNEELS.
HE PICKS UP THE SMALLER BUTCHER KNIFE
AND HOLDS IT VERY RITUALISTICALLY.

EVELYN: Juan, please. Can you put the knife down. Please? It's making me very nervous. I think you're having one of those episodes.

JUAN: Episodes?

EVELYN: That soldiers have when they come back.

JUAN: No. . .I know what those are.

EVELYN: Please. . .

JUAN: I'm definitely not having "an episode.". I was never sober, Evelyn. . .my whole tour. If it wasn't alcohol. There were two kinds of soldiers.

The alkies and the stoners and for the most part, they were mutually exclusive. I was neither, really, till I discovered opium. I started to lace the pot with the oil, right?.

EVELYN: I'm sorry. I didn't mean to pry.

JUAN: Of course you did, Evelyn. The minute you bought those dog tags on the street you were prying. And then when you started making phone calls and paying visits to people. . .you started haunting them like a ghost they thought they had buried, you were prying. You can play the innocent if you want to. . .but you're prying, okay?

HE LEAVES THE ALTAR AND WALKS OVER TO WHERE HE LEFT THE DOG TAGS EARLIER AND LOOKS AT THEM.

JUAN: Holding these again. . .

HE VERY CEREMONIOUSLY PUTS THEM AROUND HIS NECK.

JUAN: And wearing them. . .puts me right back there, right now, whether I like it or not.

EVELYN: I'm sorry if I've caused you any distress.

JUAN: But I'm not fighting it anymore, Evelyn. That's what those flashbacks are. When you're fighting them. . .they haunt you day and night. I've stopped running from them. I've stopped lying to myself about the wrong I've done.

EVELYN: It wasn't wrong to fight for this country.

JUAN: Not the way I fought it, Evelyn. A hero is a man who doesn't have the courage to be a coward. And I'm going to die trying, alright? You know who Van Gogh was don't you?

EVELYN: Yes. . .

JUAN: He wanted nothing more that to paint that last sunset. . .his masterpiece. And when he finally got to it, he knew he was done.

EVELYN: No, Juan. . . he knew he was done because he was always in so much pain and he wanted to end it.

JUAN: Says who?

EVELYN: Why do you think he killed himself?

JUAN: Because he painted the sunset he always wanted to capture. For all of his life. That's why he wrote: "My work is done. I am fulfilled. I am leaving this world contented. . . ." Can you even say that, Evelyn?

EVELYN: What?

JUAN: About your life? Your work. That you're content, going around delivering dog tags? Chasing your dead husband all the way back to Vietnam?

EVELYN IS PIERCED TO THE CORE.

JUAN: I'm the one who killed your husband, Evelyn. That's why you're here. But you don't even have the guts to say it. You have to make up some lame story about the dog tags and crap. So who put you up to it?

EVELYN: You didn't kill my husband.

JUAN: Who sent you here?

EVELYN: Nobody. I told you why---

JUAN: I was the Lt. of my tank. Which I'm sure you know. My job was to make sure the convoys that would go back and forth on any given day. . .that they wouldn't get ambushed by the NVA. Sometimes as many as twenty in each direction made their trips through our neck of the woods.

So. . .that's meant we were busy all the time. Or doing absolutely nothing but waiting. I'm talking about days and days of nothing.

EVELYN: My husband's plane went down because of a malfunction.

JUAN: So you are prying.

EVELYN: I'm trying to understand what you just said.

JUAN: He went down in Quang Tri am I right?

EVELYN: In hostile exchange with the enemy, yes.

JUAN: Is that how they put it?

EVELYN: Who?

JUAN: Whoever reported your husband missing.

EVELYN: They told me he went down near Quang Tri, his plane crashed and his body was missing.

JUAN: They had to have told you I was pretty fucked up.

EVELYN: Juan. . .they didn't tell me anything about you.

JUAN: Who are <u>they</u>?

EVELYN: How do I know? I didn't even know you. Why would they, whoever they are. . . tell me about you?

JUAN: Because. . .during those long periods of nothing that I was telling you about. . . when we didn't know when the next attack would come.   It would be quiet for days on end. . . .and then another ambush and out of the blue another attack all in one instant!. But on that particular day. . .it was March, right?

EVELYN: What?

JUAN: When your husband was killed. It was March 9, 1971. Isn't that right?

EVELYN HESITATES TO RESPOND.

JUAN: Opium is a bridge that puts you right in the mouth of nothingness, the drug of choice for my outfit, so I thought, hell. . .its a higher grade of pot because we would roll joints and then drop this local opium oil all over it. Maybe St. Sebastian himself puffed on this shit because it makes whatever is coming at you, arrows and shit feel like raindrops. . .or grade school girl kisses. . . .so there I am, gliding, inside the stars themselves. . ....when they radio us that an ambush is in progress. We are being called to do what we have done a hundred times before but the problem is this time, I can't tell west from east or south from north. And neither up from down. And what I don't know is that there's been heavy losses from the ambush all around us. Several F-4s been called in, right? I see something coming our way. This big fucking bird which in my mine is a falcon that's gonna swoop us up, honest to go, , I have no idea what's happening so I give an order to my gunner to start shooting thinking we're being attacked .

JUAN: I gave the order, well I did more than that, I pointed the fucker and---yeah, I shot it. So we see two, maybe three parachutes---

EVELYN: You shot your own---

JUAN: Friendly fire is forgivable if it's an honest mistake, Evelyn. But if you're high on junk and you can't tell your ass from your head.

EVELYN: Oh my god.

JUAN: I picked the parachutes out of the sky like---quail, I mean when you're gliding like that, I was back at my uncle's ranch and its hunting season.

HE GOES AND KNEELS ON HIS LITTLE RUG . HE TAKES THE KNIFE OUT AGAIN. SHE HAS A MOMENT TO RETRACE THE CONVERSATION. SHE FINALLY GETS IT.

EVELYN: But that wasn't my husband, Juan. You didn't shoot my husband down.

JUAN: I took somebody's husband down. Somebody's kid. March 9, 1971. Why else would you come all this way? From fucking Iowa?

EVELYN: IDAHO, Jesus! Not Iowa---Idaho! (tries to calm her self down) Juan. . .listen to me. My husband is alive. His plane malfunctioned, he radioed that in. He went down, survived and he's been left behind. The government knows that.

JUAN: No, Evelyn. That's not how it happened.

HE OPENS UP HIS ROBE, PICKS UP THE KNIFE. HE'S DETERMINED TO GET ON WITH HIS RITUAL.

EVELYN: For heaven's sake, Juan. Please. Put that goddamn knife away!

SHE TRIES TO REACH FOR JUAN'S KNIFE. HE QUICKLY HOLDS IT BEHIND HIS BACK.

JUAN: I thought you said you were afraid of knives.

EVELYN: I am! Goddammit! Please.

SHE TRIES TO TAKE THE KNIFE AWAY FROM HIM AGAIN.

JUAN: I'm not afraid to take you with me, Evelyn.

EVELYN: Then do it. Go ahead do it! You think I give a shit?

HE'S VERY CHARMED BY HER ALL THE SUDDEN. THEY STARE AT EACH OTHER FOR A MOMENT.

JUAN: I like this.

EVELYN: What!

JUAN: Your original face, Evelyn.

EVELYN: You mean scared shitless?

JUAN: Honest.

EVELYN: My husband is not dead. You had nothing to do with bringing his fighter down if that's what you're thinking.

JUAN: It doesn't matter anymore. What matters is that you're here right now, Evelyn. Giving me witness. You get to see with your own eyes that your husband did not die in vain.

EVELYN: Frank isn't dead, Juan.

JUAN: I shot him down, Evelyn.

EVELYN: You're being. . .psychotic.

JUAN: Excuse me?

EVELYN: Frank is very much alive.   I know in my heart that he was captured.

JUAN: Quang Tri, March 9. Tell me I'm wrong. That's why they sent you here with the dogtags.

EVELYN: Juan please. Just give me the fucking knife!

SHE TRIES TO TAKE THE KNIFE AWAY AGAIN.THEY STRUGGLE.

Goddammit!

*SHE BITES HIS HAND IN AN ATTEMPT TO GET
HIM TO RELEASE HER. HE DOES. BUT THEN
HE SLAPS HER. . .BY REFLEX.*

JUAN: Oh God. I'm sorry.

SHE STARTS TO CRY.

JUAN: I'm sorry.

*HE TRIES TO COMFORT HER FOR A MOMENT.
SHE HITS HARD AGAINST HIS CHEST WITH
HER FISTS WITH EVERY LOUD SOB THAT
COMES OUT OF HER. LONG PAUSE.*

EVELYN: No more insanity. No more. Please.

JUAN: I'm sorry. I'm sorry. .

*HE BREAKS DOWN LIKE A LITTLE BOY A
LITTLE BOY. . .SOBBING EVEN LOUDER AND
HARDER SHE WAS. IN A VERY MATERNAL
WAY, SHE REACHES OUT TO HIM. HE FALLS
INTO HER EMBRACE. THEY HOLD EACH
OTHER FOR A LONG MOMENT. THERE IS
COMFORT IN THAT. THEY PULL AWAY FROM
THE OTHER MOMENTARILY BUT THEY ARE
STILL CLOSE ENOUGH TO FEEL EACH
OTHER'S BREATH. AFTER A MOMENT, EVELYN
LEANS INTO JUAN. SHE TRIES TO STIFLE THE*

IMPULSE. INSTEAD OF KISSING HIM ON THE MOUTH, SHE GOES FOR HIS CHEEK BUT THEN THEY BOTH FREEZE THERE FOR A MOMENT. VERY SLOWLY, AND WITH INTENSE HESITATION ON BOTH THEIR PARTS, THEIR FACES BEGIN TO TURN INTO THE OTHER. FINALLY, AFTER A LONG, PROLONGED HESITATION, THEY KISS. THE KISS QUICKLY BECOMES HEATED, ALMOST DESPERATE.

JUAN: Evelyn. . .please. Say something. Anything. What just happened here?

EVELYN: I'm sorry. It's been---

JUAN: No apology necessary.

THEY STARE AT EACH OTHER FOR A PROLONGED MOMENT. WITHOUT EITHER LEADING, THEY BOTH MOVE TOWARDS THE OTHER. AGAIN THEY KISS. THIS TIME CLOTHES QUICKLY GET PULLED AT AND FLUNG OFF. THEY DON'T TAKE THEM ALL OFF, JUST ENOUGH TO PENETRATE THE OTHER, MUCH TO THEIR OWN SHOCK AND DISBELIEF. AFTER A MOMENT OF FRANTIC EXCHANGE, THERE IS TOTAL SILENCE. AS THEY PULL AWAY FROM THE OTHER AND QUICKLY COMPOSE THEMSELVES, AS BEST

THEY CAN, THEY MOVE AWAY FROM THE
OTHER, AS FAR AS POSSIBLE, IN THE SPACE.
EVELYN WILL NOT LOOK AT HIM HE
ATTEMPTS TO WALK TOWARDS HER.

EVELYN: Don't. Nothing happened.

THEY SIT. NEITHER CAN LOOK AT THE
OTHER. AFTER A MOMENT, JUAN GOES TO
HIS BOOKSHELF AND PULLS DOWN A BOOK.
HE HAS A PAGE EAR-MARKED. AFTER A
MOMENT, HE STARTS TO READ ALOUD.

JUAN: "For. . .'him'. . .the kiss was death, the very
death in love he had always dreamed of. The
softness of her lips, her mouth so crimson in the
darkness he could see it with closed eyes, so
infinitely moist, a tepid coral sea, her restless
tongue quivering like sea grass. . .in the dark
rapture of all this was something directly linked to
death. He was perfectly aware he would leave her
in a day, yet he was ready to die happily for her
sake. Death roused inside him, stirred."

HE STOPS. AFTER A STRAINED MOMENT, SHE
FINALLY LOOKS AT HIM.

EVELYN: I hate that book. It's sophomoric,
idiotic, psychotic. The way Mishima would incite

physical desire in the most pitiful women to prove to himself that he was normal. He was anything but.

JUAN: Okay.

EVELYN: So is that what do? Fabricate passion, bringing yourself to kiss me to then feel nothing.

JUAN: I don't call that. . .nothing, Evelyn.

EVELYN: If you think this makes you a man, think again. Just because you can entice a woman without even loving her---

JUAN: Don't put words in my mouth.

EVELYN: Just to abandon her without thinking twice about it.

HE MOVES TOWARDS HER.

EVELYN: Don't take another step. I'm warning you.

HE STOPS.

EVELYN: Lying to yourself over and over again about not loving, a pathetic excuse for your indirect refusal---forcing yourself on me to prove something to yourself?

JUAN: You think I---? I forced you to stay here, maybe, yeah you missed your plane. But you're the one who---

EVELYN: What? I'm the one who what?

JUAN: Kissed me.

EVELYN: You kissed me.

JUAN: We kissed each other.

EVELYN: You enticed me on false grounds, playing with fire for what? Tell me that?

JUAN: Who do you think you're talking to here? Your husband?

EVELYN: My husband loves me.

JUAN: You think you're talking to someone who's alive and living, Evelyn. That's your problem.

EVELYN: I hate you.

JUAN: I hate you back.

EVELYN: That's what I'm saying. Have the balls, Juan, to admit it.

JUAN: Admit what? That from this point on, I'm already dead, I'm only remembering myself?

You're the ghost here, chasing after your dead husband.

EVELYN: I hate you, I hate you, I hate you, I hate you, I hate you, I hate you, I hate you, I hate you, I hate you. I hate you. I hate you. I hate you. I hate you! (with all the venom in her soul) Nothing happened here, do you hear?

LONG SILENCE BETWEEN T HEM.

JUAN: You weren't unfaithful to your husband here. He's dead.

EVELYN (She eerily composes herself): Nothing happened. I brought you the dogtags.

SHE'S MANAGES TO PUT HERSELF BACK TOGETHER, CLOTHES WISE. SHE SITS ON THE COUCH, IN A DAZE.

EVELYN: You read me from your pathetic book and I left. Nothing happened.

JUAN: Evelyn.

EVELYN: I told you about my husband. How they never found his body.

JUAN: Can you just be here with me for just a moment?

HE TRIES TO APPROACH HER AGAIN. SHE QUICKLY STANDS UP AND MOVES AWAY.

Please--- Evelyn, look at me. For just a moment. Something did happen. Here. You're not trying to deny that, are you?

EVELYN: I'm warning you.

SHE GRABS THE SWORD.

JUAN: I'll stay over here, alright. . .just put that down.

HE WALKS AWAY AS FAR AS HE CAN FROM HER.

EVELYN: I 'm going to throw up.

HE LOOKS AROUND FOR HER, FOR A PLACE TO SUGGEST TO HER.

JUAN: The outhouse is that way. Let me have it.

SHE PACES, BREATHES DEEP AND HARD, TREMBLING, HOLDING THE SWORD. SHE SITS AGAIN.

EVELYN: Was he walking? Was Frank walking?

JUAN: Can we give it a rest, alright?

EVELYN: They didn't release every POW and you know it. (beat) Now fucking spit it out!

JUAN: We radioed for help. My gunner went to check on the two we brought down when suddenly this swarm of arrows come at us. The fucking mungs, grandmas, grandpas and tiny children started to shoot arrows at us. Fucking arrows!

JUAN INDICATES SEVERAL PLACES ON HIS BODY.

JUAN: That's what these are, scars, where the arrows went through my arms, my shoulder, my legs. My gunner, though—took one right through here---

JUAN INDICATES HIS CHEST.

died instantly.

EVELYN: What did you do with my husband?

JUAN: I didn't do anything.   To your husband.

EVELYN: When you shot him.

JUAN: There were all kinds of casualties going on. When you're getting ambushed with fucking arrows, I mean why do you think it was so easy for the dead to end up with somebody else's tags in that hell hole? I mean. . . look at the tags you came back with.. They never made it back with a body. Only a body made it back and it wasn't even necessarily the right body that some of those families buried as their own.

THE POSSIBILITY OF THAT IS TOO MUCH FOR EVELYN, SHE FEELS WEAK AND FAINT. SHE SURRENDERS THE SWORD.

JUAN: I'm sorry, Evelyn. If I could change any of it--- all of it. I would. (beat) Something did happen. Here. Between us. Just please---look at me.

FINALLY HER ANGER IS STARTING TO SURFACE.

EVELYN: Did they try you??

JUAN: What do you mean?

EVELYN: Were you charged?

HE DOESN'T RESPOND.

EVELYN: Did you serve time?

JUAN: I was dishonorably discharged.

EVELYN: For murder?

JUAN IS STUNNED, UNABLE TO MOVE.

EVELYN: You're a fucked up, psychotic you know that?

SHE CAN'T BELIEVE THE RAGE THAT'S SURFACING. SHE'S UNABLE TO CONTROL IT.

EVELYN: Who's going to try you for forcing yourself on me, huh? Tell me that.

JUAN:*DEEPLY HURT* I didn't force myself on you, Evelyn.

HE PUTS THE SWORD DOWN BETWEEN THEM.

EVELYN: You couldn't stand my faithfulness, could you? You couldn't stand how much I love my husband. How I went to the ends of the world to find him. That's why you kept me here, against my will. You're a pathetic, lonely man. You had to take it out on somebody, didn't you? Those who don't cry cause hell on others, don't you know that?

JUAN: I kept you here to make something right.

EVELYN (screaming): By taking everything that ever meant anything to me. And destroying it?

JUAN (quietly): Get out of here. Get the hell out.

HE WALKS TO THE DOOR AND VIOLENTLY TEARS IT OPEN.   SHE STAYS ON THE COUCH.

JUAN: Go. Leave!

HE TAKES THE SWORD AND TRIES TO HAND IT TO HER. SHE IGNORES HIM. HE PLACES IT NEXT TO HER. SHE STARTS TO CRY. HE THROWS HIS OWN SWORD ON THE GROUND.

JUAN: I'm done.

HE GOES AND HE KNEELS ON HIS MAT. EVELYN IS COMPLETELY PREOCCUPIED WITH HER THOUGHTS. SHE SITS ON THE COUCH FACING AWAY FROM JUAN FOR A MOMENT.SHE DOESN'T NOTICE THAT HE'S REPOSITIONED HIMSELF FOR THE SELF-INFLICTED SLAUGHTER.

JUAN: (to himself) I am done. (almost a whisper) My work is done.

AFTER A MOMENT, WE SEE AND HEAR HIS HORRIFIC SOUND OF PAIN. EVELYN IS STUNNED. SHE LOOKS BACK.

EVELYN: Oh my God! Juan! No!!!!!!

SHE TRIES TO TAKE THE KNIFE AWAY FROM HIM BUT ITS TOO LATE, HE FALLS OVER. . .CONVULSING IN PAIN. SHE RUNS TO THE DOOR. . .UNLOCKS IT.

EVELYN: Help me! Somebody help me.

AFTER A MOMENT, JUAN SITS UP VERY GRACEFULLY AND RISES IN REGULAR TIME AS EVELYN FREEZES IN MOTION AT THE DOOR. HE, STEPS OFF THE RITUAL MAT AND STANDS SLIGHTLY TO THE SIDE OF WHERE HE WENT DOWN. HE FREEZES FOR A MOMENT AS SHE IS ABLE TO MOVE AGAIN TO THE SPOT WHERE HE WENT DOWN. SHE KNEELS NEXT TO THAT SPOT AND THEN FREEZES. WHEN SHE'S STILL AGAIN, HE'S IN MOTION FOR A MOMENT. HE FACES THE AUDIENCE AND IN A VERY LIGHT-HEARTED MANNER SPEAKS TO THEM.

JUAN: (to the audience) You cannot send a man in love to war. He will say: I am so happy where I am! Where are you sending me? And why should I go and kill strangers who may be happy in their homes? It wasn't even till I felt the knife cutting my insides out that I knew love. I finally knew love for the first time. . .and perhaps . . .for all of time. I felt love for that perfect stranger that came knocking at my door. And when you love, you taste something of life. . .and in that moment I was no longer in love with killing. I wanted to write a song maybe. Or paint a picture. . . but never again. . . go rushing off madly to kill anyone who is absolutely unknown to me. . .who has done nothing. . .who is as unknown to me as I am to them. Once you know what life is you never bother about death again. You can go beyond all that. It took all of my insides spilling onto the floor. . .and hearing her sobs beside me. . . to feel my blood rushing like a mighty river into the welcoming ocean. . .and that's when I knew. . .humanity will drop war only when love enters the world again. . .(he looks down her at her for a moment) just like that perfect, perfect stranger.

BY THIS TIME, EVELYN HAS ENDED UPKNEELING BESIDE THE NOW INVISIBLE

*BODY OF JUAN AND WHERE HE FELL. SHE IS
NOW MOVING IN REAL TIME AGAIN ROCKING
BACK AND FORTH AND CRYING ALOUD AS HE
WATCHES HER. STANDING SLIGHTLY TO THE
SIDE OF HER. . . FROZEN IN TIME.*

ACT II

Scene 1. The United States. . .of mind, thirty two
years later

*EVELYN KNEELS LIKE BEFORE. SHE'S EVEN
ROCKING BACK AND FORTH, CRYING ALOUD
LIKE BEFORE. AND EVEN THOUGH IT'S
THIRTY ONE YEARS LATER, SHE LOOKS
EXACTLY THE SAME EXCEPT FOR HER HAIR IS
STYLISHLY GRAY. HER CLOTHING IS
EXPENSIVE BUT CASUAL. FRANK, A MAN IN
HIS SIXTIES, STANDS SLIGHTLY TO THE SIDE
OF HER , EXACTLY WHERE THE "DEPARTED"
JUAN STOOD AT THE END OF ACT I.
UPSTAGE, PHUN, IN HER EARLY THIRTIES
,SITS NEARBY SMOKING A CIGARETTE IN AN
OPEN BAR. SHE WATCHES FRANK INTERACT
WITH EVELYN.*

FRANK: Evelyn, please, you're going to have to
get hold of yourself, for God's sake woman.
(Evelyn cries louder.) I won't leave, alright? If

that's what it takes, I won't go. There's plenty to do around here, it's not like I need to go anywhere. Jerry and the rest of the usual suspects are doing their yearly visit. I thought it would be a good time to join them. (Evelyn continues to cry, but she's getting quieter.) But I'm not going. So there. (beat) Why don't you come with me this time? It would be a nice vacation for both of us.

EVELYN: I don't consider Vietnam a vacation, Frank.

FRANK: You've never been to Thailand. Are you kidding? It's paradise on earth. We could make it a second honeymoon, maybe, huh?

EVELYN CRIES LOUDLY AGAIN.

FRANK (to Phun): When I first got back from Vietnam, everything was a deeper shade, everything tasted better, it was like I was seeing everything for the first time ever. Especially Evelyn "Let's use this thing up!" I told her the first time we went out, "let's wear it out if we have to. So do you love me or what?" I asked her. On our first date. She looked at me like I was crazy. "Cause if you don't, I have plenty of people who do." I was talking about my mom and dad, my friend. I had never had a girlfriend. But its like I knew that there wasn't any time to waste. Or play games ever. And this was before the war. It's like something in me already knew. If you can see what it is you want, why would you give it your second best? "You think I'm gonna like you any less. . .six months from now if I love you already. Runaway with me. "But I hardly know you?" Okay, I can't argue with you about that. But that's why you have to marry me, so we have our whole lives to figure it out.

EVELYN STARTS TO CRY AGAIN. FRANK WATCHES HER AS A DEEP SADNESS COMES OVER HIM. IT FORCES HIM TO WALK AWAY. HE JOINS PHUN, LIGHTLY DISTRACTED. HE KEEPS LOOKING BACK AT EVELYN WHILE HE INTERACTS WITH PHUN.

FRANK: I'm sorry. . . I'm late. I've been trying to talk to my wife. Ex-wife. Back in the States. We keep getting disconnected. We've been finalizing our divorce. There's a lot of loose ends

FRANKS SITS IN THE OPEN AIR BAR IN UDONTHANI, THAILAND AS LIGHTS FADE OUT SLOWLY ON EVELYN. FRANK WATCHES THE LIGHTS FADE ON HER, OBVIOUSLY

DISTRACTED. ACROSS HIM SITS PHUN, A
PETITE THAI WOMAN IN HER THIRTIES.

FRANK: I can't say my wife was happy about it.
(corrects himself) My ex-wife.

PHUN: How long?

FRANK: Have I been trying or. . .

PHUN: The marriage?

FRANK: Thirty seven years. (beat) Would it be
alright to switch places with you?

*HE DOESN'T WANT TO FACE THE DIRECTION
IN WHICH HE LAST SAW EVELYN.*

PHUN: I don't know what you mean.

FRANK: I sit there, you sit here.

PHUN: Oh sure. No problem.

FRANK: I prefer walls, to lean into. When I can
have them.

THE TWO GET UP AND SWITCH PLACES.

I like to see what's in front of me. And feel what's
behind me.

LIGHTS TOTALLY OUT ON EVELYN NOW.
FRANK NOTICES PHUN'S DRINK IS EMPTY.

Would you like anything else?

PHUN: No. Thank you. Two is my limit.

FRANK: And two is my warm-up. (beat) I used to always say to Evelyn, my wife. "You don't have to worry about me getting a mistress. Vietnam is my mistress."

PHUN: Vietnam is not faithful. It has many lovers.

FRANK: And she understood, at least for the first few years. The first few visits I made over here.

PHUN: And each time you visit, you come looking for your son?

FRANK: No. I haven't. Not till I called your office last year. That was the first time I came looking for him.

FRANK IS SUDDENLY VERY
UNCOMFORTABLE.

He'd be thirty five this year, I can hardly believe that.

PHUN: Well we have one lead today .

FRANK: There has to be tens of thousands Ameriasian children out there.

PHUN: Problem is, all want <u>you</u> to be their father. It might take some time to check every claim.

FRANK: Does this one check then?

PHUN: When I verified his written statement, it did not match your description, the location.. There are many shams, Mr. Ross.

FRANK: Well then, I guess our business is done. For now.

PHUN: I'm afraid so, yes.

FRANK (more to himself): And that's too bad.

PHUN: What's that?

FRANK: That our business is done.

FRANK DOESN'T KNOW HOW TO COVER FOR HIMSELF.

I'll be here, though. I'm not going anywhere for a while. I'll be in the third jungle, second rice paddy to the left

PHUN: You're not returning? To America?

FRANK: I bought the property across the street from the old air force base.

PHUN: Oh. (beat) I see. Very good.

FRANK: Construction is underway. I'll have me a house by the end of the summer.

PHUN: A house to live? Or investment house?

FRANK: To make my home. Home sweet home.

PLEASANTLY SURPRISED

PHUN: All good. Yes. Very good.

THEY STARE AT EACH OTHER. BOTH ARE SUDDENLY SELF-CONSCIOUS. PHUN LOOKS AT HIM VERY INTENTLY, FINALLY SHE SMILES. AFTER A MOMENT PHUN RISES AND EXITS. FRANK WALKS INTO A TIGHT SPOT OF SHADOWS.. HE IS ONLY IN SOLITARY CONFINEMENT AGAIN TALKING TO A LITTLE MOUSE THAT SHARES HIS CELL..

FRANK: Jesus Christ, I'm burning up.

HE FRANTICALLY PULLS AT HIS CLOTHES. IN A FLASH, HE'S SHIRTLESS. . .AND HE'S

ROCKING HIMSELF BACK AND FORTH. BACK AND FORTH, DEEP IN CONCENTRATION. HE HAS SMUGGLED BANANA THREADS INTO THE CELL WHICH HE'S WEAVING AND UNWEAVING AS HE TALKS THE MOUSE THAT SHARES HIS CELL.

FRANK: sever lack of mobilitsever lack of mobility That's better. A lot better.

HE SWATS AT INVISIBLE MOSQUITOS. AND HE SCRATCHES FRANTICALLY AT DIFFERENT TIMES.

FRANK: I only got what's under the fingernails today, little buddy. A flake a rice maybe and you're gonna need all the strength you can round up. We're starting with the wings. That's as good a place as any. The first thing you do, we start with the ribs first. So we need, first. . .I need to build a jig to build the ribs. Let's cut the spruce strips and shape them. They're quarter inch square, see the ribs are like sticks put together with plywood gussets, they're the curve of the wing. And there are like. . .twenty. . .I'd have to go back. . .they're not all the same, there's about twenty eight ribs altogether. You have to make a jig, or modify a jig for each one that's different. .

.for the different sizes. The jig holds the pieces together when you glue and nail the ribs together. Then we're going to build the spars, little buddy. . .there's the main spar and two rear spars. Its more difficult. . .the ribs, each one is a little project in itself. Just building one is enough of a project. . .building an airplane takes years. . .just cutting out each piece, for the rib is a project. So today. . .rib number one. You have to shape the spruce, cause its curved. . .you wet the wood. . .the spruce. . .to shape it, curve it. . .and then you cut all the pieces and you put them in a jig. . .so it becomes a truss, like a bridge. . .you got a bunch of triangles, but each rib is like a bridge. . .and in the shape of the air foil and. . .where the sticks are joined, there's a plywood gusset which is glued and nailed with little tacks. . .tacks that are nailed together, that are put together with a little hammer.

LIGHTS OUT.

Scene 2. Ta-ra-ra-boom-de-aye!

A GARDEN AT A DECAYING, ANCIENT BUDDHIST TEMPLE. FRANK IS TAKING

PHUN'S PICTURE.

FRANK: I need you to move a little more to your left, otherwise it looks like you got two heads, coming out of you, the statue's head is popping right over yours. That's better. Say cheese.

PHUN: Cheese.

PHUN'S FACE DOESN'T MOVE. ITS VERY STILL.

FRANK: That means smile, Phun.

PHUN ATTEMPTS A SMILE, NOT MUCH DIFFERENCE. FRANK POKES HIS HEAD OUT OF HIS CAMERA.

FRANK: Can I see some teeth or something?

PHUN: Frank, smile is not here.

SHE DOES BAD IMITATION OF WHITE PEOPLE.

PHUN: This is scary to Oriental, it is sham, very insincere. A smile. . .if real smile. . .is here.

SHE GESTURES A BIG SMILE WITH ARM THAT RUNS UNDERNEATH HER REAST FROM ONE SIDE TO OTHER SIDE.

FRANK: Okay, if you say so. I'm gonna count to three, alright? One, two. . .three.

HE TAKES THE PICTURE, THEN SHOWS IT TO PHUN.

FRANK: That's a good one. Very good.

HE NOTICING THE STATUE BEHIND PHUN.

So what exactly does that represent?

PHUN: She female Buddha. Tara. Help overcome obstacle, when anything terrify. She take human form to help anyone who has physical, spiritual danger.

FRANK: What did you call her?

PHUN: Tara.

FRANK: Like ta-ra-ra-boom-dee-aye.

PHUN DOESN'T FOLLOW.

I'm a shit and you know it. So tell me some good news, will ya? Can we sit here, by the fountain or is that disrespectful.

PHUN: It is garden place, public place. For meditation.

FRANK: We can go to a coffee shop then.

PHUN: No, garden is good. Very good. Here.

THEY SIT. FRANK LOOKS DISTRESSED. SHE REMEMBERS.

PHUN: You want to change place with me?

FRANK: That's only when there's walls, there's no walls. I'll be fine.

HE WON'T BE. HE'S VERY UNEASY HERE.

PHUN: This week I hear mother send your son to Minh Hai to work rice paddies.

FRANK: That's very hard work, pulling the plow.

PHUN: People too poor to buy ox.

FRANK: Is that what he's doing now?

PHUN: No. His uncle, Viet Cong veteran, hate your son so much, he beat him, his head with stick when he fail to pull plow. Old woman there say boy suffer from headache.

NOTICES HOW UPSET FRANK IS GETTING.

PHUN: Boy run away soon after, back to mother.

FRANK: That was merciful.

PHUN: He beg her, hoping to take him back, but stepfather---

FRANK: He was a real sonofa bitch, her husband. There was always a bruise on her somewhere. He was a real sonofabitch that one.

PHUN: Stepfather not allow boy to stay.

FRANK: So where do you think he is now?

PHUN: We have lead in Saigon. He was seen selling dried red pepper.

FRANK: Is that a good living?

PHUN: A dollar twenty five a day.

FRANK: Jesus.

PHUN: He not living alone but with woman. They have two kids.

FRANK: So I'm a grandfather?

PHUN: If they belong to him, yes. He is living in little house inside cemetery.

FRANK: A cemetery?

PHUN: The poor can set up house, they have no beds. They sleep on floor. They have good life there.

FRANK: In a cemetery? Come on.

PHUN: He is doing better than many, if he is there. Only dead can bother him there.

UNUSUALLY AGGRESSIVE

FRANK: Well if you say so. I'll believe you. I'm paying you for that.

PHUN: My service not pleasing you ---

FRANK: Are you kidding? You've given me hope. Yes, you're pleasing me. Are you kidding? Your services, wow. (innuendo) How lucky would that be. They're pleasing alright. Your agency is top notch, your assistant. The whole sha-bang. (beat) Well worth the investment, I'm paying enough for it. Well worth the dough, whatever it takes. That's why I'm here. No problem there. (beat) Please go on.

PHUN: The boy's mother, you saw her last when?

FRANK: She'd just given birth. I was captured soon after.

PHUN: And that was merciful.

FRANK FREEZES. HE'S NOT SURE HE HEARD HER RIGHT.

To be captured, Mr. Ross.

FRANK: If you say so.

PHUN: Merciful you survive. To be here. Thirty years later, having conversation.

THEY SMILE AT EACH OTHER. PHUN LIKES FRANK A LOT. HE FEELS TOO OLD AND WEARY TO BELIEVE IT.

FRANK: Hell yes, I know too many guys who aren't here. But merciful, never! Five years weaving and unweaving banana leaves, Phun,

PHUN DOESN'T FOLLOW.

FRANK: I'd smuggle banana leaves into my cell. In solitary confinement, you have to exercise the mind or you lose it. So the banana. three eighteen inch long fibers were perfect, I would weave and unweave them. For hours and hours at a time, weave and unweave. Weave and unweave. But one day the gook spots the threads in my cell. And of course he takes them away. If they found anything on you, that even looked like entertainment, you'd get the torture rack.. That's why my arm is not exactly straight anymore.

HE SHOWS HER HIS ARM.

Merciful? Not really.

PHUN: It takes so many things, so many people, for two people to meet, two people to understand the other the way we understand. I understand you. You understand me.

ANOTHER AWKWARD MOMENT, AS LIGHTS GO DOWN. FRANK ENTERS HIS SOLITARY CONFINEMENT AGAIN BUT THIS TIME, HIS WIFE EVELYN IS WEAVING AND UNWEAVING BANANA LEAVES. FRANK IS ALMOST NCONSCIOUS, HE'S IN SO MUCH PAIN.

FRANK: The tail group is made of fabric, sweetheart. That's conventional construction. Just like the early airplanes, they had a frame, it was covered with fabric because you couldn't have a heavy wing.

EVELYN: But wings are heavy, Frank.

FRANK: Which is why you couldn't have a solid weight, that's a factor, dearest. With an airplane the strength to weight ratio is really important. You need a structure that's strong.

EVELYN: It looks like steel to me.

FRANK: You'd need a really big engine to get it off the ground if it were street, sweetheart. But if you think about it, the model for airplanes were birds.

EVELYN: And birds don't weigh a thing.

FRANK: They're light but strong. (with sexual innuendo) You're pretty light yourself, sweetheart.

EVELYN PUTS THE BANANA LEAVES ASIDE. SHE GOES AND SITS ON HIS LAP.

FRANK: I'm going to need some way to shape the ribs.

HE STARTS TO TOUCH HER TENDERLY.

FRANK: The ribs will be steel, brazed to a round leading edge.

RUNNING HIS HANDS ON HER CURVES.

FRANK: I'll strap hinges and the whole thing will have wire braces. I'll need a brake to form the ribs and braze all the parts together.

HE TAKES HER HANDS AND RUNS THEM ACROSS HIS BODY. HE CLOSES HIS EYES, AS IF STRUGGLING TO REMEMBER. . .WHAT HE HAS TO REMEMBER.

FRANK: The leading edge, the ribs, the trailing edge, we'll have the frame, skeleton, the fuselage. All fabric covered.

HE TEARS OPEN HER BLOUSE.

FRANK: And when those are finished, I'll paint them red, white and blue, like the flat, designed so it's easy to see, so there's nothing to hide. Nothing else to hide. . .ever again.

LIGHTS OUT ON FRANK AND HIS FIGMENT OF EVELYN, AS THEY BEGIN TO MAKE LOVE.

Scene 2. Heavy Wings

A few months later

PHUN STANDS IN FRONT OF FRANK'S NEW HOUSE WHICH IS UNDER CONSTRUCTION.

CALLS OUT

PHUN: This has very good shape, this home. They're doing good job. Will they put a red roof? Like that one across the street?

FRANK: (Offstage) It's not exactly required by the Neighborhood Association.. . .

- 355 -

PHUN: The what?

FRANK: (Offstage) I was trying to make a joke. (beat) And yes. It'll have a red roof like the best of them. And. . . a lagoon pool. In the back yard. Go take a look. They broke ground for it today.

PHUN TAKES A LOOK AT THE BACKYARD.

PHUN: Very luxurious.

FRANK ENTERS. HE'S WEARING A HAWAIIAN SHIRT, LOOKING DAPPER.

FRANK: A small pension goes a long way here.

PHUN: It's. . .very nice.

FRANK: For a hole in the ground. You know how much it would cost for this same hole back in US?

PHUN IS ABOUT TO ANSWER BUT HE INTERRUPTS.

FRANK: Yes sir, it's better to be old and poor in Udon than in Stanley, Idaho. It was 32 below there today and it's what. . .90 above here? I'd rather be taking clothes off any day than puttin' em on.

HE'S EMBARRASSED THINKING THAT SHE
MIGHT THINK HE'S BEING FORWARD. PHUN
ENJOYS THIS EXCHANGE. SHE DOESN'T HELP
HIM OUT.

FRANK: I like what they wear. Or don't wear. In
Thailand. This is Thailand. I mean people wear
clothes here. Just not as many. (beat) I must have
died and gone to heaven.

SMILES

PHUN: Well then I was run over, flat like
pancake--- with you.

FRANK GETS VERY SERIOUS FOR A MOMENT.

I was making joke.

SELF-CONSCIOUS

FRANK: What?

PHUN: Your face.

FRANK: I got pie on my face, or what?

PHUN: Like someone new. The face. Maybe the
way light shines. On your face.

FRANK: Unfortunately, it's still me.

PHUN: Your original face, Frank.

FRANK: Nothing original about it.

FRANK IS EMBARRASSED. SHE CHANGES THE SUBJECT.

FRANK: You see that one building behind the bamboo over there? That used to be an old hotel. An old massage club. . If you had told me back then, when I'd go up there for R&R. . .having my first experience with--- finding out for the first time that there's more to relations than the missionary position---(he laughs). ."Guess what Frank, you're gonna retire across the street one day!" Shit! Even a dog doesn't shit where it lies. So do you have kids? A husband?

PHUN: No.

FRANK: A pretty little thing like you? How did you manage that?

PHUN: They die sometimes.

FRANK: I'm sorry. (beat) So tell me some good news today.

PHUN: You son's mother, did she know of your capture?

FRANK: No. She probably thought I skipped out on her and went back to the States.

FRANK IS SUDDENLY VERY AGITATED.

FRANK: You don't got a cigarette on you, do you?

PHUN: No. I can drive to store if you like.

SHE DIDN'T REALLY SAY THAT. . .DID SHE?

ATTACKS HER

FRANK (attacks her.) : I don't pay you for that.

FRANK IS SUDDENLY DIZZY.

FRANK: I got to sit down. For a moment.
Nothing personal.

PHUN: You okay Frank? Your hand. The shaking.

FRANK: I'm a piece of shit and you know it.

PHUN: I'm sorry?

FRANK: I pay you to listen, Phun. I do not pay for anything else.

NEITHER CAN SAY ANYTHING FOR A MOMENT.

So tell me some good news today.

PHUN: I find relative of Thu Thuy.

FRANK: I don't want to know that.

PHUN: But you ask me---

FRANK: I said, she's probably dead. And I want to keep her that way. Are you deaf or what?

STUNNED

PHUN: Yes. . . of course.

FRANK: I don't know why I'm here. What the hell am I doing here? I should be dead ten times over. I'm just old, Phun.

FRANK PACES NERVOUSLY.

PHUN: Go on.

PHUN: Maybe your son is looking for you as much as you are looking for him. His mother too.

FRANK: <u>That's</u> what I don't pay you for. I don't pay you for that kind of nonsense.

PHUN: I'm sorry.

FRANK: I don't pay you to speculate. She doesn't have any relatives, or she stopped having them around, after. . .our association. I'm not interested in anyone who would have mistreated her, you understand? I don't want to know what happened to her, that's all. I thought I did. You were saying?

PHUN: Maybe your son is looking for you. My mother in high school, a student when she meet my father, American soldier stationed in Hue. He live with her for eight months after she have me.

FRANK: Wait, wait, wait one minute. Your father was a soldier?

PHUN: I am born to American soldier, Mr. Ross. That's why I say---

FRANK: That's definitely not helpful. Not to the situation at hand.

PHUN: The relative. . .not helpful?

FRANK: Okay fine, who was the relative?

PHUN: Her sister. Sister of mother.

FRANK: She didn't have a sister. Not that she talked about. So what do you know? About your father?

PHUN: My father, my mother say, was handsome, charming. I have no photos. North

Vietnamese take my mother's home of Quang Tri.
. .

FRANK: Jesus, mother of God.

FRANK SPRINGS RIGHT UP. HE HAS TO PACE A LITTLE AS IF TO GET CIRCULATION BACK INTO HIS LEGS.

PHUN: I'm sorry.

FRANK: I can't take this. It's all too much, I'm sorry. I had too much caffeine. (beat) I'm fine.

PHUN: I talk too much.

FRANK: I like your talking. I'm the one that keeps interrupting. When were you born?

PHUN: 1971. March 9.

FRANK: I'm old enough to be. . .

PHUN: My friend. At least my friend.

FRANK: Tell me the date again.

PHUN: 1971.

FRANK: The day!

PHUN: March 9.

FRANK: That is unbelievable. Fricking unbelievable. That's the day I went down. What are the chances of that? That's unbelievable. So you know your father?

PHUN: I wanted my father. I went looking. That's why I say---

FRANK: Nothing about you looks American.

PHUN: Cause I'm not. . .American.

FRANK: I know but you speak English well. . .very well.

PHUN: My father American.

FRANK: Okay. That explains everything.

PHUN: My mother's village is Quang Tri.

FRANK: That's where I went down, Jesus Christ.

PHUN: When North Vietnamese take over there, they beat her because my father.

FRANK: I took a beating too, let me tell you.

PHUN: They tear all photos.

FRANK: But they left her standing.

PHUN: Yes. It was merciful. All good, yes. We have this conversation now. Because of that.

FRANK: What is merciful about that?

SHE LAUGHS

PHUN: Do you make joke?

FRANK: I wish I could.

THE BOTH SIT QUIET FOR A MOMENT.

FRANK: So you make it to America and then what? Did you mother go with you?

PHUN: No. She died, so I go.

FRANK: The beating?

HE SITS BACK DOWN, ALBEIT RELUCTANTLY. HE'S VERY UNCOMFORTABLE.

FRANK: Is it alright to ask?

PHUN: She die with asthma, in my arms. . .I not fourteen yet so her family take my two brothers. She have two more children by then. Their father, not my father but Vietnamese boyfriend. But they want nothing with me.

FRANK: And why was that?

PHUN: I have American in me.

FRANK: Oh come on. That's fucking ridiculous, excuse my French. A mung is a mung for God's sake.

SHE CANNOT BELIEVE WHAT HE JUST SAID.

FRANK: You're one of the lucky ones.

PHUN: I'm sorry. . .what is mung?

FRANK: I'm a piece a shit and you know it. Forget it, forget that. So you got to America? On your own or what?

PHUN: In plane when America open doors to Ameriasian children

FRANK: So were you adopted or what? Why are you here? You live here, right?

PHUN: I come here looking for brothers. My last name different now, no longer same name my brothers. I can not prove my family in Vietnam because American family adopt me. I am their name. But I want my brother with me. I move back. To begin again.

FRANK: Tell me again when you were born?

PHUN: 1971. March 9.

FRANK STARTS TO PACE BACK AND FORTH AGAIN.

FRANK: Fucking unbelievable, excuse my French. What do they call the rednecks around here?

SHE HAS NO IDEA WHAT HE'S SAYING.

The word for white jerks like me. In Cantonese. Gwailo? Is that right?

PHUN: White ghost. Gwailo, yes.

FRANK: Is that what it means?

PHUN: Is that what you say?

FRANK: Yeah. White ghost. That's exactly what I'm saying. You were born on the day I went down. What are the fucking chances of that? Except in heaven, huh? Tell me that.

SHE HAS NO IDEA WHAT FRANK IS SAYING.

PHUN: Your son look for you. That's what I say.. His mother know what happen. The sister say yes.

FRANK: I don't see how that would be possible. I got my orders to Quang Tri that Friday morning, no warning, I had no way of letting her know, I mean, we had all been given a death sentence, I knew it right then. But she couldn't have known.

PHUN: So you never go back?

FRANK: Not when you wake up in a makeshift prison camp, with two broken ribs and a busted ankle and my toes on my right foot gangrened ,

PHUN: I want to verify sister. She say her American, the father of sister's son---return after that.

FRANK: Jesus Christ! She didn't have a sister, I already told you that. (beat) And here's the pisser, I can't even walk, right, I break so many bones on impact but if I don't make a run for it, I'll be left for dead, so I put all my weight on my bad leg and start walking, after peeing and shitting all over my self---I'm sorry for the graphics.

PHUN: I take no offense, Mr. Rose.

FRANK: That's why I haven't got toes, I want you to know all that, up front. I have everything else. Maybe it doesn't crank up, like it used to---

HE CAN'T BELIEVE WHAT HE'S JUST SAID.

FRANK: This is around the time that that what fuck McCarthy's running for president, I mean maybe you liked him---

PHUN SHRUGS

So there's McCarthy telling the North Vietnamese that if he becomes president, he'll sign just about anything to get us out of Vietnam. So they transfer the whole prison camp, we get driven hundreds of miles away, to the other side of the asshole--- excuse my graphics, I mean that's what our superiors made sure we understood the first time we set foot in Vietnam. "Welcome to the asshole of the world. And you, gentleman, are the toilet paper!" And that's what it felt like up there in that remote place, way up north somewhere. I never saw her again. I was never anywhere near Quang Tri after that until you and I met there, last year. That was the first time I'd set foot there---since then. If I could have found my way back there---I would have done it.

LIKE BEFORE, THE SPOT WITH THE SHADOWS APPEARS .FRANK SLOWLY RE-ENTERS THE SPOT LIKE BEFORE AS LIGHTS GO OUT ON

THE TWO OF THEM. HE PULLS A CRUMB OF HIS POCKET.

FRANK: The paint we're gonna use on the fabric is called dope, little body. Yeah, I wish. I wish. (he laughs). This dope smells like finger nail polish, that's right. I like that smell. When I was building models as a kid my mom wouldn't let me dope them in the house cause she didn't like the smell   But I always liked the smell. Its kind of a clean smell, that' sright. I'm thinking of Evelyn's fingers when she polished her nails. Her cherry colored polish. On those little girl hands. . .she does have long fingers, like they're reaching up to the heavens, the way they always painted fingers on saints hands, reaching up like that!

HE DEMONSTRATES.

FRANK: I always loved St. Judas, the patron saint of hopeless causes, little buddy. He doesn't get the acknowledgment he deserves. There's a bushy tree named after but, geez. He was the closest to Jesus, why do you think he could betray him like that? That's the kind of friend you want to have in battle with you, little buddy. Judas accepted the job and did exactly what had to be done. How else would the miracle have happened? It's the same when you're building a plane with someone, you're trusting them with your life. We're building a Whittman Tailwind here, it's a two seater. . .side by side, economical but fast, considering how little power it has. And now that we've gotten to the wing, little fella, it has to be as fine and sound as the inside of a violin. (beat) Are you with me?

Scene 3. Good Conversation

A few months later

FRANK'S NEWLY FINISHED HOUSE. THERE'S A STACK OF PVC PIPES ALL AROUND. THERE ARE ALSO WALKERS AND CRUTCHES MADE OF PVC THAT HAVE BEEN COMPLETED.PHUN PICKS UP A PAIR OF CRUTCHES AND TRIES THEM OUT.

CALLS OUT

PHUN: So this is how a day go for Frank in Udonthani?

FRANK: (Offstage) I got nothing to do, and all day to do it in, that's right.

REFERRING TO THE CRUTCHES

PHUN: This is not nothing.

FRANK: (Offstage) What's that?

PHUN: The crutches you make.

FRANK: (Offstage) Yeah? What about them?

PHUN: To help people walk.

PHUN TRIES OUT ONE OF THE WALKER, ENTERS

FRANK: We take them to cripple children in Khan Kaen.

PHUN: They need them in Quang Tri.

FRANK: I got twenty more to make for them

PHUN: And now we have conversation, Mr. Ross.

FRANK: Frank. Nobody calls me Mr. Ross.

PHUN: Frank.

FRANK: Yeah, something like that.

AGAIN, THEY'RE BOTH SELF CONSCIOUS FOR A MOMENT.

So tell me something good today.

PHUN: All bui doi want to know their father, Mr.---Frank.

THREATENS

FRANK: You can insult me all you want but you're not gonna come close to what I'm capable of. (beat) I couldn't do that to my wife.

PHUN: Bui doi's do not want disruption.

FRANK: We had three kids of our own by then. I wasn't going to jeopardize that.

PHUN: That is not what bui doi want.

FRANK: What do they want?

SHE DOESN'T KNOW WHAT HE'S ASKING.

FRANK: What are you calling them?

PHUN: The bui doi. The children of the dust. Ameriasian children.

FRANK: Bui. . .

PHUN: Bui doi.

FRANK: Bui doi, so you're a bui doi. My son's a bui doi.

PHUN: All want to know--- who are they? Everyone knows. When they see the bui doi, that there is difference. Half-breed they say to me. I take beatings. All the time. My teachers worse ones. Very cruel. Nine years old, I raise my hand, ask permission for bathroom but teacher don't let me go. I wet pants. She take my face. . . .force face down, the mess everywhere on my face, the children laugh. Say terrible, cruel thing. I never go back to school. Many years pass and all I can write is my name.

FRANK: You do more than write now.

PHUN: Because I go to America. The bui doi do better there. . Maybe your son is there?

FRANK: Give me my fucking money back then, Jesus Christ. Tell me some good news today woman! Back in the States, come on. You said yourself he was here, working the rice paddies.

PHUN: When twelve years of age, yes. (beat) Fire me, Mr. Ross, if that is best.

FRANK: Nobody is saying anything about firing anybody. And please, I know I'm old enough to be your father, but you're going to have to call me Frank.

PHUN: No good news today, Frank. I'm sorry. No good news today

FRANK: I've always had a mouth on me. I'm a piece of shit and you know it. You're doing a good job. Keep up the good work. I want to stay on task. I came here to look for my son. And that's what we're going to do.

PHUN: We are on his path. For now, it is slow.

FRANK: Cause he blowing in the wind. That's what you're saying.

PHUN: I say what?

FRANK: The dust. It blows in the wind doesn't it?

PHUN: Yes, It does. (beat) Yes.

THEY STARE AT EACH OTHER FOR A LONG MOMENT. LIGHTS OUT.EVELYN IS WAITING IN FRANK'S CELL TODAY. WHEN FRANK APPEARS, HE CAN BARELY STAND, IN FACT, THE MOMENT HE SEES HER, HE FALLS INTO HER ARMS. ANYWHERE THAT SHE TOUCHES HIM, HE EXPRESSES "WORDLESS" SOUNDS OF PAIN, AGONY. SHE STARTS TO KISS ALL OF THE BRUISES. AND EACH TIME THAT SHE

DOES, IT BUILDS INTO A DEEP, DEEP SOBBING FOR FRANK. LIGHTS OUT.

Scene 4. "War is not the answer. . . "

FRANK'S CHANGING AN ALBUM ON HIS RECORD PLAYER.

FRANK: They're a pain in the ass to lug around, but they sound better. You get more information on a magnetic tape then you can on digital, I like to hear the person breathing, if you listen real close, you can sometimes here them breathing in the background, when a song's about to start. Digital takes all that away. It feels really distant. Don't get me started. So what would you like to hear next?

PHUN: All is good. To me. (beat) Silence good too. For business.

FRANK: Right, I don't pay for this. (sits) So tell me something good today, huh? It's been a few weeks.

PHUN: Yes.

FRANK: I called my three grown kids back in the states last night, "Guess what , I'm not coming home. But what about mom?" they all asked.

They raised holy hell. "What about her?" She can't live without you. But the truth is, she can't live with me. . .either.

PHUN: Maybe she understand you.

FRANK CAN'T RESPOND.

I make joke.

FRANK: Whose side are you on?

PHUN: I'm sorry.

FRANK: When I came back from Vietnam, something had stolen her insides. When she would look at me, she wasn't seeing me. She wasn't seeing anything or anyone.

PHUN: It was joke, Frank.

FRANK: When she talked, she wasn't saying anything either and if she was, it was abrupt.

PHUN: I'm sorry.

FRANK: Made no sense. Totally hateful.

LOSES COMPOSURE

PHUN: I told you, I was making joke, Frank..

FRANK: Something was always wrong, always wrong---no matter how good things were. She'd be in and out of the hospital . I made that woman rich. We raised our kids, all good kids. But if we said more than one word to the other for the last fifteen years, it was "Pass the salt please." (beat) Okay, that's four words. On a good day. So yeah, penance is the price you pay for the wrong that you do.

PHUN: You honor her to stay with her.

FRANK: I wouldn't exactly call that honor.

PHUN: But you stay with her.. For all those years.

FRANK: I gave her the clap, twice. Always had something on the side. I'm not proud of it but you got to call a spade a spade,. I didn't do her any favors. Its like you Phun, What do you want your father for, anyway? You've made something good of yourself without him. Look at you.

PHUN: To know my flesh and blood is my desire. Don't care if he is rich or poor. If homeless, I would bring him in, take care of him.

FRANK: But look at you. You've made something important of yourself. You don't owe him a thing.

PHUN: If he wanted to give me $1, I would take it,. But ask him? No. I never ask.

FRANK: You've done better than that, you've got a successful business. Pat yourself on the back for that.

PHUN: I cry--- if I meet him, yes. I don't want him to see me cry. (beat) I wait till he go, then cry.

THEY STARE AT EACH OTHER FOR A MOMENT.

PHUN: You honorable man, Frank.

FRANK: Well then I'm not who you think I am, Phun. Why she stayed with me, under such miserable circumstances, I can't really say. Maybe American women just want a man for security. That's the one thing she DID allow me to give her.

PHUN (with humor): And Thai women do not?

FRANK: Thai women do not what?

PHUN: Thai women do not want a man for security?

FRANK: Well I don't know. You tell me.

PHUN: I am Vietnamese. . .American.

FRANK: So what do you want a man for ?

SHE LOOKS AT HIM AS IF TO ASK, "ARE YOU KIDDING ME?" HER FACE SOFTENS. IN AN INSTANT SHE IS SURPRISINGLY SEDUCTIVE.

PHUN: Con. . .versation.

THEY BOTH LAUGH.

PHUN: I want 'good' con. . .versation.

THEY STARE AT EACH OTHER. BOTH GET VERY SERIOUS. BOTH TENTATIVELY WAIT TO SEE IF THE OTHER WILL SAY SOMETHING. OR DO SOMETHING. FINALLY, PHUN BREAKS THE ICE BY REACHING OVER FOR FRANK'S HAND. HE IS FROZEN, UNABLE TO DO ANYTHING BUT STARE AT IT.

FRANK: Your hand . . .is---tiny.

PHUN: And your hand is so. . .

FRANK: Old.

PHUN: No!

FRANK: I see my grandfather's hands when I look at him.

PHUN BRINGS HIS HAND CLOSER TO HER FACE TO EXAMINE IT.

PHUN: They are wise, these hands.

FRANK: He was a drunk. Not so wise, no. But his hands could have been a concert pianist's.

SHE LOOKS AT FRANK'S PALM.

PHUN: You will live long, prosperous life.

SHE KEEPS LOOKING AT FRANK'S HAND. AFTER A MOMENT, SHE KISSES IT. HE CANNOT BELIEVE

PHUN: what is happening. Again he freezes.

And yes, Thai women want man for security.

FRANK: Security's a hell of a lot cheaper here---so what do you say?

AGAIN THEY BOTH LAUGH.

PHUN: About?

FRANK: Security.

PHUN: Security--- woman want. . man strong.

FRANK: I'm a piece of shit and you know it. . .so what do you say?

SHE TAKES HIS HAND AND GENTLY RUNS IT OVER HER FACE. SHE SMELLS HIS HAND. HE IS PETRIFIED.

PHUN: I like the smell.

FRANK: It's probably the after shave. Cheap stuff.

PHUN: Naked skin has smell like no other smell I know.

FRANK: Naked smells, I can't remember those. It's been a while.

PHUN: It's quiet smell.

FRANK: I never knew smells to be quiet.

HE LAUGHS NERVOUSLY.

FRANK: My skin's never made a peep.

PHUN: No?   When skin say, follow me? You hear nothing?

SHE KISSES HIS PALM.

PHUN: Follow me here, it say.

SHE KISSES HIS WRIST.

PHUN: To here. . . .

FRANK PULLS HIS ARM BACK, AWAY FROM HER.

FRANK: I don't pay you for that.

PHUN: There's no price for that, Frank. I speak of smell, my nose, if it say no, thank you, then I say no too..

HE IS STUNNED, UNABLE TO DO ANYTHING BUT STARE AT HER.FINALLY AFTER A MOMENT, HE IS ABLE TO ASK.

FRANK: So. . .which is it?

PHUN: Which is what?

FRANK: Your nose. ..does it know. What does it know about---what's happening here. What do you say? What does it say?

PHUN: About ?

FRANK: You and me, Jesus Christ, Phun. I'm an old man.

PHUN: It say yes. Yes.

*SHE WALKS UP TO HIM AND KISSES HIM
GENTLY ON THE MOUTH. HE RECOILS. PACES
AND THEN RETURNS TO HER WITH IMMENSE
PURPOSE.*

FRANK: You're not pulling my leg here?

*SHE SHAKES HER HEAD, NO. THEY STARE AT
EACH OTHER.FINALLY HE KISSES HER.
LIGHTS OUT ON THE TWO OF THEM.THE SPOT
ON FRANK IN HIS CELL COMES UP. HE LIMPS
INTO THE LIGHT, IN EXCRUCIATING PAIN. HE
IS BADLY 'HURT' FROM THE TORTURE HE HAS
JUST ENDURED.*

FRANK: I can't sit, little buddy, not just yet.

HE LOOKS AT HIS ANKLES IN DISBELIEF.

FRANK: That iron bar is bending up these bones
pretty good, ain't it little buddy? Does one leg
look longer than the other to you? You don't want
talk about it. Who would believe it anyway? My
arms have to be longer, they have to hang down
an inch longer. . . the way they pull those ropes,
those horrible smelling straps they lace around
your armpits, good buddy. Let's just say you
know somebody's been there before you. You can
smell them, every bit of them---Jesus. What are

- 383 -

you looking at me like that for? Did they forget to put my head back on? I don't feel my head anymore, little buddy, even when I'm touching it. They push it against my feet sohard, they've done it so many times, no one wrote a manual for this hell hole! But I didn't know it was coming, the flame out. There is just a silence when you flame out, little buddy, sssssssshhhhhhssssss---your mind goes into automatic pilot, you're no longer making choices---you're just following the book, you understand? You do every step by rote, no variations on a theme and you pray the rest will take care of itself. I find comfort in that, good buddy, I blow the canopy, then me and the seat. I let the plane go that day, buddy, the craft is gone. I crash and burn when they push my head so hard, its difficult to breathe. They tighten the ropes, and that awful gook, with the sleepy eye, he likes to stand on my back, bouncing like I'm a trampoline, and the swelling, Jesus. . .look at it---it always worse when they bring me back to you, little buddy, the swelling is so excruciating, well there's nothing else to call it, is there? That's right, that' s why we're building us a new plane---from scratch. Right now? I'm still in the harness--- the canopy just opened, I can see the enemy camp down below, but thank God there's a gusty wind blowing me further south, towards the water---the beach. That's where I want to end up, good buddy. The beach.

FRANK FALLS ASLEEP. LIGHTS OUT.

Scene 8. The Spoils

PHUN ENTERS, HALF DRESSED, QUICKLY PUTTING HER CLOTHES BACK ON. AFTER A MOMENT, FRANK ENTERS, HE'S WEARING BOXERS. HE TOO IS ICKL PUTTING HIS CLOTHES BACK ON.

FRANK: I'm a shit and you know it..

PHUN: Frank. . .

HE STOPS.

FRANK: I tried to tell you that. Didn't I?

PHUN: This was not business.

FRANK: I know what you're going to say, Phun. But don't. It's not gonna make any difference what's so ever. Just get your things and go. While we're still ahead.

PHUN: I'm not going, Frank.

FRANK: You are if you're fired.

SHE CANNOT BELIEVE WHAT FRANK IS SAYING.

FRANK: I mean it. Take off. Leave. Go on. And don't let the door hit you on the way out. And whatever you do. . .don't look back. Whatever you do. Just don't even think about it. I'm not going to. I can promise you that.

SHE DOESN'T MOVE.

FRANK: What part of go don't you understand?

HE LEAVES HER ALONE IN THE ROOM FOR A MOMENT BEFORE RETURNING WITH A BAG OF POT WHICH HE QUICKLY STARTS TO ROLL INTO A JOINT.

FRANK: You left some of your. . .lady things in the bathroom. I don't want to have to throw them out.

SHE EXITS TO BATHROOM TO GET HER THINGS. AFTER A MOMENT, PHUN RE-ENTERS.

PHUN: You are not the boss of me Frank Ross.

FRANK: I sure the hell am.

PHUN: Not if I quit.

FRANK: Then quit. Just get it straight. I pay you to be here, Phun. That's why you're here. And I'll pay you to leave if I have to. (beat) What are you looking at? For god's sake woman. Get the hell out. What?

SHE'S UNABLE TO SAY A WORD.

FRANK: You want me to pay you for. . .trying? Or what?

PHUN: We did more than try, Frank.

FRANK: And you're good. . .at what you do. You're more than good. Surely you know that. Real good in fact. Real slick. Real sincere. Very believable.

PHUN: Frank. . .

FRANK: But what did you take me for, huh?

PHUN: What is wrong in your head?

FRANK: Well at least you're discreet. I'll give you that. I didn't even see it coming.

PHUN: See what coming?

FRANK: You turn my crank like nothing I've ever know. And you know it.

HE SHOWS HER HIS HANDS. . .THEY'RE TREMBLING.

FRANK: Look at this. Is it palsy, or what the fuck?

PHUN: Frank, look at me. . .

HE RELUCTANTLY LOOKS AT HER, BARELY.

PHUN: What happened?

FRANK: You saw for yourself, didn't you? I almost strangled you, Phun. Jesus! Don't mess with me like that.

PHUN: You were having a bad dream.

FRANK: And I'm not awake yet, either. I'm a shit and you know it. For God's sake girl. This can't be new to you, surely. If you want me to recommend you, to my friends. Not Jerry though. He's crazy enough to marry <u>his</u> whore.

PHUN: What?

FRANK: I'm sorry. I don't know the translation for that.

SHE IS STUNNED.

FRANK: You heard right.

PHUN CANNOT BELIEVE WHAT FRANK IS SAYING. SHE HAS TO SIT TO RECOVER.

FRANK: Jerry's whore got a proposal out of him, the first night. I mean you've seen the guy, he's practically in a wheel chair. What's he suppose to do if a sweet, beautiful young lady throws herself at him. I mean. . . .come on. But you're smarter. More attractive and far more deadly. So go.

HE PULLS OUT HIS WALLET, PULLS OUT SEVERAL BILLS AND THROWS THEM AT HER.

FRANK: Get the hell out.

SHE STANDS UP, IGNORES THE MONEY AND AS SHE PASSES NEAR FRANK. SHE GOES FOR THE HIT.

FRANK: So how many men do you sucker in and blow in a day, huh?

SHE SLAPS HIM, MUCH TO HER OWN SURPRISE. HE SLAPS HER BACK THOUGH. BOTH OF THEM ARE SHOCKED BY IT. THEY STAND THERE STARING AT EACH OTHER.

FRANK: Jesus Christ.

FRANK PULLS AWAY. PHUN STARTS TO CRY.
SHE DOESN'T WANT HIM TO SEE HER CRY, SO
SHE EXITS INTO THE BATHROOM.

(to himself) Jesus. You fucking piece of scum.
What are you doing?

HE SITS DAZED

I didn't mean that. I don't do that. I'm sorry.

HE STARTS TO SLAP HIMSELF. PHUN ENTERS.

You fucking bastard, piece of shit.

SCREAMS AT HIM

PHUN: Stop it. Stop that.

SHE STARTS TO CRY AGAIN.

STOP! This isn't Frank, it isn't.

FRANK: You don't' know that. You don't know
me from Adam. Get the hell out! Now! Before I
throw you out.

PHUN GRABS HER THINGS AND STORMS OUT.
LIGHTS OUT.

FRANK: Scene   The Pursuit of Happiness

PHUN WALKS INTO A POOL OF LIGHT.

PHUN: Nobody wins war. Everybody loses. In the village of my mother, the guns are quiet and have been quiet for thirty years but the war in that village is not finished. For those who live there--- my relatives, my friends, my neighbors. All are disabled. Some is killed, others injured every day, for working their vegetable garden. Bombs that stay there, buried in ground, still those bombs explode, every day. The war end, Americans leave but in Quang Tri, many die every day and many like my brother, lose one leg, one arm. I can not count the many who lose the two eyes. Their bodies with marks everywhere by bombs that stay behind. But worse bomb of all, is bomb that stay inside here (gestures her head) inside the brain of people. Many go blind in my mother's village. The doctor say nothing is bad with eyes but in here (gestures her heart) the suffering. It closes the window to their soul.. Every curtain inside, closed.. And why? They cannot see the life they had before the war.. I know why the people missing say darkness is better. Its better to not see the bad. (beat) But Americans, they see different. They don't lose eyes. They go to movies. Inside their brains. They see movies here, over and over again. What is past, what happened is no different than the here and now for them. Their government tell them to follow happiness, look for happiness. They say to them, life is made good if they find happiness. When I go to America, I see that happiness or no happiness is the same. To be born with war everywhere, everywhere you live, you do not live waiting for happiness. You live life without happiness. Like sweater you put on. Inside--- happiness, outside—no happiness. It has no matter which. You stop worry. You stop considering, which side of sweater is showing? Happiness or no happiness. You put sweater on, you feel the warm of that and it does not matter which side, happiness or no happiness, is touching you--- anymore.

Scene 9. Tsunami Calling

FRANK IS BACK IN HIS CELL---BUT THIS TIME IT'S ALSO HIS NEW HOUSE IN THAILAND. THE HOUSE IS DARK, ALL THE BLINDS ARE DRAWN.

AS IF TALKING TO HIMSELF

FRANK: I don't hold it against you in any way, little buddy. No wonder you've been acting so skittish, look at you! You've doubled in size---in two days! You must be far along. I just thought you were a he, that's all. Here you go. . . Take whatever you need, there isn't much nesting material around here.

TEARS OF A PIECE OF HIS SHIRT.

FRANK: Take whatever you need, there isn't much nesting material around here, but chew this up if you have to little buddy, so you have somewhere to nest. First time mothers get confused, that's all. Overwhelmed, they feel like they can't take it on, I know. Thu Thuy was all alone in this. Believe me, I know. (beat) I know there's not enough food---for any of us. Whatever you do, don't eat those babies, I won't hold it against you. Its either you or them, I understand. I'm just saying, let me be here for you, okay little buddy? (as if responding to a question) I don't know if its talk. If we're going home I'll believe it when I wake up in Idaho. Maybe it's prison talk. . .maybe it's not. But they let the sick go first, civilians second. I'll be the last one out, you and me on that freedom bird, you and me and those babies.

THERE'S A FRANTIC KNOCK ON THE DOOR.

PHUN: Frank! It's me. Open the door.

FRANK INSTANTLY DODGES BEHIND A CHAIR, FOR SAFETY.

FRANK: Whose there?

PHUN: It's me. Open the door!

TO THE IMAGINARY MOUSE

FRANK: Of course I can smuggle you into the states. You'll fit in my pocket. No one left behind. We got a job to finish, you and I. The plane's coming along, she's a real beauty.

KICKING AT THE DOOR

PHUN: Frank! Whose there with you?

FRANK: Where the hell are my glasses!

PHUN: What's that?

FRANK: My glasses, I've lost my glasses.

PHUN: By the swimming pool, Frank?! I'll go check for you. You just open the door, okay Frank?

TO IMAGINARY FRIEND

FRANK: Not quite ready to leave the ground, little buddy, but when the engine's in place. . .the test run will be a breeze, a sweet, cool breeze from the West, taking us home, little buddy. Taking us all home. (beat) Home sweet home.

PHUN TRIES THE DOOR AGAIN. IT'S STILL LOCKED.

PHUN: Frank! You need to open door. I got your glasses Frank, now open door, please open door.

HE STUMBLES TO THE DOOR. OPENS IT.

PHUN: You left glasses on bar. By the pool. (hands them to him) Why aren't you answering phone?

HE DOESN'T KNOW HOW TO ANSWER. HE'S STILL VERY DISORIENTED.

PHUN: Can you hear me Frank?

HE JUST STARES AT HER.

Do you know who I am?

FRANK: You were going South.

PHUN: Yes, good. So you got my message?

ALL THE BLINDS ARE DOWN, ITS DARK IN THE ROOM, SHE IMMEDIATELY STARTS TO DRAW THEM OPEN.

Why so dark, Frank. It's stuffy and dark in here.

FRANK: Don't do that! I like it that way.

SHE CONTINUES.

PHUN: How long have you been in here, Frank? You don't return message, VFW friends call me, worried sick, they say they don't see you for days and days.

HE DOESN'T RESPOND.

PHUN: I thought I would never see you again. Did you get message?

NO RESPONSE

I was there, Frank. Where tsunami hit. Khao Lak hit hard Frank, I barely miss it.

FRANK: A what?

PHUN: The hotel community is gone. I would have been gone too.

FRANK: What are you talking about?

PHUN: The tsunami Frank.

FRANK: What tsunami?

PHUN: What tsunami? Its in news, the tv---
where you have been Frank?

FRANK: You're saying a tsunami hit---where?

PHUN: An earthquake Frank, in the Indian Ocean,
make killer wave, it kill hundreds and hundreds
of people, not just Thailand but all over Frank.
Its everywhere you look right now, the
newspaper, radio. What is wrong with you?

FRANK IS WALKING AROUND DAZED.

Do you remember me leaving? The letter I got.
Do you remember me showing you the letter?

FRANK SHAKES HIS HEAD.

I found your son on the West coast of the
mainland, a village that face the Andaman Sea.
He is living in fishing community. Frank, did
you hear me.

FRANK: That's great news, Phun.

PHUN: No, the tsunami is terrible news. They
were totally wiped out, Frank---all the boats and
nets all gone. The big wave has taken villages,
hundreds, maybe thousands of people, Frank.

FRANK: What do you mean a big wave?

PHUN: What is wrong with you? I went to investigate the letter. I was in Khao Lak. Its here somewhere, the letter. I left you message. Frank. . .look at me.

HE CAN'T MOVE.

PHUN: I was there to investigate, I had appointment with boy, well man, now, he's not a boy ---your son was there to meet me in Khao Lak. But before we meet, I get evacuated, I do not know what happen to your son. His fishing community is gone, Frank. Maybe we save his life to call him to Khao Lak.. His village was hit harder, Frank. But it doesn't look good, for anybody, Frank.

NOT QUITE SOUNDING LIKE HIMSELF

FRANK: My fucking teeth are falling out.

PHUN: Frank. . .

FRANK: I'm vomiting blood, little buddy. I can't even stand.

PHUN: Frank, have you been hearing anything I say?

FRANK: These wretched cramps in my bones, Jesus. help me, please.

PHUN: Frank, look at me.

FRANK: My muscles, they're tearing like paper, Phun. Look at this? I can't even   scratch myself without hurting myself, the bruises. Look. . .look at my arm? .

HE'S SOMEWHERE ELSE AND SHE KNOWS THAT.

We got to hurry now. I know, not everyone can build an engine, little buddy. Many people start. These are home built airplanes. Amateur built.

PHUN: Frank---

FRANK: Home builders adapt car engines. But we're using aircraft engine designed for an airplane. Some overhaul engines but to actually one is beyond most builders.

PHUN: Can you hear me?

HE DOESN'T.

FRANK: We need a Continental 0200. build the engine mount It's easy but let's cut the tubing, shape it and weld it together.

PHUN GOES UP TO FRANK. SHE GETS RIGHT IN FRONT OF HIM.

PHUN: Frank listen to me.

FRANK: We can build the engine mount, it's easy. But cutting the tubing, to shape it and weld it together---

PHUN: Just listen! For a goddamn moment, hear me.

SHE ATTEMPTS TO TOUCH HIM. HE MAKES A SOUND AS IF HE JUST HURT HIMSELF.

FRANK: That sonofabitch has caught wind of our project. Hide the propeller---!. (screams) Hide!

HE STARTS TO WHISPER AS HE MOVES AWAY FROM HER.

I don't think they can see us here. I think we can finish where we left off. We're gonna have to put it all together, quickly though.

HE'S DUCKING BEHIND THE CHAIR.

We're safe right here but they're gonna come back. We're gonna have to hurry. We got the wings, the fuselage, the tail. . .but there's the instrument panel---

PHUN: Just do this—

SHE NODS TO DEMONSTRATE

if you can hear me, Frank.

FRANK: They're gonna be moving us out any moment. I don't want to forget anything.. And the hurry-ered I get, the slower I go.

PHUN FINALLY SITS DOWN, SOMEWHAT SHOCKED. SHE WAITS AND WATCHES FRANK GO THROUGH HIS MOTIONS.

FRANK: It's final inspection, buddy. Take the cowling off, so they can see the engine installation.

HE LOOKS DIRECTLY AT PHUN. HE ADDRESSES HER.

I know why you're here.

PHUN DOESN'T RESPOND.

Scene 10. The Funeral

Five months later

PHUN: Authority find three people, remains--- five month after tsunami, bodies suck down to bottom of waste water treatment plant. Frank want to see for himself what happen to Khao Lak where his son go to meet me. Frank take picture, me standing with big police boat that come inland, tsunami put boat on top of trees.. Authority say they leave bus there in trees as memorial. Frank take my picture standing there with bus in tree, behind me. We see people everywhere we go, roads full, camps everywhere you look. Frank say it feel like war, like he in service--again. We walk to ocean in Khao Lak, Frank say ocean look better than it has done for twenty year. Tsunami wash all debris away. People, there on beach, many from Sweden, which suffer more death than any nation outside Asia, they stand there together to remember the dead. Frank want to be there with them, for ceremony.. But his boy not die here, I say to Frank. Boy they find at bottom of waste water maybe not his son, but Frank say, he know, in his heart, boy, is <u>his</u> boy.. I am done," he say. No more search. Only sorrow. And here sorrow unite with people from Sweden. So we wait by beachside for sun to break through clouds of passing rainstorm. We take shoes off, walk into ocean with all clothes on, we send krathongs into sea. Krathongs little small floats, made from banana leaves, small floats carry incense, candle and flower. . .drifting to ocean. We stand for long time, till they disappear. Later that night, under one tree by beachside, where family from Sweden put flowers, teddy bear toys beneath picture of children who die in killer wave, Frank sit for long time. I sit nearby, on beachside---waiting.

LIGHTS OUT ON PHUN.

Scene 11

And. . .finally, the Wedding

Six months later

OFFSTAGE A THAI WOMAN SINGS HAUNTINGLY, A BEAUTIFUL MELODY. LIGHTS UP ON FRANK FACING THE AUDIENCE, SUPPOSEDLY WATCHING THE WOMAN SING. HE IS DRUNK AND STILL DRINKING. AFTER A MOMENT PHUN ENTERS. SHE SITS ON THE OTHER SIDE OF THE STAGE. THEY ARE BOTH DRESSED UP IN NICE CLOTHES, HAVING JUST ATTENDED A MUTUAL FRIEND'S WEDDING. THEY ACKNOWLEDGE EACH OTHER WITH A NOD BEFORE GIVING THEIR ATTENTION BACK TO THE SINGER.

FRANK: And Jerry thought no woman would have him after his wife died last year. Just look at him now. (calls out) Go Jerry! Go! Here's to you good buddy!

FRANK DOWNS A WHOLE DRINK.

 FRANK: He's discovered Thailand alright. He fell for the first woman he met.

POINTS TO A DECORATIVE TREE NEARBY.

But tell me this. . .why a Christmas tree for the wedding? Can you tell me that?

PHUN: That's not a Christmas tree. It is a Bah-Si-Su-Kwa.

FRANK: You can't tell me it doesn't look like a Christmas tree. Surely you've seen them, a Christmas tree. Can you tell me that it doesn't look like a Christmas tree?

PHUN: That is a traditional Thai wedding tree.

FRANK: But with fucking banana leaves? Jeez.

PHUN: Yes, why not banana leaves? With jasmine flowers. You want to file a complaint? Do it.

FRANK IS OBVIOUSLY UNEASY WITH THE WHOLE THING.

FRANK: I was just asking. I'm a piece of shit and you know it. I didn't mean anything by it.

THE WOMAN OFFSTAGE FINISHES HER SONG. CLAPPING IS HEARD. FRANK CLAPS TOO. AN OFFSTAGE VOICE ANNOUNCES OVER THE P.A.:"WE ARE GOING TO INVITE TOASTS FOR THE LOVELY BRIDE AND GROOM. AFTER EACH SONG, PLEASE. . .WE INVITE TOASTS, BUT ONLY IF YOU'RE STANDING." LAUGHTER AND CLAPS ARE HEARD. FRANK MANAGES TO STAND UP.

(to Phun) After you.

SHE SHAKES HER HEAD VEHEMENTLY.

Ladies first.

SHE IS VERY EMBARRASSED THAT HE IS INSISTING.

FRANK: Okay then, I guess I'll go first. Being that I'm the best man and all. (to Phun) I'll make a goddamn toast for the two of us, sure. Get the show on the road. Here we go. (to the unseen crowd) First, I want to say congratulations, especially to you good buddy! Jerry, you've chosen a fine, fine woman in Yen. God knows we've been to hell and back to get as close as we can to this side of heaven. (addressing the crowd)

Jerry and I met in Vietnam, no surprise there. Right here in Thailand where we would come for R&R, he from his job---loading the bombs, the fact that he's standing right here, right now, so many years later, after so many. . .

FRANK GETS UNEXPECTEDLY EMOTIONAL.HE HAS TO STOP TO COLLECT HIMSELF.

FRANK: I'm sorry. This beer, something's wrong with this beer. . .this cup has been drinking. maybe I need to start with a new one.

HE TAKES A MOMENT TO RECOVER AGAIN.

FRANK: Like I was saying. There are old explosives men and there are bold explosives men, but there are no old, bold explosives men. Except in the bed, we hope, good buddy, if your ammo's still in place. (crowd laughs) We both know how fortunate he is to be here. . . how I'm even standing here, well. . .barely. But hey, we're celebrating. And for that --and our return to the place where we found rest and relaxation, once upon a time, may it stick, this time, good buddy! Thais recover better than anybody I know, be it rain, tsunami or more. I want to wish for you the greatest luck in the world, good buddy. I hope you have a long and enjoyable life and may all your checks arrive on time.

FRANK RAISES HIS GLASS, CLAPS ARE HEARD.
PHUN RAISES HER GLASS AS WELL, EACH
SEPARATELY.

FRANK: And to Yen, dear sweet Yen, who could
have been the daughter that Jerry never had---God
bless you too. . . . may you have a long and happy
life and never stop loving Jerry.

AGAIN FRANK GETS EMOTIONAL. HE STOPS
TO RECOVER.

FRANK: And. . . would you please quit spending
all his money so he has some left over for beer?

AGAIN FRANK RAISES HIS GLASS. CLAPS AND
LAUGHTER ARE HEARD. HE WALKS OVER TO
PHUN TO TOAST BUT WHEN HE TRIES TO
CLINK HIS GLASS ON HERS, SHE PULLS HERS
AWAY, OFFENDED. BACKGROUND THAI
MUSIC IS HEARD AGAIN. A BAD BLUES
BROTHER IMITATION

FRANK: "What did I say to piss you off this time. .
.baaaaaaaby?"

PHUN: You. . . are an old, sad fool.

RAISES HER GLASS TO HER

FRANK: Okay. I'm old, I'll give you that. Here's to old then.

SHE IGNORES HIM. HE DOWNS THE DRINK.

FRANK: You think everybody loves you for your money.

FRANK: Well they don't hate me for it, that's for sure.

PHUN STARTS TO TEAR OFF A BRACELET OF STRINGS ON HER WRIST.

What the hell. . .is that?

PHUN: I don't want blessing.

FRANK: It took all day for those women to tie them on you, the whole long day, jeez. You don't want hurt their feelings, do you?

SHE CONTINUES TO TEAR OFF ALL OF THE STRING BRACELETS.

PHUN: Weddings in Thailand are a mating dance for everyone else who hasn't yet found a partner, Frank.

HE DOESN'T KNOW WHAT TO MAKE OF THAT.

FRANK: Is that why you're taking them off? You found a partner?

PHUN: It means I don't want one.

FRANK: *VIOLENTLY*

FRANK: You think it's easy to pass you up goddammit!

PHUN (vehemently): I didn't ask you to pass me up.

FRANK: I'm doing you a favor. You should be thanking me. I'm a broken, old man, Phun. Maybe Jerry can fool himself.

SHE SHHHHHSSS HIM. HE TRIES TO WHISPER.

 But I can't. And I won't. (back to normal) Don't you fucking get it? I'd only be trying to make you the living ghost of a lost love. That wouldn't exactly be fair, would it?

PHUN: If you say so.

*IN THE BACKGROUND, A TRADITIONAL THAI
TUNE CAN BE HEARD. A THAI WOMAN SINGS
HAUNTINGLY ANOTHER BEAUTIFUL
MELODY. AFTER A MOMENT, PHUN STANDS
UP AND SLOWLY BEGINS TO SWIRL, HER
ARMS REACHING HIGH IN THE AIR, FINGERS
CURLED BACK. HER DANCE IS PART HULA,*

*PART BARONG. FRANK WATCHES HER,
BAFFLED.*

FRANK: (embarrassed, maybe titillated) What the
hell are you doing?

PHUN: I dance before you. And I dance after you.
. .what do you think?

*SHE CONTINUES HER DANCE. SHE IS
BEAUTIFUL AND FOCUSED AND AMAZINGLY
UNCONSCIOUS. IT BECOMES TOO PAINFUL
FOR FRANK TO WATCH.*

FRANK: You're making a fool of yourself.

PHUN: Only a <u>bigger</u> fool --- would know.

*HE THROWS HIS DRINK AT HER, IT SHOCKS
AND WETS HER FACE COMPLETELY. THE
STARE AT EACH OTHER FOR A LONG,
EXTENDED MOMENT. LIGHTS OUT SLOWLY
ON BOTH OF THEM AS THEY COME UP ON
EVELYN, WHO CAN STILL BE SEEN ROCKING
LIKE BEFORE AS FRANK, STILL IN HIS
WEDDING GARB, FINDS HIS WAY BACK TO
HER.HE STANDS EXACTLY NEXT TO HER,
WHERE JUAN STOOD BEFORE, FOR HIS FINAL
MONOLOGUE IN ACT I.*

FRANK: (to the audience) There are times when I
look at Evelyn, whenever I remember her. . .and I

swear I am looking at the youngest, most fragile part of her being. The way she looked originally, when we first saw---the other. It's that moment when you look at someone and you're pretty sure that's its going to fly. But it's untested. You've built it and now something in you knows that, you've been working on this plane for a long time and you don't want anything to happen to it which is a silly thing to think about. Because you always have to accept the possibility of losing the airplane if it means saving your own life but. . . .you just go through it in your mind---what you plan to do---you've got a tremendous amount of adrenalin flowing, so you try to remember everything you're suppose to do. But if you're not an experienced pilot, you probably get another person to fly it. But in my case, I have enough experience to fly myself. So. . .you get in it, put on the shoulder harness and seat belt and start the engine and make sure that everything is working properly, taxi out to the runway, maybe remember to check for traffic, and then you taxi out. . .and. . .then finally---take off. (Frank kneels in exactly the place, where Juan's body went down.) What happened, sweet buddy, I'll ask. What happened to us? How did we make living ghosts of the other? And when the loving arms that would comfort us appear. . .why do we send them empty-handed on their way---without us? What happened to us? And what would it take to make it right?

EVELYN CONTINUES HER ROCKING BACK AND FORTH AND SLOWLY BUT SURELY HE MIRRORS HER, MOVING ALONGSIDE HER.TOGETHER THEY ATTEMPT TO FIND COMFORT---IN THAT AS JUAN APPEARS AND STANDS QUIETLY BESIDE HIM, LOOKING AT EVELYN AS LIGHTS FADE.

END OF PLAY.

Esmeralda Blue: La Mujer Moderna

(The Modern Woman)

A Play in Three Acts

(with Song)

"Whoever finds love beneath hurt and grief

disappears into emptiness with a thousand new
disguises."- - -Rumi

This play won the "Best Female Protagonist"
Award from the Mae West Festival, Seattle
Washington, 2007

Characters: (5 m/ 4 f):

Patti Santiago. . .late thirties (also doubles as Carmen Stansell and Ruby the nurse)

Jairo Vasquez. . .forty five

Dolores Casas. . .late thirties

Daniel Scarth. . .early forties

Clara Cisneros. . .late forties

Francisco Olvera. . .in his seventies, also doubles as the therapist

Augustin Julian Saenz. . .circa 1880, preserved in his late twenties, doubles as the guitarist who provides the musical accompaniment

Esmeralda Saenz. . .circa 1950, a Mexican Donna Reed; also doubles as Adela, . .circa 1911, a soladera who fought for Pancho Villa preserved in her late twenties.

Emil Holmdahl. . .circa 1910, the true historical figure

Time: the early 2000s

Place: NYC and San Diego, Texas

<u>Music</u> – accompaniment should be one guitarist only and ideally the musician should double as Augustin Julian Saenz.

I wish to acknowledge John Reed's "Insurgent Mexico" (1914) for providing me with the impressions I needed to borrow and build upon. I wanted the composite (albeit fictional rendition of Holmdahl) to give authentic testimony to the "hidden beauty of the visible world" even in the guise of the barbaric wars of our days. Nobody would believe it---otherwise.

Act I: The Departure:

Scene 1: The Ordinary World

A KNOCK IS HEARD. AND THEN A DOORBELL.

JAIRO: Hello! (beat) Anybody!? It's me.

AFTER A MOMENT, PATTI SANTIAGO, LATE THIRTIES, APPEARS.

PATTI: Jairo?

JAIRO: I locked myself out.

PATTI WALKS UP TO THE DOOR AND PROCEEDS TO UNLOCK IT. JAIRO "HI-ROW" VASQUEZ, 45, ENTERS. HE'S CARRYING SOME FRESH FLOWERS.

JAIRO: I had a last minute walk-in and left my keys on the---is Dolores alright?

PATTI: It took six hours to drive twenty miles.

JAIRO: But you got there. I guess that's all that matters. So she's alright?

PATTI NODS.

I really wanted to be there.

PATTI: She knows how demanding your work is.

JAIRO: She didn't want me there, Patti. I would have gone. I offered. Pleaded.

JAIRO AND PATTI STARE AT EACH OTHER FOR A MOMENT. IT'S A STRAINED MOMENT.

Did she say anything about how it went. . .for her?

PATTI: Not really. She didn't talk very much. I did all the talking there. And back. She's excited about going to Texas though.

JAIRO: Nobody inherits the state of Texas, Patty.

PATTI: I didn't even know she had relatives in Texas.

JAIRO: She's getting five hundred acres or something ridiculous like that. The guy hated his contemporaries, his living relatives, so he willed his fortune to his family. . five generations later.

PATTI: That's unbelievable.

JAIRO: Not's not even counting the gold coins.

PATTI: The what?

JAIRO: They found a couple of crates full of 17th century Spanish gold coins. On the land. (beat) I'm gonna need a vase.

PATTI STARTS LOOKING AROUND AS DOLORES CASAS ENTERS. SHE LOOKS AT PATTI AND JAIRO SUSPICIOUSLY.

DOLORES: (to Jairo) When did you get home?

JAIRO: Just now.

PATTI: He locked himself out.

DOLORES: Again?

JAIRO GOES UP TO DOLORES AND KISSES HER ON THE CHEEK. DOLORES BRISTLES A BIT. HE HANDS HER THE FLOWERS.

JAIRO: How you feeling?

DOLORES: He had a fisherman's cap on his head. I mean how tacky is that?

NEITHER PATTI NOR JAIRO KNOW WHAT SHE'S TALKING ABOUT.

The doctor. He had a fucking fisherman's cap on his head. (to Patti) There's a vase in the bedroom.

PATTI EXITS.

JAIRO: Should you be up and around? I mean, shouldn't you be. . .resting.

DOLORES: I am resting.

JAIRO: They probably don't want you on your feet very much.

DOLORES: Did you hear what I said?

JAIRO: I'm sorry. . .

DOLORES: The fisherman's cap---on his head and he looked like Bill Clinton.

JAIRO: So are you in any kind of pain?

DOLORES: I think I would know that, wouldn't I?

JAIRO: Right now I mean.

DOLORES: If I was in pain, I would know. Don't you think I'd be the first one to know, Jairo?

JAIRO: I was talking about physical pain, Dolores.

DOLORES: When they first fish it out of you. . .sure. There's pain. Like a cigarette burn. And it sounds like a garbage disposal sucking up your insides and grinding them down into mush. But that lasts a whole five seconds. Maybe. So. . . right now? This moment? No. There's no pain.

PATTI ENTERS.

DOLORES: (to Patti) How would you describe it?

PATTI: What?

DOLORES: The procedure.

PATTI: I don't know. I've never. . .

DOLORES IS DIGGING AROUND FOR A SNACK. DOLORES FINDS SOME CRACKERS. SHE DEVOURS THEM.

DOLORES: But you've had kids, right? Labor and all that?

PATTI: Yeah. (beat) I fixed you both a light dinner. It's in the fridge.

JAIRO: That's very nice of you. Thank you.

PATTI: It's nothing fancy.

JAIRO: Are you kidding? The way you cook' nothing fancy' is tremendous.

DOLORES: I'm really not hungry.

PATTI: I fixed the soup with greens you like, Dolores. And a salad. It's no big deal. Really. But that way you don't have to go out. (Pause) If you don't want to. Go out. It'll be in the fridge for later.

DOLORES: I'd like to get some fresh air.

JAIRO: But there's ice everywhere, Dolores. Everything's closed down.

DOLORES: I like the cold.

JAIRO AND PATTI EXCHANGE A LOOK. PATTI LOOKS AT HER WATCH.

PATTI: Oh my God. I have to get going before the last train.

JAIRO: Thank you again, Patti. Dolores loves your green soup. (to Dolores) Don't you, honey? Wasn't that nice of Patti?

DOLORES STARES AT BOTH OF THEM. SHE GRABS AN APPLE, AND THE CRACKERS SHE'S BEEN MUNCHING ON.

DOLORES: I'm not that hungry.

JAIRO: You might be in shock, Dolores.

DOLORES: Cause I'm not hungry?

JAIRO: A painful experience just happened to you. Yes, you reacted quickly, put up whatever defenses you could. . . .

DOLORES: Please don't start.

JAIRO: If I'm hearing you right. . .

DOLORES: You're not.

JAIRO: I'm not what?

DOLORES: Hearing me right.

JAIRO: *CAN NO LONGER CONTAIN HIMSELF*

JAIRO: And why I am not hearing you right? Because you happen to carry a vial of spite with you. Everywhere you go. And when you're not doing that you put the vial in a box and you wrap the box in a bigger box, sealing the box with electrical tape, putting the box in a safety deposit box—that's what. Never mind that the goddamn deposit box is full of other vials. That's what you do, Dolores. Only this time, you've got witnesses. Patti and I are standing right here watching you carry the box to a cave where you dig an even a bigger hole.

DOLORES: What the hell are you talking about?

JAIRO: You're taking the vial, sealing it, surrounding it with a barbed wire fence <u>and</u> an armed guard or two.

DOLORES: *(to Patti)* You see what I mean?

JAIRO: And. . . if that wasn't enough. . .you've put the 'Do Not Trespass' billboard up on top of that and then renamed the goddamned location "Peaceville!" That's what you do, Dolores.

PATTI GATHERS HER THINGS. SHE BEGINS TO LEAVE.

DOLORES: *(TO PATTI)* You can't stay for your own dinner?

JAIRO: (to Patti) Thank you for driving Dolores there. And back. Thanks for the nice meal. (to Dolores) That was really nice of her. (Patti) Thank you for all your help.

DOLORES EXITS. PATTI AND JAIRO WATCH HER LEAVE.

You've been such a good friend. (pause) To Dolores. Thank you.

LIGHTS FADE.

Scene 2: The Call to Adventure

*DOLORES AND DANIEL SCARTH ENTER.
DANIEL IS PROBABLY IN HIS FORTIES TOO.
BUT HE LOOKS YOUNGER.FOR A FEW
MOMENTS THEY WALK TOWARDS EACH
OTHER BEFORE TURNING, STOPPING AND
FACING THE AUDIENCE.*

DOLORES: I found him in the variations section of the Village Voice.

*DANIEL STANDS LOOKING AT THE AUDIENCE
QUITE SIMPLY.*

DOLORES: His simple ad read: a single WM, 40 male seeking height/weight proportionate female with all or some of these ingredients: adventurous, sexy, erotic, exhibitionist, Bi, petite, fun. No drugs/smoke. Age/race unimportant. Short/long term. And no talking, ever. " (pauses) It was the no talking ever. . . that caught my eye.

DANIEL: What do you mean, "no talking ever?" she wrote me in her first e-mail. (faces Dolores) I quickly wrote back, I mean, "real connection comes only in silence" I underlined silence.

DOLORES: (faces Daniel) So do you mean we won't talk during. . .our encounters?

DANIEL: (to Dolores) During. . . before and after. We agree on a time and a place and we meet there weekly till we don't.

JAIRO ENTERS. HIS FOCUS IS ONLY ON DOLORES AND NOTHING ELSE.

DOLORES: I have to say, that appealed to me. . .(back to the audience) very much.

JAIRO: You're not very talkative, my dear. You know that?

DOLORES: Jairo, my ex-boyfriend. . .was a shrink.

JAIRO: You've buried your emotions and now they have to be validated. . .

DOLORES: He would talk this way at the grocery store.

JAIRO:. . .and expressed. People with your kind of disorder, and it is a disorder.

DOLORES: We could be standing in line at the movies.

JAIRO: All the time, this disorder makes you do really stupid or desperate things. . . .

DOLORES: Even dining at the finest restaurant, he would ruin a perfectly expensive dinner.

JAIRO:. . .in an effort to meet the emotional needs of your BPSOs. . .the intention is to 'give him what he wants' to make the craziness stop. Isn't that right?

DOLORES: (to Jairo) Why can't you just talk English to me?

JAIRO: Dolores, you're a sane person dealing with an insane disorder. You didn't cause it, you can't control it and you can't cure it.

DOLORES: (to audience) I didn't know how to break up with Jairo exactly. He was the father I never had.

JAIRO: (to audience) I suggested a period of "no contact" whatsoever to Dolores

DOLORES: So I answered Daniel's personal ad instead.

JAIRO: (to audience) We would need a necessary cooling off period of course.

DOLORES: And I met Daniel the following Thursday at 2:00. in the afternoon.

DANIEL: (to Dolores) I found an inexpensive hotel in the upper west side. Not much of a view.

A bed. . .and with very little room on either side.

JAIRO: And its very important that no contact occur. . . directly or indirectly.

DOLORES: And every week Daniel would reserve a room at this place in the upper west side. Kind of a youth hostel but more private.

JAIRO: No phone calls. . .

DOLORES AND DANIEL WALK TOWARDS EACH OTHER.

No visual sightings. No e-mails.

DOLORES: I didn't know Daniel's real name for at least six months. I only knew him by his e-mail address: "Dear tall dark and lonesome69: "Won't it be great to never have to say to the other 'I think you should,'" I wrote him on the first day. "I can't even imagine a relationship without the punishing 'how come you didn't?' Or the narcisstic- - - "That's nothing, wait'll till you hear what happened to me!" Or the know it all: "this could turn into a very positive experience if you just couldn't, wouldn't, shouldn't!" I definitely won't miss the kiss ass "But it wasn't your fault, you did the best you could!" Or the self referential, "this reminds me of the time. . .!" And definitely. . .not the platitudes: "Cheer up, don't feel so bad," or better still, the ridiculous pitying "oh, you poor thing!" Or- - - the diagnostic: when did this begin?" Can you imagine if we never have to offer each other the excuses: "I would have called but. . . ." And of course, my personal favorite: "that's not how it happened my love!"

DANIEL: Dear Esmeralda Blue: Someone is putting a spell on me.

DOLORES AND DANIEL KISS PASSIONATELY.

JAIRO: (to the audience) The no contact rule is the only thing that gives you the opportunity to get out of the crazymaking of the BPD/NonBPD dynamic. The fact that she agreed to the no contact rule showed progress I thought. Perhaps she was finally going to stop spending time, energy and even money attempting to prove that she was not being controlling, emotionally abusive or unfaithful.

Scene 3: The Refusal of the Call

DOLORES IS TAKING DOWN THE CHRISTMAS TREE. PATTI IS READING A MAGAZINE.

PATTI: "Today during the day you are inclined to keep your feelings and innermost thoughts to yourself. A sense of loneliness or isolation frequently accompanies this period of time and depression and a general sense of pessimism."

DOLORES: You sound just like Jairo.

PATTI: I'm reading my horoscope. For the month of January. Will you let me finish? "Domestic problems may also accompany this influence, usually because you feel that in some way your domestic life is not giving you what it should."

SHE THROWS DOWN HER MAGAZINE IN A HUFF.

Fuck that. I've never been happier.

DOLORES PICKS UP THE MAGAZINE. SHE STARTS TO READ.

DOLORES: What does it say about mine?

PATTI: Let me see that. I read yours earlier.

DOLORES: How come?

PATTI: I read about all my friends. I always underline mine. And yours. Here we go.

"You're feeling slightly out of sorts. Your real problem is either that you are cut off from your emotions or that your emotions are too unpleasant to deal with."

DOLORES: Is that you or me?

PATTI: "This influence, dear Scorpio, may force you to briefly experience what you consider to be your negative side. There is a strong conflict between what you think of yourself and what you think you should be."

DOLORES: Say that again. The part about the conflict.

PATTI: There's a strong conflict between what you think of yourself and what you think you should be.

DOLORES EXTENDS HER HAND OUT FOR THE MAGAZINE. PATTI HANDS IT OVER.

DOLORES: If I'm about to inherit a million dollars, its bound to change something.

PATTI: You can't be serious.

DOLORES: And I've been thinking--- what will I do with it and I thought of you.

PATTI: What about me?

DOLORES: You'd be someone I'm gonna give money to. To start the flower shop you've always wanted.

PATTI: Well that's nice. . .of you.

DOLORES: But then again, we may never see any of it. Most of the land has been utilized by the state for years. Its going to be in court for a while. And did I tell? They're turning my crazy relative's house into a museum and since I'm one of the direct ascendants, I've been invited to the opening.

PATTI: Now tell me again where this place is?

DOLORES: San Diego, Texas. From what I hear it's a ghost town with people still living in it. I need a vacation, so I'm going.

PATTI: Is Jairo going with you?

DOLORES: It's a vacation. No.

PATTI: What about the guy you're fucking?

DOLORES: Excuse me?

PATTI: The guy you've been meeting with. You're not taking him are you? I mean, Jairo would have had that baby with you, Dolores. And been the perfect father for it too.

DOLORES: I would not have inflicted Jairo on any baby of mine.

PATTI: Shut up! You love Jairo so much.

DOLORES: Like a father, Patti. And that's fucked up. At least my relationship with

SHE DOESN'T KNOW WHAT TO CALL HIM

. . . my new friend- - -

PATTI: What's his name anyway? Your new friend?

DOLORES: We've agreed to respect each other's anonymity.

PATTI: You don't know his name. He hasn't told you his real name. That is so fucked up, Dolores.

DOLORES: Patti, this is the best relationship I've ever had.

PATTI: Right, with this guy who doesn't even know your fucking name.

DOLORES: It irks you that my circumstances never repeat. I'm always new to him. And he's always new to me.

PATTI: Oh come on. There's only so many ways to do it, for God's sake.

DOLORES: Only if you believe the shit you read in this magazine. Like this woman-on-top crap. (reading) "Seems that the sight of you playing cowgirl in his saddle is enough to burn him up with lust."

They base their articles on surveys, Dolores. They're not just making shit up.

DOLORES: Right, like some guy's going to take the time to fill out a survey about women riding his bronco. They're calling a man's penis a bronco, Patti. Is this where you're getting your ideas about bliss and beyond?

PATTI: You can't possibly call what you do with that guy a relationship, Dolores! Jairo was at least willing to commit to you. Marry you. Settle down and have a family with you. Your new friend doesn't even want to know what you do for a living. I mean you can't call that a relationship, alright?

DOLORES: He doesn't imprison me in his memory, Patti. What the hell does that mean?

DOLORES HAS PULLED OUT A SENTIMENTAL ORNAMENT.

DOLORES: He doesn't have ideas about me. Like Jairo does. To Jairo, I'm a label, a disorder. Something he can only hope to fix. (referring to the ornament) I've had this since the seventh grade. I made it in Sister Janie's class. Do you remember her?

PATTI: The guy's probably married. Your new friend.

THERE'S A PAUSE.

He's married isn't he?

DOLORES: I'm clear about the nature of my desire. And that's all I care about.

STILL PONDERING THE ORNAMENT

PATTI: The nature of your desire- - - hello? What the hell is the nature of your desire?

DOLORES: I had a huge crush on Sister Janie. Even back then, I was clear about the nature of my desire. We would make out all the time.

PATTI: Why are you telling me all this?

DOLORES: I'd help her after school, we'd wait till everyone was gone and we'd.

PATTI: You don't even talk right anymore. You seem to derive some kind of sick pleasure out of watching me squirm.

DOLORES: Watching you squirm?

PATTI: You say things just to shock me, you know you do. How can you live with yourself knowing there's some poor woman somewhere out there who stays up late at night wondering where the fuck her husband is. And then you stand there bragging about messing around with some nun, for God's sake, Dolores! You're having a mid-life crisis.

DOLORES: I never see him at night.

PATTI: So's he's married isn't he? How can you live with yourself

DOLORES: I don't let second hand information influence me.

PATTI: Second hand information?

DOLORES: You're the one making it all up, Patti. I don't know that he's married. No. In his ad he originally said he was single. So whatever you're saying is shit that you yourself are afraid of. You're the one that stays up all night wondering where the fuck Hector is.

PATTI: I don't care how you try to rationalize it, babe. You're not in reality, okay? And Hector is home every night be eight.

DOLORES: Its only reality or morality if you're willing to accept repetition, Patti. To have stayed with Jairo, I would have been motivated by security. The way you are with Hector. You're motivated by compensation.

PATTI: Compensation?

DOLORES: You like the life he provides for you. And your children. But there's no living in the moment, ever.

PATTI: That's not true, Dolores. We're very attentive to each other. Even after all these years.

DOLORES: You're not the owner of what you have, Patti. Not your husband, your children and even your house. But you have this idea that being Hector's wife, my friend, your children's mother is all that you are at every given moment. Every situation is colored by these ideas that you have of yourself. When I meet with this man, my new friend, we have no defined role with the other. And when our bodies meet it is for no particular end but the act of meeting love. In each other.

PATTI: You've always resented me. Because I'm a happily married woman. And have been that for almost twenty years.

DOLORES: So happy that you're totally fixated with Jairo?

PATTI: Jairo?

DOLORES: Jairo. Everything you're accusing me of. Most of what you are thinking I should do for myself with Jairo. . .is what you're actually wanting for yourself

PATTI: I don't think of Jairo. . .in that light.

DOLORES: No, but you think of Jairo. . .in the dark. Late at night. When you're alone. When you're bored to death with Hector plowing you and you just lay there playing dead. If you could be honest with yourself, drop the security of all your repetitions, Patti. Your patterns. You'll finally be free to pursue Jairo. That's what this is all about.

PATTI STARTS TO PACK UP HER STUFF. SHE IS BESIDES HERSELF.

PATTI: I feel so sorry for you. I really do.

PATTI EXITS.

Scene 4. Supernatural Aid

DOLORES STEPS INTO A SPOTLIGHT. DANIEL INTO ANOTHER. THEY NEVER FACE EACH OTHER. THEY SPEAK OUT TOWARDS THE AUDIENCE, IN DEEP REVERIE. THEIR EXCHANGE SHOULD BEGIN QUIETLY, SLOWLY AND THEN BUILD INTO A "CLIMAX." IT IS, FOR OUR PURPOSES, THEIR LOVEMAKING.

DOLORES: We peel every layer of skin off, the room cold---

DANIEL: The days of late colder than usual---

DOLORES: So we wrap around the other under the blankets, his hand wanders. . .

DANIEL: I go right to the lip of her, lowering myself on the long side. . .

DOLORES: His fingers, his tongue, one in, one out, . .

DANIEL: Her nipple catches my fancy, her hip. . .

DOLORES: His breath like an echo, calling me back, always back. . .

DANIEL: Into total liquid…

DOLORES: I'm going to pee on myself. .
.(feverishly) don't stop!

DANIEL: Her wetness in my mouth, like I'm
kissing her mouth. . .still.

DOLORES: I take charge. . .hanging over, hanging
onto the bedframe. . .

DANIEL: Her light rain on my face.

DOLORES: I am laundry on the line. . .Who are
you. . .

DANIEL: Who are you. . .

DOLORES: Who are you, we're drawn. . .

DANIEL: Her eyes. . .

DOLORES: Oh loss, I feel loss. . .

DANIEL: But not one word. . .

DOLORES: Between us. . .

DANIEL: She moans, we climb. . .

DOLORES: Distrust. . .and still my hips move
shamelessly

DANIEL: Higher, she scratches

DOLORES: Faster, don't stop. . .

DANIEL: Higher, faster. . .

DOLORES: Don't stop!.

DANIEL: Release. . .

DOLORES: Don't stop, please. . .don't. . .to fall---

DANIEL: To fall. . .

DOLORES: Surrender, my weary but satiated bones. . .

DANIEL: Surrender,

DOLORES: This total perfect stranger. My heart. .

 DANIEL: I must distract.

THEY TAKE A MOMENT TO RECOVER THEIR BREATH.THEY TURN TO FACE THE OTHER. THEY ARE INSTANTMESSAGING THE OTHER.

DOLORES: Dear Tall, dark and lonesome 69:

A COMPUTER SCREEN PROJECTION BEHIND THEM TYPES THEIR CONVERSATION IN A DIFFERENT "PROGRAM." MAYBE ONE LOOKS MORE LIKE MUSIC WAVES, OR PERHAPS

HEIROGLYPICS. . .AND THE OTHER IS A FOREIGN "COMPUTER" LANGUAGE.

I hope you haven't reserved a room for next Thursday.

DANIEL: I have.

DOLORES: Can we skip a week?

DANIEL: Was it something I "said"?

DOLORES LAUGHS.

DOLORES: Very funny. I do wonder about that.

DANIEL: What?

DOLORES: Your voice. What it sounds like.

DANIEL: So why a week?

DOLORES: I have to go to Texas.

DANIEL: (*unexpectedly jealous*): What's in Texas?

DOLORES: Family. (beat) That I've never met.

DANIEL: That's adventurous.

DOLORES: And. . .a buried treasure.

DANIEL GETS VERY STILL. DOLORES WAITS FOR ARESPONSE. FINALLY SHE CONTINUES.

DOLORES: You won't be placing any ads while I'm gone. . .will you?

DANIEL: Not till you're back to respond to them.

THEY BOTH ARE AT A FAMILIAR LOSS OF WORDS.

DANIEL: I like your mouth.

DOLORES: I like your mouth too.

DOLORES AND DANIEL TURN BACK TOWARDS THE AUDIENCE. THEY SMILE TO THEMSELVES. LIGHTS OUT.

Scene 5. The Crossing of the First Threshold

A DOORBELL IS HEARD. JAIRO APPEARS. HE'S STILL IN HIS PAJAMAS. HE LOOKS VERY DISTRAUGHT AND UNKEPT. THERE ARE SEVERAL SEALED JARS OF WATER STARTING TO STACK UP IN THE CORNER OF THE ROOM.

JAIRO: Patti, is that you?

PATTI: Yes.

JAIRO OPENS THE DOOR. SHE'S SHOCKED TO SEE JAIRO LOOKING THIS WAY.

PATTI: I came as fast as I could. You look. . .

JAIRO: Like shit. I know. But I want you to see something.

HE POINTS AT THE JARS IN THE CORNER OF THE ROOM.

JAIRO: I'm running out of jars.

PATTI: I'm sorry?

JAIRO: I've been collecting the rain.

PATTI: What rain?

JAIRO: What do you mean what rain?

PATTI LOOKS UP AT THE CEILING.

PATTI: There's a leak in the ceiling Jairo.

JAIRO: Call it what you want.

PATTI: Have you called the landlord?

JAIRO: About what?

PATTI: The leak. It's the snow, melting.

JAIRO: He won't believe me. Nobody believes you if you talk about holy water. I'm gonna need more jars.

PATTI: Jairo. . .I'm worried about you.

JAIRO: Because. . .

PATTI: I don't know what you're saying. About the holy water.

JAIRO: Dolores is sleeping with someone.

PATTI: (lying) I don't think so.

JAIRO: As soon as the rains came, I knew.

PATTI: What do you mean?

JAIRO: I knew to open her fucking e-mail. She's been meeting some guy. . .every Thursday. I knew the minute the rain started. . . .I started to hear clearly. See clearly. I've known exactly what to do. And when.

PATTI: About. . .

JAIRO: About. . .whatever needs to happen next. Do you know the guy?

PATTI: What guy?

JAIRO: That Dolores is sleeping with.

PATTI: I don't think she's sleeping with anyone, Jairo.

JAIRO: Oh yeah? Then why does your lip curl up like that?

PATTI: My lip does what?

JAIRO: It curls up on the side. It only does that when you're trying to hide something. But it's okay. You're only lying to me because you care about me. You don't want me to hurt more than I have to hurt right now.

THEY STARE AT EACH OTHER FOR A LONG MOMENT.

Do you have extra jars at home? (beat) I've been out pricing guns all morning.

PATTI: What?

JAIRO: I went on a walk. Something inside me, after the rain started, knew I had to go somewhere. I ended up at the pawn shop. The one around the corner.

PATTI: Yeah. . .

JAIRO: I didn't plan to go there but then somehow I knew I had to take a walk. So I do. And where do I end up? At the pawn shop. And just like I know your name and the names of your family. . .I knew I had to walk in there. When the clerk asks me what he can do for me, I tell him the truth. I don't know I say. Because I didn't. Not in that moment. But as I'm saying this I'm standing over the counter where they keep the hand guns. "Are you looking for one of these?" he asks. And because I am standing right there. And I'm staring right at them I say. "I think I am." "Is it for sport?" he asks. I had already forgotten why I was there. Was it? Was it for sport? And if so. . .who was I hunting down? And the more I thought it out it, I could say yes. Kind of. Yes, I told him. "I need something that would take my sport down. In one shot." Is that a four legged? Or a two legged? I guess he was talking code. Two, I say. Two. . .two leggeds. And when I say that. . . he doesn't even blink. He pulls out three handguns and lays them out on the counter in front of me. "This one. . .even if you aim just right won't necessarily hurt them. At least not bad. But this one. . .you'd have to know what you were doing. And if you did know what you were doing. . .it would definitely do the trick. But this one would blow them completely away even if you didn't aim at that them directly you know what I'm saying?" But of course I didn't. . .but I was suddenly very interested.

PATTI: Jairo. . .

JAIRO: I started to feel good for the first time in days. Weeks even. And do you know why? Because this jerk with two charm bracelets and a gold chain around his neck was listening to me Patti. He wasn't questioning me. Judging me. He was really listening. I felt really listened to. (notices a change in Patti) What?

PATTI: I'm not comfortable hearing this.

JAIRO: Hearing what?

PATTI: That you went out looking for guns.

JAIRO: I didn't go out looking for guns. I came upon the guns. But that's exactly what I'm talking about. Do you see that? That's exactly what I'm saying. You're not really listening to me.

PATTI: I'm definitely listening.

JAIRO: To what?

PATTI: You haven't been to work in a week, Jairo.

JAIRO: It hasn't been a week.

PATTI: I've called your office for a week.

JAIRO: But if you were listening. . .really listening, you would have heard me say something totally completely different.

PATTI: Like?

JAIRO: Like. . . that I get it. For the first time in my professional life. I get it that I'm been a fake. A fucking fake at my job. I get paid to listen to people all day but not once have I really been listening. Not like the guy at the pawn shop. What I've been doing is assigning a prognosis. And that's not really listening. That's deciding ahead of time. . .what something is. So that I don't have to deal with it. Like right now, if you've already decided that I was out pricing guns with the intent of actually using them. . .then you missed the entire point that I was trying to make.

PATTI: I'm sorry. . .but look at you!

JAIRO: Look at me. . .why?

PATTI: You look. . .

JAIRO: I look. . .what?

PATTI: Disturbed.

JAIRO: Really?

PATTI: Really.

JAIRO: And that means. . .what exactly?

PATTI: Jairo, please. Stop with the bullshit.

HE BURSTS OUT LAUGHING.

JAIRO: Wow! And I'm thinking the total opposite. I'm finally speaking the truth. I'm finally getting it. I'm getting myself, Patti. For the first time ever. And you're calling that bullshit.

PATTI: Did you buy the gun?

JAIRO: Why? You see how you stopped listening. . .you see that? You already decided something about me. . .that I bought the gun maybe. And that I'm going to use it and so you're treating me accordingly.

PATTI: You haven't been to work all week, there's a leak over your fucking head that you're calling holy water and. . . .you're wearing your pajamas.

JAIRO: In my own house.

PATTI: But its four o'clock in the afternoon.

JAIRO: And that means. . .

PATTI: Did you buy the gun?

JAIRO: No. I didn't buy the gun.

PATTI: Why don't you come and stay with Hector and I at least. And the kids. You know how much they love you. We can keep you company. Make sure you're fed at least.

JAIRO: I can't stand to be around anybody. No offense. It took everything I had to call you.

PATTI: You're a fucking shrink, Jairo! Pull yourself together! Use your own goddamn medicine.

JAIRO: Are you kidding? This is the best thing that could ever happened to me!

PATTI: What?

JAIRO: Up until this point, the disorder has been somewhere out there. Somewhere else. Far away. Somewhere safe. . . outside me. Going postal is something my clients do. But not me.

PATTI: Okay. . .

JAIRO: Allowing myself to price guns, Patti. If anything. . .that was my own goddamn medicine! And I didn't have to kill somebody to do it.

PATTI: And who would that somebody have been?

JAIRO: The guy she meets on Thursdays. Who else? I know she must have told you something about him. She tells you everything. And who knows? Maybe after I'd be done with him. She would have been next.

THEY STARE AT EACH OTHER.

JAIRO: You look. . .really great by the way. You always do. But there's something else about you today. Maybe it's the sweater. The color. The way it brings out your eyes.

PATTI IS UNABLE TO MOVE. SHE'S UNABLE TO LOOK AT HIM.

You look really good. Even when you're so unhappy.

PATTI: I'm not unhappy.

JAIRO: Hector doesn't touch you enough. Not anymore.

PATTI: He touches me. Enough.

JAIRO: No. I mean. . . like he means it. Not out of obligation. Not because he has to so that you'll pick up the kids at gymnastics or do the laundry or make it okay for him to stay out late. . .night after night. You don't even ask him about it anymore, do you?

PATTI: I have to go. Do you need me to call the landlord? Or not? About the leak?

SHE DOESN'T MOVE.

JAIRO: I know how unhappy you are, Patti. I just want you to know. You deserve better.

That's all. I knew this before the rain ever came by the way. And no. . .you don't need to call the landlord. I like collecting the holy water.

PATTI: Its probably somebody's water heater upstairs. And they're gone for the holidays. And there's nothing holy about it. Somebody needs to know. Before. . .

JAIRO: Before. . .

PATTI: The fucking ceiling caves in.

JAIRO: How perfect would that be?

PATTI: (She looks at him.) If it's all going to fall anyway. . .why not just let it?

THEY STARE AT EACH OTHER FOR A MOMENT. JAIRO APPROACHES PATTI. SHE DOESN'T MOVE. THEY STAND THERE. . .VERY CLOSE TO EACH OTHER. HE VERY GENTLY TAKES HIS HAND AND RUNS IT LIGHTLY OVER HER FACE. SHE DOESN'T MOVE.

If takes the worry away- - -sure. . .call the landlord. The number's on the refrigerator. It's a twenty four hour line. (pause) I know how much you care about me. I've always known it. And for that. . .I'm one of the lucky ones.

SHE LOOKS AT HIM STRAIGHT ON AND THEN EXITS. LIGHTS OUT

Scene 6. Tests, Allies, Enemies

*CLARA CISNEROS, FORTIES, AN ARCHIVIST
FOR THE UNIVERSITY OF TEXAS INSTITUTE
OF TEXAN CULTURES, ENTERS. DOLORES IS
WITH HER.*

CLARA: As you can see your greatgrandfather built this place out of massive blocks of *sillar*---limestone, which is native to the region. But if you notice, the proportions are huge, not quite the pyramids, but he built everything in such strange configurations, nobody's been able to understand how he could have done it single-handedly.

*DOLORES IS LOOKS AT THE STRUCTURE
DUMBFOUNDED.*

DOLORES: He couldn't have moved these by himself.

CLARA: But he did. (beat) Is this your first visit to Texas?

DOLORES: I've never been further south than Pennsylvania, yes. I'm not sure what I expected exactly.

CLARA: Cowboys on horses. . .maybe?

DOLORES: I didn't expect the palm trees at the airport.

CLARA: Oh right. That's right. Well, we're very excited to have one of the only direct living descendants of Augustin Julian Saenz here with us. I want to thank you again for responding to our invitation. Even 60 Minutes is here. They plan to film part of the opening festivities. They've requested an interview with you, but you're not obligated in anyway.

DOLORES: An interview. . .about what?

CLARA: You're great, great grandfather Augustin.

DOLORES: I only know what you're telling me. About him. Up until your phone call and letter, I had no idea I had family here. I've only talked to my biological mother once.

CLARA: Esmeralda.

DOLORES: Yes. And she wouldn't agree to meet with me. We just talked on the phone. I'm adopted, as you know. And I grew up thinking I was Cuban. Raised in Florida, and then my family moved to New York City when I was a teenager, so all of this is rather---unexpected. And exotic.

CLARA: Esmeralda is the one who gave us your name. She didn't want to talk to us either, even though she lived here till she was a teenager. I can see the resemblance. Between the two of you.

DOLORES: Really? I've never seen a picture of her.

CLARA LEADS DOLORES TO AN EXHIBIT

Is that her?

A BEAUTIFUL WOMAN ENTERS DRESSED IN 1950S CLOTHING. SHE SHOULD LOOK LIKE A LATIN VERSION OF DONNA REED BUT IN HER TEENS. SHE MOVES ABOUT THE STAGE IN RUNWAY MODEL AFFECTATIONS AS THEY TALK ABOUT HER.

She's beautiful. (very moved) So beautiful.

CLARA HANDS HER ANOTHER PHOTOGRAPH. A VERY DISTINGUISHED MAN WITH A LONG WHITE BEARD AND CLOTHES CIRCA 1880 ENTERS WITH A GUITAR. HE SITS AND AFTER A MOMENT BEGINS TO PLAY SOFTLY.

CLARA: And that is Augustin, your great, great, grandfather. He was born in Mier, Mexico, as I was telling you. His family was given over a thousand acres of land grants and he came here to settle his share. The plan was to build his fiancé a house. But when he returned to Mier to get her, she had supposedly married somebody else.

A VERY ATTRACTIVE MAN IN HIS MID-SIXTIES, FRANCISCO OLVERA, ENTERS. HE DOESN'T SEEM COMFORTABLE IN THE SPACE.

FRANCISCO: I don't know where you expect people to park out there. I would call the gas people to check the lines, it smells like natural gas out there. Maybe sewage.

CLARA: Mr. Ramirez. Please. Come in. I'm sorry about the disruption.

FRANCISCO: You're already attracting every kind of con man around, have you noticed the campers parked out there? All wanting to claim their share, I hope you know what you're doing.

CLARA: I would like to introduce you to the daughter of Esmeralda Saenz, Mr. Ramirez. This is Dolores. She's the daughter of Esmeralda Saenz.

FRANCISCO: (to Dolores)The daughter of who?

CLARA: Your stepdaughter Esmeralda.

RIGHT ON CUE, ESMERALDA BLUE WALKS PAST HIM. FRANCISCO IS OVERWHELMED TO SEE ESMERALDA HERE.

FRANCISCO: There's no blood between us.

CLARA: What's that?

FRANCISCO: Esmeralda came with the package. There was never any blood between us.

DOLORES: So you're my mother's--- stepfather?

CLARA: Yes

FRANCISCO: Tell me again who your mother is?

DOLORES: My biological mother is Esmeralda.

DOLORES WATCHES ESMERALDA DIRECTLY AS SHE WALKS BY OBLIVIOUS TO EVERYONE IN THE ROOM.

CLARA: Your stepdaughter. (to Dolores) Esmeralda lived with Mr. Ramirez when she was a little girl.

FRANCISCO: Esmeralda was never a little girl. Not that girl.

CLARA: Dolores is here all the way from New York City, Mr. Ramirez. For the museum's opening.

FRANCISCO: Is that where Esmeralda ended up?

DOLORES: No. I'm from New York.

FRANCISCO: She was a wild devil child that girl.

DOLORES: Esmeralda lives in Phoenix.

CLARA: Before it gets too late for me, I want to give both of you a walking tour of the place.

FRANCISCO: Frankly I think these museum people are grasping at straws. Proud of the sensationalism they're setting into motion. (to Clara). I just think you're publicity stunt in the paper today is a disgrace Miss Cisneros. A total disgrace.

CLARA: Mr. Ramirez, I wouldn't believe everything you read in the papers if I were you.

FRANCISCO: It's going to sell a few extra tickets to the freak show, if that's what you're after.

CLARA: The timing of that story is very unfortunate for the museum. If its alright with you, Mr. Ramirez, I have very little time to get a lot of things done. I have spoken to Dolores about the artifacts. And I'd like her to see them.

AUGUSTIN HAS SET HIMSELF UP IN FRONT OF A SMALL STAND WITH A PLAQUE THAT TELLS ABOUT HIM. HE IS NOW FROZEN IN PLACE. DOLORES GOES UP TO HIM LIKE SHE WOULD A MUSEUM PIECE. SHE READS ABOUT HIM AS WELL. ON THE OTHER SIDE OF THE STAGE, ESMERALDA HAS ALSO FROZEN IN PLACE AS WELL.

FRANCISCO: Somebody needs to tell the press that the emperor has no clothes.

CLARA: I beg your pardon?

FRANCISCO: You're trying to use this place to justify your indiscretions. (to Dolores) Your poor great grandfather is being villianized, to distract from this woman's wrong-doings.

CLARA: Mr. Ramirez! You're out of line.

FRANCISCO: I think that's calling the kettle black, wouldn't you say? I seriously doubt your judgment. (to Dolores) You need to look at the newspaper. And if I were you, I would totally disassociate myself from this woman and her efforts.

CLARA: I think this conversation is over, Mr. Ramirez.

FRANCISCO: If. . .if the old man

INDICATES THE OLD MAN STANDING THERE FROZEN

FRANCISCO: was as crazy as they say he was...let him be. Let him rest in peace.

CLARA (to Dolores): I'd like to get started if we could. These are the steps that lead to the basement where they found your great grand father's journals.

FRANCISCO: Surely that's why you're here. . .Ms.

DOLORES: Dolores. Please. Call me Dolores.

FRANCISCO: Those coins are worth thousands of dollars. Why do you think they're tearing up the whole street out there? (to Clara) I'd watch out for looters if I was you.

CLARA: We hired a plumber a few months ago to fix a sewer line after we started to remodel the building.

FRANCISCO: I lost this place to back taxes a few years back. And these people jumped in like vultures. Them and all of their goddamn lawyers.

CLARA: After we got the house designated into a historic monument and started the process last fall. . .the plumbers found the crates. (to Francisco) Not before.

FRANCISCO: I'm planning a countersuit.

HE MOVES TOWARDS THE 1950S WOMAN AND EXAMINES HER LIKE A MUSEUM PIECE.

To protect your mother's property. Maybe you have no interest in doing that. But I do.

CLARA: I'm afraid there's a legal dispute going on. About the coins themselves. I think our attorneys sent you that letter.

FRANCISCO (to Dolores): And if you think you can pull into town and suddenly start claiming the coins like everybody else you got another thing coming, you understand me? (referring to Clara) Besides, you should know who you're dealing with first. This woman has no scruples.

CLARA: Mr. Ramirez! My personal life has nothing to do with anything. Especially the museum and the coins.

FRANCISCO: Those are some very serious allegations they're charging against you. (to Dolores) She has enough legal problems of her own without getting you involved.

CLARA: I'm going to have to ask you to leave, Mr. Ramirez.

FRANCISCO: She's going to read it in the Corpus Christi Caller anyway! (to Dolores) And have they told you what they're making public about the old man?

HE NOW STANDS IN FRONT OF THE OLD MAN.

CLARA (to Francisco): The journals, as you yourself witnessed. . .are more than a hundred years old. They're mostly undecipherable. . .that's true. Mold has gotten the best of them.

FRANCISCO (to Dolores): But does that keep these overly educated people from reading into them? For their own purposes (to Clara) Tell this woman what you plan to tell the world about the crazy old man. I mean, he's not even blood. . .to me. . .but when I put myself in his place. . .

THE OLD MAN GESTURES FOR FRANCISCO TO TAKE HIS PLACE AS CLARA EXITS. AUGUSTIN RETURNS TO HIS GUITAR AND BEGINS TO PLAY "WITH THE FATHER."

 (to himself) I can feel him turning in his grave!

FRANCISCO FREEZES MOMENTARILY IN WHAT WAS AUGUSTIN'S PREVIOUS PLACE. DOLORES LOOKS AT HIM AS IF LOOKING AT A MUSEUM PIECE. AFTER A MOMENT, SHE WALKS AWAY AS HE SLOWLY COMES TO LIFE AS A SPOTLIGHT FEATURES HIM SINGING: WITH THE FATHER.

I can tell you how

How to cut somebody's throat

I've never even spoken to

I can tell you how

How to gut out the insides of a man

I've never even known

I can tell you how

How to take the head of things

Into your own hands

But I don't know how

How to hold, really, hold

A woman in my arms

Chorus: I must be the son of Abraham

Felt my father's blade

Rest too closely on my throat

God waging, God gambling,

Betting his all on holy wars

And the souls, of his many

Lost children, turn to gold

Turn to gold, their souls

I cannot tell you how

How to win a woman's love

Her name I've never even known

I cannot tell you how

How she makes my life complete

To have her, is to have myself

I cannot tell you how

How to fall down on your knees

And give yourself to Love

But I want to hold, really, hold

A woman in my arms

LIGHTS UP ON DOLORES AND DANIEL,
INSTANT MESSAGING.

DOLORES: (addressing tall, dark and lonesome)
Have I broken the rules?

DANIEL: What rules?

DOLORES: Bringing in some history about myself.
Into the e-mails?

DANIEL: I like knowing you by what's "relative."
(beat) Can it really be about you. . . if its history?

LIGHTS OUT ON THE LOVERS AS EMIL
HOLMDAHL ENTERS. ALTHOUGH HE'S
DRESSED LIKE MOST AMERICANS AT THE
TURN OF THE CENTURY, HE WEARS A
PANCHO VILLA DESERT HAT AND CARRIES A
WINCHESTER RIFLE WHICH DISTINGUISHES
HIM.

EMIL HOLMDAHL: If you're going to give a
mercenary value to things, you can't be surprised
by who or what shows up for the job. I was pretty
green when I did my first tour in the Philippine
Islands. But I got my first real dose of soldiering
there. And it came from watching these crazy
monkeys in the jungle close to camp. From what I

could figure, there was the one big monkey who was the leader of the pack because all the women monkeys and their babies would sit at his feet. And whenever any other monkey tried to touch one of those females, he'd get a good swing across the head and go flying straight into the bushes. The big monkey had won that position for himself. . .beating out every man monkey I suppose for his throne. But then one day, I see this pack of younger man monkeys near by. They'd get together to stare down the big monkey that was getting all that special attention from the ladies. It was about a week later that I watch the most horrific battle I have ever seen. . .and I've been to several wars. And several bloody scenes. But never have I seen something this vicious. It was the day that the group of males attacked the leader of the pack. . .all at one time but the way they did was to take every little baby monkey in sight. They grabbed them from the mothers and tore them apart by stomping on them, bashing their heads against the trees. I even saw some being thrown off the cliff. When I saw the big monkey just walk away, after seeing every little baby mutilated and the lady monkeys go berserk because they were helpless, that's when I understood soldiering. The lady monkeys had no choice but to follow the new pack of victors. Which got me believing one thing. Wars are about the children. Like those slaughtered baby monkeys. When you go into battle you're either saying you're protecting the children or you go right for the kill. . .you slaughter the babies because <u>then</u> you have the mothers. The lady monkeys were nobody without their babies. They were nothing but an empty vessel for bringing in another monkey into the world, the next monkey that would lead the pack. And so on and so forth. I saw something similar when I joined Lee Christmas in the jungles of Honduras. And there was quite the mess up there with that revolution and just like in the Philippines. . deep, deep in the jungle, there was a group of savages that pretty much did what those monkeys did to their own people and it wasn't even my job to care about that. My job was to be one of General Manuel Bonilla's monkeys, which lead to other successful exploits in Central and South America at the time. And the bottom line was always the same. Take the children and you have won the war.

Act II: Woman as Temptress:

Scene 1. Approach to the Inmost Cave

CLARA IS WORKING AT HER DESK. DOLORES IS READING THROUGH A TRANSCRIPT.

DOLORES: This is fucking---I'm sorry. This is unbelievable.

CLARA: Which part?

DOLORES (reading): "No man, who has loved a woman with every cell of his being, can call himself of good faith unless he can admit that he'd rather see his mistress dead than unfaithful." He didn't kill her, did he?

CLARA: In every room of the house. Over and over again, he did. Come with me.

CLARA LEADS DOLORES TO THE OTHER SIDE OF THE ROOM.

As you can see, this room has more than one level. The purpose of that, we think, was to create more of an imbalance, or at least that's what he says in the journal. He describes filling the room up with down, silk pillows, imagining that she'd come into this room, not able to resist its luxury, its elegance and of course throw herself onto the pillows, unaware. He, though, planted a long rusted railroad spike underneath one of the pillows.

CLARA SHOWS DOLORES SOMETHING IN THE GROUND.

That's what this is. It was to hold up a railroad nail, somewhere underneath ,where in his deranged mind he hoped she would inevitably impale herself.

CLARA POINTS TO SOMETHING IN THE TRANSCRIPT THAT DOLORES WAS READING.

"The imagination is where all of my pleasures arise. The sharper, the crueler is the delight if I can pierce and tear open her skin. I would offer to help clean the wound out, into which, I would pour melted hot wax."

DOLORES: But he never saw her again.

CLARA: Not face to face, no. Only in these rooms, where he visited her demise, daily, devising yet one more way to sodomize her. Day in and day out. You've read these pages.

DOLORES NODS, OBVIOUSLY DISTURBED BY IT.

DOLORES: So why, in Gods name, would you want to immortalize that? In a museum?

CLARA: That is what Mr. Ramirez would like you to think, but that is not the purpose of the museum. We're honoring your grandfather's unusual, if not miraculous masonry. By anybody's books, the building itself speaks to something more human and heroic that that. It speaks to the wits and courage he had to survive in a rattlesnake infested, waterless, dry terrain. From this perch, your granddad got to see the Confederate war, it came right up to his moat walls. Had Santa Ann decided to take a right turn, instead of left the whole history of the Alamo might have configured itself quite differently. It could have very well have played itself out here. The dimensions of the buildings are the same. The Army came very close. You have to remember that the Alamo itself, while hosting a battle, was a glorified myth in itself that high society white woman devised a hundred years after the battle, taking the "Remember the Alamo" cry as excuse for racial purity.

DOLORES: I don't know anything about . . .the Alamo, except for the John Wayne movie, I'm afraid.

CLARA: And the John Wayne movie does the best job of telling that story and from that bias. Villain-izing the Mexicans, who were only defending their rightful property, was the purpose of turning that building, into a shrine.

DOLORES: So what are you defending here? I still don't get the significance of a museum to glorify my grandfather's. . .perversions.

ADELA, CIRCA 1911, A SOLADERA WHO FOUGHT FOR PANCHO VILLA ENTERS, PRESERVED IN HER LATE TWENTIES. SHE POSES AS A MUSEUM RELIC.

CLARA: The woman your father loved, is the real hero, in my book.

THE TWO WOMEN APPROACH HER LIKE AN EXHIBIT.

CLARA: Your grandfather was a Mexican national who became part of the Republic of Texas, over night. By no choice of his own, he woke one day to find himself designated as a "Tejano." A Texan, who white Texans, saw as a subordinate and not as a native. The fact that he could build this miraculous structure, that defies engineering, speaks to the kind of spirit it took to tame this rugged, merciless grassland.   In his mind, he was torturing this woman, definitely. And that aspect I have very little interest in glamorizing, to answer your question, but if you let him represent more than that, he speaks to the broken dreams of a people that were colonized when this land became the Republic of Texas. And if you ask me, the real hero of this tale is Adela. The woman he tortured in his very messed up mind.

DOLORES: This woman was a soldier?

CLARA: A revolutionary soldier, yes.

DOLORES: In what war?

CLARA: The Mexican revolution. She fought in Pancho Villa's army.

DOLORES: Who fought in the Alamo?

CLARA BURSTS OUT LAUGHING.

I'm a New Yorker for God's sake.

CLARA: Let's just say this woman defied what was expected of her. As a woman. For that time. Adela was even sentenced to death for it.

DOLORES: By my grandfather?

CLARA: Oh no, the United States government was going to hang her. This is a woman who President Taft freed at the very last minute, okay? And by then, she had already put the message out to the masses. . .loud and clear. . .that the birth of the modern woman had indeed occurred even in the sticks of nowhere, Texas. And its motherland, Mexico. Your grandfather, of course, would have preferred to see her dead.

DOLORES: For her political beliefs?

CLARA: No, for rejecting him. When he returned to Mexico to marry her, she had already traveled across the border to the U.S., as part of Villa's efforts. She found protection on the American side of the border for a while where she wrote propagandic pamphlets. We found several of them in your grandfather's journals. Did you see the pamphlets in the main exhibit upstairs?

DOLORES: I saw them, I just didn't know what they were.

CLARA: This woman never married. Not like he told himself over and over again that she did. She was a. . .well a very modern woman. She preferred the company of. . . .women.

DOLORES: She was a lesbian?

CLARA: Let's just say that's she's a modern, even radical woman.

DOLORES: What?! Wait a minute.

CLARA: The donors, in this town and my current situation do not allow it.

DOLORES: And what exactly is your current situation? Is that what Mr. Ramirez was talking about?

CLARA: Why do you think 60 Minutes is in town? They're here to cover my situation. Unfortunately, they now want to include the museum as part of their story since I work here. And they want to feature the supposed, lewd writings and sadism of your grandfather as if there's any connection between the two.

*CLARA HANDS OVER THE NEWSPAPER.
DOLORES IS CONFUSED. CLARA POINTS OUT
THE ARTICLE ITSELF. DOLORES READS A
LITTLE BIT OF IT.*

It made the front page this morning. I'm really
sick about it.

*CLARA IS EXTREMELY EMOTIONAL ABOUT IT
BUT DOES HER BEST TO COPE.*

 I've worked very hard, for the last five years to
make this museum a reality and now. . . they're
trying to desecrate its historical relevance because
of my. . .situation.

DOLORES: What exactly are the charges?

CLARA: They're saying I. . . abused. . .someone.
My girlfriend. They're saying I---raped her.

LIGHTS OUT.

<u>Scene   .The Road of Trials</u>.

LIGHTS UP ON WHO EMIL CONTINUES TO SHINE AND READY HIS ASSORTED WEAPONRY.

EMIL (to the audience): When someone hires me to fight their cause my question to them is: how much will that bring me? Because bottom line. . .with money--- a person can procure anything. Money is my baby. That's why I went to Mexico for the first time in 1909. I served in the Rurales under Emilio Kosterlitzky there, but once there, I changed allegiance to Madero after the fall of Juárez and joined Pancho Villa and then Obregon soon after. And even though they were saying some pretty low down things about Villa at the time in the American papers. . .from my vantage point, this was a man who wasn't looking to get paid. This man played with money. He threw it at the poorest people imaginable and that's why they loved him so much. If you ask me. . .that was reason it was impossible to ever hunt him down. He also traveled with only one faithful companion, he camped in desolate spots and then would dismiss his guide. He'd leave a fire burning and then ride all night to get away from the faithful companion. He never slept. . .or if he did, he was a cat about it. When you least expected it, he would show up like he did one night to see if we were doing our job and then in the morning he'd come back from a totally different direction. No one, not even the most trusted officer of his outfit knew his plans until he was ready to spring into action. It happened pretty unexpectedly one morning, that after fighting right along side him in the battle of Ojinaga. . .there comes an order from Villa himself to discharge all the Americans in the ranks and ship'em back to the border! Now I'll be the first to admit that those fellas from the U.S. were nothing but bums, most were not even welcome back home, but there was an occasional exception like myself who put in a pretty good effort on his behalf. And he gave us nothing but our honorable discharges to show for it. Overnight! We had no place to sleep and nothing to eat, but somehow, and it wasn't easy, I made it back to the U.S. and started working as a taxi driver, anything I could find, really. But then I heard talk about Pershing being sent out to punish Villa. I needed the money so I re-enlisted. Now you might say, "you were changing allegiances like underwear," but if you ask me, war is never about two different sides. It's the same coin, you understand? I told Pershing myself, "you're never gonna find Villa alive," and that ended up being prophesy. For me. Because when I finally came across Villa again myself, it was at his grave a few years later. I was out of money again so I started prospecting in Mexico one more time. But as luck would have it, I got arrested right as I got there. Someone had desecrated Villa's tomb and someone told the authorities they had seen me there a day or two before, so they throw me in the dungeon and throw away the key. If it wasn't for a wealthy group of fellas up east that liked collecting skulls, I would have rotted there. Turns out those skull boys had the Apache Chief Geronimo's skull in their cellar and I guess they wanted Pancho Villa's head as well. . .for their collection. These fellas were up in New Haven. . . the one that paid me was a serious fella named Prescott Bush. . .who personally offered to pay me $25,000 dollars for Villa's skull which at the time, was enough for someone like myself to buy a sheep farm. And it was obvious that these skull fellas knew all the right people in all the right places, even as far and nowhere as Mexico. They arranged my release like I was some V.I.P. with the understanding that I would send the skull to the states. The truth is, the Mexican officials didn't really ever have any evidence, they never could find Villa's head to prove it. I had buried it, like bears do, when they take their prey apart and bury the rest for later. I had put the head in a little church yard, where it stayed, till I came and packed it up real good, like an expensive set of dishes. And that's when I sent to those fellas in New Haven. And I never had to prospect another day in my life. And frankly, I never could figure out why they would pay that kind of money, for that kind of rot.

Scene 2: Woman as the Temptress

A KNOCK IS HEARD. DANIEL OPENS THE MOTEL DOOR.

DANIEL: Yes. Can I help you?

JAIRO: May I come in?

DANIEL: I'm sorry. . .you have the wrong room.

JAIRO: Isn't this where the two of you meet. . .at this hour. . .every Thursday?

DANIEL: I think you're mistaking me for somebody else.

JAIRO: Tall, dark and lonesome 69?

DANIEL CANNOT RESPOND OR DENY.

You've been sleeping with my fiancée asshole.

DANIEL: You're definitely mistaking me for somebody else.

JAIRO: Please don't insult my intelligence.

DANIEL: I have no earthly idea who you are or what you're talking about.

JAIRO: I broke into her e-mails. I'm the one who e-mailed you last night telling you I was back in town. Isn't that why you're here? Thinking you'd be seeing Dolores at the usual time and place? But she's still out of town. Back in Texas.

DANIEL DOESN'T SAY ANYTHING BUT HE GESTURES FOR JAIRO TO COME INSIDE. JAIRO MANAGES TO ENTER WITHOUT INCIDENT BUT THE MOMENT HE WALKS INTO THE ROOM HE TURNS AROUND AND BELTS A HARD PUNCH TO DANIEL'S FACE KNOCKING HIM TO THE GROUND. IT HURTS JAIRO MORE THAN DANIEL.

JAIRO: Jesus to heaven and God.

*DANIEL THOUGH GRABS JAIRO'S FOOT AND
TRIPS HIM TO THE GROUND. THE TWO MEN
BEGIN TO WRESTLE IN A MESSY WAY.*

DANIEL: I told you. I don't know who you're
talking about.

JAIRO: Oh yeah.

DANIEL: Yeah. I don't know your fiancé.

*THE WRESTLING CONTINUES ALONG WITH
GROANS AND SOUNDS OF STRUGGLE.
DANIEL FINALLY HAS JAIRO PINNED DOWN.*

I don't know a Dolores, alright? I know a dark
haired woman with no past. No name.

No fucking story. . .you understand?

JAIRO: So you meet someone here every week. . .
right?

DANIEL: Yes. I have.

JAIRO: And you came today because you thought
she'd be here.

DANIEL: (Daniel hesitates.)Yes.

*THE SCUFFLE BEGINS AGAIN. AGAIN DANIEL
GETS THE UPPER HAND. JAIRO IS IN PAIN.*

JAIRO: That fucking hurts.

DANIEL: Yeah?

JAIRO: I can't breathe.

DANIEL: If I let you loose. . . we're done with the punches you understand?

JAIRO: I understand.

THEY STARE AT EACH OTHER DEFIANTLY FOR A MOMENT.DANIEL FINALLY LETS GO. JAIRO STAYS ON THE FLOOR   RECOVERING. DANIEL PULLS AWAY TO RECOVER HIMSELF

I can't believe she never told you about me.

DANIEL SHAKES HIS HEAD.

That fucking bitch.

DANIEL: We don't talk.

JAIRO IS ABOUT LUNGE AT DANIEL AGAIN BUT THIS TIME DANIEL GRABS THE CHAIR QUICKLY AS IF TO SAY 'I'LL CRACK THIS ON YOUR HEAD.

We don't ever speak. I'm warning you. That's our agreement. To not say a word to the other.

JAIRO: But you had to speak to meet. For the first time?

DANIEL: I placed a personal ad in the Voice for a single woman.

JAIRO: She answered a personal? Oh my fucking God. We've been together seven years. You think you know someone.

DANIEL: Can you ever really know anybody?

JAIRO: Shut the fuck up.

DANIEL: Look. . .

JAIRO: I'm sorry. I'm way out of line. Way out of character. Way out of my league, you understand? I'm a fucking psychotherapist for heaven's sake. I've always done. . .the right think, okay? And this. . .is. . .well, it didn't used to be the right thing. . . .I'm not so sure it's the right thing now. But. . .here I am. Losing my fucking mind. I've never been in so much pain. Never. Not even when my mother died. I'm sorry.

DANIEL: I'm sorry.

JAIRO: Go on. Please.

DANIEL: I asked for a single woman. I assumed.
. . .

JAIRO: Right. And for the record. . .we're
separated. Are you in love with her?

DANIEL: I'm not involved with her. . .in that way.

JAIRO: But you're. . .(in great pain.)

DANIEL: We have sex. Yes.

*JAIRO HAS YET ANOTHER REFLEX. DANIEL
REACHES FOR THE CHAIR. JAIRO FALLS TO
HIS KNEES WAILING. DANIEL WATCHES HIM.*

JAIRO: I don't know what it is. (between sobs) But
this woman. . .has fucking destroyed me. I mean
maybe its not even her. Maybe I'm finally. . . .(he
starts sobbing again) I didn't shed a single tear.
For my mother. I mean that's what I would tell
someone. Anyone. A client if they came to me
devastated. . .like this. Like Mr. Epstein. Last
week. . .when he came to my office for the first
time. . . .he'd never been to a therapist before. He
was just recounting the facts of his life. In fact he

was seeing me because his wife was making him. If he didn't get therapy she was leaving him. So there he was reporting that when his mother died. He didn't cry. So when he says to me: "I never mourned my mother" I look at him straight in the eye and I say to him: "You didn't have to. You married her." The look on the poor man's face. What people do years and years of therapy for. To get that one big "ah ha." And he got it. Right there in one session. And with that one response. From me. He could cry for the first time in twenty years. And how did I know to say the one perfect thing? I was talking to myself. That's all. I didn't marry Dolores. But now that's she's left me. It's my mother dying all over again. And this time. . . .(he starts to wail again.) I can finally feel her absence. But now. . .to add insult to injury. . . you don't even love Dolores.

DANIEL: I'm not saying that.

JAIRO: So do you?

DANIEL: What?

JAIRO: Love her asshole. I'm sorry. I'll refrain from the name calling. I'm sorry.

DANIEL: At those times. . .when she's right here. . .standing right in front me. . .maybe. Yes. Maybe I feel that kind of affection. But since we don't say a word.

JAIRO: Wait, wait. . .wait. Please. You don't say a word. . .literally?

DANIEL NODS.

I just thought you meant. . .we don't talk. . .we just fuck.

DANIEL: Well we do.

JAIRO: No. (Jairo slams something hard. Finally he regains himself.) I meant. . .because we fuck all the time. . .whose got time to talk. I thought that that was what you were saying.

DANIEL: Oh. . .I see.

JAIRO: Is that what you mean?

DANIEL: We stare at each other. For long periods of time. Is that what you mean?

JAIRO: Instead of fucking?

DANIEL: Along with. . .or after. And. . .before. Since we don't talk. . .I don't. . .I didn't. . .even know her name. Till you said it.

JAIRO: Unbelievable. So you don't know anything about her?

DANIEL: I know about her crazy great, great grandfather in Texas.

JAIRO: What great, great grandfather in Texas?

DANIEL: Her dead relatives. The guy they're building the museum about. Her great, great grandfather.

JAIRO: I don't know about a great, great grandfather. You see what I mean. You already know parts of Dolores. . .that I don't know anything about.

DANIEL: I just told you what I know. In total. And that's because of the e-mails. But that's it. Really.

JAIRO: That's fucking unbelievable. I get her bad mouthed self. For seven years. I get all the stories she uses to keep distance between us. Day in and day out. You know what I mean? The day in and day out crap we can disagree about. Like who picks up the clothes at the cleaners or whose suppose to take the trash out. Crap, nothing but crap bullshit. So that we don't have to deal with each other anew. You know what I mean? And then you. . .get the best of her. In bed. I mean I'm assuming she lets herself go there. She's a fucking. . .goddess in bed or was. Till we started living together. I mean have you ever even disagreed with her?

DANIEL: About?

JAIRO: Exactly. If you're not talking to each other. . .what is there to disagree about? That's what I'm saying. I get all her disagreements. Because of all the talk we've done. I ought to fucking kill you.

DANIEL REACHES FOR THE CHAIR ONE MORE TIME JUST IN CASE.

JAIRO: I mean. . .I'm not going to. Okay? I've already done it. Right here. (points to his head) I priced the gun and everything.

THEY STARE AT EACH OTHER FOR A MOMENT.

JAIRO: I can't fucking believe it. You've had the best of her.

DANIEL: I don't know if that's . . .

JAIRO: If you kept coming back here to have her. Please. Give me that. That's all I'm saying.

THEY STARE AT EACH OTHER FOR A LONGER MOMENT.

JAIRO: I'm sorry. . .for barging in here. And if I did any damage.

DANIEL: (Daniel touches the bruise on his face.) It took me back. To grade school. It's fine.

JAIRO: I should really be thanking you. . .I'm sure.

DANIEL SHRUGS.

JAIRO: I'm serious. I see exactly now what happened. I lost Dolores over time. And I see why.

DANIEL: I'm not interested in her that way. I have no intention of continuing my relationship with her.

JAIRO: Why?

DANIEL: Because. I know too much about her now. Too much that would get in the way--- eventually.

JAIRO: Not if you don't talk about it.

DANIEL: Even if we didn't talk ever. . . .there's you.

JAIRO: But we're not together. . .she and I. . .we're done.

DANIEL: It doesn't matter. You're part of the picture now. I couldn't be with her. . .without taking you into consideration. I'm not interested in her story. . .you understand?

JAIRO: Story? What the hell are you talking about?

DANIEL: I have a story now. About you. And her now. And. . .it's no longer just about her and me.

JAIRO: Now wait a second. You don't have to disqualify her because of me.

DANIEL: Disqualify her?

JAIRO: I mean. . .she's quite the woman. . .

DANIEL: I'm just saying. . .you're the end of the story. Between she and I. You're the end of it. Everything has a beginning, a middle and an end. To go beyond the natural "end" of anything. . .is to not be in reality with it. Had it not been you. . .it would have been something else. Somebody else. Maybe death itself in time. Even if she and I had met every Thursday till one of us passed away. . .we would still have passed away. . .from the other. I didn't seek her out in the first place to keep her. . . .to make a habit out of her, you understand?

JAIRO: If I disturbed something significant. Between the two of you. . .it's not right. Really.

DANIEL: You didn't disturb anything. You just defined it. And when something is defined. . .it's over and done with. That's all.

The two men stare at each other as the lights go out.

Scene 7: The Meeting with the Goddess

(Emil, in long johns, begins the slow, meticulous task of putting on his new, improved military outfit.)

EMIL HOLMDAHL: I tell you what. . . the way men and women found each other in Mexico was different than anything I had ever seen. When a man and a woman fell in love they would fly to each other without the formalities of a courtship---and when they tired of each other, they simply parted. Marriage was costly (six pesos to the priest) and was considered a very swatter extra and it was no more binding than a casual attachment. But of course jealousy was a stabbing matter. But more often than not, if a girl caught a man's fancy, he slipped a lover's note into her hand as she went by and she answered with a smile if she liked him. That meant meeting later, a long talks in the darkness and then they would be lovers. But it was a delicate business, this handing of notes. Every man carried a gun and every man's girl was his jealously guarded property. It was a killing matter to hand a note to someone else's girl. But it was hard to tell with the Mexican gals out on the field because they were soldiers. . .doing their share of the battle sometimes <u>and</u> the field work out there. They'd carry the water jugs on their heads and when they would unwind their shawls, they'd be carrying around this heavy little stone trough that they would husk the corn into. That to one side and a rifle to the other. One time I run into this very dark skinned Indian girl, about twenty five years old, with the squat figure of her race, pleasant enough features, hair hanging over her shoulders in two long braids, big shining teeth when she smiled. . .and I never knew if she had been a peon woman working when the attack had come or whether she was a camp follower. But I saw this one girl trudging behind the Captain who never spoke to her, never looked back. When he'd get tired of carrying his rifle he'd hand it back to her, for her to carry. . . .somebody later said that he had found her earlier that day wandering around aimlessly after the battle, apparently out of her mind. But needing a woman, the Captain had ordered her to follow him. Which she did, without question, which was the custom of her sex and country. On this day, I happen to be walking past her when she says to me, "Listen *senor*, whoever you are! My lover was killed yesterday in the battle. This man. . .(meaning the Captain). . .is my man," she said, "but by God and all the saints, I can't sleep with him this night. Let me stay then with you." Now I wasn't getting that she was being a coquette with me. With her dead lover barely in the ground, and me being nothing to her and she nothing to me. . . .that was all that mattered. So she starts walking with me when we hear "Where you going?" It was the Captain. "I'm going with this *senor*. I'm going to stay with him. To which the Captain says to me, "*Oiga, senor.* . .this is my woman here!" And I'm standing there stuck in the middle so I say "she looks pretty tired to me and not well. I've offered her my bed for the night." "Oh. . . but that is very bad, *senor*." But then in a loud voice from this little tiny little woman I hear her say to him "Until the next time, *senor*!" And then she grabs my arm and pulls me away. I can still hear the captain behind us saying "I am telling the Colonel! This gringo has taken anyway my woman! It is terrible insult." But I hear the Colonel say very calmly back, "if they both want to go, I guess there isn't anything we can do about it, eh?"   But now here's the strange thing. As we walk past everyone, the soldiers and the wounded, they sit up and start making rough talk as if this was a marriage between us. It wasn't coarse talk. . .it more like happy talk. They were glad for us. So right then this old man leads us to this little house at the end of the camp. And from the looks of it they had put new linen on the bed, lit the candle in front of the altar of the Virgen and someone had even hung paper blossoms over the doorway. It made no difference to them who we were or what our relation was. Here was a man and a maid and to them it was a bridal. "May you have a happy night," the old man tells us and then he leads us to the room. So we get in there and she starts putting out the candles right away as we hear some music playing outside the window. Someone had actually hired the village orchestra to serenade us and I could hear them moving tables out of the way in the next house where the serenade was quickly becoming a *baile*, a dance for everyone else. So I'm starting to get pretty nervous about the whole thing. And then without any embarrassment she lays down beside me. Her hand reaches over for mine. She snuggles against my body and says, "Until morning." And that was it. She went right to sleep faster than I could say goodnight. When I woke up the next morning, she was gone. I later found her near the fire patting *tortillas* for the Captain's breakfast. And he was back to snapping orders to her about how late his breakfast was, saying we'd be leaving camp in an hour. "Are you going?" I ask her. "Seguro! she says. "He is my man."

(Emil shrugs.)

I was a little confused. . .of course. From the looks of it, she had forgotten her dead lover. And I. . . had. . .made it possible for her to get a good night's sleep.

Scene 5. Reward (Seizing the Sword)

(La Hacienda Nursing Home. Clara sits besides CARMEN STANSELL who sits up on her hospital bed. Carmen is played by the woman who earlier portrayed Esmeralda. Carmen is in her early fifties.)

CARMEN: I don't know why that strange man likes coming into my room like that. He just barges in. I'm going to have to call the police on him.

CLARA: He's your brother Jessie.

CARMEN: I don't have a brother.

CLARA: You have two sisters. And a brother. Jessie.

CARMEN: Are you my sister?

CLARA: No.

CARMEN: Who did you say you were again?

CLARA: Clara.

CARMEN: Clara. And how do I know you?

CLARA: We're in love, Carmen.

CARMEN: Women don't love other women. . .unless they're sisters. Are you my sister?

CLARA: If you want me to be. Yes. Can I hold your hand?

CARMEN: You're my sister. Of course.

CLARA TAKES CARMEN'S HAND. SHE STARES AT HER FOR A LONG MOMENT. FINALLY SHE TAKES CARMEN'S HAND AND KISSES IT GENTLY.

CLARA: I love you with all my heart.

CARMEN: Who did you say you were?

CLARA: I'm the one who loves you and takes care of you, sweetheart.

CARMEN: So you can tell that man. . .

CLARA: Your brother.

CARMEN: I don't have a brother. I'm talking about the man with red hair. He has to stop coming here. I know he dyes his own hair. That's why it's so damaged. You can see the horrible roots.

CLARA: Yes. You can.

CARMEN: You'll tell him. . .for me. . .not to come by here or I will have to call the police.

CLARA: I will. I will ask him to stop coming by.

CARMEN: You promise?

CLARA: I promise.

CARMEN: You have very soft hands.

CLARA: You can kiss my hand if you like?

PAUSE. AFTER A MOMENT CLARA TAKE CARMEN'S HAND AND KISSES IT.

CARMEN: I can smell the Jerkin's crème on your hands.

CLARA: I know.

THE TWO WOMEN SMILE TENDERLY AT ONE ANOTHER.

Can I kiss your cheek? We have to be very quiet about it.

CARMEN: Quiet as mice.

CARMEN NODS. CLARA LEANS OVER AND KISSES HER CHEEK.

CLARA: Do you like kisses on your mouth?

CARMEN NODS. CLARA OBLIGES.

CARMEN: You lips are very soft.

CLARA: Yours are very soft too.

CARMEN: Can you do that again?

CLARA: I can.

SHE DOES.

CARMEN: One more time for the road?

CLARA: One more time for the road.

CARMEN: One for the road.

THERE'S A KNOCK ON THE DOOR.

CLARA: Shhhhh. Remember you cannot tell anybody I'm here. It's a game remember?

CLARA QUICKLY HIDES. ANOTHER KNOCK.

VOICE (o.s.): It's Ruby, Carmen.

A NURSE POKES HER HEAD IN. RUBY THE NURSE IS PORTRAYED BY THE ACTRESS WHO PLAYED PATTI..

It's time for the lights to go out. Do you need anything before I put the lights out?

CARMEN: I'd like another kiss from my sister.

RUBY: I'll see what I can do. She called this morning.

THE NURSE TUCKS HER IN.

CARMEN: She's right here with me right now. Only I'm not suppose to say she's here.

RUBY: That will be our little secret then, yes?

CARMEN SMILES AND NODS.

Here's your medicine.

CARMEN TAKES IT.

That's very good. And now. . . it's time to turn the lights out, okay? It's bedtime.

CARMEN: Okay.

THE NURSE TURNS THE LIGHTS OUT.

RUBY: Now you have a good night, you hear?

CARMEN: I will, now that my sister is here. It's always a good night when she's here.

RUBY: That's good. I'm glad. Goodnight.

THE NURSE EXITS. AFTER A MOMENT,CLARA REAPPEARS.

CARMEN: You are so silly when you play hide and seek like that.

CLARA (very serious): And you are so naughty to tell her that I'm here.

CARMEN: Can I have another kiss? On the mouth?

CLARA: Only if we're very quiet.

SHE KISSES HER.

CLARA: I've got some medicine for you.

CARMEN: More medicine?

CLARA: Yes. I'm going to take some too.

CLARA POURS THEM BOTH SOME LIGUID.

It's not going to taste very good. But since we're both going to both take it, let's see who can drink it the fastest.

CARMEN: You look sad.

CLARA: I've never been happier. It makes me so happy to be with you. I want to always be with you.

CARMEN: Okay.

CLARA: So take the medicine.

CARMEN: You said we would take it together?

CLARA: Yes. Okay. . .but you have to close your eyes.

CARMEN CLOSES THEM.

Are you ready? Get set. . .go!

CARMEN DRINKS UP THE LIQUID, CLARA DOES NOT.

CARMEN: Oh my God! That is the ugliest tasting medicine I have ever taken.

CLARA: It's pretty bad. Here's some water to chase it down.

CARMEN: I feel like I want to throw up.

CLARA: Don't throw it up. Chew on this. It's peppermint gum. It will help settle your tummy.

CARMEN TAKES IT AND CHEW IT UP QUICKLY.

CLARA: Would you like to play another game?

CARMEN: The one we play in the dark?

CLARA: The one we play in the dark.

CLARA PUTS THE LIGHT OUT.

CARMEN: I like this game. Very much.

CLARA GETS INTO CARMEN'S BED AS THE STAGE LIGHTS GO OUT EXCEPT ON EMIL WHO KNOW SHINES HIS SHOES.

EMIL: Pancho Villa had at least twenty two wives. That's how the American papers liked to tell it but as far as I know, he had only two. One that had been with him since his outlaw days. She stayed in El Paso once he was a revolutionary. The other is the one I would see. She was this cat-like, slender young girl, who ran his house in Chihuahua. He was pretty open about this fact. It wasn't till the more educated, conventional Mexicans started to gather around him that they tried to hush up the fact but among the peons, it was not only usual but customary to have more than one mate. I asked one of his closer companions one day, if it was true that Villa violated women the way the papers said he would and his compadre said, "He never takes the trouble to deny such stories. They say he's a bandit, too. But tell me, have you ever met a husband, father or brother of any woman that he's violated? Or even a witness?" And I really couldn't say I had. There was a young reporter that was traveling with us at the time and he asked Villa one day if Mexican women would be able to vote in the new Republic of Mexico? What do you mean vote, Villa asked. Do you mean elect a government and make laws? The reporter explained to him that women were already doing that in the United States. Well, if they are doing it in the United States, I don't see that they shouldn't do it down here too. He seemed very amused by the question. "It may be as you say," he said, "but I have never thought about it. Women seem to me to be things to protect, to love. They have no stern of mind. They can't consider anything for its right or wrong. They are full of pity and softness. A woman would never give an order to execute a traitor.: "I'm not so sure about that, mi General," I piped up. Women can be crueler and harder than men." I don't know why I said that, but I did. "Maybe the gringas are like what you are saying." In that moment, his wife was setting the table. "Olga," he said, "come here. Listen. Last night I caught three traitors crossing the river to blow up the railroad. What shall I do with them? Shall I shoot them or not?" She took his hand and kissed it and said, "Oh, I don't know anything about that. You know best." "No," he said, "I leave it entirely to you. They were traitors, federales. . .what shall I do? Should I shoot them or not?" "Oh well, shoot them," she says. I had never seen Villa laugh so hard. "There is something in what that gringo says," he told everybody! And that's the most that we ever said to one another.

Scene: 6 The Road Back

NEXT MORNING. DOLORES IS ON THE PHONE IN CLARA'S OFFICE.

DOLORES: I'm just trying to get somebody to check the apartment upstairs. That's all. Maybe even save you a few dollars. Look. . .I can't do anything more than that. I'm in Texas right now. Please call me back.

HANGS UP THE PHONE AS CLARA ENTERS. CLARA HAS BEEN UP ALL NIGHT AND LOOKS IT. SHE'S WEARING THE SAME CLOTHES TODAY.

My fucking landlord. The ceiling to our apartment is caving in. Water is pouring down into our place. And I can't get anybody to deal with it. Apparently my ex is having a nervous breakdown.

CLARA: I brought you some coffee. And some Mexican sweet bread.

DOLORES: Thank you.

CLARA: I don't have much of an appetite right now. Thanks.

DOLORES: Are you alright?

CLARA: I know what steps I want to take for myself. Under the circumstances. So yes, I'm doing good, thanks.

DOLORES: Well. . .good.

CLARA: And you want to know something else? If I had to do it all again, all of it, I would do it exactly the same way.

DOLORES: Not everybody can say that.

CLARA: No they can't. And if it's alright with you, I'd like to clear the air if I could. I'd feel better about it anyway.

DOLORES: Okay. Sure.

CLARA: The story in the paper isn't accurate.

DOLORES: I didn't think it was.

CLARA: Carmen, my girlfriend, has her wits about her. I figure you're from New York so I can talk pretty straightforwardly to you about our relationship. People are out there. But down here, it's not the same. That's why her family wants everyone to believe that Carmen doesn't function at all.

DOLORES: And Carmen is your girlfriend.

CLARA: Yes, the woman. . .at the nursing home. That they say I. . .violated. She went to the nursing home after she had a stroke. . .it affected her memory, of course. But she's doesn't have

Alzheimer's. Yet. She's in the earliest stages, I guess.

DOLORES: Oh I see.

CLARA: I volunteer at the nursing home. That's how we met. We very quickly became friends. And then we started to have deeper exchanges. . .together. But I never forced myself on her, like they're saying. It was an exchange. Between two consenting adults. That's exactly what happened. And just because she doesn't remember things. . her family is insisting that I. . .took advantage of her.

DOLORES: So Carmen remembers you? When you visit? My mother, the one that raised me, had Alzheimer's.

CLARA: Carmen doesn't have Alzheimer's.

DOLORES: I'm sorry, I was just trying to say that my mother had memory challenges. She would ask me who I was every time I visit.

CLARA: Yes. Carmen does that. Maybe she doesn't remember every detail about our exchange. But we love each other very much.

And that. . .is what they want to ignore. Or avoid. Or at least deny.

DOLORES: What do you mean she doesn't remember every detail?

CLARA: She doesn't know what they're talking about right now. If you try to ask her about it.

DOLORES: So how did they even know. . .an exchange happened?

CLARA: I told them. When they started to treat me like I didn't exist. What difference does it make that she didn't have memories like everyone else? Does that mean she doesn't have needs or a soul anymore? I mean Carmen knows that her memory is. . .challenged. She's still coping with the aftermath of the stroke so for her a degree of denial is essential. Together we're like two people drinking hot coffee together. We sip the truth of her condition gently. And while its true that one day Carmen is able to do something and the next day she's not. . . we spend a lot of time enjoying the moments when she can do something. And that's how we fell in love in the first place. She's only 58 years old. She told me when we first met, "I don't know who I am, I don't know. It comes and it goes." But since I didn't know her before.

Before the car accident. That's what brought the stroke on. I only knew who she was now. It didn't really matter to me whether she knew who she was, you know what I mean? And I think that's what her family objects to. They look at her and say: you're not yourself. But what is that? The self they don't recognize is the self I'm in love with. Does that make any sense at all?

DOLORES: Oddly. . .yes. I'm having a similar relationship right now with someone. We're not memory challenged but. . .I'm sorry, I'm interrupting. Please. . .go on.

CLARA: This is a woman who never had. . .a. . pleasurable experience, you know what I mean? For fifty eight years! Not until she and I . . .went there. Together. I'm not taking credit for that, I'm just saying. . .in her case. . .because she was able to forget who she was before. She was able to respond to me genuinely. With her whole body. And not have her mind get in the way. You know what I mean?

DOLORES: I do. I really do. The relationship I was talking about. We leave the mind out of it as much as we can.

CLARA: Really. . .

DOLORES: He's an acquaintance, a friend with whom I have no immediate history with, I guess you could say.

CLARA: How do you manage that?

DOLORES: We don't talk about. . .who we are. We don't talk. We email but we try to keep, as much as possible, to the where and when. To plan our next time together.

CLARA STARES AT HER.

Does Carmen remember her other family members?

 CLARA: Not really. But she always remembers who I am. If it was Alzheimer's. . .or the beginning of. . . I'm not naïve. I know that the disease eventually destroys her personality. I took care of my aunt till she died and she definitely had Alzheimer's. So when my girlfriend's doctor tells me that she might someday become violent or try to hit the road without me.

DOLORES: And that definitely happens. I lost my mother one time. She just took off. We found her on a ferry boat.

CLARA: I guess what I meant was, that when the doctor says she's going to hit the road without me, I say to him: isn't that true for everyone? At some point. We can't know that someone's gonna stay with us even if they have their memory, you know? It's not like there's any guarantees with anybody. . .even without the memory loss.

DOLORES: So. . .what's the problem then? Why the charges?

CLARA: They have charged me with rape because Carmen doesn't remember details and the details are what they keep asking her about, they're saying that constitutes rape.

DOLORES: Details like. . .

CLARA: How it all came to pass.

DOLORES: Did somebody catch you. . . .

CLARA: No. I was the one who told her daughter.

DOLORES: You told her daughter. . . what?

CLARA: That I had spent the night with her. This was after she was released from the nursing home for a time. . .shortly after her accident. We had only recently consummated our relationship. In her home. But now they've readmitted Carmen as of last week. . .saying her disease is progressing too quickly now and that they don't want her living by herself. They're saying she can't take care of herself. But the truth is they know I'd be over there. With her at house. If they didn't commit her. And since they're Baptists with a lot of political pull in this community.

DOLORES: That's terrible.

CLARA: Yeah. And now on top of that,   the museum is taking the brunt of it. . .after I've worked so hard on making your grandfather's place a reality. I've been focused on that house for two years. And we're this close to making it happen.

DOLORES: That's terrible.

CLARA: It's the malicious publicity I hate. Its hurting my credibility as a professional person. And it couldn't be worse timing for the museum. I'm really sorry about that most of all. Because for me personally. . .it's a done deal.

DOLORES: Meaning. . .

CLARA: I wasn't going to just sit here and watch them take the little bit of life and happiness left in her and have them imprison it at that filthy place.

DOLORES: But maybe. . .as far as the museum goes. . .considering what you've told me about my grandfather, maybe the publicity is a good thing right now. You can take it and use it for your own cause.

CLARA: I don't know about that. It seems to be making it worse. Somebody sprayed painted the side of your great grandfather's house. . .the museum last night. Something about Satan and sodomy.

DOLORES: Is this considered the Bible belt. . . down here?

CLARA: Not really. This town is way bellow the belt. . .so to speak. It's just a superstitious little town. Hypocritical, about "funny" people. That's what they call gays down here. "Funny." Somebody egged my car a couple of days ago. And then smeared dog shit on top of that. And I have an idea who it was too. And the really sad thing is that person crosses lines himself. With the truckers passing through town. So that's what I'm talking about. When you can't accept who you are. . . .you start to do damage to other people you think are doing what you're not admitting.

DOLORES: Say that again.

CLARA: What?

DOLORES: What you just said! When you can't accept who you are. . . .

CLARA: You start to do damage to other people you think are doing the very thing you're not admitting.

DOLORES: Oh my God, Clara. You have no idea how true that is.

CLARA: But so what? What I've been building through this museum. . .it's what I've wanted to do for my whole life. And now its all gone.

DOLORES: But it's not gone.

CLARA: The main funding, a private donor. . .has pulled out. She's afraid of the 60 Minutes story, they came to her house. She wants nothing to do with it. That means we don't get the matching funds. So yes, it's over and done with. I brought you out here for nothing. There's no opening. No nothing. That's what I came to tell you. It's all being cancelled.

DOLORES: I don't care about that. That's what I'm trying to tell you. I'm sorry for you, all your hard work. All the time.

CLARA: I took care of Carmen, Dolores.

DOLORES: That's good then.

CLARA: I made sure she was taken care of. .Now I just have to take care of myself.

DOLORES: That's true for all of us!

CLARA: I have no choice. . .now.

THE TWO WOMEN STARE AT EACH OTHER AS THE LIGHTS GO OUT.

Act III: Return

Scene I: Resurrection

PATTI SITS ALONE IN THE DARK IN JAIRO AND DOLORES' PLACE. SHE'S BEEN DRINKING. AFTER A MOMENT, JAIRO ENTERS AND FLIPS ON THE LIGHTS.

JAIRO: Jesus to heaven and God!

PATTI: It's me! I'm sorry. I let myself in.

JAIRO: You nearly gave me a heart attack. I thought you were Dolores.

PATTI: I thought you were going to say a burglar. That you thought I was a burglar.

JAIRO: Same thing. (notices Patti is tipsy) Are you alright?

PATTI: Yeah! Why?

JAIRO: Have you been drinking, Patti? I've never known you to drink.

PATTI: You've never known me then. (Pause.) Dolores was right. She was right all along.

JAIRO: About?

PATTI: Everything. You. Hector. Me.

JAIRO: I don't know about that.

PATTI: Hector fucks whores, Jairo. The same whore. Regularly. When he says he's in his studio working.

JAIRO: How do you know that?

PATTI: I took her out to lunch. The whore.

JAIRO: You took the whore to lunch? Patti, how much have you drank?

PATTI: Remember the day I was over here and you were showing me the holy water and you said Hector never touched me.

JAIRO: I'm really sorry about that. I had no right to say that.

PATTI: But it was true. He doesn't touch me anymore. So anyway. . .I drove directly to his studio. He was out of town. I never go there. I have no reason to. Or maybe I just never wanted to. . .know what I know now. Anyway, I let myself in, to his studio and I started to look around. Really look. . .like you were talking about that night. Really see things. Hear them. So the first thing I notice is the phone machine blinking. It had several messages. . .he'd only been gone a day right? And supposedly he'd been working at his studio the night before he left so who in the hell would be calling him? Maybe it was some kind of emergency. I should make sure. So I hit the play button and I hear this woman say, "Hey hot stuff. . .It's Tuesday. . .are we meeting up?"

JAIRO: You're kidding.

PATTI: And so she leaves her number right? And she had already left more than one message and I could just tell that it was a business arrangement between them. . .albeit it. . .sexual of course. . .so- - -I can't believe I did this. But I did.

JAIRO: What?

PATTI: I call her number and I say I'm a friend of Hector's. A journalist. And I'm writing a piece about prostitution. Would she be willing to talk to me?

JAIRO: But how did you know she was a prostitute?

PATTI: I didn't. I just had a hunch. I figure if she wasn't a whore, I'd just hang up, right?

JAIRO: Wow! I'm impressed.

PATTI: Why?

JAIRO: I just didn't picture you. . .

PATTI: Being a pathological liar?

JAIRO: Exactly. It's very sexy.

SHE GIVES HIM A LOOK.

I mean. . .you are. Sexy. And I don't know why I'm saying that right now. I'm sorry.

PATTI: I actually appreciate it though. Maybe that's why. You're saying it. Thank you.

JAIRO: When you lie like that. . .I mean it.

PATTI: Mean what?

JAIRO: It doesn't matter. Go on. Please.

PATTI: What has happened to you?

JAIRO: What do you mean?

PATTI: You're just saying whatever comes to your mind these days.

JAIRO: I'm finally telling the truth. So of course I would love a liar. That's all. Please. I'm joking. Go on.

PATTI: 'kay. So she agrees to meet me. The whore woman. And I interview her about what she does. She tells me about the ins and outs of her job. . .(she bursts out laughing at the pun!)

JAIRO: That's pretty good.

PATTI: Yeah. And I'm not even trying. And then at some point I say. . .so with a client like Hector, for example. . .and then she just goes off about him.

JAIRO: You're kidding.

PATTI: She thinks we're friends and that I probably know all about him anyway. So she explains they have a weekly arrangement and have for the last couple of years. And it turns out her name is Tuesday.

JAIRO: Oh my God. . .

PATTI: So on her messages when she says, "Hi. . it's Tuesday" I'm thinking she's got an arrangement like Dolores does with that guy.

JAIRO: So you did know.

PATTI: What?

JAIRO: About the guy.

PATTI: Yeah.

JAIRO: So you are a liar.

PATTI: Jairo. She made me promise.

JAIRO: It doesn't matter anymore. Go on. Can you share what she said about Hector.

PATTI: Well it's not even just about Hector, from the way she made it sound. She talked about men like she was an expert. How they need to have a fantasy life and she plays those roles out for them. At some point she asks me if I'm married. I say yes. And she says. Look, no offense. . .but what you're wearing isn't gonna do it for him, okay? Check me out. . .and she stands up (Patti stands up) and shows me how her outfit is geared exactly for what he. ..and everyone like him. . .is going to go for.

JAIRO: And what is that? Cause as far as I'm concerned. . .what you're wearing right now. . works for me.

PATTI: Really?

JAIRO: Oh yeah.

PATTI: You're always so sweet to me, Jairo.

JAIRO: Not really. I'm just telling you how it is.

PATTI: I mean, maybe if it was a little shorter. . .

SHE RAISES HER SKIRT UP A LITTLE AND THEN PUSHES UP HER BREASTS SO THAT SHE SUDDENLY HAS CLEAVAGE.

. . .and I was flaunting it. . .you wouldn't like that even more?

JAIRO: Ah. It would scare me to death actually. In a good way, don't get me wrong. Yes. . .I'd like it...definitely. But more. . .(hesitates) possibly.

PATTI RAISES HER SKIRT UP. SHE UNBUTTONS HER BLOUSE AND PUSHES UP HER CLEAVAGE AGAIN.

What are you doing?

PATTI: What I should have done the first time I saw you?

JAIRO: Patti. . .you've been drinking, probably a little bit too much I'm thinking. . .and you're probably a little bit in shock right now.

PATTI: Shut up, Jairo. Don't start turning psychotherapist on me. That's what ruined your relationship with Dolores.

JAIRO: You're right. I'm sorry.

PATTI: Talk dirty to me instead.

JAIRO: Patti. . .you're definitely scaring me.

PATTI: Good. I'm scaring myself. I'm feeling alive for the first time in twenty years. Talk dirty to me. Now.

BLACK OUT EXCEPT FOR A SPOT OF EMIL WHO IS VERY METICULOUSLY GETTING INTO HIS SOLDIER GEAR.

EMIL: On one occasion, the priest of the hacienda church. . .they were called the *cura*. . .sat at the head of the table and lead the meal like it was a church service. But first he got the best *viands*, helping himself first, sometimes passing what he didn't want along to the rest of us. Everyone there, especially the priest, was drinking *sotal*, when I notice that he's making away with the whole bottle of looted *anisette*. And this was after he had started to talk about the virtues of the confessional, especially where young girls were concerned. He made it known that he possessed certain feudal rights over the new brides. "The girls here are very passionate," he started to brag but that's when I notice how deadly quiet the room was getting. Even the drunk priest sobered up pretty quick when he saw all the soldiers staring at him. So he excuses himself but he hasn't even left the room when one of soldiers starts hollering: "I know that dirty son of a *puta* and my

sister. . . .!" he didn't finish what he had to say.
He starts banging his fists on the table! Mad as a
hornet! "The *Revolucion* will have something to
say about these *curas*!" It was no secret that Villa
hated the *curas* and the Catholic church. And that
the church was one of the first things Villa was
going to get rid of. But it was on this particular
occasion that I noticed this rather unusual woman
for the first time, sitting off the side. Young,
slender woman. .handsome on the outside. She
would sit and write long, long letters, keeping to
herself on every occasion. And when we would
get to the next town, she would round up all the
women together and sometimes they would ride
off. . .we wouldn't see any of them for days. The
reporter told me later she would take the women
across the border to the US and then speak out on
her political beliefs about the revolution while the
ladies cheered her on. She would pass out
pamphlets to the crowds. Even after reading it
more than once, I still couldn't get what she was
talking about. It went right past my abilities. I
remember one pamphlet in particular, it was
called "La Mujer Moderna" (the modern woman)
and even though I wasn't much of the ladies man.
. . I mean she was womanly in her soldier attire
and all, even if I never saw her smile and never

heard say a gentle word. I could tell she was poison to you if you tried to make conversation with her, if you were a man. . . I knew to stay away from her too because if anybody would have been able to get me to work for them without having to pay me anything for it. . .it would have been this gal. I later heard she got arrested on the American side for saying it was "the rich Americanos who wanted to rob the Mexicans, just like the rich Mexicans wanted to rob the poor ones." She was all ready to get hung when at the last minute President Taft set her free. It made all the papers at the time And I tell you what. She made the papers for all the same reasons I am talking about. There's nothing more dangerous than a woman who can act and even look like a pretty man and still. . . when you really look at her---she makes your legs feel like taffy at the knees. That's what this gal was capable of. She was dangerous to every man she ever knew.

Scene 2. Return with the Elixir

DOLORES IS ALL PACKED. SHE SITS ON ONE OF HER BAGS, WAITING. FINALLY A KNOCK ON THE DOOR.

DOLORES: Clara. Is that you?

FRANCISO: It's Francisco Ramirez. We met at the museum.

DOLORES LETS HIM IN.

DOLORES: I'm afraid I don't have much time. Clara is picking me up and driving me to the airport.

FRANCISO: I'm the next of kin so they called me to come. Clara isn't coming.

DOLORES: Next of kin to who?

FRANCISO: You. Apparently Clara was found this morning. Dead.

DOLORES: What?

FRANCISO: She blew her head off.

DOLORES: What?

FRANCISO: They found her dead in the parking lot at the nursing home. But first she poisoned the poor invalid woman at the nursing home that she was abusing.

DOLORES: She never abused her.

FRANCISO: I tried to tell you that woman was psycho.

DOLORES IS IN TOTAL SHOCK. SHE SITS DOWN.

The museum wanted me to drive you to the airport. I have a bad back otherwise I would offer to carry your bags.

DOLORES: I just need to sit down for a moment.

PAUSE.

Is there a shuttle I can take?

FRANCISO: Look. . .it's the least I can do.

DOLORES: I don't want to inconvenience you.

FRANCISO: Since I'm the next of. . .kin. It's the least I can do.

DOLORES: We're not even related.

FRANCISO: I was your mother's stepfather.

DOLORES: A mother I barely know. That I just met. She's a total stranger to me.

FRANCISO: But she's your blood.

DOLORES: I guess.

FRANCISO: There's no guessing to do about it.

DOLORES: Look. . .I'd rather catch a shuttle, really.

FRANCISO: Did she ever talk to you about. . . your father?

DOLORES: No. I consider my real parents my adopted parents.

FRANCISO: But she's your blood. Blood is. . .the real thing whether you like it or not. Its what decides who you are. How you are. And how you're going to be.

DOLORES: Look. I think I'd like to change my reservation. And spend a little more time. . .digesting everything. If you don't mind, I'd like to be alone right now.

FRANCISO: If you could meet your father, would you do it? Wouldn't you think it would explain a few things? About yourself to yourself? I mean why did you bother coming out here to find out about this great, great grandfather if you didn't care about that sort of thing.

DOLORES: I wanted a vacation, okay?

FRANCISO: It was all about the gold pieces then.

DOLORES: The gold pieces? Oh God no. That will never be resolved. I don't expect to get a single cent of that.

FRANCISO: They're going to be worth thousands and thousands of dollars, you do understand that?

DOLORES: Look. . .it's. . .all too much for me right now. So no. . .I mean, if I knew I was inheriting some money. . .no strings attached sure, I'd take it. Same thing with my dad. . .if I knew he existed. Sure. . .I guess it wouldn't hurt to know who he was but I'm not going out of my way to find out right now.

FRANCISO: Would you let drive you to the airport?

DOLORES: What?

FRANCISO: I don't think I'll ever understand what exactly happened to your mother. If I hadn't experienced it myself. . .I would not have believed it.

DOLORES: Experienced what?

FRANCISO: We don't ever decide who we love, Miss. . .can I call you Dolores?

DOLORES: Sure.

FRANCISO: I don't know whose name you took. Did you take your mother's name?

DOLORES: No. I told you, I never even knew Esmeralda was my mother.

ESMERALDA ENTERS ON CUE. AGAIN SHE DOES HER STRANGE, GHOSTLY WALK ON A TRACK LIKE BEFORE.

FRANCISO: I don't admire cowards. I detest them, you understand?

DOLORES: I'm sorry?

FRANCISO: I lost all dignity over this situation a long time ago. I would have been a totally different man had I been able to stand up for her. For your mother. I made her the shell she is. I hear she barely talks to anyone. And when you're with her it's like you're talking to a ghost. Is that true?

DOLORES: She's definitely quiet but. . .nice enough.

PAUSE.

FRANCISO: She was like a wild stallion when she was a kid. All fire. All graceful. She would look you in the eye. She was strong too. But I let her down. I denied her and the whole town the truth. I paid for her bus ticket and I threatened her to never, never come back. And I meant it. She knew I meant it. She left fearing for her life.

FRANCISCO SUDDENLY GETS VERY EMOTIONAL.

FRANCISO: I have never loved anyone as much as I loved that girl. And she wasn't even my blood, you understand? But nobody would have ever known it. Especially her. And when people force things, they say they do it out of hatred. I'm sure that's what she thought at the time because I never spoke to her about it. After that day. Even on that day. That one time we were all alone. We just knew to look at each other. I did everything I could to walk away from her but when she took my hand that way. And she kissed it.

DOLORES IS A LITTLE OVERWHELMED BY WHAT SHE THINKS SHE IS HEARING.

FRANCISO: Maybe if her mother hadn't disowned her . . .who knows? When she told her mother she was. . .with child. She didn't say who the father. We all thought it was one of the many young men that pursued her at that time. That's what I thought too. But when I drove her to the bus that day. And she told me . . .I had been the first. . . I didn't believe her. I slapped her. I called her horrible, horrible names and I told her never, never to come back.

HE BURSTS OUT CRYING LIKE A LITTLE BOY.

When I look at you now. . . .it's like I'm seeing her standing right there. Right now.

THE TWO SIT VERY QUIETLY TOGETHER FOR A LONG MOMENT AS ESMERALDA CONTINUES HER GHOSTLY PRANCE.

That's why I'm asking. Did you know who your father was?

DOLORES SHAKES HER HEAD.

And would you let him drive you to the airport? If you did?

LIGHTS FADE OUT SLOWLY.

Scene 3: The Magic Flight, too

DOLORES IS ON HER LAP TOP AT THE AIRPORT. SHE'S ON INSTANT MESSENGER.

DOLORES: Dear Tall, Dark and Lonesome 69:

Why aren't you responding to my e-mails?!!!!!!

SHE WAITS.

Alright then. . .I'll talk to myself. I'm headed back to New York City. I wanted to let you know that I won't be meeting you on Thursdays anymore.

DANIEL FINALLY RESPONDS.

DANIEL: Ditto.

DOLORES: So you are there! Hi! Is it something I said?

DANIEL LAUGHS.

DANIEL: Yes. But tell me more.

DOLORES: Why ditto?

DANIEL: I'm in agreement with you. No more Thursdays.

DOLORES: Why?

DANIEL: It just feels that way to me too.

DOLORES: I need the man I'm involved with to talk. On a daily basis.

DANIEL: You mean like your boyfriend.

DOLORES: Why do you say that?

DANIEL: He's pretty talkative.

DOLORES: He can be.

DANIEL: So are you? Going back to him?

DOLORES: If he'll have me back. Yes. (beat) I met my real dad. In South Texas.

DANIEL: Yeah?

DOLORES: I can't really tell you why or how. . .but somehow it changed everything. I wish I knew more than that. But I don't.

DANIEL: I met your boyfriend.

DOLORES: What?!!!!!!

DANIEL: He came to the hotel.

DOLORES: You're joking.

DANIEL: He punched me in the face.

DOLORES: Oh my God! How did he know where to find you?

DANIEL: Get him to tell you the gory details.

BOTH JUST STARE AT THEIR SCREEN UNABLE TO WRITE ANYTHING.

But since the rules have been broken.

DOLORES: What rules?

DANIEL: Bringing in some history. . .

DOLORES: Can it really be about you if its. . .

DANIEL: YES!

DOLORES: But I don't know any thing relative of yours.

DANIEL: My great, great grandfather fought with Pancho Villa. How do you like that?

DOLORES: But you're not Mexican. (pause) Are you?

DANIEL: No. And neither was Emil Holmdahl.

DOLORES: You're telling me your name.

DANIEL: I'm telling you <u>his</u> name. He was a soldier of fortune.

DOLORES: You mean he was paid to fight. (beat) I guess there's wilder. . .crazier things.

DANIEL: Like you.

DOLORES: Like you!! (beat) I'm going to miss you.

DANIEL: ----

DOLORES: I think I loved you. On Thursdays.

DANIEL: I think I loved you too. On Thursdays.

DOLORES: Should we be talking? I mean should we meet? To have closure?

DANIEL: No.

DOLORES: Why?

DANIEL: Because I want to love you. . .still. (beat) If we start talking we're liable to ruin everything we had.

DOLORES: You don't know that for sure.

DANIEL: Oh yes I do. I know myself.

NEITHER CAN WRITE ANYTHING FOR A LONG MOMENT.

DOLORES: Okay.

DANIEL: And. . . that also means no more e-mails.

DOLORES: Alright already! Go fuck yourself!

DANIEL: I'll have to.

DOLORES: I'm sorry.

DANIEL: But I'll think of you when I do.

DOLORES: I'm finding it hard to. . .stop. Writing.
I want to see you. Any suggestions?

DANIEL: No.

*THEY BOTH STARE AT THEIR SCREENS. AFTER
A MOMENT, SHE FINALLY TYPES.*

DOLORES: Okay then.

*DOLORES GETS EMOTIONAL. SHE LOGS OFF.
THE MESSAGE: "ESMERALDA BLUE IS NO
LONGER ON LINE" APPEARS. DANIEL STAYS
ON LINE A LITTLE BIT LONGER, STARING.
AFTER A MOMENT. . .HE TYPES.*

DANIEL: I really did. . .(he stops, erases and then
replaces it with) "do". I really do love you.

HE TYPES "ON THURSDAYS" AT FIRST. BUT THEN STOPS, ERASES AND THEN CORRECTS IT.

(repeats) I really do love you. . .whenever I think of you.

HE THEN LOGS OFF TOO. DANIEL AND DOLORES STAND IN THEIR SEPARATE SPOTLIGHTS. THEY SING: A SIGH DEEPER THAN WORDS.

DANIEL: If I have forgotten how to pray

Spirit comes

And prays on my behalf

In a sigh deeper than words.

DOLORES: What is it that I am asking?

To be earth,

ready to receive.

Even in its driest, hardest place

the ground remembers the rain.

Come.

Come, rain.

Come, shine.

Come in a sigh deeper than words

for words never had anything to say

to either of us.

DANIEL: I'm mouthing this prayer

knowing

Spirit comes

and says it aloud on our behalf.

In a sigh deeper than words.

DOLORES: Can you hear the feel of asking?

The innocence of wanting?

The delicate blossoms between us.

That

we've always understood.

What if there is a garden

where all of our roots meet?

The garden has an address

A location in time

DANIEL: If. . .

I have forgotten how to pray

Sprit comes and prays on my behalf.

DOLORES: Can you hear the compost of me?

The food I have become

All thrives in

Around me, eat.

Eat till you're full. . .

Eat till your fat

DOLORES and DANIEL: With all that is good between us.

Scene 4: Rescue from Without

DOLORES LETS HERSELF INTO JAIRO'S APARTMENT. A VERY RUMPLED JAIRO ENTERS WITH JUST A TOWEL AROUND HIS HIPS. HE'S SUDDENLY VERY NERVOUS.

JAIRO: I wasn't expecting you.

DOLORES: I wasn't expecting me either.

PATTI (offstage) : High! Can you grab the tequila while you're out there?

DOLORES AND JAIRO LOOK AT ONE ANOTHER.

DOLORES: Is that. . .Patti?

A LONG SILENCE. JAIRO STARES AT HIS FEET.

I'm impressed. I would have never thought she had it in her.

AFTER A MOMENT, PATTI ENTERS WRAPPED IN DOLORES' ROBE.

I'd rather you wear the blue terrycloth one. I'm kind of attached to that one.

PATTI: I'm sorry.

DOLORES: I am too.

PATTI: I'll go change.

DOLORES: I'm kidding.

JAIRO: I didn't expect you to come back.

DOLORES: I didn't either.

PATTI: Dolores, I'm really sorry.

DOLORES: I'm not. (she looks at both of individually) I'm not.

HE LETS HERSELF IN BY KICKING OFF HER SHOES AND MAKING HERSELF MORE COMFORTABLE.

I didn't think I would miss home. My home. But I did. (she looks at Jairo)

I do.

PATTI: I really should be going.

DOLORES: Please don't.

JAIRO: You think you can just let yourself in here and just start making yourself comfortable? Like nothing ever happened? Are you nuts? I met your psycho lover.

DOLORES: That's all over and done with.

I know. He didn't want anything to do with you.

I'm the one who broke it off with him.

JAIRO: Right. Just like you were the one to break it off with me. You always have to be the one in fucking control.

DOLORES: Are you two in love?

JAIRO: It's none of your fucking business.

DOLORES: I just wanted you to get this thing between you out of your systems, that's all. And now. . . I just want things to go back to normal.

JAIRO: Normal?

PATTI: Jairo. . .

JAIRO: Shut up. I mean. . .please Patti. . .can you stay out of this?

PATTI: It's a little late for that.

JAIRO: I'm sorry. But I'm talking to Dolores right now.

PATTI: I'll just get my things and go.

DOLORES: Don't go, Patti. Please. You're my best friend.

PATTI: I just fucked your boyfriend.

JAIRO: Ex-boyfriend.

PATTI: She's obviously here to reconcile.

JAIRO: Reconcile what? I can't reconcile this?

DOLORES: Jairo. . .please.

JAIRO: You were fucking a total stranger when we agreed to have "no contact" with each other and other people.

DOLORES: And Patti isn't other people?

JAIRO: All bets were off after I met your fling.

PATTI: I'm finally leaving Hector, Dolores.

DOLORES: So?

PATTI: And I'm not two-timing him. I just wanted you to know that.

DOLORES: So you want a gold metal or what? You mean he knows you're leaving him or now that you fucked Jairo. . .you know have to leave him but Hector doesn't have a clue yet? Which is it?

PATTI: He's been screwing the same whore for two years.

DOLORES: Because he loved you. What do you think? He didn't go starting a real relationship with someone. He chose a whore for God's sake. Don't you get it? He just wanted to get kinky.

PATTI: That's exactly what she said.

DOLORES: Who?

PATTI: The whore!

JAIRO: Takes one to know one.

DOLORES: Hector is crazy about you. Why do you think he has stayed this long?

PATTI: Well I'm sorry. I'm just old fashioned I guess. I require honesty. At the very least fidelity.

DOLORES: How can you expect anybody to be honest with you when you aren't even honest with yourself?

JAIRO: Who made you the judge of her, Dolores?

DOLORES: And who made you her protector? Oh. I see. I get it. You two can idealize each other to death and call it honesty. Fine. Fuck you both.

JAIRO: You've got some nerve, that's all.

DOLORES: Yeah. That's about all I've got.

SHE GRABS HER THINGS AND STARTS TO HEAD FOR THE DOOR.

PATTI: I'm not in love with Jairo, Dolores. (to Jairo) I love you, yes. . .but not that way.

JAIRO: What exactly were you doing in that bedroom with me then? What is it you were saying to me?

PATTI: What I'm saying now is. . .I love my husband. I just wanted to understand what he's needing from that whore. I wanted to be that with someone else.

JAIRO: A fucking whore?

PATTI: Yeah. So I could let him off the hook.

JAIRO: Well congratulations. And fuck you both. Get the hell out of my apartment.

DOLORES: Our apartment.

JAIRO: My apartment. My lawyer is calling you now that you're back.

DOLORES: Jairo. . .please. Can I at least tell you what I've been through? What I have realized at least?

JAIRO: Pay somebody else to listen. I'm not going to be the one to do it for free.

DOLORES: I love you. I finally know that. That's what I have come to realize.

JAIRO: I don't need that kind of love, Dolores? That's what I have realized. Not from either of you. I'm asking you nicely. . .get the fuck out of here. Both of you before I call the police.

HE STOMPS OUT.

LIGHTS FADE.

Scene 5. Master of the Two Worlds

THE ACTOR WHO PORTRAYED DOLORES' GREAT GRANDFATHER NOW PLAYS THE THERAPIST IN THIS SCENE. HE LISTENS INTENTLY TO DOLORES WHO HAS A FIRE ABOUT HER THAT WE HAVEN'T QUITE SEEN BEFORE.

DOLORES: Tell me if I'm wrong. Please.

THERAPIST: It's not my place to tell you whether you're wrong, you do know that.

DOLORES: I need somebody to try.

THERAPIST: For what purpose?

DOLORES: So that I stay alive in this body for another day. Or two.

THERAPIST: Are you feeling suicidal?

DOLORES: It's just a figure of speech. Okay. I'm not going to pull a Clara, okay?

THERAPIST: A Clara?

DOLORES: The woman I met in South Texas.

THERAPIST: You're going to have to fill me in on that one.

DOLORES: She's this woman who poisoned her girlfriend and then poisoned herself.

THERAPIST: So you are feeling suicidal?

DOLORES: Don't you ever just want to start all over again?

THERAPIST: Is that what you're wanting?

DOLORES: Isn't that what life is requiring? But we think we have to repeat ourselves day in and day out? We think we have to master the same fucking lines and be in the same fucking dramas with the same fucking people?

THERAPIST: I have no problem with the word fuck, Dolores. . .but I think you're feeling angry right now and I would love to hear you say what you really feel as simply as possible.

DOLORES: I'm fucking angry.

THERAPIST: Okay.

DOLORES: Because I'm a fucking freak. Did I tell you my father raped my mother who was fourteen at the time and then called it love?

THERAPIST: Do you want to tell me more about that?

DOLORES: Or that my great, great grandfather spent his life torturing the woman he loved. . .in his mind- - -by building this incredible monument of hatred as a testament to his love?

THERAPIST: Are you feeling like these concerns are causing all of this anger right now?

DOLORES: I'm saying. . .I've inherited a full, fucking plate of psycho DNA to contend with, yes. I am saying. . .we don't have as much choice in the matter as we'd like to believe. I am saying. . .you are the last therapist I will ever have a relationship with. I don't even know why I'm here. I don't believe you can help me. I don't believe that what we inherit from the ancestors has to be fixed, okay? It just has to be digested. So if you don't mind. I want to leave now. And I'm happy to pay you for the full hour. But I think you're full of it And frankly, I came here out of habit more than necessity. My psychotherapist boyfriend won't take me back. . .I'll thank him for it one day soon I'm sure. . .but I needed someone to talk to me. . .the way he used to talk to me. So that I could have the fucking courage. . .once and for all- - -to just walk away from it. And. . just stay gone this time.

THE THERAPIST STANDS UP AND OFFERS HIS HAND. SHE DOESN'T TAKE IT.

I don't need to let you drive me to no fucking airport, okay?

SHE EXITS. BLACK OUT.

Scene 6: Freedom to Live: The epilogue

A LONE SPOTLIGHT APPEARS. IT HAS A LOT OF BLUE IN IT. SHE TALKS

DIRECTLY TO THE AUDIENCE.

DOLORES: I got a letter in the mail today. (Emil enters.) A registered letter from a lawyer in South Texas. Apparently, I am the legal heiress to the Spanish gold they found in my great, great, grandfather's house. (the grandfather enters.) They estimate the coins are worth at least a hundred thousand dollars. (Francisco enters.) Francisco, who supposedly is my real father, dropped his claim on the gold which means, my mother Esmeralda (Esmeralda enters.) and I get to inherit all of that good fortune. I called her on the phone yesterday to ask if she had received her registered letter and she told me she had but that she doesn't open anything that comes from South Texas. So she took her bic lighter and torched it in the bar-b-que pit. Was it something important she asked. No, I said. Not because I wanted to keep the money. But grateful that I too could let go of all that money by donating it to the museum itself. That's where they found it. That's where it should stay. After the big donor pulled out and they lost all of their funding, that meant that my grandfather's house was just going to sit there and rot without Clara working to preserve it. (Clara enters.) This way they could hire somebody else to do that. So I wrote the lawyer back and asked if I could donate it towards that cause? He's looking into it. But I had another request, as well. I wanted to come and see and touch and hold the gold with my own hands. . .if I could please do that before turning it over to the U.S. Treasury who would then cut me a check for its current amount, I might have a chance at holding something eternal in my hands. Isn't gold one of the few things that passes the 'acid test' of time? It doesn't even tarnish. Regardless of the circumstances. I told myself. . .if I can touch something eternal with my own hands. . .it will change me forever. I don't know why I know that. But I do.

ADELA IN FULL SOLADERA REGALIA APPEARS IN HER OWN SPOTLIGHT AS DOLORES' SPOT SLOWLY FADES TO BLACK. ADELA WEARS RED, BRIGHT DANCING SHOES. SHE SINGS:

WINDBLOWN.

Carry me wind on your breath

Carry me wind at night

I have all things I desire

No one to need

No one to miss

No mouth to feed

No hand to kiss

As long as you're there to move me

> Chorus:

> Wind, please have your way with me

> There's rapture in my hard, rock places

> Scatter me, make dust of me please

> Oh wind please spend one day with me

> In your time that's eternity

> I'll be the canyon to your warm caress

DOLORES APPEARS. SHE SINGS THE SECOND VERSE.

Carry we wind on your breath

Carry we wind at night

I am no longer afraid

I'm not alone

I'm so at home

I'm free to come

And free to roam

As long as you're there to move me.

TOGETHER THE TWO, WHO NEVER MAKE DIRECT CONTACT, SING THE CHORUS.

END OF PLAY.

Biographies

AMPARO GARCIA-CROW is a multi-disciplinary artist who acts, sings, directs and writes plays, screenplays and songs. As a playwright, Garcia-Crow has been developed at South Coast Repertory Theatre and has had world premieres Off-Broadway, Actor's Theatre of Louisville, Latino Chicago and various theatres and universities in the Southwest. A former James Michener Fellow, Amparo won the Larry King Playwriting Award for her play, *Cocks Have Claws and Wings to Fly* and most recently the national Mae West Festival's "Best Female Protagonist" award for her play *Esmeralda Blue: La Mujer Moderna.* Her *Unknown Soldier: The New American Musical of Mexican Descent* was recently featured in Hector Galen's documentary: "Visiones (Visions): Latino Art and Culture" on PBS and currently in development as a major motion picture. Other films include "The Death Rattle" and "Loaves and Fishes" which aired on Texas PBS after premiering at SXSW Film Festival and the Los Angeles Latino International Film Festival. As an actress Amparo has performed at the Kennedy Center and other regional theatres in the Southwest, various independent films, commercials and industrials. As a director, she has been an NEA/TCG Director's Fellow, produced independent musical releases of her original compositions and been a Professor of Theater and Dance at University of Texas and Austin Community College where she's taught acting, directing and playwriting. Most recently, she served as the inaugural Program Manager and designed the grand opening for the City of Austin's new sixteen million dollar Mexican American Cultural Center.

JOSE E. LIMÓN holds the BA in philosophy, the MA in English and the PhD in cultural anthropology/folklore from the University of Texas at Austin where he now serves on the faculty. He is the Mody C. Boatright Regents Professor of American and English Literature as well as Professor of Mexican-American Studies, American Studies, and Anthropology. He is also the Director of the Center for Mexican-American Studies. In addition to some thirty scholarly articles, he has authored three books. <u>Mexican Ballads and Chicano Poems : History and Influence in Mexican-American Social Poetry</u> (University of California Press, 1992) received an "Honorable Mention" award for the University of Chicago Folklore Prize for "distinguished contribution to folklore scholarship" and <u>Dancing with the Devil: Society and Cultural Poetics in</u>

Mexican-American South Texas (University of Wisconsin Press, 1994) was named as the winner of the 1996 American Ethnological Society Senior Scholar Prize for "a vital and contentious contribution to ethnology. His most recent book is American Encounters: Greater Mexico, the United States and the Erotics of Culture (Beacon Press, 1998). At present he is writing Neither Friends, Nor Strangers: Mexicans and Anglos in the Literary Making of Texas. Working with the Recovering the Hispanic Literary Project at the University of Houston, he has also edited the writings of Jovita Gonzalez.

OCTAVIO SOLIS is a playwright and director living in San Francisco. His works *Lydia, Man of the Flesh, Prospect, El Paso Blue, Santos & Santos, La Posada Mágica, El Otro, Dreamlandia*, and have been mounted at the Oregon Shakespeare Festival, the New York Summer Play Festival, the Dallas Theater Center, the Magic Theatre, Intersection for the Arts, South Coast Repertory Theatre, the San Diego Repertory Theatre, the San Jose Repertory Theatre, Shadowlight in San Francisco, the Venture Theatre in Philadelphia, Latino Chicago Theatre Company, La Compania de Albuquerque, Teatro Vista in Chicago, El Teatro Campesino, the

Undermain Theatre in Dallas, Thick Description, Campo Santo, and Cornerstone Theatre. He is the recipient of the 2000-2001 National Theatre Artists Residency Grant from TCG and the Pew Charitable Trust for Gibraltar at the Oregon Shakespeare Festival. His new anthology, *Plays By Octavio Solis* is issued by Broadway Play Publishing. He has also completed "Prospect," an independent feature film which he wrote and directed. Solis is a member of the Dramatists Guild and a New Dramatists alum.

NoPassport

NoPassport is a Pan-American theatre alliance & press devoted to live, virtual and print action, advocacy and change toward the fostering of cross-cultural diversity in the arts with an emphasis on the embrace of the hemispheric spirit in US Latina/o and Latin-American theatre-making.

NoPassport Press' Dreaming the Americas Series and Theatre & Performance PlayTexts Series promotes new writing for the stage, texts on theory and practice and theatrical translations.

Series Editors:

Jorge Huerta, Otis Ramsey-Zoe, Caridad Svich

Advisory Board:

NoPassport *wishes to thank Antonella Fernandez And Stephen Squibb for copy-editing help for this volume.*